4

Break
of Dawn

Rita Bradshaw

Break of Dawn

headline

First published in 2011 by
HEADLINE PUBLISHING GROUP

1

Cataloguing in Publication Data is available from the British Library

Hardback ISBN 978 0 7553 5938 7

Typeset in Bembo by Palimpsest Book Production Limited,
Falkirk, Stirlingshire

Printed and bound by
CPI Group (UK) Ltd, Croydon, CR0 4YY

Headline's policy is to use papers that are natural, renewable and recyclable
products and made from wood grown in sustainable forests. The logging and
manufacturing processes are expected to conform to the environmental
regulations of the country of origin.

HEADLINE PUBLISHING GROUP
An Hachette UK Company
338 Euston Road
London NW1 3BH

www.headline.co.uk
www.hachette.co.uk

For our infinitely beloved grandson, Reece Benjamin Bradshaw, born 26 July 2011; precious baby son for Ben and Lizzi, beautiful new cousin for Sam and Connor, Georgia and Emily, and Lydia. You were prayed for and wanted more than you will ever know, little one, and we praise the Lord for his treasured gift and give all thanks to God for you. 'Weeping may endure for a night, but joy comes in the morning.'

And I couldn't let this moment go by without mentioning Bailey, our dear grand-dog, who was going to be put down simply because he's a Staffie cross and his face didn't fit, before Ben and Lizzi took him in. He's the most endearingly daft canine in the world, an utter softie and a comic genius without knowing it!

Acknowledgements

In the twenty-first century, few people think twice about women having the vote along with equality before the law in Britain, particularly in the divorce and custody courts, but these rights were won at great cost.

In the Victorian and Edwardian eras and beyond, courageous women from all walks of life and all classes rose up to fight for what we now take for granted. Many women's movements existed, among them the Actresses' Franchise League featured in this story.

I've gathered material from many sources, but particular thanks go to Julie Holledge for her wonderful history of women in the Edwardian theatre. Her book, *Innocent Flowers*, was quite a revelation.

It is of the Lord's mercies that we are not consumed, because His compassions they fail not. They are new every morning: great is Your faithfulness.

Lamentations 3, v. 22–3

Contents

PART ONE

The Homecoming

1880

Chapter 1

Every jolt of the coach was torture. She didn't know how she had stood the journey thus far, but this last leg was the worst. Or perhaps it was that she knew she was going home.

Esther Hutton, or Estelle Marceau as she liked to be known, attempted to ease her swollen body into a more comfortable position on the hard wooden seat, but it was no use. She gritted her teeth, opening her eyes – which she had kept closed for much of the time since leaving London in an effort to avoid conversation with any fellow passengers – and sat staring out of the grimy window. The November afternoon was dark and overcast. The weather had got progressively colder over the long, tedious days since she had left her lodgings in Whitechapel, and for the last forty-eight hours, squalls of wintry rain had battered the coach roof and stung the travellers' faces when they had hurried into the various inns for a meal or overnight stay.

How she hated the north – and her home village in particular. Her full, somewhat sensual lips curled. From as long as she could remember, Southwick's residents had successfully fought off attempts by Sunderland's corporation to integrate the village into the township, as though there was something worthy in remaining separate. She had been brought up listening to her parents talk about the dregs of humanity 'across the river', as though poverty and disease and squalor didn't exist in Southwick. The hypocrisy, that's what she couldn't stand. All right, her family might be middle class, her father being a vicar and all, but his work must have brought him into contact with the seamier side of life in the village. When she had been able to escape her mother's obsessional control and run wild in Carley, the area closest to the vicarage, it was the smell and flies she had noticed the most.

Esther swallowed hard, the memory of the ash middens rising up in her throat as the child inside her kicked as though in protest at her thoughts. The children she had played with on those occasions had never seemed to be aware of the stench filling the back lanes, but once, when she'd had no choice but to use one of the back-yard privies shared by several families or soil her drawers, the excrement was piled up practically to the top of the wooden seat and she had thrown up the contents of her stomach right there on the rough stone floor. Some of the children had even played in the field where the scavengers who cleared the human muck each week dumped their grisly load. Flies lived in their millions on the dung hill and during the summer months they invaded the tightly packed terraced houses closest to the farmer's field, resting on food and getting into jugs of milk and crawling on babies' sticky faces.

She swallowed again as her stomach churned, telling herself to think of something else.

How would she be received when she reached the vicarage? The grey landscape mocked the foolishness of the question. Why ask the road you know? Her father would be full of icy fury and her mother beside herself as to what people would think. To have their daughter's sin paraded in front of their eyes was their worst nightmare. She glanced at the cheap gold band on the third finger of her left hand. She had bought the wedding ring before leaving London. It wouldn't fool her parents but it gave some semblance of respectability to her homecoming.

Her gaze wandered and she caught the eye of the wife of the young couple sitting opposite. The woman immediately dropped

4

her gaze to the neatly gloved hands clasped in her lap, her sallow cheeks flushing. Since leaving London, Esther had had to change coaches several times. This one, which had left Middlesbrough early that morning, held yet another different batch of travellers. Besides the young couple, a portly, red-faced man was sitting dozing next to the husband, and an elderly gentleman with snow-white hair and a frock coat was sitting reading from a book of prayers on the seat beside Esther.

All her fellow passengers were dressed soberly and the woman in particular was the very essence of propriety, her dark-brown coat and hat and high-buttoned black boots speaking of dignified refinement. Esther appeared like a bright exotic bird that had somehow found itself among a group of sparrows, and the young wife's fascinated and covert glances as the journey had progressed had made Esther very aware of her mistake. Among the company she had mixed with in London her blue brocade dress and matching coat with its elaborate fur collar would have been considered almost dull. It was the most subdued outfit in her wardrobe, which was why she had chosen to wear it for her imminent arrival in Southwick, but too late she realised she should have pawned a couple of the dresses one or other of her 'gentlemen' had bought her and used the money to buy something plain and serviceable.

She looked out of the window again, studying her reflection in the glass. Her hat with its sweeping blue and silver feathers brought out the deep violet of her eyes and pretty tilt of her chin, but she lamented the loss of the paint and powder she had used regularly for the last decade. Her mother would have become apoplectic at the faintest suggestion of such wickedness.

The coach lurched drunkenly, its wheels struggling over the thick ridges of mud and deep icy puddles in the narrow road they were travelling on, and Esther banged her forehead on the window, knocking her hat askew. Suddenly hot tears pricked at the back of her eyes, not because of the bump which had been nothing in itself but because of the position she found herself in. She had vowed never to come back to the north-east when she had left it fifteen years ago, but what choice did she have? Her hands rested for a moment on the mound of her stomach. None. The music-hall audiences didn't want to see an actress heavy with child entertaining them, and her admirers had vanished one by one over the last months as her pregnancy had progressed. She had sold every bit of jewellery she possessed and the lovely fur coat one of her gentlemen had bought for her in the early days, and she still hadn't been able to pay the rent for the last few weeks. A moonlight flit had been her only option and she had left with the remainder of the clothes she hadn't sold for her coach fare packed in her carpet bag and little else.

She blinked the tears away and sat up straighter. But she would return. Once the child was born and she had rested and was strong again, she would plan her escape. She had managed it fifteen years ago and she would do it again. Her parents would take care of the baby, they would see it as their Christian duty however much it stuck in their craw. She would make her way back to London and with her figure her own again she could take her life up once more. She was still pretty, and what she didn't know about pleasing a man and catering for their more . . . unusual desires wasn't worth knowing.

Her whole stomach shifted as the child changed position, and as she had done so many times, she silently cursed its existence. She hadn't been able to believe the non-appearance of her monthlies at first, but once she had accepted that the preventative measures she had been instructed in by an older actress at the beginning of her career in the halls had failed, she had tried everything she could to get rid of the thing growing inside her. Bottles of gin, scalding hot baths, jumping down half a flight of stairs and lifting weights so heavy she thought her eyes would pop out of their sockets, she had done it all. All but visiting one of the old wives, of whose dark arts every actress knew. She had seen too many girls die as a result of their ministrations over the years to go down that route.

She shut her eyes, exhaustion uppermost from the last few days spent on uncomfortable seats in lumbering, swaying coaches and nights tossing and turning on bug-infested mattresses in wayside inns. She was cold and tired and hungry, and already homesick for

London and the life she had led before this disaster had overtaken her.

She didn't doubt that not a thing would have changed in Southwick; except, perhaps, the streets which had begun to spread eastwards from the village green five years before she left might have increased in number. But the glassworks, shipyards and all manner of industry that jostled for space with the lime kilns built to take the stone from Carley Hill would still be lining the river banks, and smoke and filth from the factories would continue to hang ominously in the air. Wearmouth colliery would still be dominating the western part of Monkwearmouth which led on to Southwick, and cinders and ash blown in the wind from the pit would inevitably find their way on to the washing of Southwick housewives.

Of course, the air could be thick with smog and the gutters running in filth in London, but it was different somehow, Esther thought drowsily. The taverns and coffee-houses, the theatres and exhibitions and concerts, the galleries and waxworks were all so vibrant and exciting, and the shops . . . Oh, the shops. Full of the latest Paris fashions and so elegant. Shopping being one of the few amusements considered suitable for unaccompanied women, she and her music-hall friends had often indulged themselves as far as their purses would allow. And if it had been one of the times when a group of upper-class young rakes had patronised the theatre the night before, looking for fun after the show, their purses might be very full indeed.

A small secret smile touched the corners of Esther's mouth. The stories she could tell . . . But why shouldn't she live life to the full? You were only here once. And when a woman got married she was finished. She was a slave to her husband, and unless she married well she was a slave to the home too. But in either case her freedom was curtailed, restraints came in their hundreds and all merriment was gone. Not that she intended to end up like one or two actresses she knew, reduced to working in one of Soho's 'pleasure halls' where carnal depravity and unimaginable licentiousness was the order of the day. No, she would get out before her

7

looks began to fade, take herself off somewhere in the country and pose as a genteel widow to snare some yokel who was wealthy enough to see to it she didn't have to lift a finger.

She snuggled deeper into her warm fur collar, the rocking and swaying of the coach adding to the overwhelming weariness. And then she slept.

'The Lord giveth and the Lord taketh away, and it is not for us to fathom the mind of the Almighty, Mrs Skelton.' Jeremiah Hutton placed a large bony hand on the shoulder of the little woman standing next to him. 'Life and death is in His hands and His alone.'

A snort from the corner of the room where a wrinkled crone was sitting huddled in front of the glowing range with a sleeping baby on her lap caused Jeremiah to turn his head. This was the old grandmother, and he had had occasion to cross swords with her before. Shrivelled and skeletal, and possessing black teeth which protruded like witch's fangs whenever she opened her mouth, she was nevertheless a force to be reckoned with and, in Jeremiah's opinion, profane and godless. 'You wish to say something, Mrs Woodrow?' he said coldly, aware of Mrs Skelton at the side of him flapping her hand silently at her mother in an effort to keep the peace.

She might as well have tried to stop the tide from flowing in and out. 'Aye, I do, an' stop your flutterin', our Cissie,' the old woman added to her red-faced daughter. 'All this talk of the Almighty an' Him decidin' what's what don't wash with me, Vicar. It weren't Him who had Alfred standin' on a plank weldin' thirty feet off the ground, now was it? There's not a day goes by that some poor so-an'-so don't cop it in them blood yards, an' you know it – but the owners aren't interested in safety or workin' conditions. Not them, in their fine houses with their lady wives takin' the air in their carriage an' pair.'

'Mam, *please*.'

'Weeks he's bin bitin' down on a bit of wood at night to keep from cryin' out an' frightenin' the bairns, his legs smashed to pieces. You know – you saw 'em, Vicar. An' when the gangrene set in an' they brought the maggots to feast on his flesh, even then he didn't give up. Fought to the last, Alfred did, poor devil. Well, he's fightin' no longer.' The old woman's rheumy gaze moved to the wooden trestle against one white-washed wall of the kitchen, a bucket standing beneath it to catch the drips from the body lying above. 'God rest his soul.'

Jeremiah had remained still and silent throughout this discourse as befitted someone of his standing. He was not about to enter into a debate with Mrs Woodrow on the nature of her son-in-law's untimely death; he had learned to his cost in the past that the irascible old woman had an answer for everything. His face impassive, he merely stared at her, wanting nothing more than to be gone from the two rooms the family of ten called home which smelled strongly of death and bleach. But his duty had brought him to the house to discuss the funeral the day after tomorrow, and he had never shirked his duty in his life.

He was grateful that most of his parishioners came from the better part of Southwick but there were a few, like this family, living in Low Southwick on the doorstep of the shipbuilding yards and marine engineering and glass bottle-works who worshipped at his church rather than attending a chapel or a smaller church in the district. Jeremiah looked on such folk as his cross to bear and prided himself that he did it with fortitude.

The tenement building in Victoria Street was all stairs and passages, and in this street and others like it, the front and back doors were always open, being thoroughfares for the numerous residents. It wasn't unusual for each room of the two-up, two-down terraces to house entire families, but the Skeltons were fortunate inasmuch as they rented the downstairs of this particular house, comprising of the kitchen and front room, the latter used as the family's communal bedroom.

Turning his pale-blue eyes on the bereaved widow, Jeremiah reminded her of something else she had to be thankful for as he ignored the old woman by the range. 'It's a blessing Adam and Luke are in employment, Mrs Skelton,' he said stiffly, referring to the woman's eldest sons who worked alongside their father in

Pickersgill's shipyard, or had done until their father was careless enough to get himself killed. 'It must be a great comfort to know you are sure of two wages coming in each week.'

There was another 'Hmph!' from the corner by the range. 'Aye, an' young Luke already havin' lost a finger an' him only sixteen.'

'*Mam.*'

This time her daughter's voice held a note that caused her mother to narrow her eyes and suck in her thin lips, but she said no more in the few minutes Jeremiah remained in the house.

When he emerged into Victoria Street, the afternoon light was fading fast and the earlier rain had turned to sleet, but Jeremiah stood breathing in several lungfuls of the bitterly cold air before he began to walk briskly northwards. The stench of death had got up his nostrils, he thought irritably. It would quite spoil his appetite for dinner.

His thick black greatcoat and hat and muffler kept out the chill, and by the time he had walked along Stoney Lane and turned on to the green, he was sweating slightly. The usual tribe of snotty-nosed and barefoot ragamuffins hadn't been playing outside the houses from whence he had come today, much to his relief. The worsening weather had sent them indoors. And now, as he made his way through the streets of High Southwick towards the vicarage, he relaxed a little. There might be some rough types hereabouts, especially among the Irish contingent in Carley, but they couldn't hold a candle to the scum in Low Southwick.

He gave a self-righteous sniff, tucking his muffler more securely in his coat although it was perfectly all right as it was.

That dreadful old hag back there, daring to address him without a shred of respect for his position! Even the Carley O'Rileys, bad as they were, held him in the esteem due to him. It was a great pity the two Skelton boys were of an age to be in employment, since the workhouse would have soon brought their crone of a grandmother to heel and taught her to respect her betters.

He passed a group of ruddy-faced men leaving their shift at the Cornhill Glassworks, and as one man they doffed their caps to him. Their deference went some way in soothing his ruffled feathers, but he was still smarting a little as he opened the wrought-iron gates which led on to the drive of the vicarage.

He regretted not taking the pony and trap now, but the last time he had used it to visit one of his parishioners in Low Southwick Bess had been as skittish as a foal on the way home, something obviously having upset her. Sprites of Satan, some of those children were. But it gave emphasis to his standing, the horse and trap. He must remember that in the future when dealing with such as Mrs Woodrow.

In the last few minutes, the sleet had turned into fat flakes of snow which were beginning to settle as the temperature dropped, but Jeremiah's mind was on something more serious than the weather as he reached his front door. The reverence given to a man of the cloth such as he, was surely a courtesy of the utmost importance and he could not, he *would* not allow the common rabble to display such impertinence. For their own sakes. Where would society find itself, if dishonour and insolence were allowed free rein? The Woodrow woman's indictments against the shipyard owners – several of whom he counted among his personal friends – could not be tolerated. It was his clear Christian duty to have a quiet word in the necessary ears. It stood to reason, if the father had been stirring up anarchy within his own home, the sons must be tainted with the same brush. The old grandmother couldn't have come to such conclusions on her own, she was merely a woman, after all. She must have heard talk. Rebellious talk.

Jeremiah breathed in deeply, exhaling slowly as he turned to look back over the pebbled drive and neatly manicured lawns and flowerbeds either side of it. The vicarage was a substantial building of three storeys and set in half-an-acre of ground. It was situated a few hundred yards from the main village, the church rising up behind it like a sentinel keeping watch over the grids of streets running down to the River Wear. He had been born in the master bedroom thirty-eight years ago, and apart from his time at ecclesiastical college he had never lived anywhere else. Just weeks after he had left college, his father had contracted cholera from one of his parishioners in Low Southwick, and within days he had died, his mother passing away of the same disease within the week. Jeremiah had remained in good health, something he had felt was God's provision, especially when the bishop of the diocese, a family friend, had made it plain he wished him to continue in his father's place.

Taking off his hat, Jeremiah banged it against his leg before turning and opening the front door. Immediately a strong smell of beeswax and lavender oil met his nostrils, and as he stepped into the tiled hall he exhaled again, this time with a feeling of satisfaction. His home was one of order and discipline – he would not tolerate anything else – and with his wife being of like mind, their existence together was harmonious. When the bishop had made it clear he expected Jeremiah to find a wife post-haste in view of his changed circumstances, introducing his niece at a dinner party shortly afterwards, Jeremiah had taken the hint and within twelve months he and Mary were wed. It didn't matter to him that Mary was plain and severe in outlook – probably the reason she'd had no suitors at the age of twenty-five – she was domesticated and of good breeding and perfectly suited to her role as a vicar's wife.

Such was his passionless nature he could have continued quite happily through life without a mate, but he had performed his husbandly obligations every so often and in due course Mary had given birth to their son, John, five years after they were married – a respectable interval, they had both felt. Matthew had followed two years later, and the twins, David and Patience, four years after that. By unspoken mutual agreement they had decided that their procreation function in the sight of God was adequately discharged, and both had felt relief that that side of marriage – obligatory but slightly distasteful – was over.

He was taking his coat off when Bridget, their little maid, came through the door at the end of the hall which opened into a corridor leading to the kitchen and servants' quarters. His father had employed a cook and a maid, and Jeremiah had grown up in a very comfortable household along with his sister Esther, but his initial salary as a young vicar had not been such to afford servants. When he had married Mary, the bishop had seen to it that his niece could continue to live in the manner to which she was accustomed, and so Bridget, her mother Kitty who was cook and father Patrick who took care of the grounds and any odd jobs, had joined them. That had been twelve years ago and Jeremiah didn't pay the little family a penny more than when he had first taken them on. He considered that they were adequately fed and clothed and had a roof over their heads; their wage was something he secretly resented.

Jeremiah's eyes narrowed as he registered the start the little maid gave when she saw him, and as she scurried to his side he could see something was amiss.

'Oh, sir, we didn't know you were back,' she said in a loud whisper. 'The mistress asked me to keep an eye open for you, but then she wanted some more hot water for the pot and—'

'What is it?' He had no patience with Bridget's gabbling; the girl was a constant irritation to him, but thankfully it was Mary who mostly dealt with the servants.

'It's her, sir. The – the lady who's in with the mistress. She says . . .' Here Bridget's speech seemed to fail her and she gaped at him for a moment, before continuing, 'She says she's your sister, come to visit, sir.'

Jeremiah's sharp ears didn't miss the infinitesimal pause. He stared into the earnest rosy-cheeked face, his mind racing. Esther? Esther had come home? But it had been fifteen years and no word. Not that he, or his parents before they had passed away, had wanted one, not after the note she had left saying she intended to go on the stage. They had told no one of that, of course. His father had let it be known that his daughter had gone abroad for her health, and after a suitable time had intimated that she had decided to live permanently in warmer climes.

Becoming aware that Bridget was waiting for him to speak, he pulled himself together. 'I see.' He glanced at the silver hot-water jug which had been part of the fine tea set the bishop had bought the happy couple as a wedding gift. 'Take that into your mistress and tell her I'll be along shortly.'

'Yes, sir.' Bridget seemed glad her duty was done, whirling round and scampering across the polished tiles to the drawing room even before he had finished speaking.

The drawing room and morning room were on the ground floor of the vicarage. The first floor was taken up with the dining room, Jeremiah's study and the children's schoolroom. The top floor consisted of six bedrooms, with a less grand and space-consuming staircase than that which connected the ground and first floor.

Jeremiah had visited more lavish premises when calling on clergy friends, but also many less spacious, and overall he was pleased at the accident of birth which had destined him to live in the vicarage after his parents had died. When they had been alive the morning room had been the dining room, and his mother's sewing room had occupied the present dining room on the first floor. On entering the house, Mary had immediately declared that an informal sitting room on the ground floor was essential. His position dictated a morning room where Jeremiah could see parishioners in private, or she could receive women friends who called for morning refreshments. He hadn't argued. And so their meals had to come up one flight of stairs and be kept hot, which involved placing serving dishes in scalding water and perfect timing when a dinner party was in progress. But that was Kitty and Bridget's problem. Servants were readily available, and could usually be replaced without difficulty if they failed to meet the required standards.

Jeremiah eased his starched clerical collar and smoothed the strands of sparse ginger hair either side of his head before looking towards the drawing-room door. He felt no excitement at the prospect of his sister's return, merely anxiety. Esther had been a wayward child, given to flights of fancy and extreme precociousness, and as she had grown, so had her brashness. She had run rings round their mother, and her boldness with his friends had caused him much embarrassment. She had possessed none of the modest virtues appropriate for the daughter of a well-to-do vicar, and had stated quite emphatically that she had no intention of becoming the decorative wife of a boring provincial husband but would follow her own star. He had put much of her prattle down to her youth, but when she had skedaddled at the tender age of fifteen it hadn't come as much of a surprise to him, although their parents had been mortified.

His brows drew together. And now the black sheep of the family was sitting in the drawing room with his wife, who knew nothing of the true circumstances surrounding Esther. He had been too ashamed to tell Mary the truth. The door to the drawing room opened and Bridget re-emerged, the girl's expression changing to one of wariness as she saw him still standing there. He beckoned her over with a crooked finger and when she was standing in front of him, said tersely, 'The children? Where are they?'

'Me da's lookin' after 'em in the schoolroom for the present, sir. The mistress said for me to go and take over once I'd served tea.'

'And have you served tea?'

'Aye. I mean yes, sir. I have.'

'Then go and do what your mistress told you.'

Jeremiah waited until Bridget had disappeared upstairs before walking across the hall. He opened the drawing-room door with a flourish and stepped inside.

Chapter 2

Esther had scarcely been able to believe it when after knocking on the door of the vicarage and demanding to see Mrs Hutton, a stranger had come into the morning room where the maid had shown her. She had stared at the thin, colourless woman in front of her and the woman had stared back, before taking a deep breath and saying, 'You wish to see me?' her tone making it quite clear she did not expect the meeting to last long.

The woman's barely concealed distaste had the effect of straightening Esther's backbone and lifting her chin, but behind her cool facade her mind was racing. Where was her mother? Had her father married again? He must have. But to this frump? And if her father had taken a second wife, that must mean her mother had died.

The woman hadn't asked her to sit down and Esther's swollen feet were aching and her back breaking, but she gave no sign of her physical discomfort when she answered the usurper in an equally cold tone, 'I was expecting to see my mother. I am Esther. Perhaps my father has spoken of me?'

'Your father?' For a moment the steely poise faltered but immediately the woman collected herself, gesturing at one of the small armchairs in the room as she said, 'Please be seated. Am I to understand you are Jeremiah's sister?'

Esther continued to stand straight and still as she inclined her head. Jeremiah. Of course. This pikestaff of a woman must be Jeremiah's wife. 'Where are my mother and father?' she asked quietly but fearing the answer.

Mary was at a loss for perhaps the first time in her life. When Bridget had knocked on the door of the schoolroom where she was listening to John and Matthew's tutor, Mr Maxwell, take the boys through the alphabet after she had settled the twins for their afternoon nap, and told her they had a visitor, she had excused herself forthwith and followed the maid on to the landing. There she had been slightly nonplussed when Bridget had practically barred her way, whispering, 'Ma'am, it's a − a lady − an' she's expectin' a bairn. I thought you ought to know.'

Something in the way the maid had spoken had caused her to lower her own voice. 'A lady from hereabouts?'

'I don't think so, ma'am. At least I've never seen her afore an' she's dressed . . .' Here Bridget seemed to be searching for the right words. 'She's not dressed like folk round here, ma'am. And she wouldn't say her name. Just repeated all haughty-like for me to fetch you.'

'All right, Bridget.' Mary had thought quickly. 'I will see this lady but come immediately I ring for you.'

And now it appeared that their visitor was none other than Jeremiah's sister who, she understood, was living somewhere on the continent having made an impetuous marriage to a Frenchman without asking her parents' permission and thus incurring their wrath. When Mary had ventured a suggestion, shortly before they had wed, that Jeremiah might like to extend an olive branch to his sister now his parents had gone, and invite her and her husband to the wedding, he had not welcomed the idea, and the subject was never discussed again.

Making a swift decision, Mary forced a smile. 'Shall we go through to the drawing room where it's more comfortable?' she said graciously. 'And I'm sure it's time for afternoon tea. We can talk in front of the fire.'

She only noticed the large carpet bag when Esther bent to

pick it up, and said immediately, 'Leave that. Bridget will see to it shortly.'

All that had been over two hours ago. Now, as Mary glanced at her husband as he entered the drawing room, her hazel eyes were chips of flecked ice and her lips a thin line across her face. She was angry, more angry than she had ever been in the whole of her life.

Jeremiah had lied to her. Not only that, this sister of his was an actress in the music halls in the city of London. Everyone knew what *that* meant. Actresses were scarlet women soliciting from the stage rather than the streets, and the music halls were beds of iniquity. She had known there was no husband once Esther had begun to divulge her story, and it had only taken a few searching questions to persuade Jeremiah's sister to admit it. And this – this *woman* was her children's aunt, related to them by blood. The whole situation was quite intolerable.

After one look at his wife, Jeremiah didn't glance her way again as he walked across the room, his eyes on the sister he hadn't seen for fifteen years. In truth, he wouldn't have recognised her if he had passed her in the street. The Esther who had run away that far-off day with the money from his mother's cash-box and several pieces of jewellery which had been passed down to his mother from her mother, bore no resemblance to the plump, brightly dressed woman sitting on the sofa next to Mary. If he had had to describe the girl Esther he would have said she was pert and saucy, but with a fresh innocence that reflected a sheltered upbringing. The woman in front of him, her gown cut to show the curve of her breasts and her golden hair carefully styled in elaborate waves and curls, was neither innocent nor fresh. Her worldliness was apparent in every inch of her, but especially in the expression of her violet-blue eyes.

He swallowed against the shock and outrage and did not return her smile, nor did he address her as he would any other person who was a guest in his home. Looking down at her, he said tightly, 'Why have you come here, Esther?'

She didn't seem at all taken aback by his attitude, and as her smile died she answered him as directly as he'd spoken to her. 'I am going to have a baby and I am temporarily without funds. I had nowhere else to go.'

Her voice was still the same, clear and beautifully modulated with a hint of the soft breathlessness which had captivated all his friends when they were young. His mother had insisted Esther attend elocution lessons when they were children, worried that her daughter would pick up the north-east dialect. The result had been very successful, the child's distinct pronunciation and articulation devoid of any idiom or accent. After Esther had run away, their father had accused his wife of planting the idea of becoming an actress – albeit unwittingly – by her actions, something Jeremiah knew his mother had never forgiven his father for until her dying day.

Remembering the turmoil of that time, his voice was a hiss when he said, 'And the father? Your husband?'

Afterwards he thought he might have believed there was some hope for her if she had lowered her head in shame or wept, but when she stared him straight in the face and said evenly, 'The two are not synonymous,' it was all he could do not to take her by the throat and throttle the wickedness out of her.

'Esther is not married, Jeremiah.' Mary spoke for the first time since he had entered the room, each word a snap. 'And we have ascertained that paternity is not possible to pin down.'

He would never have imagined Mary would speak so bluntly about such matters. The fact that she had done so shocked him nearly as much as the inference her words held. 'You mean . . .' He cleared his throat, unable to go on.

'It's normal for the girls to have several admirers.' Esther's tone was not defensive, more matter-of-fact. 'No one thinks anything of it. Everything's different in London.'

Jeremiah felt a heat rising up in him made up of fury, embarrassment and shame. And yet he had known, hadn't he? The minute he'd set eyes on her he had known what she'd become. The seed of it had always been there, it had merely needed the watering of it to make it grow, and from what he had heard about the music halls and theatres in the capital, it was Sodom and Gomorrah. There were words bubbling in his head, profane, coarse, foul words that he wanted to spit into her face, but by an effort of will he had not known he was capable of, he subdued what he perceived as the flesh and the devil. 'There is no place for you here,' he said through gritted teeth. 'You broke our mother's heart and sent her and Father to an early grave. As far as I am concerned, I have no sister.'

'I understand from your wife that Mother and Father died of the cholera.' Esther's voice was low now and weighted with scorn. 'Even *you* cannot imagine I had a hand in that. And I am not so naive to believe that my leaving home affected Mother's heart one way or the other. We never liked each other, as you well know. I am sure that once you had all covered my tracks with the story of a trip abroad and my subsequent marriage to this Frenchman, there was a sigh of relief all round that I was gone.'

There was an element of truth in what she said but Jeremiah would have sooner walked on hot coals than admit it. He stared into the face which was still lovely in spite of the life of debauchery, and he had the urge, almost overpowering, as it had been once before, to strangle the life out of her. Clearly, Mary had told his sister the explanation they had put about regarding her sudden departure, but that did not trouble him. It was the fact that his wife was fully aware of this shameful and humiliating part of his life that had his stomach in knots. After Esther had left he had prayed daily for years that she was dead and burning in hell, and eventually he had persuaded himself that the Almighty had answered his pleadings.

'You're a common slut, worse than the dockside whores. At least they are driven to do what they do in the main just to survive. But you, you were a gentlewoman of good birth and breeding, the daughter of a minister with fine connections.'

'Good birth and breeding and fine connections?' Esther gave a contemptuous laugh. 'Most of my gentlemen can boast the same, along with refined, cultured wives, but that doesn't stop them coming to me for pleasures the like of which you have no idea of.

Every man is the same under the skin – even you, my dear brother.'

Jeremiah almost choked, so great was his fury. If he had ever been in doubt that the devil could enter a human being he doubted it no more. His sister was possessed, it was the only possible answer to such fiendish depravity. 'You will leave this house this instant,' he began, only to be checked by his wife rising to her feet.

For only the second time since he had entered the room he looked at Mary, and she seemed to take on the form of an avenging angel before his maddened gaze. 'Esther will be residing here until the child is born,' she told him. 'Your sister will take her meals in her room and will exercise only within the grounds of the house if she wishes to take the air. There will be no contact with the children, nor with any visitors who may call. This has been agreed.'

'But—'

'We will fulfil our Christian duty, Jeremiah.'

Helplessly he stared into the forbidding face of his wife. Gone was the compliant, amenable spouse he had shared his life with for the last twelve years, and in her place was a tight-lipped, angry woman who felt she had been ill-used. But how could he have told Mary the truth? And he had never dreamed that Esther would have the temerity to return to the place of her birth if she was still alive. Weakly now, he mumbled, 'Mary, listen to me. This is impossible. Your uncle—'

'*Do not speak his name.*' She actually took a step towards him before she checked herself. 'He is a good man, a righteous man, and you have repaid his patronage with a web of deceit and deception. He would not forgive you, Jeremiah, and neither can I.'

She stopped the response he'd been about to make with an upraised palm, and after one last scathing glance at him, turned to Esther, who had had the good sense to remain silent during the exchange between husband and wife. 'Bridget has lit a fire in your room and will bring you a tray later,' she said with icy politeness, pulling on the bell-cord at the side of the fireplace. 'As far as the servants are concerned, the story my husband and his parents circulated will hold true. You are the wife of a French nobleman who unfortunately met with an accident recently, and after his untimely death it was discovered that the estate was deeply in debt. You wished to be with family when your child was born.'

Esther nodded. She wasn't about to look a gift horse in the mouth, and it would seem this dried-up stick of a woman was the one she needed to appease. Nevertheless, her sister-in-law's overt condemnation rankled, and Esther vowed that before she left this house she would see her day with the pair of them.

'While you are under this roof you will be known as Mrs Esther Lemaire,' Mary added, her back as straight as a ramrod, 'and you will conduct yourself accordingly. I want no mention of your stage name, Marceau, in this house. I will not have a breath of scandal contaminating my children. Is that clear? One indiscreet word and you will live to regret it.'

After a perfunctory tap at the door, Bridget entered the room, glancing uncertainly at the *tableau vivant* facing her. Again it was Mary who took control, her voice cool and without emotion when she said, 'Mrs Lemaire is tired after her journey and wishes to retire for the night. Show her to her room and see to it a dinner tray is provided at eight o'clock.'

'Yes, ma'am.'

Jeremiah waited until the maid and his sister had left the drawing room, the latter sweeping past him as though she was the lady of the manor, and the moment the door was shut, he said, 'Please listen to me, Mary. I had no idea Esther was still alive, I swear it.'

'And that makes your subterfuge acceptable? I think not.'

'You didn't have to let her stay.'

'Don't be so ridiculous.' She had never spoken to him in such a tone before. 'If we had not offered your sister refuge in her condition, what do you think the servants would have thought? Not only thought but said, Jeremiah. Gossip travels like wildfire, make no mistake about that, and human nature being what it is this tasty morsel would have kept folk well-fed for years. She is dressed like' – here Mary's speech failed her for a moment – 'like a strumpet, but by keeping to the story of marriage to a Frenchman, this can be explained by the fact that the fashions in France are more flamboyant than in England. I have made it clear what I expect of her and that for most of the time she will stay in her room. The servants will not think that unreasonable in view of her condition and the long journey she has undertaken.'

'The servants.' There was a note of irritation in Jeremiah's voice now. 'What does it matter what they think? And they wouldn't dare breathe a word, I'd make sure of that.'

Mary shook her head slowly, and again she spoke to him as she had never done in twelve years of marriage. 'You are not a stupid man, Jeremiah, so don't act like one,' she said acidly.

And it said much for how the balance of their relationship had changed in just a few short hours that her husband made no reply . . .

It was a week later and the blizzards that had arrived the night Esther had come home had finally died out. The snow lay thick and the keen north-east wind had gathered it into deep drifts which in places could swallow horse and cart whole.

Esther had made no attempt to leave her room, not because of the weather which would have made it impossible for her to walk in the gardens of the vicarage, but because she had felt unwell and wanted nothing more than to lie in a warm bed and watch the flickering flames of the fire which Bridget raked out and lit every morning. Normally possessed of a vitality which enabled her to function on no more than four or five hours' sleep a night, she felt drained and exhausted and slightly nauseous, eating only a few mouthfuls of the meals brought to her and sleeping most of the time when the child in her womb allowed her to do so.

For the first morning since Esther had arrived at the house a weak winter sun was shining when Bridget brought her breakfast. After the maid had plumped up the pillows behind her back and placed the tray containing a bowl of creamy porridge and a plate of bacon and eggs across her lap, Esther said quietly, 'I think I may get up today, Bridget, and sit by the window in the sunshine.'

'Oh aye, I would, ma'am. Makes you feel better, don't it, a bit of sun. Would you like to come downstairs to the drawing room? I've just lit a nice fire in there.'

Esther smiled. She liked this cheery young soul with her warm brown eyes and curly light brown hair which always seemed to be trying to force the little lace cap off her head. 'No, I won't come downstairs today, but perhaps you would be good enough to move the armchair over to the window so I can see out.'

'Of course, ma'am, an' I'll sort out a nice blanket for your legs. Always nippy round the legs in the warmest room, I find.' Bridget bustled about, hauling the high-backed leather armchair from its place next to the bed to the window, and then delving into the oak blanket box at the foot of the brass bedstead for a thick wool blanket. That done, she came to stand by the bed when Esther murmured, 'You may take the tray now, Bridget.'

'Oh, ma'am, can't you try an' eat a bit more?'

'I've had sufficient, thank you.' And then, in case Bridget took her words as a rebuff and not wishing to hurt the girl's feelings, Esther added, 'Perhaps I'll find my appetite again once I'm up and about. All I've done for the last week is sleep.'

'Best thing, ma'am, if you don't mind me saying so, what with the long journey and your condition an' all.'

It was the first time her pregnancy had been mentioned and Esther nodded but didn't comment.

Bridget hesitated a moment, and then said tentatively but with an eagerness she couldn't conceal, 'I hope you don't think I don't know me place, ma'am, but can I ask you what France is like? Is it very different to England? Me da, he's always had a yen to travel but he's never bin further than over the water from Ireland to these parts, bless him.'

It wasn't often Esther's conscience made itself felt but as she looked into the maid's trusting brown eyes she found it difficult to lie. 'I think your father would find most places in most countries differ only a little,' she said at last. 'France is beautiful but then so is England. Every country has its strengths and weaknesses, and people are the same the world over.'

Bridget nodded. 'Me mam always says that wherever you go the rich get richer an' the poor get poorer. Oh, not that I mean anything by that, ma'am.'

'I know what you mean, Bridget.' Esther smiled. 'And I agree with your mother. Life is rarely fair.'

Again Bridget hesitated before saying softly, 'We're right sorry about what's happened, ma'am. Me and me mam and da, I mean.'

For a moment Esther was at a loss and then she realised Bridget was referring to her supposed French husband. 'Thank you,' she said just as softly.

'The babbie'll be a comfort, ma'am, when it comes.'

'Yes, I'm sure it will.'

'Would you like me to help you get dressed, ma'am, if you're going to sit by the window?'

'I don't think I'll bother to get dressed, Bridget. The room is lovely and warm, and with the blanket you've provided I'll be as snug as a bug in a rug. You get on with what you have to do and I promise I'll ring if I need anything.'

'Right you are, ma'am.' Bridget nodded and smiled at the woman she privately termed as 'that poor soul', but once on the landing she stood for a moment before making her way downstairs to the kitchen with the tray.

'What's up with you, lass?' Her mother was standing at the large range which was the heart of the vicarage kitchen. Bridget had been thirteen years old when she and her parents had been taken on as servants, and for months before that they had been tramping the roads looking for work. The memory of that time, the cold, the gnawing hunger and terror she had felt at being homeless was burned deep inside her soul, as was the sheer bliss of their first night at the vicarage when her mother had got the range going and she'd toasted her feet on the fender whilst eating girdle scones dripping with butter. She had thought she'd landed in heaven that day, and still the security and comfort the two-oven range gave was something she would have been unable to put into words.

The kitchen itself was a fairly large room, the walls whitewashed and the floor made up of flagstones. Its ceiling was irregular and somewhat grimy, with several beams running across it. Besides the range, the rest of the furniture comprised of a long scrubbed table with a low wooden bench either side of it, a row of floor-to-ceiling cupboards the length of one wall, and two old Windsor chairs which sat on the clippy mat in front of the range. On the left wall was a doorway, without a door, leading to the scullery in which vegetables were prepared and washing-up done, and beyond this was a small walk-in larder with stone slab shelves which were an asset in summer in keeping food and milk cool. They were also dark and hard to clean, a playground for mice and beetles.

Once daylight began to fail, the kitchen was lit by candles and oil lamps – as was the whole house. There were certain establishments in Sunderland where gasoliers had replaced chandeliers in the drawing room, and gas geysers had been installed for heating water. The vicarage could not boast such modern inventions, but Bridget and her parents did not object to this. They had heard reports from other servants that gas lighting was messy, smelly and noisy, and had no wish to use a commodity they considered intrusive and dangerous.

'Bridget?' Kitty O'Leary left the soup she was preparing for lunchtime and took the tray out of her daughter's hands. 'What's the matter? You look like you've lost a penny and found a farthin'.'

'It's her, the master's sister, Mrs Lemaire. She don't look right, Mam.'

'Don't look right?' Kitty put the tray on the table and then returned to the range where she poured her daughter a cup of strong black tea from the teapot permanently stewing on the hot plate. Handing it to her, she said comfortingly, 'She's all right, lass. Her time's about due, most likely.'

'I've seen the mistress when she had her bairns an' I tell you, Mam, something's wrong. Mrs Lemaire don't look the same as she did when she first came here. She's all puffy an' swollen, an' she's eaten next to nothin' again.' Bridget plumped down on one of the wooden benches. 'She's not right,' she said again. 'Her lips have got a blue tinge. Like an old man's.'

'She's tired, lass. She came a long way, after all, and in her condition. And the loss of her husband and home must have hit hard. Not only that, she finds her mam an' da have gone and everything's changed. It's enough to send anyone doo-lally-tap, if you ask me.'

26

Bridget stared into her mother's round, rosy face. She couldn't explain the feeling of unease that had grown stronger over the last day or two, but she knew Mrs Lemaire was ailing. And the master and mistress didn't seem to care. The master hadn't looked in on his sister once, as far as she knew, and the mistress paid a brief visit each evening before dinner but that was all. There was something queer about all this, and Mrs Lemaire never spoke about her husband or cried as you'd expect.

Kitty sat down beside her daughter. 'I'm sure if the mistress thinks anything's wrong she'll send for Dr Lawrence.'

'Are you, Mam? Sure, I mean?'

The two women stared at each other for a full ten seconds before Kitty said weakly, 'She's his sister, lass, an' blood's thicker than water. Anyway, you can't do nowt and likely she'll be as right as rain in a day or two. Now drink your tea an' then go and clear the breakfast things in the dining room before you see to the twins.'

John and Matthew were considered old enough by their mother to dress themselves and join their parents for breakfast every morning, but it was one of Bridget's many jobs to wake David and Patience, change their nappies and get them ready for the day before giving them their morning bottles and bowls of porridge. Bridget didn't mind that as the family had grown, so had her duties, which meant she now rose at five o'clock every morning and was rarely in bed before midnight. She loved the children, who were all very well-behaved and docile – all but Patience, that was. Even at a year old the little girl had the upper hand with her twin and a far stronger will than John and Matthew had ever shown.

Swigging down her tea in a few gulps, Bridget rose to her feet. She'd see to the bairns same as normal and carry out the rest of the day's tasks, but that wouldn't stop her popping her head round Mrs Lemaire's door every so often and asking if she wanted anything. Her mam was a great one for believing the best in folk, she'd make excuses for Old Nick himself, would her mam, but Bridget wasn't so sure about the master and mistress in all of this. They might have taken Mrs Lemaire in but they hadn't done it willingly, and she couldn't see them putting themselves out for the poor soul. Aye, she'd keep an eye on her today, just to be sure.

In spite of her good intentions it was nearly eleven o'clock before Bridget knocked on the door of the guest room. David and Patience had been fractious first thing; the twins had heavy colds and seeing to them had taken twice as long as usual, and although she had hurried through her chores she felt as though she had been chasing her tail non-stop. It was her mother, who had prepared an elevenses tray with teacakes warm from the oven and a glass of hot milk, who alerted her to the lateness of the morning. 'Leave that ironin', lass,' Kitty called into the scullery where Bridget was tackling a basketful of the children's clothes, 'and take a bite up to the master's sister. She didn't have but a mouthful of porridge this mornin' and she didn't touch the bacon and eggs as far as I could see.'

Bridget knocked gently on the bedroom door. The twins were having their long morning nap and John and Matthew were at their lessons in the schoolroom with their tutor, who had battled through the snow for the first time in a week, but the master and mistress, although ensconced in the morning room, had ears like cuddy's lugs and she would prefer not to attract their attention.

She knocked twice before she heard a weak, 'Come in,' and when she opened the door Mrs Lemaire was not in the chair by the window but in bed. Even from the doorway Bridget could see her face looked colourless. She hadn't appeared well that morning, but now she seemed ten times worse.

Crossing the room rapidly, Bridget placed the tray on the bedside table and bent over the still figure. 'What is it, ma'am? Shall I call the mistress?'

'No.' Esther reached out her hand and caught that of the maid's, holding it with a strength that belied her appearance. 'I think sitting by the window for a while wasn't such a good idea. I'm tired, that's all, and the chair has made my back ache.'

'Do you think you could eat a little, ma'am?'

'Not just at the moment, thank you, Bridget. I'll sleep and maybe have some lunch later.'

Once the maid had left the room, Esther found she couldn't

sleep though. She was suffering some sort of cramping seizure in her back and felt strangely uncomfortable. When Bridget returned with her lunch an hour or two later she still managed to put on a brave face, but by evening the pains had moved round to her stomach and she knew the baby was coming. It was three weeks early by her reckoning, but such was the ferocity of the pains she knew there was no doubt, and when Bridget insisted the mistress must be told, she did not protest.

By midnight the baby still hadn't been born and Esther was in a state of collapse, drifting in and out of consciousness between the pains which were racking her body with relentless regularity. She was aware of very little besides her agony, but she knew Bridget was kneeling by the side of the bed and holding tight to her hand. At one point she thought she heard the little maid arguing with Mary and demanding that a doctor be called to the house, but then she told herself she must have imagined it. Bridget wouldn't dare to tell her mistress what to do.

Aeons of time later, or was it just a few minutes – she was beyond telling – a kindly face bent over her and a deep male voice said, 'Mrs Lemaire, can you hear me? I'm Dr Lawrence and I've come to take care of you, m'dear. Everything is going to be all right, you're in safe hands.'

The baby, a little girl, was born three excruciating hours later. As the infant took her first breath, Esther breathed her last. The doctor and Mary were dealing with the child so it was only Bridget who was aware of Esther's passing. A deep breath, a flutter of her eyelashes and she was gone.

'Dr Lawrence?' Bridget was still holding Esther's hand but it had gone limp in her grasp, and the note in her voice caused the doctor to spin round and bend over his patient.

It was a minute or two before he straightened, and then his voice was sad-sounding. 'There's nothing I can do. She was not bleeding unduly and although the child took its time it wasn't a particularly long labour. I can only think her heart was not strong.'

Mary had come to the foot of the bed, holding the baby wrapped in a blanket, and after a moment she said, 'I understand from my husband that his mother had another child two years after he was born who only lived six months. It was thought there was a problem with that child's heart.'

Dr Lawrence nodded. 'It could well be a defect of some kind that was passed down. Mrs Lemaire might have lived to old age had she not had children, but both carrying a child and bringing it forth fatigues the mother, and in this case it was too much. I'm very sorry.'

Bridget was listening to the conversation above her head but she could not bring herself to let go of the slim white hand in hers. Mrs Lemaire was dead; after all that pain she was dead – and she hadn't even seen her daughter. And the baby, it would never know its mother, poor little mite, and its father dead too. What a start to life.

Bridget watched as her mistress drew the doctor to the other side of the room, there to confer with him in low whispers. She caught a few words: ' . . . husband recently died and left destitute,' and then ' . . . do our Christian duty to the best of our ability,' but as she laid the still warm, soft hand on the coverlet and stood stiffly to her feet, she could make out nothing more.

'Take the child, Bridget.' Mary's voice was quiet as she held out the bundle, but behind her sombre facade she was feeling heady with relief. She had been in turmoil ever since Jeremiah's sister had entered the house, and had laid awake most nights worrying what the outcome of this catastrophe would be. Now it appeared her frantic prayers had been answered. The problem was taken care of. Of course, it would have been more beneficial if the child had died with its mother, but it was clearly strong and healthy, which was a pity. But she would not shirk her responsibility. The child would be brought up in the sight of God, and any badness thrashed out of it before it could take root and grow, as it had with the mother.

She glanced at the still figure on the bed, at the golden hair fanning out in a mass of silky curls and waves across the pillow, and her mouth tightened into a thin line. History would not repeat itself. Not while she had breath in her body.

Chapter 3

'She's bonny, isn't she, Mam? Have you ever seen a bonnier babbie in all the world?' Bridget gazed down in rapt adoration of the sleeping baby in her arms, the small face with its silky smooth skin and tiny eyelashes and rosebud lips enchanting. 'The mistress's bairns were nothing like this. Skinned rabbits they were and they've all got her nose.'

It was a full week later. Esther had been buried in the churchyard next to her parents that afternoon, and although the day had been dark and overcast and bitterly cold, it had kept dry until the last guest had gone home. Now, at nearly midnight, the wind was howling like a banshee and rattling the windows, and the second bout of snow they had been expecting for the last day or two was coming down thick and fast.

The funeral had been a quiet one, attended by a few older folk who remembered Esther as a child and had come to pay their respects at the church service, and several colleagues of Jeremiah who sat with him on the local Board of Guardians for the Sunderland workhouse among other things. They and their lady wives were invited back to the vicarage for refreshments. The villagers were not.

Dr Lawrence had been one of the guests. When he had asked

after the deceased's child, he had been told she was feeding well and thriving. The baby was to be christened Sophy Miriam in the spring, after her dear grandmother, and they did so hope Dr Lawrence and his wife would do them the honour of becoming the child's godparents, Mary had added. The doctor had happily consented. 'Such a fortunate little girl,' he had commented on the way home to his wife, 'to have devoted guardians like Jeremiah and Mary.'

Bridget now carefully placed the sleeping baby in the old wicker laundry basket which Mary had delegated as the child's crib. The lace-bedecked Moses basket which had been made for her own babies was stored away in the attics, and she had looked askance at Bridget when she had suggested fetching it down.

'She's a picture,' Kitty agreed, joining her daughter and stroking one tiny velvet cheek, 'aren't you, my precious? It's a cryin' shame, my little flower. A cryin' shame.'

Bridget didn't need to ask what her mother meant. The mistress had made it abundantly clear from day one that she was far too busy to see to a newborn baby, neither did she want her niece intruding into their family life. The child would do far better being kept in the kitchen in front of the range where it was always warm, and if she survived the next weeks, which of course one never could tell with such a small baby, either Bridget or her mother would attend to her needs.

'She'll survive,' Bridget had said grimly to Kitty when her mother had related the mistress's instructions. 'If I have to feed her every hour, day and night, she'll survive, poor little mite.'

In fact, the 'poor little mite' was doing exceedingly well. She fed lustily on the pap bottles she was given every two or three hours, and slept like an angel between times. And she was, without doubt, as bonny as Bridget declared, her milky smooth skin and delicate features doll-like, and her small arms and legs plump and rounded in spite of the fact she was so tiny.

On the second day after her birth, Jeremiah had come into the kitchen to see his niece. He had stood gazing down into the wicker basket which Patrick had placed on two orange boxes to protect it from draughts, and he hadn't said a word. The baby had been awake and, unusually for her, had begun crying after a moment or two. When Bridget had come forward to pick her up, Jeremiah had left as silently as he had arrived, leaving Bridget and her parents staring at each other.

Bridget had cradled the tiny bundle to her as she'd whispered, 'What do you make of that?'

It was Patrick who had put into words what they were all thinking. 'If he had his way, that bairn'd be six foot under alongside her mam.'

After that the three of them made sure Sophy wasn't left alone for a moment, and Bridget had asked her father to carry the lumpy flock mattress off her narrow iron bed into the kitchen where she had taken to sleeping at night. In truth it was no hardship. The kitchen was lovely and warm compared to the little icebox of a room that was hers, situated next to her parents' – equally cold – larger room, and she slept well, secure in the knowledge she would hear Sophy when she awoke for a feed.

'She's already fillin' out a bit,' Kitty said, as the two women stood, arms linked, gazing down at the sleeping baby. 'All thanks to you, lass. No mother could take more care of their little one than you're doin' with her.'

'I love her,' Bridget said simply. She had long ago resigned herself to the fact that she was destined to be an old maid. After one brief affair of the heart when she was eighteen years old, seven years ago now, which had ended badly, she hadn't had another beau. Working all hours as she did, she rarely made use of her half-day off on a Sunday afternoon, which made the chance of meeting someone non-existent. But now the void in her life was filled with Sophy. The tiny baby – she couldn't weigh more than five pounds – had had her heart from the moment she'd set eyes on her, still covered in blood and slime from her mother's womb.

'Aye, well, it's a good job someone does.' Kitty patted her daughter's arm before turning away. 'I'm off to bed, lass. Your da's already snorin' fit to wake the dead, bless him.'

''Night, Mam.' Bridget stood looking down at Sophy for another moment or two before beginning to get ready for bed. In her cold little cell of a room she had always whipped off her dress and apron as fast as she could, and pulled her thick flannelette nightdress over her shift and petticoat. Even with the feather-filled eiderdown she had treated herself to a few winters back to augment the coarse brown blankets on her bed, she'd lain shivering for half an hour or more, no matter how tired she was. Now she undressed in front of the range, relishing the warmth, and was always asleep as soon as she snuggled under the covers heaped on the mattress. Sophy sometimes snuffled and sucked at her fingers but she didn't mind that; it was comforting and flooded her with a quiet joy to know the baby was close at hand.

After laying her clothes on one of the armchairs and pulling on her nightdress, Bridget knelt down to say her prayers. Her parents had been born and raised as staunch Protestants in Ireland, leaving the Old Country for a new life in England before she was born, and had brought their only daughter up to believe unquestioningly in a Protestant God. Kitty had been sad when there were no more babies after Bridget, but had accepted it as God's will and got on with her life, and there was much of her mother's pragmatic approach to life in Bridget. Her prayers reflected this. First, she recited the Lord's Prayer as she did each night, following this with requests for protection for each member of the household, lingering longer over little Sophy. The last third of her prayers centred on her own needs and since Sophy had been born, they were simple. 'Please let the master and mistress keep her but let me look after her because You know they don't really want her, dear God. I love her and I know her mam would have wanted me to take care of her. Bless Mrs Lemaire now at peace with You, in Your Holy Name. Amen.'

After putting out the oil lamp in the centre of the kitchen table, Bridget snuggled into bed by the faint light given out by the range and was asleep as soon as her head touched the pillow.

Not so Jeremiah.

It was pitch black in the bedroom; Mary insisted that not a chink of light was allowed into the room, and the heavily-lined

34

velvet curtains at the window were closed against the storm raging outside. The storm inside his being was another matter. For the first time in his life he had been cast in the role of a transgressor and he was burning with righteous indignation.

He lay stiff and silent, listening to his wife's steady breathing and small, ladylike snores.

Mary had made him feel like a sinner, like the worst kind of miscreant – and why? he asked himself for the thousandth time. Because he had wished to spare her the knowledge of his sister's ignominy, that was all. No good purpose would have been served by offending her delicate sensibilities, and if things had remained as they were – as he had expected them to remain – she would never have known the shameful truth. He had *told* her that it had been his parents' decision to explain Esther's leaving with the story about warmer climes and a French husband, and that he had merely been respecting their wishes, that he had never – would never – keep anything from her in the normal way of things, that he had only been thinking of her tender emotions and the pain such a revelation would cause to one brought up as sensitively as she had been.

Mary had listened to his explanation in silence, her eyes gimlet hard and her face stony with condemnation. Then she had made the pronouncement which even now, two weeks later, had the power to make him squirm.

'You have betrayed the trust my uncle placed in you when he introduced us, in the worst possible way. You are a false man, Jeremiah Hutton, and it gives me no pleasure to say so. I shall not disclose your cruel trickery to the bishop, nor to my parents or the rest of the family, not for your sake but for theirs. But do not expect me to condone such deceit by absolving you of your crime because I will not.'

Crime. Jeremiah ground his teeth. He had been made to feel like a criminal in his own home, sure enough. And now his sister's bastard was to be raised in this house, a constant reminder of his fall from grace in Mary's eyes.

Did she expect him to continue begging and pleading for her

understanding in the coming weeks and months? Probably. Certainly she was displaying a spitefulness of which he would not have thought her capable, disguised under a pietistical facade which made his blood boil often as not.

He wouldn't be able to stand it if this state of affairs continued. He stared into the blackness, self-pity choking him and causing him to swallow against the lump in his throat. He was a good husband. Mary had had no cause to complain in twelve years of marriage, and he doubted if there were many women who could say that in this town. And now, when he was asking for just a drop of the milk of human kindness, she had none to give. Well, so be it. He now knew where he stood. If she wanted to drive a permanent wedge between them, she was going the right way about it. He'd had enough, more than enough, in the last weeks. Mary would see another man to the devoted husband she was used to over the next little while, and she had no one to blame but herself. If she had thought to crush him with her attitude, she was in for a shock. He would not be browbeaten in his own home and neither would he plea for her understanding again.

And as for the living evidence of the trouble which had ripped their family apart, he would continue to pray each day that the child born of sin would not see its first year. Every time he looked at it he would see and hear Esther as she had been the night she had come home, brazen in her shame.

His guts writhed and he lay for a moment more before quietly sliding out of bed. By feel he found his dressing gown on the chair by the side of the bed and put it on, but he left his slippers where they were and crept barefoot out of the bedroom. Once on the landing it was possible to see shapes and shadows, the large landing window being uncurtained, but he still had to watch his step as he made his way downstairs.

He would make himself a drink of warm milk and take it to his study where he could work on his sermon for Sunday in peace, he told himself as he reached the kitchen door. There had still been a good fire in there last thing; it wouldn't have gone out yet and a couple of logs would soon bring it to a blaze.

He opened the door as silently as he had come downstairs and stood for a moment, his eyes fixed on the raised laundry basket in front of the glowing range. It was only then he acknowledged the real reason for the midnight sojourn, the thought that had been there from the second the child had taken breath. His heart began to race, pounding in his ears.

He took a step into the room, then another, unaware of the icy chill from the stone flags under his bare feet, and then he froze as a rustle and sigh from a black mound by the kitchen table caused his gaze to shoot down. For a moment he couldn't believe his eyes as he took in the mattress and the figure sleeping under the covers. That girl. What on earth was she doing sleeping on the floor of the kitchen?

Without making a sound he backed towards the door, and it .was only when he was standing in the corridor leading to the kitchen with the door shut that he let out his breath. He found he was shaking, whether from the enormity of the deed he'd been about to do or the fact that Bridget might have awoken and found him there, he didn't know.

He leaned against the whitewashed wall, moving one lip over the other, his head swimming. He remained there for several minutes until the nausea which had risen from his stomach into his chest subsided.

He wouldn't have done it. He ran a hand over his face which was damp with perspiration in spite of the freezing cold. He wouldn't have. Would he? No, he wouldn't, he wouldn't. He told himself the same thing several more times before he could move, and then he stumbled upstairs to his study and fell into the big leather chair behind the fine walnut desk which had been his father's. He drew in a great breath of air, as though he had been running for miles, and then put his head in his hands as he began to cry.

PART TWO

The Child

1890

Chapter 4

Little had changed in Southwick over the last ten years. True, Southwick's Local Board had defeated another Sunderland act to absorb the growing township, and as if to cock a snook, Southwick had seen to it that a cricket and bicycle club was formed, along with a tennis club and a rowing club later in the decade. Southwick now boasted its own purpose-built Coffee Tavern at the east end of the green, something the Temperance Society considered a huge step forward in its fight against the demon drink, and the Liberal Club had opened new premises at High Southwick. All in all, Southwick residents felt their independence as a separate entity was justified. They could manage their own affairs and didn't want Sunderland muscling in where it wasn't wanted.

Outwardly, little had changed at the vicarage too. The vicar still visited his parishioners when the need arose, sat on various local Boards involved in good works, and preached fire and damnation from the pulpit every Sunday morning. Inside the house, however, the catalyst which had been dropped into their midst ten years before in the shape of one small baby had continued to bring changes which even now rippled an undercurrent within the family.

It would be fair to say the vicarage was a house divided, and the divide came in the shape of Sophy. On the one hand Jeremiah, Mary and Patience made no secret of their loathing of 'the child' as Mary continued to call Esther's daughter, but John, Matthew and David held their cousin in deep affection and the little girl was Bridget's sun, moon and stars. Unfortunately for Sophy, the three sons of the family were at private boarding schools for a great part of each year, and she was left to the tender mercies of Patience, whose chief delight was finding new ways to torment her. And in this Patience was ably assisted by her mother.

With each passing year Esther's daughter had grown more beautiful and similarly, so had Mary's hate of her niece grown. She lost no opportunity in physically punishing the little girl for the slightest fall from grace − of which there were many because Sophy was a spirited child − using her correction cane with righteous zeal and unerring accuracy for maximum pain. A word spoken out of place, a chore not carried out to her satisfaction, a glance she considered insolent − all brought forth retribution of the harshest kind. It was one of Mary's regrets that she couldn't find fault with the child's aptitude for her lessons. Patience and Sophy were taught by a governess for four hours each morning, and although Patience was fourteen months older than her cousin she didn't have half of her intelligence or natural proficiency. Once the lessons were over for the day Sophy was consigned to Bridget's care with a list of chores from her aunt as long as her arm, and both Mary and Patience had taken to checking that these were being carried out at odd moments of the day, suspecting that Bridget was too lenient with her small charge.

Jeremiah had little to do with the workings of the house and none with domestic arrangements. When he was at home he buried himself in his study, emerging only at mealtimes or when they had guests. At those times anyone would have been hard put to guess the state of enmity existing between husband and wife. Most of the time he ignored Sophy's existence, and when he was forced to acknowledge her presence, his granite profile concealed a bitter resentment which had grown like a canker over time, souring every aspect of his life.

As for Sophy herself, it would be true to say that but for Bridget and her parents the little girl's life would have been unbearable. As it was, she accepted her lot, if not stoically – she had too much of her mother running through her veins for that – then with a fortitude which enabled her to be happy some of the time, although the older she got the more she questioned the unfairness of her position.

As she was doing right at that moment whilst helping Bridget clean the household silver on the scullery table. 'I'm going into double numbers tomorrow, aren't I, Bridget?'

'That you are, my lamb.'

'Patience and David had a party when they went into double numbers. Do you remember the frock Aunt Mary bought Patience, the pink one with the silk sash?'

Bridget nodded but didn't comment. The mistress had spent a fortune on the dress from one of the la-di-da shops in Bishopwearmouth, but all it had done was to accentuate Patience's extreme plainness ten-fold. No expensive frock could disguise the fact that Patience was the spitting image of her mother, in nature as well as appearance, Bridget thought darkly.

'It was a bonny frock,' Sophy murmured wistfully, glancing down at the plain grey serge dress her aunt made her wear every day except for the occasions they had visitors.

Bridget sniffed. 'Bonny is as bonny does.'

Sophy stared into the round, rosy face of the person she loved most in all the world. Bridget sometimes said things which didn't make any sense at all.

'Kitty's making me a birthday cake but we've got to keep it a secret,' she whispered conspiratorially. 'She said I can help decorate it and write my name in pink icing sugar.'

'Is that so?' Bridget knew she didn't need to emphasise that the bairn's aunt and uncle mustn't catch a whiff of it, and Miss Patience, too, of course. She'd often thought it was a great pity Patience wasn't a boy, because there was no doubt a major part of her fierce hatred of this child was down to the green-eyed monster. And she could understand how Patience must feel in

43

part, because if Mrs Lemaire had been pretty, her daughter was beyond bonny. Sophy's skin was pure milk and roses, her wavy hair a bright golden auburn and her lips full and perfectly shaped, but it was the bairn's eyes that took your breath away. They were like none she'd seen before in a human face, being a burned honey colour and as clear as amber, with thick sweeping lashes and fine curving brows above.

'If my mother was here she'd have bought me a new frock.'

It was a whisper but Bridget heard it and put her arm round the slender shoulders. 'That she would, me bairn. That she would. And a matching one for herself, no doubt, then you'd have been two peas in a pod.' She was exaggerating a little but felt it was called for. 'Just like her you are, hinny.'

Sophy nodded. And that was why her aunt and uncle didn't like her. She had learned much from listening to Bridget and Kitty's chatter as she had grown, especially when they thought she was asleep in her pallet bed in the far corner of the kitchen. She knew her mother had been her uncle's sister and that she had married a French nobleman of whom her family had dis-approved. Her mother had been beautiful, like a fairy princess, and her father very handsome. She had added that last bit herself but she knew it to be true, for why else would her mother have left everyone and everything she'd known to marry him? It was like a story, even if it had ended badly with her father dying and her mother having to come home to her Uncle Jeremiah. Her aunt and uncle hadn't liked her mother and they didn't like her. She had said that once to Bridget, and Bridget had answered that her aunt and uncle didn't like anyone, including each other, but then Kitty had shushed Bridget and told her to hold her tongue.

She also knew that Bridget was wholly hers in a way no one else was, and this was often balm to her bruised heart when her aunt had been particularly harsh. Only last night she'd heard Bridget and Kitty talking at the kitchen table over a cup of tea before they retired for the night, Patrick ensconced in his chair by the range smoking his pipe.

'Cryin' shame, I call it,' Bridget had said softly. 'She'll be ten the day after the morrer and still sleeping like a dog in the kitchen. What other man would hold with his own sister's bairn being treated as scum, I ask you? She's worse off than we are, at least we get paid for the work we do' – here Kitty had snorted, and Bridget had amended – 'even if it is a pittance, and we have our own rooms, Mam, now then. That little bairn has never been allowed to play, and she was made to slave from when she could walk. A pallet bed in the kitchen – it's not right, not when the guest room is empty year in and year out, 'cept for when the bishop comes to stay for a few days.'

'I know, lass, I know, but it's none of our business. We work here, that's all, an' we could be out on our ear afore you could say Jack Robinson.'

Bridget had been silent for a moment and Sophy had risked peeking out from under her blankets. Bridget was slowly shaking her head, her face sad but her voice angry when she'd murmured, 'Makes my blood boil, the things that go on in this house, and all the time them actin' the holy Joes. I'd like to take that little lass to one of his damn committees and show them what his lady wife does when she's of a mind. Last time she caned her, she was black an' blue all over.'

'Wouldn't make any difference if you did.' Patrick had entered the conversation, which was rare. He was a man who didn't say much. 'The nobs stick together, as you well know. Like your mam says, it's none of our business an' you'd do well to remember that, lass.'

This had effectively finished the conversation but it had left Sophy feeling warm inside that Bridget cared about her so much. Reaching up now, she whispered in Bridget's ear, 'I love you.'

'An' I love you, hinny.' Bridget's gaze rested on the shining hair which was strained into one tight plait so that not even a curl escaped. The mistress had insisted on it as soon as the baby mop of curls had grown, along with the dull dresses and ugly, thick-soled boots the little girl was made to wear, but nothing could disguise Sophy's beauty, Bridget thought for the umpteenth time with great

45

satisfaction. And that was something that stuck in the mistress's craw all right, cruel devil that she was.

As though her thoughts had conjured the mistress up, Bridget heard her mother say, 'Good afternoon, ma'am,' a moment before Mary appeared in the scullery doorway. She and Sophy stood to their feet, it was one of many niceties the mistress demanded but Sophy knew better than to stare at her aunt and kept her eyes lowered.

Mary Hutton's cold reptilian eyes swept over the silver on the rough wooden table. 'Haven't you finished that yet? It's' – she consulted the small silver pocket-watch pinned to the bodice of her thick linen day dress – 'almost four o'clock and we have guests for dinner tonight.'

'Nearly done, ma'am.' Bridget dipped her knee just the slightest.

'See to it the dining table is set with the silver and my best crystal, and use the new damask cloth I bought last week, the one with the roses and leaves. Eight places. And the fire in the drawing room needs attending to. It was almost going out when I left.'

'Yes, ma'am.' Bridget knew this to be untrue, since she had piled up the coal in the large grate only an hour before, but not by intonation or expression did she reveal this. The mistress was never satisfied, and if there wasn't anything to find fault with, she'd make something up. It had always been the same. 'Do you want the best candelabra in the centre of the table, ma'am? The one with the crystals hanging from it?'

'Of course, girl.' It was a snap. 'I told you it's a dinner party.'

And if I'd put the best one out you'd have said you wanted the second best that the bishop bought, Bridget thought grimly.

Mary stood a moment more, surveying the maid. She hadn't glanced directly at Sophy but each feature of the child's face was burned on her mind, day and night. It was through this creature that the gulf between her and Jeremiah had come about – she had long ago glossed over her own actions in the matter – and her marriage had been ruined. She had been forced to lie to the bishop and the rest of her family – the truth would have brought unthink-able humiliation – and continue the deception year after year. And the child herself, she was the very embodiment of the mother's provocative predilection for lasciviousness, with her great saucer eyes and Titian hair. She had watched her own sons soften towards the girl despite her warnings that they should have little to do with her, and the scut was a cross that her poor Patience had been compelled to bear daily. From a small child the girl had displayed the same waywardness as the mother – it was in her every glance, the tilt of her head, the pout of her lips. But she would break her spirit, Mary thought; the creature would not get the better of her.

She now turned about, her petticoats swishing and her carriage ramrod straight as she left the kitchen after checking a few details about the evening meal with Kitty. Sophy sank down on the bench and continued to rub at the silver plate she had been cleaning when her aunt had made her entrance, Bridget disappearing to see to the drawing-room fire.

She liked it when her aunt and uncle had a dinner party. Kitty always let her stay up late and have a taste of the different dishes, just a mouthful, before Bridget whisked them up to the dining room, and often there were five or six courses instead of the normal three the family had. She slid off the bench and sidled into the kitchen where Kitty was occupied in expertly filleting a whole salmon. 'What are they having for dinner, Kitty?' she said, standing by the kitchen table.

Kitty smiled. She knew what Sophy was really asking. 'Salmon puffs to start with, like they had when the bishop came last time, do you remember?'

Sophy nodded. Kitty had done a whole extra puff for her and the filling – a mix of salmon flakes, cream, butter, flour, eggs and spices – had been mouth-watering.

'Then soup, chicken fricassée, followed by lamb cutlets. The hot pudding is pears in ginger sauce, and the cold is Charlotte Delight, and I've made some of my shortbread to go with their coffee. Does madam approve?'

Sophy nodded, grinning. Pears in ginger sauce was her favourite pudding.

'An' aye, before you ask, you can stay up, as long as you're in your nightie in case the mistress takes it on herself to come down for any reason.' Kitty had the notion the mistress was beginning to suspect that on such occasions the odd treat or two found its way into Sophy's small frame.

Sophy nodded again, her eyes alight as she hugged herself in anticipation. Pears in ginger sauce, and her birthday tomorrow. Last year Bridget, Kitty and Patrick had bought her a sketchbook and coloured pencils which she kept hidden under her bed away from prying eyes. They always bought her something. One year it had been a whole box of chocolates to herself, another, a picture book which resided with the sketchpad and pencils and had been looked at so often it was falling apart. Her favourite present, though, was one she'd received when she was five years old, a cloth dolly she'd named Maisie. She slept with Maisie every night and in the day tucked her well down under her blankets on the pallet bed, knowing if Patience or her aunt ever became aware of the doll's existence, that would be the end of Maisie. 'I'll stay in bed and look at my picture book and if we hear anyone coming I'll hide it under the covers and pretend I'm asleep.'

'Aye, that's right, hinny, you do that.' Kitty's voice held a tinge of sadness, and as she had done countless times before, she thought, You poor little mite. There was this bairn, as bonny as a summer's day and as sweet as a nut in nature despite the way she was treated by her own kith and kin, and then there was Miss Patience, as spiteful and mean-minded a little madam as ever had been born, who was spoiled rotten by the mistress.

'Kitty?'

'Aye, me lamb?'

'Do you think my mother can see me? From heaven, I mean?'

Kitty stopped what she was doing and stared down into the earnest little face. 'Whatever's brought that into your head?' she said softly. 'Of course your mam can see you, hinny. She watches over you every day, I'll be bound.'

Sophy nodded but without conviction. 'Uncle Jeremiah said in his sermon last week that there's a divide between heaven and earth like there is between heaven and hell, and that when you're in heaven you don't care about earth any more and you just praise God all the time.'

'Did he?' Kitty had to confess she turned off once the master got on his bandwagon in the pulpit.

'He said God and the angels can see us but not real people who have died. They're not allowed.'

'Not allowed my backside.' Kitty didn't have a clue one way or the other, but her voice was adamant. 'Your mam *can* see you, hinny, an' don't let anyone tell you different. I'd stake my life on it. All right?'

Sophy gave a small smile. 'All right.'

'An' preachers an' suchlike, even ones like your uncle, they don't know everything,' Kitty added, hoping she wasn't perjuring her own soul. 'Their own take on things comes into it and the master, well, he isn't the most merry of men, now is he? If there's a black way to look at something, he'll find it, but it don't necessarily mean it's right.'

Sophy took a few moments to consider this. She hadn't looked at it like that before. Her expression lightened and now her voice carried more confidence when she said, 'I think my mother can see me. Heaven is somewhere where all your wishes come true and she would want to see me if she could, wouldn't she?'

'Aye, for sure, hinny.'

Two small slender arms went round her middle and Kitty found herself hugged briefly before Sophy disappeared off back to the scullery. Kitty stared after the child for a moment before getting back to the salmon. Whatever next? she thought with wry humour. You never knew what that little 'un was going to come out with. Bright as a button she was. Fancy her listening to the master's sermon like that when most of his parishioners, including herself, couldn't have repeated a word the minute they'd left the church.

She shook her head, dropping the filleted fish into a dish where it would poach in a drop of milk with a dash of vinegar before being flaked.

She was a thinker, was little Sophy, and knowing with it. That didn't bode well for any woman in what was definitely a man's world, but Sophy's position was worse than most. She was between two worlds, neither gentry nor servant, and likely to remain there until she was wed. And what sort of husband would the master and mistress choose for the lass? Likely some dusty old widower who would incarcerate her in a life of toil bringing up children who were not her own, or some psalm-singing hypocrite like the master, who preached one thing and did another.

Eeh, where had that last thought come from? Kitty shook her head again, but this time at herself. A few minutes with the bairn and she was thinking all sorts of things. But it was true. In spite of how he was, she had respected the master at one time, him being a man of the cloth an' all, but since the child had been born she had seen another side to his pious nature that couldn't be ignored. He knew full well how his lady wife treated the bairn, yet he let her get on with it – and why? Because he'd disapproved of Sophy's mam marrying a Frenchman. Now she wasn't learned like the master, and she dare say he'd forgotten more about the Good Book than she'd ever know, but to hold a grudge all these years? It wasn't right. Whatever way you looked at it, it wasn't right. One day, chickens would come home to roost and then the roof would go off this house – she could see it coming. Aye, the older the bairn got, the more she could see it coming.

Settling her chin into the ample folds of her neck, Kitty continued with her preparations, not dreaming that that day was closer than she had imagined.

The dinner party had gone off splendidly. Mary had been trained by her mother in the arts of being a good hostess and it was something she excelled in and thoroughly enjoyed. The other three couples – Dr Lawrence and his wife, Mr Longhurst, a local magistrate, and Mrs Longhurst, and the Williamsons – he was standing for Parliament this year and Mrs Williamson was involved in a string of good works – knew each other very well and the conversation at the dinner table had been merry. Jeremiah had roused himself to join in the general joviality, even making the odd quip or two, which was unusual.

Bridget had sensed the convivial atmosphere and seen how her mistress was basking in her success when silently serving the various courses, all of which boded well for the next little while. When one of the mistress's social functions didn't pass as smoothly as Mary would have liked, the whole household, but in particular Sophy, suffered the brunt of her frustration for days.

By the time the Williamsons' carriage and pair and Dr Lawrence's neat little pony and trap had been brought round to the front of the house from the stables by Patrick, it was clear that several members of the party were a little intoxicated. The women were giggling and fussing as Bridget helped them on with their coats and furs, and the men's voices were over-hearty. The Williamsons and the Longhursts were travelling together, and Mary and Jeremiah walked the three couples across the drive to the waiting conveyances, but Dr Lawrence, who was slightly behind the others, stopped midway and came back to Bridget, who was standing in the doorway in case she was needed.

'I forgot to give this to your mistress.' He handed her a small slim package. 'It's just a little thing for the child, Sophy, but I wouldn't like her to think I've forgotten her this year. She always writes such a formal little note of thanks. We don't buy for the others' children' – he gestured with his head towards the group talking by the carriages – 'so one has to be discreet, but as Sophy is our god-daughter . . .'

'Of course, sir.' Bridget dipped her knee as she took the gift and slipped it in her apron pocket, her mind racing as Dr Lawrence joined the others. Sophy had never received a present from Dr Lawrence and his wife and had certainly never written to thank them, so that meant . . . How could she? How *could* the mistress be so mean? To withhold the doctor's presents like that, it was stealing, that's what it was. Did the master know? And him a clergyman. But she wouldn't put anything past the pair of them where that bairn was concerned, so why was she surprised? And even when Sophy was occasionally summoned to the drawing room with Patience when visitors arrived, ostensibly to keep up the pretence that she was treated as a member of the family, she had noticed before that this never happened if the guest was Dr Lawrence. And now she knew why. He might mention something.

The carriage was drawing away, the trap following, and as a few desultory snowflakes drifted down in the bitterly cold night, Mary and Jeremiah walked towards the house. Bridget made up her mind quickly. She wouldn't say a word about the present, not until she'd given it to Sophy anyway, and then she would mention it casually when she was serving the mistress's elevenses in the morning room tomorrow. No doubt she would get into trouble, but that didn't matter. She could make out that the doctor had given her the gift when she was busy with her duties, and she'd put it in her pocket and forgotten all about it till morning when she'd found it and given it to the bairn.

Mary and Jeremiah walked past her without acknowledging her presence, their personas having changed radically now there was no longer any need to keep up the pretence of being a happily married couple. However, Mary did manage a tight smile as she paused at the foot of the staircase to say, 'Tell Cook the meal was most satisfactory, Bridget.'

'Yes, ma'am. Thank you, ma'am.'

'The ladies on my committee for the Sunday School Christmas party will be meeting here at ten-thirty tomorrow morning. Please see to it refreshments are served promptly at ten forty-five.'

'Yes, ma'am.'

'And the young masters will be home for the Christmas holidays in five days' time. You may start airing their bedding tomorrow morning and lighting a fire in their rooms.'

'Yes, ma'am.'

'That is all. Once you have put the drawing room to rights, you may retire.'

Considering it was nearly midnight, she should think so an' all, Bridget thought, her voice without expression as she said again, 'Yes, ma'am.'

Nevertheless, as she stacked the coffee tray, plumped the cushions on the sofas and tidied up crumbs of shortcake from the carpet with a little dustpan and brush, the small, gaily-wrapped parcel in her pocket banished any tiredness. She could just imagine Sophy's face tomorrow morning when she had a present from the doctor. And there were the books she and her mam and da had bought the bairn too. The old picture book was falling apart, Sophy had looked at it so much, besides which the lass hadn't been reading so well then. She hadn't known which book to choose – Hans Christian Andersen's *Fairy Tales* or Lewis Carroll's *Alice's Adventures in Wonderland*, when she had nipped into the little toy shop close to the dairy in Southwick Road. Conscious of the list of shopping in her pocket from the mistress, she had bought them both and she didn't regret it. The bairn had little enough.

She would have dearly loved to buy Sophy one of the richly dressed dolls she had seen, their porcelain faces and long hair curled in ringlets similar to those in Miss Patience's room, or maybe one of the magic lanterns which could project hand-coloured scenes on slides, but both would have been difficult to conceal. The books would give her the greatest pleasure. She nodded to the thought. And no doubt before too long she would know the stories off by heart.

Bridget's parents had already retired to their room when she finally finished in the drawing room and walked through to the kitchen. The room was in semi-darkness. Kitty had extinguished the oil lamp but left two candles at either end of the kitchen table, and by their flickering light Bridget gazed down at the child sleeping under her mound of blankets. Sophy was so finely boned and slender she often appeared small for her age but in fact this wasn't so.

Crouching down beside the pallet bed, Bridget smoothed a stray silky curl from the velvety forehead. Long thick lashes rested on milky white skin and the rosebud lips were slightly apart. The child was so lovely, the ever-present worry Bridget felt about Sophy's future rose to the fore once more. She was going to be a beautiful young woman in a few years, and a girl as enchanting as Sophy needed a father's protection, or at the very least a guardian's covering between her and a world full of men.

And then Bridget's common sense intervened. The bairn was only ten years old. There would be more than enough time to worry about such things in the future, but for now she was safe enough.

Standing upright, Bridget eased her aching back, the tiredness she had felt earlier suddenly overwhelming. She had been on her feet since five o'clock, not an abnormal occurrence, but tonight she felt every one of her thirty-five years and a good few more besides. She needed her bed. It had been three years after Sophy's birth before she had felt able to return to her room, and even now she occasionally felt uneasy about leaving the child sleeping in the kitchen, but this night she didn't even bother to undress before falling into bed, and was asleep as soon as her head touched the pillow.

Chapter 5

When Sophy opened her eyes the next morning, her first thought was of her birthday, and the second that she still felt full from the forbidden delicacies Kitty had slipped her way the previous evening. Kitty had given her a little bit of most of the dishes, but had made her a whole pear smothered in ginger sauce all to herself, the taste of which still lingered on her tongue.

Sophy glanced across the kitchen to where Bridget was busy persuading the range fire into a cheerful blaze. Sitting up, she rubbed her eyes. 'It's my birthday. I'm ten years old.'

'That you are, my pet.' Bridget smiled at her. 'Why don't you hurry up and get dressed, and then you can lay the table in here while I see to the fires in the house.'

Sophy nodded, scrambling out of bed. She liked the beginning of each day more than anything. The family were still asleep when she and Bridget and Kitty and Patrick ate their breakfast at the kitchen table, and it was always quiet and peaceful. She had never told a living soul – not even Bridget from whom she normally had no secrets – but she always pretended each morning that Bridget was her mother, and Kitty and Patrick her grandparents, and that they were a proper family eating together. To have said it out loud would somehow be a betrayal of her real mother, but just thinking it was all right.

By the time Kitty and Patrick rose at half-past six, the fires in the drawing room, morning room and dining room had been lit, and the first of the two pans of porridge which Kitty always left soaking overnight was simmering on the hob. Once they had eaten, Kitty would begin to prepare the family's breakfast which was served in the dining room at eight-thirty sharp after the whole household had met for morning prayers in the drawing room.

Porridge was always followed by a full English breakfast for the family. It had been something Mary had been used to when she lived with her parents and had continued into her marriage. Along with freshly baked breakfast rolls accompanied by various preserves, dishes of all kinds were sent up to the dining room: grilled bacon and broiled kidneys, boiled eggs — cooked for exactly four minutes by the kitchen clock — mushrooms from Patrick's dark little forcing house behind the south wall of the garden, and a hash of potatoes cooked the night before, to which onion and seasoning was added before Kitty shaped the end result into small squares and warmed them on the griddle. Occasionally, kromeskies — a kind of fritter — were also sent up to the dining room. When the boys were home, the dishes invariably returned to the kitchen empty. Other times, if anything was left, Kitty was expected to use it for the servants', and Sophy's, lunch.

Mary had a bee in her bonnet that the breakfast beverage had to be cocoa. Her father had always insisted that because cocoa contained cocoa-butter and starch, it would make up for the waste which had occurred during the fast of the preceding night, and would also maintain the body during the day. Tea was drunk at breakfast only when the bishop was a guest, since he had a dislike of cocoa.

Another of Mary's pet hates was pre-packed coffee. Although tradesmen were forbidden by law to adulterate coffee with chicory, Mary didn't trust them, therefore she insisted that the family's coffee was roasted and ground in the kitchen. Every three of four days, Kitty would take half a pound of the raw coffee berries, put them in a clean frying pan with a little fresh butter and stir them round and round until the whole was done, before grinding them immediately. Kitty often complained to herself during this process, muttering that the freshly packed coffee was just as good and she had enough to do as it was, but Sophy loved the mornings when the roasting coffee beans filled the kitchen with their luscious aroma.

Porridge, followed by thick wedges of Bridget's crusty bread spread with butter and two rashes of bacon apiece was the servants' breakfast as decreed by the mistress of the house. However, Kitty saw to it that a boiled egg – two for Patrick – along with several of the potato hashes, was added, having little time for what she called 'the mistress's parnicketies'.

It was one of Sophy's jobs to wash and prepare the vegetables for the whole household's meals each morning before the servants' breakfast. Kitty left the required amount in the scullery's huge square sink every evening before she retired, and Sophy always got to work as soon as she was up. She had to stand on an orange box to reach the sink, and however warm the kitchen was, the scullery was always freezing and gloomy, but with Bridget bustling about seeing to her various tasks the time passed quickly enough. Today though, Sophy had had to clean and scour a couple of pans and kitchen utensils left over from the dinner party the previous night before she could start on the vegetables. As far as Mary was concerned, it was one of Sophy's many duties to scrub all the stewpans, saucepans, sauté pans, frying pans and other kitchen equipment each day, but between them Bridget and Kitty saw to it that the majority of this was taken off Sophy's small shoulders. If the child had been forced to carry out all of Mary's orders, it was doubtful if she would have got to bed each night before the early hours of morning.

Sophy had just finished the last of the vegetables when Kitty called her through to the kitchen for breakfast, and when she took her place at the table there were two packages by her bowl of porridge, a slim long one wrapped in bright paper and another bulkier one in brown paper tied with string. She glanced at Bridget whose soft brown eyes were waiting for her. 'Happy birthday, hinny.' And then, as Sophy leaped up and hugged her, planting a kiss on her cheek, before doing the same to a smiling Kitty and Patrick, Bridget added, 'Now afore you open 'em, the smaller one is from the doctor, Dr Lawrence.'

'Dr Lawrence?' Sophy returned to her seat, her eyes wide, touching the bright paper as though it was going to bite her. 'Why would Dr Lawrence buy me a birthday present?'

After talking the matter through with her mother in hushed whispers while Sophy finished the last of the vegetables, Bridget had decided to say nothing of the past gifts, feeling it would somehow take the shine off the present. Now she cleared her throat before saying, 'I suppose it's because you're ten and that's quite a landmark, and you are his god-daughter, after all.'

Sophy stared at Bridget in amazement. It was the first time she knew of this. 'I am?'

'Aye, you are. When you were a little babbie you were christened by your uncle, and Dr Lawrence and Mrs Lawrence were asked to be your godparents.'

It was the biggest surprise of Sophy's young life. Again she trailed a finger over the doctor's present. 'Did my mam ask them?'

It was rare Sophy used the local idiom. Mary insisted she speak as she termed 'properly' and any lapses on Sophy's part had resulted in a brutal use of the cane.

'No, hinny.' Bridget's voice was soft. 'I don't think so.'

Sophy nodded. 'But she liked the doctor?'

'Oh aye, he's a grand man, the doctor, and he was the first one to see you when you were born. I think your mam would have been very pleased.' Bridget's voice was over-bright; the expression on the child's face was paining her, and even Patrick had a lump in his throat at the transparent wonder lighting Sophy's face. 'Come on then, let's see what you've got.'

Sophy's small hands hesitated over the doctor's package, and then she reached for the brown-paper one. 'This is from you all?' she asked, her clear amber eyes flashing over their waiting faces. And at Bridget's nod, 'Then I'll open this one first.'

There was another round of hugs after she had opened their present, and then she carefully separated the edges of the thick embossed paper. It fell apart to reveal a swathe of pale pink tissue paper, and when she lifted out the lengths of ribbon – two white, two violet and two scarlet – Sophy and the two women drew in their breath in a long *oooh* of delight.

'Aren't they beautiful?' Sophy lifted shining eyes to the others. 'Feel them, Bridget. They're like silk.'

'They're bonny.' The look on Sophy's face brought a feeling of recklessness and Bridget jumped up, coming behind the child as she said, 'Let's see what they look like in your hair, shall we?' and she began to unplait the tight golden-red braid.

'She won't be able to wear 'em in front of the mistress.' It was Patrick who spoke and his voice was cautionary. 'You understand that, don't you, hinny?' he added to Sophy as Bridget finally loosened the waist-length hair which spilled over the child's slender back in a mass of glowing waves.

''Course she does, she's not daft.' Bridget was combing out the thick, silken locks with her fingers. 'But that don't mean she can't have a few minutes now, does it? It's a cryin' shame, keeping all this hidden day after day. Beautiful, your hair is, me bairn. Just like your mam's.'

Bridget reached for one of the violet ribbons but she never got to pick it up, a gasp from her mother causing her to spin round. And there, standing in the doorway, was Mary Hutton.

Mary had suspected for some time that her orders concerning the child were not carried out to the letter. Bridget took too much on herself, she had been saying the same to Jeremiah for the last two or three years, but his response had been chary. The O'Learys did the work of double their number and he would be hard-pressed to get a gardener-cum-handyman, let alone a cook and maid, for what he paid each month, he had warned her. He didn't want her preoccupation over Esther's daughter spoiling things.

But now she had her proof. She was well aware it was the child's birthday and had timed her early morning visit to the kitchen to maximum effect. She walked slowly into the room and looked down at the child who was the bane of her existence, crouching into the maid for protection. 'What are these?' She flicked the paper containing the ribbons with one finger, but with enough force to send them fluttering on to the stone slabs, the sight of the child's hair increasing her fury. 'You did this,' she said to Bridget who had frozen at her entrance. 'You bought these.'

'She didn't.' The only thought in Sophy's head was that Bridget mustn't be blamed. 'The doctor gave them to me. It was him.'

'The doctor?' Mary's voice was thin and high. 'Don't talk such rubbish, girl. When have you seen the doctor?'

'Dr Lawrence asked me to give Sophy a present from him and his wife last night.' Bridget didn't add 'ma'am'; something told her they were beyond that. 'He'd forgotten to give it to you, *as usual*,' she added meaningfully.

She couldn't have said anything more guaranteed to incense the furious woman in front of her. The fact that this maid, a person so below her in the social strata, was daring to criticise her actions, inflamed Mary to the point of madness. Grabbing hold of Sophy she dragged the child from the kitchen bench, shaking her hard for good measure. 'You come with me, and you' – she turned her blazing eyes on Bridget – 'I'll deal with you later.'

'It's not her fault.' The look on the mistress's face was frightening and Bridget had lost all restraint. 'The doctor gave the present to me an' I just passed it on, that's all. You leave her be.'

'You dare to speak to me like this?' It was the final straw. 'I want you out of this house by nightfall. Do you hear me?'

'If she goes, we all go.' Patrick, his face as white as a sheet, spoke for the first time. 'My lass has worked hard for you, missus, we all have, as well you know. We're not as daft as you think we are. There's many a cook earnin' double what you pay Kitty, an' I do the work of two – three – men. We'd have slung our hook long before this if it wasn't for the bairn.'

'*Then go.*' Mary so forgot herself as to scream the words. '*Now! Today!*' as she hauled Sophy out of the kitchen, by which time Kitty and Patrick had moved to hold on to Bridget, who was fighting them to get to the child.

Mary found Sophy had turned into a whirling dervish as she dragged the little girl along the corridor and into the hall. When they reached the morning room which housed the cupboard with the dreaded correction cane, Sophy began to kick and claw at her aunt in a paroxysm of terror. She was still struggling wildly when the first vicious stroke of the cane hit her across the top of her legs, causing her to fall on the floor, her hair cascading about her shoulders. And then the cane came again and again, striking the small body with enough force to make it bounce. With each stroke Mary was flaying Jeremiah and his lies, the ruination of her marriage, Esther and her wickedness which had brought the seed of badness into her own family, and not least the sickness she felt whenever her sons were home and in close proximity to that seed.

By the time Sophy's screams had brought Jeremiah, still in his nightshirt with his dressing gown thrown hastily about his shoulders, to the morning room, Mary had locked the door against intruders. Sophy was merely a whimpering, semi-conscious heap when Mary reached for the pearl-handled knife she used to open any letters or packages delivered to the vicarage. She sawed at the long strands of golden-red hair with savage satisfaction, and each time the small head fell forwards it was jerked up again.

It took Jeremiah a couple of minutes to force the door, and by then Mary had all but completed her grisly task. She sat straddling the senseless child, surrounded by a cloud of silky hair which had feathered into the air and settled about her, her face lit by an unholy gratification and her breath coming in short gasps.

Jeremiah stood stock-still, unable to believe his eyes. It was Patience, coming up behind her father, who brought Mary to her right mind. Patience's voice was a whimper when she said, 'Mother? Mother, what have you done?' and something in her child's tone reached the enraged woman, causing her eyes to focus. Slowly Mary stood up, letting the knife fall from her clenched fingers.

'Take your mother upstairs and make her lie down, Patience.' Jeremiah looked neither at his wife nor daughter as he spoke, his eyes fixed on the small figure at Mary's feet. Sophy's dress had been almost ripped off her back in the struggle, along with her petticoat and shift, and the criss-cross of blue-red weals on her back and legs were startling against the white flesh. But it was the bloody scalp, shorn of most of its hair, which was turning Jeremiah's stomach. The child looked as though an animal had attacked it and he could hardly credit his wife, his contained, sanctimonious, self-righteous wife with perpetrating such an outrage.

He had been conscious of shouting from the direction of the kitchen whilst he had been trying to get into the morning room and now, as Bridget burst into the hall, he quickly pushed his wife and daughter out of the room and shut the door, blocking the entrance with his body.

'What's she done to the bairn?' Bridget's cap was askew and her face tear-blotched, and as Kitty and Patrick appeared panting behind her, Patrick caught his daughter's arm as she lifted it as though she was going to strike her mistress. Such was the severity of the situation that Jeremiah didn't think to reprimand Bridget. Repeating his earlier order to Patience, he said, 'Take your mother upstairs,' before he faced the servants. 'The child is perfectly all right. Please go about your duties.'

'Our duties?' Bridget was beside herself. 'The mistress has given us our marching orders and I want to see the bairn.'

He stared at the maid, his face blank but his mind working overtime. If he wasn't going to lose all credence in the town, this matter had to be defused. Keeping his back firmly against the door and his hand on the door knob, he said, 'My wife has disciplined the child but that is all and I am dealing with her now. We will discuss this later.'

'Later my backside.' Patience had led her mother to the foot of the stairs but now Bridget swung round, pointing at them as she said, 'She's a maniac, that's what she is, and all over a few ribbons.'

'Ribbons?'

'The doctor gave me a present for the bairn last night, and she' – again Bridget sent a burning glance towards the stairs – 'she went barmy when she saw them.'

Jeremiah's aplomb was returning. Drawing himself up, he said coldly, 'I am aware you are distressed but that does not excuse your impertinence to me or your mistress. We will deal with our ward as we see fit, do you understand?'

'Oh aye, I understand all right.' Bridget's Irish side was to the fore and nothing could have stopped her now. It had taken all of Kitty's and Patrick's strength to hold on to her when she had heard Sophy screaming, and when she had finally been able to fling them off and make for the hall, the silence from the morning room had been worse than the child's cries. 'Your lady wife beats her half to death and works the bairn like a dog, and you turn a blind eye. I'm sure some of your high-falutin' friends would be interested to hear what really goes on in this house.'

'How dare you.' Patience and Mary had reached the landing, and confident that his wife wasn't going to further complicate matters, Jeremiah was now every inch the master of the house. 'If you don't want to find yourself up before the magistrate, who happens to be one of those *high-faluting* friends you spoke of, I suggest you put some good distance between this town and your-selves. Slander is a serious offence and carries a custodial sentence, and I would make sure you and your parents get the maximum penalty. I don't know how you would fare in prison but I do know they are most unpleasant places with a large portion of unsavoury characters.' It had become obvious to him that there was no way he could retain the servants, so the only alternative was to put the fear of God in them. 'And at your parents' age', he glanced icily at Kitty and Patrick standing at their daughter's elbow, 'the only place from there would be the workhouse, which is perhaps more unpleasant than prison in some cases. Do I make myself clear?'

Bridget's high colour had drained away and she looked pale, but she still said stubbornly, 'I want to see the bairn.'

'Come away, lass.' Kitty pulled at her daughter's arm. 'You can do nothing here.'

'I will give each of you a month's pay, which is extremely generous in the circumstances, but I want you out of this house by lunchtime and on your way.' Jeremiah was praying the child wouldn't rouse herself and begin to cry out. 'And if I hear so much as a whisper about the affairs of this house I promise you will regret the day you were born. All of you.'

Patrick hadn't said a word thus far but had stood, his jaw working, listening to the others. Now he looked Jeremiah straight in the eye. 'And references, master?'

Jeremiah stared back at him. 'I have never found any fault with your work and Kitty is a good cook. Yes, I am prepared to give you references – even you, Bridget.'

Bridget knew what he was saying. Without references they would be hard-pressed to find good employment, especially her parents. She might find something, she was young enough, but them . . . The master had mentioned the workhouse and she knew it was a spectre that haunted her parents, even though she had promised them she would never see them put into one of those hell-holes. But would she be able to keep that promise without the master's references? He was bribing her, he knew it and she knew it. But the bairn, she couldn't leave the bairn.

It was Kitty, tugging on her arm again, who settled the matter. 'Come away, lass,' she repeated softly. 'The bairn'll be all right and after all, she isn't yours. You have no rights concernin' her and you can't do nowt. I always told you it was wrong to get over-fond of her, didn't I?'

It hurt, not so much what her mother had said but the way she had said it, because it suggested her mother held her responsible for the fact they were being turned out on their ear. Knowing she was beaten and a pain tearing her apart that couldn't be worse if she was being disembowelled, Bridget's voice was weak when she said, 'She'll do for the bairn one day, the mistress. You know that, don't you? She's not right in the head where that little 'un's concerned.' She swung round to face Jeremiah again. 'And it'll be *you* God holds responsible, because you can't pretend you don't know what's goin' on after this.'

Under other circumstances such disrespect from an inferior would have made Jeremiah incensed, but although he said icily, 'I think that's more than enough, Bridget. Go and pack your belongings and I will see the three of you in my study in an hour,' inside he was greatly afraid that his wife had indeed 'done for the bairn'. There had been no movement from within the morning room, not a sound, and the child had been unconscious when he had seen her. What if she wasn't unconscious but dead? Dear God, don't let it be so. They would never survive the scandal.

When the servants trooped away, Patrick with his arm round his daughter who was sobbing audibly, Jeremiah waited until he was sure they were in the kitchen before taking a deep breath and opening the morning-room door. The child was lying exactly as he had seen her before. Through forcing the door, the locking mechanism was broken beyond repair so he dragged Mary's small bureau against the door to prevent anyone bursting in. The way the maid had carried on, he wouldn't put anything past her.

Kneeling down, he stared at the small body and when he saw the child was breathing the relief was so great he put his hand to his head for a few moments. He could see now that some of the blue weals had bled and a wave of sickness swept over him, but he forced himself to gently turn her over on to her back and still she didn't stir. The little shorn head with a few tufts of hair remaining was shocking enough, but the child had a livid bruise on her forehead as though her face had been repeatedly banged against the floor, and maybe it had, he thought grimly.

Carefully he slid his arms under Sophy's legs and shoulders and lifted her on to one of the two dark green sofas, propping her head on a cushion, at which point the heavily lashed eyes fluttered and opened and the child gave a soft moan as she shrank from him.

For the life of him Jeremiah didn't know what to do or say. The child needed a doctor, that much was evident, but how could he call Dr Lawrence to the house and let him see the state of her? When a knock sounded at the door in the next instant and Patience's voice called softly, 'Father? Father, can I come in?' again relief was paramount. He heaved the bureau to one side and opened the door, moving it back once his daughter had entered.

Patience was beset by a whole host of emotions as she walked over to the sofa and knelt down beside her cousin. All her life she had resented Sophy's presence in the house. She knew her brothers liked Sophy more than her, even David who was her twin. Whenever the boys were home they sneaked down to the kitchen at every opportunity in spite of it being out of bounds, and the way they were with Sophy – gently teasing her, laughing with her, telling her stories of their life at school – was so different from their attitude to her. And Sophy was clever too. She was their governess Miss Brown's favourite, even though Miss Brown tried to hide it. When the three of them had read *A Midsummer Night's Dream* this year and Sophy had acted out her part, Miss Brown had told her she was wonderful and had a natural ability for getting inside a character which was a true gift. They had been going to read another of Shakespeare's plays next year but her mother had had a blue fit when she had discovered how Miss Brown was teaching English literature and had forbidden it. But it was Sophy's appearance – her large beautiful eyes, her skin, her hair, especially her hair – which she hated the most. But now . . .

Patience put out her hand and touched Sophy's arm, and like her father she felt physically sick at what her mother had done.

'It's all right,' she whispered. 'Mother's not here.' Sophy shivered, whether from the mention of her attacker or because she was cold, Patience didn't know, but she said, 'Shall I get you a blanket?' but received no answer from the colourless lips in the chalk-white face. 'I'll get you something.' She stood up and as she did so, said in an aside to her father, 'She needs Dr Lawrence.'

'That's out of the question.'

'But Father—'

'Can you see to her? If I carry her up to the guest room out of the way, can you take care of her? I can bring you what you need and I've got some laudanum left from the bottle I had for the abscess in my tooth. A few drops of that will settle her.'

'But what if—'

'*Please*, Patience.'

She hadn't heard that note in her father's voice before and more than anything else it brought home to Patience the seriousness of the situation. Her heart in her mouth, she looked down at Sophy for a long moment. She had enjoyed the times her cousin was in trouble with her mother and had done her part in seeing Sophy got the cane on lots of occasions, but this – this was altogether different. Patience didn't have the vocabulary to describe how she felt, but she knew that this last act of her mother's had gone far beyond merely chastising her cousin. 'All right.' She nodded. 'Shall I tell Bridget to light a fire in the guest room and bring some warm water, soap and towels?'

'The servants are going shortly.'

'Going?'

'I have dismissed them, it's the only way. I will see to their replacements as soon as I can, but until then we will have to manage.'

Patience stared at her father wide-eyed, bewildered at how rapidly her world had changed. 'She needs to be kept warm,' she said weakly.

'Then stay here with her.' Jeremiah pulled the sofa closer to the fire as he spoke before straightening and adding, 'I'll see to everything upstairs as soon as I can.'

When her father had left the room, Patience turned and looked down on Sophy again. The amber eyes were open and tears were seeping from them but Sophy didn't make a sound. Patience stared at her helplessly. 'Are you cold?'

Sophy made the slightest movement with her head; even so, it caused her to wince.

'Here.' Patience slipped off her thick, woolly dressing gown and placed it over the trembling body of her cousin. 'It'll be all right. I'll look after you.' And then, aware that this might not be much comfort, she added, 'I promise I won't let Moth— anyone, hurt you ever again. I promise, Sophy.'

When Sophy closed her eyes Patience wasn't sure if she had understood her or not, but anyway, it didn't matter. She had meant every word.

Bridget, Kitty and Patrick left the house at ten o'clock with a month's wages apiece and the precious references. By then Sophy was heavily sedated with a generous dose of Jeremiah's laudanum and consequently unaware of their departure. The family carried all their worldly possessions in three carpet bags, but due to the back-door trading which went on with most cooks and itinerant traders who presented themselves at the kitchen door at certain days in the month, they weren't as destitute as they could have been. Beef dripping, rabbit skins, feathers and bones were all disposed of into willing hands, and over the time Kitty had been at the vicarage she had made a tidy sum for 'a rainy day'. This did not comfort Bridget in the slightest; she was bereft at leaving the child she considered her own, but it would cushion the three against the perils of homelessness while they looked for employment.

A thin dusting of snow lay on the frozen ground from a brief fall the night before, but as Jeremiah watched the small family trudge down the drive from his vantage point at an upstairs window, he felt not the slightest remorse for turning them out in such bitter weather. On the contrary, he was more than a little peeved at having to pay out good money for nothing – as he described it to himself, ignoring the fact that he knew he had underpaid the three for years.

After he was sure they had departed, he looked in on Sophy and Patience now ensconced in the spare room. Sophy was lying as still and white as a small corpse under the heaped covers of one of the two single beds the room held, and Patience was sitting in a chair by the fire reading.

'Go and get yourself something to eat.' Jeremiah walked over to the bed and stood looking down at his niece for a moment. 'She'll sleep for some time yet.'

Patience didn't need to be told twice, and once his daughter had disappeared downstairs Jeremiah made his way to the bedroom he shared with his wife. Mary hadn't moved from the armchair in front of the fire where she had placed herself on entering the room with Patience earlier. When he had come to get dressed before he had carried the child to the spare room she had said not a word and neither had he, but her glance had carried its normal disdain when she had looked at him. Now, as he opened the bedroom door, she again looked at him in the usual dismissive way, but his opening words caused her thin, tight body to sit straighter. 'The servants have gone, as you directed, so I suggest you get yourself down to the kitchen and start preparing an early lunch.'

She stared at him as though he was mad. 'I will not.'

He carried on as though she had not spoken. 'After which you will carry out the duties Bridget normally attends to, as well as seeing to dinner tonight. And until I can replace the O'Learys, this will continue, so let us hope it can be soon.'

Mary had now risen to her feet, her bony hands joined in front of her waist. 'Have you lost your mind, Jeremiah?'

'No. For the first time in years I am thinking clearly, Mary.' His calm demeanour was holding by a thread and Mary must have sensed this as she took a step backwards. 'You've excelled yourself today, my devout, God-fearing wife. And I am partly to blame, I accept that. I have allowed you sufficient rope to hang yourself, but it wasn't you who was caught in the noose, was it? It was all of us. You would have destroyed my standing in this community without a second thought because of your obsession regarding the child. But no more. I will not be ruined on the altar of your fixation. Of course this all depends on whether the child lives or dies, because you have taken her to the edge, do you realise that?'

'Don't you dare speak to me in this fashion.'

'I dare much more than this.' It was a low growl. 'The child will reside in the guest room with Patience for the time being until I can arrange for her to attend a private school in Newcastle along with Patience.'

'No, you won't take Patience from me.'

'Of course this will mean we have to cut back a little, my dear, so thriftiness will be called for.'

Mary's breath was coming in gasps. 'I – I won't discipline the child again.'

'Indeed you won't.'

'There is no need for such measures.'

'There is every need.' Jeremiah spat the words into her stiff face, and only in that moment did Mary realise how far she had pushed him. 'I see now I cannot trust you around the child and so she needs to be removed from your presence. You will not destroy my good name, Mary. Not while I have breath in my body. Sophy will go away to school and Patience will accompany her. Anything else would raise suspicions as to why we are educating our niece above our daughter. And while we are talking like this, you had better write to your uncle and inform him that his New Year visit will not be convenient this year. The guest room will be occupied.'

'You – you devil.'

'I am but what you have made me, Mary.'

Jeremiah turned and walked out of the room, and if his wife had still had the pearl-handled knife in her possession she would have used it.

PART THREE

Destiny

1896

Chapter 6

'Aren't you even a little bit pleased to be leaving school for good, Sophy? I mean, no more arithmetic and French and embroidering those wretched samplers. If I have girls when I get married I shall make sure they never have to do any sewing.'

Sophy smiled at her friend. Charlotte Gilbert-Lee had shared much of the last six years of her life and she was very fond of her, but Charlotte was the only daughter of Mr and Mrs Gilbert-Lee and her father was a prominent solicitor who doted on his offspring. Charlotte went home every weekend to be thoroughly spoiled, and her holidays were spent in a round of entertainment and fun. They were worlds apart, and yet from Sophy's first week at Miss Bainbridge's Academy for Young Ladies, Charlotte had taken the frightened and unhappy newcomer under her wing and smoothed Sophy's path. Sophy and Patience had only gone home to the vicarage at holiday time – Jeremiah had maintained that a weekly trip to Newcastle to bring the girls home every weekend was too much – but neither of them had minded this. In the four months from Mary's assault on Sophy until Jeremiah had got them into Miss Bainbridge's Academy, the open warfare which existed between husband and wife had made life at the vicarage unbearable. And this had only got worse over the years.

Thinking of this now, Sophy said quietly, 'I like it here, I always have, and I've enjoyed everything.'

'That's because you're good at everything,' Charlotte said without a trace of envy. 'Even the pianoforte with old Potty.'

Miss Potts was the music teacher and Charlotte had been the bane of the poor woman's life; no matter how Miss Potts tried, she was unable to make Charlotte grasp more than the mere rudiments of the instrument. As Charlotte herself cheerfully proclaimed, where the piano was concerned she had two left hands. Charlotte did have a beautiful singing voice, however, as did Sophy, and the two of them had often performed a duet at the musical soirées Miss Bainbridge put on for family and friends at the end of the summer and Christmas terms. As both girls were very pretty and their voices harmonised perfectly, they had been in great demand.

Sophy had loved those occasions; in fact, she sometimes felt they were the only times she was truly alive, along with the dancing and drama classes taken by Miss Bainbridge's sister. She could become someone else – anyone else – rather than Sophy Hutton, orphan. She had once daringly asked her uncle why she couldn't be known by her father's name of Lemaire, since it was so much more satisfying than plain old Hutton, but he had told her not to be so impertinent and that was the end of that. She knew why, of course. It was because her aunt and uncle had disapproved of her mother's marriage and were determined to stamp out even the memory of her father's name. But they wouldn't. She was determined about that. She often pictured them, her mother and father, when they had been young and in love. Her mother had had deep blue eyes, Bridget had told her that, so she must have inherited her father's unusual amber eyes. She liked the thought of that. She could see him in her mind's eye – a tall, dark, handsome Frenchman with black curly hair and a captivating smile. And he was of the nobility, even if he hadn't had any money. But more than that he had loved her mother, and he would have loved her too, if he hadn't been taken so suddenly.

'Miss Gilbert-Lee? Your father is here.' Miss Bainbridge stuck her head round the door of the refectory where the young ladies were waiting for relatives or friends to collect them for the journey home, and the two girls looked at each other for a moment before hugging.

'Don't forget we're going to write every week.' Charlotte was suddenly tearful. 'And I'll get Papa to ask your uncle if you can come for a visit over the New Year. We mustn't lose touch, Sophy. Promise me we won't.'

Sophy patted her friend's arm. 'Of course we won't.' She didn't believe it. The Gilbert-Lees had made numerous requests over the last six years, asking that Sophy be allowed to come and stay, but her uncle had refused every one. Patience, on the other hand, who had been in the year above her and who had finished her schooling twelve months ago, had been given her mother's permission to accept any invitation which came her way. And Charlotte was off to an expensive finishing school in the spring to prepare her for entry into fashionable society when she reached the age of eighteen; she would make new friends, girls who would invite her to their homes and who would be invited to Charlotte's. Sophy knew this was the end of an era.

After more hugs and tears, Sophy watched her friend depart before sitting down in a vacant chair in the refectory, her valise at her feet.

She didn't want to go back to the vicarage. She drew in her upper lip, biting down hard to prevent giving way. It hadn't been so bad having to spend the holidays there because she had known she would be returning to the school again, but now . . .

She rubbed at her eyes with the back of her hand, something Miss Bainbridge would have deemed unladylike. There were many things Miss Bainbridge deemed unladylike.

It had been Patience who had broken the news of Bridget's departure from the house six years ago, and to be fair to her cousin she had tried to be kind. Patience had even gone so far as to rescue Maisie and her other hidden treasures from under the blankets on the pallet bed, along with the two new books, although the ribbons had disappeared, never to be mentioned again.

At first, Sophy had been unable to believe she would never see

Bridget and her parents again, but when it had sunk in that they had gone for good, she had been bereft. She had only really begun to recover from the heartbreak of losing the only people in the world she loved and who loved her, when she had come to the school and Charlotte had befriended her. Charlotte had been her protector in those early days too; although her hair had begun to grow back, Sophy had still had to wear a mop cap for some time, which had been explained by saying she had been very ill and her hair had fallen out. Some of the girls had teased her most spitefully until Charlotte had let it be known that anyone who upset Sophy upset her too, and Charlotte was a favourite with everyone.

She had never told anyone the truth about the loss of her hair, not even Charlotte. It wasn't out of any sense of misguided loyalty to her aunt, but because the whole episode had made her feel painfully debased and ashamed. It still did.

Sophy raised her hand to her hair, neatly secured in a shining chignon at the back of her head. All of Miss Bainbridge's young ladies wore their hair in this fashion from the age of fourteen – it was part of their preparation for womanhood; although when she was at home her aunt insisted she scrape her hair back into a tight plait. She had complied with this order thus far, but had vowed when she was sixteen and had left the school, she would tell her aunt she was wearing her hair how she liked. And her sixteenth birthday had passed two weeks ago.

Sophy's beautiful eyes narrowed. There were going to be battles ahead. She didn't know exactly when she'd ceased fearing her aunt, but gradually her dread of the woman who had treated her so cruelly had been replaced by hatred, and lately contempt had been added to the mix. Her aunt hadn't touched her since that day six years ago, but Sophy knew now that if she attempted to do so again, she would fight her tooth and nail. She'd been a slight child at ten, finely boned and thin. She was still finely boned, but now slender rather than thin, and she was tall for her age. Moreover, she knew she was strong inside, where it counted. She'd had to be. She nodded mentally to the thought. Her aunt would not subjugate her again; she would kill or be killed first. That was how strongly she felt about it.

Dear, dear. Suddenly Sophy's irrepressible humour came into play. Whatever would Miss Bainbridge do if she knew that one of 'her girls' was capable of thinking such things? Expire on the spot, most likely, or certainly indulge in a ladylike fit of the vapours.

Sophy glanced round the crowded refectory where excited girls were running hither and thither or clustered together in chattering groups, their faces alight with the anticipation of going home for Christmas.

She wasn't like any of these girls, she was different. Not just because she was an orphan, but deep inside, in her heart and mind. From when she'd first set foot in this place with Patience, Miss Bainbridge had taught them that a woman's place in life was to be a decorative and useful asset to her husband. Furthermore, expensive objects were to be coveted, representing as they did, symbols of status and lifestyle. Miss Bainbridge had been adamant that gentility and morality were one and the same, and a woman's identity lay firmly in the man whose wife she was. A woman, any woman, rich or poor, could only be happy fulfilling her sacred role of pleasing her husband in everything. These were the precepts Miss Bainbridge and her team of spinsters drummed into each girl from her first week at the school until her last, and it was true to say that all her classmates, even dear Charlotte, accepted such principles without too much trouble.

Sophy frowned, turning to gaze out of the window which over-looked the square of lawn and neat flowerbeds which was the girls' exercise area when the weather permitted. Today, with only ten days until Christmas, the lawn was buried under an inch or two of snow which had fallen during the night and frozen, creating a scene which looked as though it had been painted in silver. But Sophy wasn't seeing the garden or the mother-of-pearl winter's sky above, she was remembering passages from the book each girl leaving the school had been presented with two days ago: *The Manual of Home-Making and Fine Etiquette.*

A wife and mother, the book had stated, was called upon to be agreeable at all times, and any talents she possessed should be developed for the edification of her husband and sons. As she packaged the dinner to please her husband's tastes, with skill and care, so she should package herself and particularly her intellect to avoid being too clever in the company of her menfolk. The purposes of a woman's intelligence should be limited by the expectation of her husband. A husband would not bring his problems home with him to be discussed with his wife, but wives, nevertheless, with gentle intuition, were to understand that such problems existed and do all they could to mitigate them.

She had read that bit out to Charlotte, half-choking on the words, and Charlotte had looked at her strangely. 'But everyone knows men don't like clever, opinionated women,' she had said reasonably. 'That's all it's saying.'

'And you think that's right? That women should pretend to be stupid, or at the very least less intelligent than they are?' she'd asked hotly.

Charlotte had shrugged. 'I don't suppose so, but does it matter?' she'd answered, before leaping up as the dinner gong had sounded, at which point the conversation had ended.

But Sophy had thought about it several times since and now she sighed deeply. It *did* matter. Of course it mattered. Another passage in the book had stated that should the man of the house come home in a fractious mood or appear unreasonable or even tyrannous, then the wife's course was clear. She must bear all things with a meek and quiet spirit and thus spread the balm of her humility and gentleness over troubled waters. *Reverence your husband,* the manual had stated, *and remember at all times he is the breadwinner and his authority is not to be questioned. Your reward will be the knowledge that you have done your duty to the best of your ability. And this same duty,* the passage went on, *also applies to the 'private' side of marriage. A husband's needs must be accommodated without complaint.*

What these needs were, the book hadn't explained, and none of the girls in Sophy's year had any idea what they consisted of. Belinda Wynford had said she thought if you kissed a boy on the lips it made a baby – but when Charlotte had commented that couldn't be true because what about male cousins and brothers? – Belinda had admitted she didn't know. It was all very confusing. And Amelia Middleton had caused them all to become silent when she had whispered that her eldest sister who had been married for some years had told her there was a personal side to marriage 'in the bedroom' that was highly distasteful and far too embarrassing to talk about, and if she had known what it entailed she would have chosen to remain a spinster all her days.

'Sophy, dear?'

A gentle hand at her elbow caused her to come out of her reverie and glance up into the sweet face of her favourite teacher, Miss Bainbridge's sister. It wasn't just that this Miss Bainbridge taught dancing and drama, her favourite subjects, but she was the only teacher to unbend enough to call the girls by their christian names.

'I understand you are travelling by the stagecoach to Sunderland where your uncle is meeting you? It is due in five minutes so I suggest you go downstairs and wait in the vestibule.' Primrose Bainbridge smiled into the face she likened to that of an angel. She had said the same to her sister once, and her sister had come back with the remark that no angel had eyes the colour of Sophy's, nor her mass of Titian, flame-coloured hair either. Which was probably true. Primrose had always tried not to have a preference for one pupil, but she had failed with Sophy. And to see the girl when she was reading poetry or dancing or acting in one of the little plays the school put on was sheer delight; she had a natural talent the like of which Primrose had never come across before. She would miss this girl. She now pressed a little box into Sophy's hand, saying, 'This is just a small memento to remind you of the happy times we've had in class, my dear. Think of us sometimes, won't you?'

'Oh, Miss Bainbridge. Thank you, thank you.' For the second time in as many minutes Sophy was close to tears.

'Now get yourself downstairs and make sure the coach driver provides you with a rug for the journey; it's very cold.'

'Yes, Miss Bainbridge.' Sophy picked up her valise and then on impulse leaned forward and kissed the teacher on the cheek before making her way out of the refectory. She left Primose Bainbridge staring after her with moist eyes. Yes, she would miss Sophy Hutton more than a little. Her classes wouldn't be the same from now on.

For once the coach had been a little early, and after Sophy had climbed aboard and wished the other three occupants a good morning, she settled back in her seat by the window and opened Miss Bainbridge's box. It contained a small silver brooch in the shape of a ballerina, and she immediately pinned it to the lapel of her winter coat, her heart full. She felt as though she was leaving her home and travelling into alien territory, rather than the other way round, which perhaps wasn't too far from the truth.

It wasn't only the school she would miss, she had enjoyed living in the fast-growing, thriving town of Newcastle too. Miss Bainbridge's establishment was situated in central Newcastle, and Sophy had found the life and vigour of the town fascinating. At the weekends the girls were taken in small groups to places of interest now and again, after which they had to write reports describing the background to what they had seen. She knew that the medieval town of Newcastle had grown up around the castle, the first wooden castle being built by the son of William the Conqueror, and that when in the fourteenth century a wall had been built around the town, it had constricted the growth of Newcastle for the next five hundred years. But it was the present town which excited Sophy, the noise and bustle, the wealth of churches and monasteries, the music halls such as Ginnett's Amphitheatre and the People's Palace, as well as Hancock Museum in Barras Bridge where the girls had had to write an essay on the large collections it housed from the Natural History Society and Mr John Hancock himself, a world-renowned naturalist. Charlotte had had the class in fits of laughter when she had – quite innocently – described Mr Hancock as a naturist, and Miss Bainbridge had had to explain, with scarlet cheeks, the different meaning of the two words.

Sporting pursuits were catered for by a riding school, a racquet court in College Street and a number of tennis courts and bowling greens. There was also a swimming pool, but the young ladies of Miss Bainbridge's Academy were not allowed to partake of anything so vulgar; however, they were encouraged to walk in the parks the town contained, two-by-two, in a long line, with a teacher at either end of the crocodile. Leazes Park and Brandling Park were nice enough, but it was Exhibition Park – formerly known as Bull Park because bulls had once been kept on this part of the town moor – that Sophy liked the best. An exhibition had been held there for Queen Victoria's Golden Jubilee nine years before, and at this time the reservoir had been turned into an ornamental lake, with a bridge over it. According to Miss Bainbridge, who always relayed the history of everywhere they visited, no matter how many times they had been before, the bridge was a reproduction of the Old Bridge which had spanned the River Tyne at Newcastle for upwards of five centuries. Sophy didn't care so much about that, she just enjoyed watching the wildlife on the lake and the families with small children playing by the edge or sitting having picnics on the grass.

She would find it hard to settle in the small confines of Southwick after the bigness of Newcastle, she thought, as the coach trundled its way southwards through the mucky streets made slushy by the wheels of carriages, carts and horse trams. She had never felt overwhelmed by the size of the town; on the contrary, she had embraced it wholeheartedly, feeling as though she belonged somehow. Of course, she had never visited the areas such as Sandhill or Pipewellgate, slums which held such grotesque squalor there had been talk of clearing them for years. One of the housemaids Miss Bainbridge employed lived in Pipewellgate, and although Gracie was always as neat as a new pin, she lived in a house which contained eight other families and was right next door to one of the slaughterhouses. Charlotte, who inevitably returned to school after the weekends with a generous amount of chocolate and sweets from her doting parents, always made sure Gracie went home with most of the confectionery.

It began to snow again when they reached Gateshead, thick starry flakes falling from a sky which had turned from mother-of-pearl to an ominous pale grey. One or two of her fellow travellers expressed anxiety about getting home safely, but Sophy wished the journey could continue for ever. She wouldn't mind if they got stuck somewhere. Anything was better than the vicarage and her aunt. And the kitchen was no refuge now. Bridget and her parents had been replaced by a cook, Mrs Hogarth, who was as thin and disapproving as her aunt, and a maid called Molly who seemed a bit simple and wouldn't say boo to a goose. A man from the village came once or twice a week to see to the garden and any odd jobs, which had meant Patrick's mushroom house and his lovely greenhouse were sadly neglected, although the vegetable patch still produced vegetables for the household and the fruit trees yielded a good crop each year.

Fortunately, just after she and Patience had gone away to school, John had started work in the office of the Wearmouth Colliery and had now risen to the position of Under-manager. Matthew had been studying at law college but had left in the summer and was now training to be a solicitor with a very respectable establishment in Bishopwearmouth.

When Sophy was home from school she was expected to work for her keep, although she now ate with the family in the dining room rather than taking her meals in the kitchen with the servants. Her sleeping arrangements had changed too. She occupied a corner of Patience's bedroom, a narrow single bed having been moved in there once she was well enough to leave the guest room.

All this left her in no-man's-land inside the vicarage, emphasising, as it did, that she belonged neither in the servants' camp, nor wholly within the family circle. If it wasn't for John, Matthew and David, and – to be fair – Patience, too, these days, her life would have been unbearable, because her aunt never lost an opportunity to belittle her and make her feel the poor relation. Not that she minded working hard at any number of household jobs, she didn't, but she did mind that her aunt talked to her as though she was less than the dirt under her shoes. She was sure the writer of the manual in her valise, had she been asked to comment on the situation, would have advised displaying a sweet and submissive spirit to her aunt as befitted a well-brought-up young lady, and that was probably right and proper. She just didn't think she could do it – even to keep the peace. She didn't *want* to do it. She wanted— oh, all sorts of things, but mainly to escape the confines of the vicarage and that of the village also.

The coach stopped at an inn in Washington, a large colliery village west of Sunderland. The travellers were told it would be the last stop before they moved across country to Sunderland, which was the most tedious and difficult part of the journey due to the fact they would be using country lanes and narrow by-roads. The coachman advised everyone who was continuing with him to partake of a hot toddy to keep out the cold. The journey from Newcastle to Washington had already taken an extra half-an-hour longer than usual, due to the worsening weather, and he couldn't guarantee that the next leg wouldn't be worse.

Everyone trooped obediently into the inn parlour where Sophy tasted the first drop of alcohol of her life in the form of the innkeeper's rum toddy. She didn't like it but she sipped it slowly and found it warming, and she was glad of it once they began the journey once more. The snow was coming down thicker than ever and the poor horses, their heads down, plodded laboriously through what was fast becoming a full-blown blizzard.

Twice the coach driver and a youngish man who had joined their party at Washington had to dig the wheels free, and all the time one of the passengers, a middle-aged lady who reminded Sophy of her aunt, lamented the fact that she had not made the journey by train. Everyone else silently lamented that she hadn't done so too.

They arrived in Bishopwearmouth in an early winter twilight, and the coach driver wasn't the only one who breathed a sigh of relief that they'd reached their destination. He was anxious to get the tired horses settled in their stables at the back of the Maritime Alms Houses between Crowtree Road and Maritime Place and hurry home to the hot meal his wife would have waiting. Sophy knew she'd have to walk the rest of the way, crossing the Wearmouth Bridge into Monkwearmouth and turning west into Southwick. Normally she would have enjoyed the freedom of being out by herself, but with the atrocious weather and having to carry her heavy valise, it wasn't such an adventure. When Patience had still been at school with her, her uncle had taken and fetched them every time, but as soon as she had been on her own this convenience had stopped and she had been dispatched to and from the vicarage by courtesy of public transport. Again, she hadn't minded this, since anything was preferable to spending time in her uncle's company, but tonight it would have been nice to have made the journey in comfort, door to door.

Once she had said goodbye to her fellow travellers, however, she squared her shoulders, picked up her valise and began to trudge through the snow which now reached the top of the neat, above-the-ankle button boots which all Miss Bainbridge's young ladies had to wear. She had left Crowtree Road and turned into High Street West and then Bridge Street, and was approaching the bridge, when a voice calling her name caused her to turn and blink through the snowflakes.

'Sophy, I thought it was you.' Matthew came panting up behind her, his face beaming. 'Here, let me take that,' he added, whisking her valise out of her hand before hugging her. 'You've picked a good day to come home.'

'Matthew, what are you doing here?' She was so glad to see him; the walk to the vicarage had appeared a huge battle just moments ago. Now it was fun.

'We've all been sent home early because of the snow.' He tucked her arm through his. 'Frightful, isn't it? Everyone's saying it's going to be a bad winter, but then they always say that and it mostly is.' He grinned at her. The snow had settled on his hat and overcoat, but he looked every inch the young gentleman, and she was suddenly aware he wasn't Matthew the schoolboy any longer but a grown man earning his living. She couldn't have been more proud of him if he was her brother.

'Come on,' he said cheerfully. 'You can tell me all you've been doing and I'll fill you in on the latest at home. Did you know John is courting and it's serious? Her name is Flora Irvin and she's a miner's daughter.' His voice hardened. 'Mother's throwing a blue fit but John's determined she's the one, and Flora's a lovely girl.'

A miner's daughter. Sophy could imagine how that had gone down with her aunt. She was forever parading the daughters of her friends in front of the boys, listing their pedigrees as though the girls were cows at the cattle-market. Superior cows though. 'How long has John been seeing her?'

'Ages, apparently, but he had more sense than to let on. One of Mother's friends saw them at the Palace a few weeks ago though, and the game was up. I'd told him it was only a matter of time.'

'You knew then?'

'He told me in the summer when I left law college. I've been his alibi a few times.'

He grinned at her again and although Sophy smiled back, part of her was saddened. John and Matthew, probably David too, didn't like their mother. She'd known it for some time. Worse, they didn't love her either. She would have given the world for her own mother to have been alive, but then, her mother wouldn't have been like Mary Hutton. How could anyone love her aunt? But her uncle must have done at one time or else he wouldn't have married her.

'Flora's got a sister,' Matthew added, deadpan.

'Matthew?' Sophy stopped dead, staring at him.

'Verity's her name and she's seventeen years old and just . . . perfect. I haven't mentioned her at home yet, though. I thought I'd let the heat over John die down a bit first.' Matthew started walking again, drawing her along with him. 'What do you think?'

'I think whenever you tell your parents I'd rather not be around, if it's all the same to you,' said Sophy, and she was only half-joking. Whatever her aunt's reaction, she would bear the brunt of it somehow or other.

'So, tell me what you've been doing,' Matthew kept her tucked into his side as they marched on. The cobbled road across the bridge was deep in snow by now, the evidence of horses clear enough in the furrows left by cart and coach wheels and the odd steaming pile of horse manure. Most folk had wisely retired indoors, and the normally bustling town was hushed and still. Even the river was quieter than usual, the sound of the paddle-wheel blades on the tugboats beating the water muffled, and the smell of industrial smoke suppressed by the falling snow.

They talked all the way to the vicarage, slipping and sliding once or twice and convulsed in giggles when one or the other of them nearly went headlong. Somehow they reached home without mishap, both of them flushed and bright-eyed as they scraped the ice and snow from the insteps of their boots on the mat of the porch before Matthew opened the front door and they stepped into the warmth of the hall, just as Mary came out of the drawing room. Her eyes flashed from Matthew's laughing face to Sophy's, and then back to her son's as she said sharply, 'What are you doing home at this hour?'

'Mr Routledge closed the office early due to the snow.' Matthew bent down to place Sophy's valise on the floor before helping her off with her coat. Neither of them were surprised that Mary hadn't acknowledged Sophy's presence in spite of it being four months since she had left for her last term at school. 'I met Sophy near the bridge and we've walked home together.'

'I can see that.' Mary moved closer, sniffing, her long thin nose practically quivering. 'Have you been drinking?'

'Drinking?' Matthew said in surprise.

'Alcohol, boy. Alcohol.'

'The innkeeper made us all a hot toddy when we stopped for a while at Washington,' Sophy said quietly. 'The coach driver said it would keep the cold out.'

Matthew, no vestige of laughter remaining and red in the face from being called 'boy', spoke stiffly. 'You shouldn't have had to travel by McCabe's coach, Sophy. Father should have come and collected you. It's not right, a young lady journeying by herself.'

Mary opened her mouth to speak, took in her son's angry face and thought better of it. But she would privately reprimand Matthew later for speaking to her that way in front of the girl. Sophy had now been elevated from child to girl in her mind, and with her maturing, the fear which had begun years ago when she had seen how beautiful her niece was becoming had been magnified a hundred times. She wanted the girl out of this house and out of their lives as soon as possible, but due to Jeremiah's ridiculous interference she was on the horns of a dilemma. She had always intended to put the girl into service in the kitchens of a big house, somewhere miles from Southwick, but that was no longer possible with the education she had received. And she was too young to take the post of a governess somewhere. But something would have to be done.

Matthew took his cousin's hand, drawing her past his mother as though she didn't exist as he said, 'Come into the drawing room and sit by the fire and get warm. I'll ring for Molly to bring us some tea and cake – it's a while until dinner.'

Mary stood where she was until the drawing-room door had shut behind the two, her body rigid but the sick panic she felt every time Sophy came home to the fore. John seemed to be out of the equation now, although he would marry that miner's girl over her dead body. She couldn't believe John had stooped so low as to entertain such a thing, but it wouldn't happen. She would make sure of that. But Matthew was still fancy free and young and silly enough to act rashly if he imagined himself in love. Look at the way he had championed the girl this evening and the way they had been laughing when they'd come into the house . . .

Mary found she was wringing her hands and immediately stopped, composing herself before she went upstairs and entered Jeremiah's study without the courtesy of knocking. He was sitting hunched over his desk working on his sermon for Sunday morning and looked up in surprise at her entrance.

'The girl is back,' Mary said flatly. 'She came in with Matthew a few moments ago and he insisted on taking her into the drawing room for tea and cake.'

Jeremiah nodded without commenting. He might have known it would have to be something to do with Sophy for Mary to willingly come into his presence. That his wife hated him, he had no doubt. She had told him so often enough in the last six years since he had sent the girls away to school. But he was also in no doubt that she hated Sophy more, and he had to admit he didn't understand this. The day she had nearly killed the girl – it had been touch and go for a time and he had suffered the torments of the damned wondering if the child was going to pull through – he had realised there was a sickness in Mary. There were many times he had wished, and still did, that things were different and that Esther had never come home to have the child, since this in one way or another had been the bane of his life. That apart, he couldn't see why Mary was so against his sister's child. Women were supposed to be the softer of the sexes, weren't they? And Sophy had displayed none of the badness which had been in her mother. It was unfortunate she looked like she did, admittedly – such beauty in a woman always caused problems in his experience – but it would doubtless be an asset in getting her married off early.

'Did you hear what I said?' Mary's cold flecked eyes were fixed on him and he saw now she was upset about something or other by the patch of colour in each cheek.

'You said Sophy was home.'

Mary drew in a thin breath. 'I *said*' – she stressed the last word as one might do when talking to a recalcitrant child or a dimwit – 'Matthew brought her home and the two of them are in the drawing room.'

Jeremiah was genuinely puzzled. 'What of it?'

'Oh, give me strength.' Her cool manner gone, she glared at him. 'Isn't it bad enough that you had no idea of John's behaviour until one of my friends had to alert us to the fact he was consorting with a common miner's daughter?'

Jeremiah was beginning to lose patience. His sermon wasn't going well; he'd had indigestion from the amount of fat in the cold pork Mrs Hogarth – who wasn't a patch on Kitty – had served for lunch; he'd heard of nothing but John and this girl, Flora, for weeks from Mary, and now she was playing guessing games. 'If you have something to say, say it. Otherwise kindly leave me in peace until it is time for dinner,' he said through partially clenched teeth.

'The girl and Matthew. Can't you see what's under your nose without me having to spell it out?'

'*What?*' She had his attention now. Jeremiah sat bolt upright, staring at her. 'Don't be so ridiculous, they're first cousins.'

'And that would stop her, would it? The daughter of a whore with her mother's blood running through her veins?'

'Don't talk like that. Esther was my sister.'

'Oh, I know Esther was your sister, Jeremiah. If anyone knows that, I do. And we both know *what* she was, besides which, as you are well aware from dealing with your parishioners, there is many a girl given a child by her father or brother, let alone a cousin.'

Jeremiah went white. 'You're saying Sophy is expecting Matthew's baby?'

Mary shut her eyes for a moment. Was he being deliberately stupid just to annoy her? 'Of course not. Would I be standing here talking to you so calmly if that were the case? But there is something between the two of them, I know it, and it needs to be nipped in the bud. What are you going to do about it?'

Jeremiah had relaxed back in his chair as though all the air had left his body, which was exactly how he felt. For a moment he had thought— He shut his mind to what he had thought and looked at his wife. 'Are you sure about this?' he asked weakly. 'That they have those sort of feelings for each other?'

'Of course I am sure,' Mary bit out. 'And I hold you responsible in part, Jeremiah. If you hadn't insisted on educating the girl above her station, giving her ideas, she wouldn't have dared to make cow's eyes at Matthew; she wouldn't even have been here now. She could have been put into service at thirteen and off our hands a long time ago. But no, you had to have your way and send Patience and the girl away to school, an expense we could ill-afford.'

'You know exactly why it was necessary to get Sophy out of this house, so don't give me any of that. Your behaviour that day was inexcusable and could have had repercussions which would have destroyed us both. I had no alternative but to make sure it didn't happen again.'

Mary flicked her hand scornfully. 'A little discipline never hurt anyone. Spare the rod and spoil the child.'

'A little discipline? She was barely conscious for days and her body will bear the marks of your particular rod for the rest of her life in one or two places. There is something in you which is unnatural, woman.' There, he had said it. He had thought it for years and now he had said it.

Mary's thin body seemed to swell and he really thought she was going to spring on him, so great was her fury. She stared at him for some moments, her hate a tangible thing, and then walked to the door where she stood and surveyed him again. 'You are a spineless nothing of a man and I rue the day I ever laid eyes on you, but I say again, what are you going to do about the girl? Let me tell you, if you ignore this like you do everything else you'd rather not face, you will live to regret it. I promise you that.'

For some minutes after Mary had left, Jeremiah continued to stare across the room and then he placed his head in his hands. What *was* he going to do about Sophy?

Chapter 7

Christmas, never a particularly merry affair at the vicarage, was even more dismal than usual that year. John and his mother were barely on speaking terms, Matthew tried to spend as little time as he could at home and made the office his excuse, saying pressure of work meant he needed to do extra hours, and the atmosphere in the house was so tense generally it was painful. Even David, home from school, was subdued.

Sophy had found Patience to be out of sorts, depressed and miserable at her life within the four walls of the vicarage. On further questioning, Sophy had discovered the old curate had retired in the summer and a new young man had taken his place who had set Patience's heart a-flutter. Unfortunately, her feelings didn't seem to be reciprocated. In fact, Patience said, Mr Travis had taken to avoiding her and she wasn't imagining it. Following this revelation, relations between the two girls became strained when, at the Christmas Day service, Mr Travis made a beeline for Sophy and tried to chat to her for some time, in spite of all her efforts to cut the conversation short. In the end she had had to be somewhat impolite to make her escape.

A couple of days before the New Year, when her aunt was out with Patience one morning calling on friends, Sophy felt an overwhelming urge to escape the vicarage. Apart from attending her uncle's church service she had barely been out of the house since she had arrived home, the inclement weather making even the shortest journey difficult. It had snowed on and off since her first day back in Southwick, and even today the sky looked heavy and low again. Her aunt had left her a basket full of mending to do; quite different to the variety of fancy needlework Patience and her mother spent their time doing, along with a little painting in fine watercolours and drawing in charcoal.

She was fully aware the basket of mending was a subtle insult by her aunt, a reminder that she was little more than a servant, but she would actually prefer to be doing something useful rather than stitching netting purses, embroidering pen cases or decorating handkerchiefs, things of limited use and value. But today she felt she would go mad if she didn't go outside for a while, and so she ran upstairs to Patience's bedroom and put on an extra layer before donning her winter coat, hat and gloves. She was just about to leave the house when David, who wasn't due to go back to his private school for another week, appeared from the direction of the kitchen munching on a piece of Christmas cake.

Sophy smiled at Patience's twin. He was tall for his age and gangly with it, and always ravenously hungry. That he was Mrs Hogarth's favourite was in no doubt, since he was the only one in the family who could scrounge anything from the cook between meals, but that was David all over. He was as sunny-natured as his twin was dour, and at seventeen years of age possessed of a gaiety which was infectious. He was also in the grip of what Charlotte would have called a 'mash' on her. Sophy had been aware of this to some extent in the summer, but since she had returned home, the poor boy stammered and blushed and nearly fell over his own feet whenever he saw or spoke to her. For this reason she had tended to avoid him to some extent, for his sake not hers, not wishing to embarrass him. Now though, seeing her dressed for the outdoors, he rushed towards her as eagerly as a puppy, saying, 'Are you going for a walk? I was just about to do the same. Perhaps we could walk together?'

She didn't have the heart to refuse him. Apart from her uncle, who was ensconced in his study as usual, the house was empty, John and Matthew being at work, and no doubt David was as bored as she was.

She waited while he threw on his hat and coat and then they set off, walking north away from the village towards Carley Hill Farm and the quarries and more open countryside. The air was bitterly cold but wonderfully fresh and clean, and although the snow was deep in places it had been trodden down over the last ten days or so to provide a narrow walkway in most places, with great drifts piled up either side of the paths. The going got harder after they passed the old quarries, but they were young and energetic, and once David had got over his initial shyness at having the girl he dreamed about every night all to himself, they chatted and laughed together, much as Sophy and Matthew had done the night she had come home.

They walked as far as Boldon, a mining town some three or four miles north of Southwick, following the old dry-stone-walled lanes until they came to the growing township and West Boldon Mill. This had been seriously damaged by fire three years previously: a storm had caused the sails of the mill to rotate so fast that when the brakes were applied, such heat was generated that a fire broke out and all but the stone tower was destroyed.

'We'd better start back.' They had stood staring at the remains of the mill for some moments, catching their breath, and it dawned on Sophy that they would be hard-pressed to be back before her aunt and Patience finished their round of calls. Not that she and David were doing anything wrong in taking a walk together, but she knew instinctively that her aunt wouldn't like it. Her aunt had been even more cold and abrupt than usual over Christmas and had given her a hundred and one jobs to keep her from spending time with the family. The trouble was, Mrs Hogarth resented anyone but Molly in 'her' kitchen, and when Sophy was told to do the mountain of ironing that accumulated day by day in the scullery washing baskets, or to help prepare meals or clean the range, the cook viewed this as gross interference, reflected in her attitude to Sophy.

Sophy sighed deeply. She needed to get away from Southwick, but although her education had been a good one for a girl, it had merely prepared her for running a comfortable and peaceful home for her future husband, the destiny of any well-brought-up young lady. And the thing was, more and more of late she knew she didn't want to tread the path expected of her. She didn't want to get married, well, not for years and years anyway, and she certainly didn't want to spend the rest of her days occupied like her aunt and so many of her aunt's friends, making a round of calls every morning and sitting embroidering useless items every afternoon. And once children came along, a woman's life became even more limited and restricted.

She had played with the idea of giving elocution lessons, or maybe teaching ballet or the rudiments of music, but that didn't appeal either. She would still be forced to live at the vicarage for one thing until she could build a name for herself and maybe afford to take rooms somewhere, and she couldn't see her aunt allowing any part of her home to be used for such vulgar purposes. But besides the mechanics of the idea, she didn't actually *want* to teach. She wanted to give free rein to the feeling which always rose in her breast when she was dancing or singing or acting, for it was only then she truly felt herself. But she hadn't dared mention this to a soul. Even Charlotte, sweet as she was, would have been horrified at the notion, and regarded her as mad. And perhaps she was. No one else she knew was like her and she didn't understand where this urge to perform had come from.

'What's the matter?' David had heard the sigh and as they began to retrace their steps towards home, he glanced at Sophy. She was wearing the grey serge coat which was part of the uniform for the school she had attended. Patience had at least two other coats, but Sophy was limited to the one. Her fur bonnet had been a present from John for Christmas though, and it was lined and trimmed in a dark gold satin. This framed her lovely face perfectly and brought out the burned honey of her eyes in a way that made him catch his breath now.

Unaware of his rapt gaze and her eyes on the road ahead, Sophy said quietly, 'I was just thinking, that's all.'

'What about?'

'All sorts of things,' she prevaricated.

'Has Mother upset you again?'

His voice had hardened in the same way John's and Matthew's did when they spoke of Mary, and Sophy said quickly, 'No, no she hasn't. It's just . . .' She fiddled with her gloves for a few moments as they walked. 'I've finished school now and I'm not sure what's going to happen.'

David stared at her, alarm rising. 'Why does anything have to happen? You'll live at home like Patience, won't you?'

Sophy shook her head. 'David, Patience is your parents' daughter. I – I was foisted on them when my mother died, and your mother has never let me forget it, as you well know. I have to take responsibility for my own future. I can't expect them to keep me now I'm old enough to work.'

'Work?' He sounded as shocked as though she had said something indecent. 'But you can't work, Sophy. You'll stay at home until you get married.'

'I can work and I will.' Her voice brooked no argument. 'I've been thinking of various things I might do, although I must admit nothing particularly appeals. But then, why should it? Thousands of people have to work every day at jobs they don't like. Think of the mines and factories and mills.'

'Those are men and it's right and proper they earn a living.'

'Women work just as hard as men, David. Harder. And not just in the home caring for their family either. Lots of women have to take in washing or needlework, and some work in the factories and milliner establishments, the mills, all sorts of places. They do a day's work and then go home and start there.'

'Those are working-class women, not someone like you.'

She stopped dead, staring at him. He was probably the gentlest of the brothers, and undoubtedly kind and caring, but the way he had spoken grated on her. Her voice was uncharacteristically sharp when she said, 'We're all the same under the skin, David. Queen and washerwoman. It's just an accident of birth that separates the lady in her big house with umpteen servants and the pauper starving in one room.'

David blinked. He hadn't heard Sophy talk like this before and he didn't know what to say. 'But — but that's just how things are, how they've always been.'

'It doesn't mean it's right or that it should continue. In fact, lots of things should change. People laugh at women who say we should be able to vote the same as men, but why not?'

'Is this the sort of stuff they've been teaching you at Miss Bainbridge's Academy?' David was completely out of his depth but fascinated by her vehemence and flushed cheeks.

Sophy, who had been about to elaborate further, stopped, and then giggled. 'Goodness, no. Miss Bainbridge would have a fit. She even vetted the books we read and the list of what she considered improper was endless. But Jessica, one of the girls in my dormitory, had a brother who used to give her the newspapers he bought and she smuggled them in for us to read. Most of the girls didn't bother, but I found them interesting. I learned more about life from them than I ever did from Miss Bainbridge and her team of old spinsters.'

'Good gracious.' David found he was more in love than ever. 'Like what, for instance?'

They continued to discuss the merits of social and political reform, Gladstone's dealing with the Irish situation, the controversy over women's suffrage and a whole host of other issues on the walk home, both of them enjoying themselves immensely. It was the first time Sophy had been able to voice her opinions and arguments, and although such matters were part of David's education, he had never heard a woman's point of view before. Indeed, he would never have imagined the female sex concerned themselves about anything other than the latest fashions and the price of a new bonnet. He knew there were a few, what were considered 'strange' young women in the country, who attended the Lady Margaret Hall in Oxford, all from upper-and middle-class families, but his tutors had been scathingly dismissive of this establishment, and his conviction that a woman's place was in the home had never been seriously shaken. Now he was having to think again, and it both excited and worried him. But excitement prevailed.

Sophy was a wonderful girl, he told himself, as they neared the vicarage gates and she laughed at a joke he had made, making him feel ten-feet tall. Just wonderful. And the next moment, surprising himself as much as her, he pulled her into his arms and kissed her full on the lips, dislodging her bonnet so it fell to the back of her neck where it dangled, held on by its silk ribbons.

It was over in an instant. Sophy jerked away, her outraged 'David!' bringing him immediately to his senses. And there it might have ended. A brief second of boyish ardour.

But to Mary Hutton, rounding the corner of the lane in the pony and trap with Patience sitting at her side, it confirmed every last fear she'd had about Jeremiah's sister's child. The trap reached the pair who were now standing some three feet apart in moments, and her face livid, Mary raised her ornamental whip with the intention of bringing it down on the golden-red head. It was only Patience, grabbing hold of her mother's arm and refusing to let go, who deflected the blow.

'*You hussy.*' Mary didn't shout, she didn't have to. The words came like molten steel between her clenched teeth, and when David tried to explain she cut him short, saying, 'Get into the house, both of you, now.'

David's face was chalk-white as they followed the trap up the drive, his muttered, 'I'm sorry, Sophy,' shaky. 'I'll tell her it was me, don't worry,' he added, as they mounted the three steps leading to the open front door.

Sophy said nothing but she was trembling inside, not because she was afraid of her aunt, that time had gone, but to be faced with such hatred was unnerving. They'd heard Mary screaming Jeremiah's name as they'd reached the house, and as they entered the hall her uncle came hurrying downstairs, his irritated, 'What now?' receiving no answer.

They followed Jeremiah into the drawing room. Mary was standing with her back to the roaring fire still dressed in the brocade and fur ensemble she wore when she went visiting, and Patience was sitting in a chair on the other side of the room, her face as white as theirs, mainly because her mother's rage had brought back the horror of the time six years before. She had never been able to view her mother in the same light again after that, and although she still resented Sophy's beauty at times – especially recently after Mr Travis had practically drooled over her – she'd always felt protective of her cousin.

It was to Patience Mary turned as she said, 'Tell him. Tell your father what you have just seen.'

'Mother—'

'I said tell him.'

'You tell me.' Jeremiah could see Mary's face was suffused with dark colour and that she was shaking with fury, and he had noticed the pony and trap was still standing on the drive when he had come downstairs. The horse should be in its stable.

'I told you, didn't I? I told you what would happen and I have been proved right. Not only does she want the elder brother but she has corrupted the younger, too. She's vile, wicked, and I told you.'

Jeremiah glanced at Patience for an explanation, but it was David who stepped forward and faced his father. 'Sophy and I went for a walk and – and I kissed her. It was my fault, she had nothing to do with it.'

'Nothing to do with it? Oh, you foolish boy.' Mary's voice was rapier-thin. 'She encouraged you, don't you see? A girl like her knows a thousand tricks to lead a man on. It's in her blood, she was born to it.'

'That's enough, Mary.'

Far from deflating her rage, her husband's voice fanned it. Beside herself, Mary took a step forward, looking straight into Sophy's stiff face, her own features contorted as though she was looking at something repulsive. 'A whore born of a whore, that's what's been nourished in this house. That is what my children have been forced to consort with all their lives. Your mother was a scarlet woman, do you hear me? And she took her lovers by soliciting from the stage instead of the streets. She couldn't even put a name to which one had sired you, there were so many.'

'Mary.'

'Don't "Mary" me. You, you'd let your sons be defiled by her, wouldn't you? Your own sons. That – that *harlot*.'

'It's not true.' Sophy spoke for the first time, her voice strangely flat-sounding. 'My mother was married to a French nobleman and he died.'

'Your *mother* was an actress in the music halls in London, a hussy who flagrantly displayed herself to any man who could afford her,' Mary said relentlessly. 'She might have had the odd nobleman or two, but they paid like everyone else.'

The crack of her husband's hand across her face sent Mary reeling backwards, and but for the ornamental fireguard she would have fallen into the fire. As it was she landed with her hands stretched either side of her and resting on the oak mantelpiece, her thin body stretched backwards.

For a moment everyone was rigidly still. Jeremiah fully expected Mary to retaliate by word and action but she simply looked at him, a look of such loathing and bitterness it was a wonder it didn't burn him up where he stood. And then without a word she slowly straightened away from the mantelpiece and walked out of the room.

Jeremiah stood exactly where he was, his head thudding. He was not a violent man. He had never raised his hand to man, woman or child before this day. And now he had hit his wife, he had struck Mary. Dear God, what had possessed him? And why wasn't he feeling remorse? He should, shouldn't he? He was a man of the cloth.

'Father?'

David's face was white and shocked but Jeremiah's glance passed over his son to the slim young girl standing silent and still. He had never felt so inadequate in his life. 'Your mother wasn't as bad as your aunt has painted,' he said softly. 'Come and sit down and let me explain. David, can you leave us. You, too, Patience.'

'No, let them stay.' Sophy still didn't move. 'Is it true? What she said?'

Jeremiah cleared his throat. Patience had gone to stand with Sophy and had put her arm round her cousin, her face as shocked and horrified as David's. 'Your mother was always determined to follow her own star, Sophy,' he said, struggling for words. 'Even as a child she wasn't happy in the village, she wanted more, but it led to her being taken advantage of.'

'So she was an actress in the music halls?'

He nodded. 'She ran away from here when she was fifteen years old.'

'And my father? Did – did she know who my father was?'

'Like I said, your mother was taken advantage of. It happens to the best of women when they are in a vulnerable situation.'

'So I am a—'

'You are my niece.' For the first time in sixteen years Jeremiah went some way in redeeming himself. 'And part of this family.'

'No, I have never been part of this family, Uncle.' Sophy glanced from Jeremiah to Patience, whose eyes were swimming in tears, and then David. When her cousin couldn't meet her gaze, it brought home to her what she could expect if anyone found out the truth about her.

She bent, picking up her fur bonnet which had loosened and fallen to the floor at some point in the proceedings, and then straightened. Quietly turning away, and ignoring Patience's anguished, 'Sophy, wait,' she walked out of the room, shutting the door carefully behind her.

Chapter 8

Sophy left in the middle of the night. She would have gone without saying goodbye to anyone, but after she had packed her clothes in her valise and stuffed Maisie and a few other personal items she possessed into an old carpet bag, Patience stirred on the other side of the room. Sophy was halfway to the door when Patience sat up in bed. 'Sophy? What are you doing?'

'Ssh.' She walked quickly over to Patience's bed. 'Keep your voice down.'

'What's happening?' Patience peered at her in the dim light from the window, the white world outside reflecting the moonlight. It had snowed a little that afternoon but the evening had turned clear and a heavy sparkling frost had fallen which sat on the snow like diamond dust. 'What have you got your coat on for? You're not— No, you're not thinking of leaving!'

'I have to.' Sophy sat down on the end of the bed. 'I can't stay, not after today. You must see that.'

'No, I don't. I don't, Sophy, and Father wouldn't want you to go like this.'

'I don't think that's quite true. One way or another, I think I've caused quite a bit of trouble for him over the years. Anyway, I want to go. I've wanted to for ages.'

'But you can't.' Patience reached out and grabbed her cousin's hand, her lank brown hair which was drawn with excruciating tightness each night into curling papers bobbing as she knelt up. 'I won't let you. We're friends now, aren't we? And I've been longing for you to come home. It's so awful here with just Mother and Father all day, and the boys are hardly home at all in the evenings. I don't blame them, I wish I could escape too.'

Sophy smiled sadly to herself. Since the revelation about her mother, Patience had been as nice as pie to her, which was kind of her, it really was, but she couldn't help feeling that now she was no longer a perceived threat where Mr Travis was concerned – for no respectable curate would dream of declaring an interest in a girl with her background – it had coloured Patience's attitude somewhat. The thought of her mother weakened Sophy; she had deliberately put everything out of her head but packing and escaping the confines of the house while she had been getting ready to leave. She would think about her mother when she could bear to, but not now.

'I can't stay,' she said again, extricating her fingers from Patience's hand. 'I have to go.'

'But how will you manage? Where will you go? And it's the middle of the night. At least wait till morning and let Father take you somewhere.'

'I – I don't want to see anyone.' For a moment Sophy's voice almost broke, but then she cleared her throat and a trace of bitterness showed through when she muttered, 'My mother managed perfectly well, didn't she, and she was a year younger than me when she ran away.'

Her uncle had come and sat with her earlier that evening and explained exactly what had happened to his sister, the life she had led, and the events which had driven her to seek refuge in her old home just before Sophy's birth. He had tried to be kind as well as honest, but nevertheless, his abhorrence at his sister's defilement had shown through. He had told her it had been his wish that she never find out the truth about her mother, but in a strange way Sophy was glad she had. It explained so much, not least the passion that burned in her when she sang and danced and had acted in the little plays and soirées the school had put on. She was her mother's daughter. Her eyes took on the hardness of polished amber. But she would never let herself be used by men as her mother had. She would die first.

'Sophy, please stay.' Patience tried one last time. 'No one has to know about your mother; everything could be the same as before.'

They both knew that wasn't true. Pandora's box had been opened and there was no going back. Besides which, Sophy told herself fiercely, she wouldn't live another day under the same roof as her aunt. 'I can't,' she said for the third time, her voice stronger. 'I'm sorry, Patience.' She leaned forward and hugged her cousin briefly, before standing up. 'You go back to sleep.'

'Wait.' Patience had slid out of bed. 'You'll need money. Wait here a minute.'

Before Sophy could stop her, Patience had flitted out of the room like a little white ghost in her voluminous nightdress, leaving Sophy in an agony of suspense and frightened that her cousin might rouse the house. She needn't have worried. Patience was back in two or three minutes. 'Here.' She thrust a handful of notes into her cousin's hands. 'This will give you a bit of a start at least.'

'I can't take this.' Sophy couldn't see clearly but it felt like a good deal of money. 'Where did you get it?'

'Out of Mother's cash box. Don't worry, I shall tell her I gave it to you, I promise. She owes you far more than this, Sophy, the way you have worked for her for years, and I know she has quite a bit hidden away from her housekeeping elsewhere too. I saw her once, when she didn't know I was about, counting notes into a cloth bag which she concealed in the back of her wardrobe, and since the boys have started work they give her their board too. She's always going on about the cost of things and what she has to pay out to the tradesmen and so on, but there's quite a lot in that bag, I can tell you.'

'But why would she do that? What can she possibly be saving it for?' Sophy asked in amazement.

Patience shrugged. 'Who knows?'

Bridget had always used to say that there was nowt so queer as folk, and she was right, Sophy thought. What was the use of piles of money in a bag at the back of the wardrobe?

'Anyway, take what I've given you. You'll need it.' Patience now hugged Sophy, holding her close for a long moment which touched Sophy more than anything else. 'And write to me when you're settled and let me know you're all right.'

Sophy didn't reply to this. Heartsore and smarting from her aunt's revelation, which had made her feel she didn't know who she was any more, she wanted to cut all threads which held her to the Hutton family and Southwick. Instead, she whispered, 'I can't take this money, Patience.'

'You can and you are going to, else I'll wake the whole house and tell them you're leaving. You've earned it, Sophy, you know you have. And I shall tell Mother exactly that. *And* that I know about the bag in the wardrobe. She won't make a fuss if she knows I'm on to that.'

The boys, and Patience too. Her aunt had no one who cared about her, but right at this moment in time Sophy couldn't feel a shred of pity for the woman who had made her life a misery whenever she could, and who'd ripped her apart with her tongue earlier.

She stuffed the notes into the carpet bag and put on her bonnet, wanting to get away before it was light. Normally she would have been in fear and trepidation at the thought of leaving the vicarage in the middle of the night and walking into Bishopwearmouth, but now it was as nothing. And the money Patience had given her *would* enable her to put a good distance between herself and Sunderland.

A little while ago she had imagined herself begging a lift on one of the dray carts or farmers' wagons out of the town, it didn't matter where, just so long as she got away. There were bound to be barns where she could sleep. She hadn't thought what she would do about food; or at least she *had* thought about it but put it from her mind, but now that immediate worry was gone. She had money. She would survive.

'Goodbye, Patience.' The two girls didn't embrace again before Sophy left the bedroom, holding her boots and the carpet bag in one hand and the valise in the other. She trod carefully down the wooden stairs, which creaked and grumbled at the best of times, but then she was in the hall where she stopped and put on her boots.

The bolts on the front door rasped a little but not too loudly, and when she pulled it open the cold icy air took her breath away for a moment but also sent the adrenaline flooding her system. She shut the door quietly but her back was straight and her chin up as she walked down the drive, pausing only for a moment at the gates which led out on to the lane. But she didn't look back. Instead she took a deep breath, squared her slim shoulders, and walked on.

'What did you say?'

'I said Sophy left for good early this morning and I gave her the contents of your cash box to help speed her on her way. I didn't think you'd mind, considering you've wanted rid of her for years, Mother.' Patience had been dressed for some time but had waited until the hall clock struck eight o'clock before walking into her mother's room. This had once been the spare bedroom but her mother had moved into it shortly after she and Sophy had gone to school. Now, when the bishop came to stay, which was more and more infrequent due to his advanced years, he had David's room and her brother shared with Matthew for the duration of the bishop's visit.

Her mother had been sitting up in bed reading when she had knocked at the bedroom door. A book of devotional prayers. Now she slung the book aside and swung her legs out of bed as she cried, 'Are you mad, girl? There was over four pounds in that box. Help me get dressed, I need to tell your father to go after her.'

'There was four pounds and ten shillings to be exact, Mother. I counted. Of course, how much is in the bag in your wardrobe I have no idea. You would know that better than me.'

Mary froze. Her body remained rigid but her head turned, her eyes boring into those of her daughter's. 'You've been snooping in my room?'

'Not exactly. The door was ajar one day and I saw you, that's all.'

'How dare you.' Mary's voice was low but deadly.

'I haven't said anything to anyone – anyone except Sophy, that is. She didn't want to accept the money from the cash box but I explained you had plenty more, besides which she was owed a lot more than four pounds if you count all the years she has worked for nothing.'

For a moment Patience thought she'd gone too far. Her mother looked as though she was going to expire on the spot. She'd turned a dark shade of purple and her eyes appeared as though they were going to pop out of her head. 'You stupid girl,' Mary hissed. 'You stupid, stupid girl. It would have been the workhouse for her mother if we hadn't taken her in, have you considered that? And the girl would have been brought up within its confines. Far from being hard done by as you infer, she has been most fortunate, having a roof over her head for sixteen years and an education into the bargain.'

'Can't you call Sophy by her name even now when she's gone for good?'

Mother and daughter stared at each other, neither liking what they saw. 'Get out,' Mary said at last. 'Get out of my sight.'

Patience got out, but knowing that for the first time in her life she'd had the upper hand with her mother and things would never be the same again. Walking downstairs, she went into the drawing room where Molly was knelt at the huge hearth seeing to the fire. After a brief, 'Good morning,' she stood with her back to the room looking out over the snow-covered grounds beyond the house. The garden was bathed in a pale pink glimmer as the winter dawn rose in a crystalline sky and the light banished the darkness, and the hard frost caused the snow to glint and glow. Her heart swelled with the beauty in front of her and she remained for a long time soaking it in.

If she had had the courage, she would have gone with Sophy, but she wasn't made like her cousin. Nevertheless, she wasn't going to settle for living here and being at her mother's beck and call, just waiting to become an old maid. And that was what often happened to plain daughters like her; they were seen as potential nurses for their parents in their old age. Neither was she going to demean herself again like she had with Mr Travis, manoeuvring moments where she could speak to him and hanging on his every word like a lovesick fool.

She would find herself work outside the home. Her heart beat faster, colour staining her sallow cheeks. Thanks to her education at Miss Bainbridge's Academy she wasn't a total dunce, even if she'd never grasped higher arithmetic and the rudiments of French and Italian as well as Sophy. Perhaps she could apply for the post of a librarian or train to be a schoolmistress, and in the meantime, which would soften the blow for her parents at the thought of their daughter taking up employment, she could do voluntary work at the Sunderland Royal Infirmary or maybe the Eye Infirmary in Stockton Road. She had always been fascinated by what she had read about Florence Nightingale and the work she had undertaken in the Crimean War. Whatever, she wasn't going to waste another day of her life. If Sophy could brave leaving Southwick altogether with next to nothing, then she could take this step. This day was a new beginning for them both.

The fire was now crackling and burning brightly in the heavily carved fireplace, Molly having long since left the room, and Patience walked over to the flames and held out her cold hands. But she wasn't feeling cold inside. Suddenly she felt she had been presented with new possibilities, a direction to her life she would never have considered but for Sophy's departure, and she wasn't going to let anything or anyone change her mind.

The boys would back her. She nodded mentally to the thought. They knew full well what her mother was like and how miserable she'd been of late. Yes, they would speak up for her if necessary, but with or without them, she was going to do this.

The tall clock tower of Sunderland Central station could be seen from most of the town, and when Sophy set her eyes on it after crossing the Wearmouth Bridge, it drew her like a magnet. Suddenly she knew exactly what she was going to do, and excitement briefly banished the sick, lost feeling she'd felt since the day before. It wasn't just the truth about her mother which had caused her to feel she was floundering in an alien world but the fact that the man she had thought of as her father – the tall, handsome Frenchman with amber eyes and black hair and a warm smile – had only existed in her imagination. Her mother had been unmarried and her father could have been any one of a number of men, according to her aunt; there was no way she could ever know, and the secret dream that she'd carried in her heart, that one day she would try and find her father's relatives in France was over. She was illegitimate. 'Scum', as her aunt had called her. That's what people would think if they knew the truth about her beginnings.

She was one of the first of the early morning passengers when she entered the station by the main entrance off High Street West just after six o'clock. She stopped on the left of an archway by the weighing machine, wondering how best to proceed. She had never travelled by train before or even entered the railway station, although she knew the great iron-framed glass roof was a marvel.

She had only been standing there for a minute or two when a young couple with a little boy came into the station, the child immediately declaring he wanted a turn on the weighing machine and then a gadget whereby you could stamp out your name and other details on a metal tag. The mother, who seemed somewhat harassed, gave in to the child's demands without protest, and once the boy was satisfied, Sophy followed them and did what they did at the ticket office, where she was asked her destination by the cheerful little man with his peaked cap.

She took a deep breath and then spoke clearly and firmly. 'London, please.'

Chapter 9

Sophy stood staring about her. The attic room at the top of the four-storey terraced house in one of the maze of streets in Holborn was dark and grimy, the only daylight coming through a tiny window which was so filthy it was impossible to see out. The bare floorboards were devoid of even a humble clippy mat, the open fireplace hadn't been cleaned in years, and the pervading smell – a mixture of damp, age and old man's pee – had her stomach turning. A single iron bed with a heavily stained flock mattress stood against one wall, a small square wooden table with two hardbacked chairs against another, and on the shelf above the table sat a kettle, a couple of pots and a frying pan, and an oil lamp. A piece of wood with a number of hooks nailed into it had been fixed on to the wall next to the window.

'See that there.' The landlady pointed to a large black hook which could swing out from the grate over the fire. 'You can put your pots on that an' cook for yourself if you've a mind, and the kettle boils in no time on the steel shelf at the back of the fire. The lav's in the yard along with the washhouse an' tap.'

Sophy nodded. She couldn't have spoken at that moment.

'Old Mr Ferry, bless him, he lived here for years after his wife died. No trouble, he was. But being eighty odd, the stairs were too much for him in the end.'

'He – died here?' Sophy looked askance at the bed.

'Died in this room? Dear oh dear, lovey, whatever put that in your head? No, he's gone to live with his married daughter in Paddington, somewhere between the railway and the canal, he said. Mind, that isn't an area I'd want one of my daughters living in, I can tell you. Slums mostly, and with all sorts of goings-on once it's dark, if you know what I mean.'

Sophy wondered what this street and the ones around it were, if not slums. But she couldn't afford to be choosey. Since arriving at King's Cross station three days ago she had been staying in a small guesthouse close to the station while she got her bearings, but at three shillings a night for bed, breakfast and evening meal, she'd quickly realised she had to find inexpensive lodgings somewhere or the rest of her money would be swallowed up in no time.

'Well, lovey, do you want the room or not?' The landlady folded her arms over her dirty pinny. 'It's a week's rent in advance, mind. Two bob it is, an' that's a bargain. It's an extra tanner a week for the rooms down below, but they're a bit bigger, mind. Still, it's only you, isn't it, so this should suit you fine.'

Sophy looked again at the soiled mattress. 'Could you arrange to have that taken away? I – I shall be bringing my own mattress, thank you.'

The landlady nodded, the man's pipe that was sticking out of the corner of her mouth bobbing. 'I'll get my Jim to see to it, dearie. When do you want to move in?'

'Would tomorrow be convenient?'

Again the pipe bobbed. 'If you don't mind me asking, lovey, what's a girl like you doing in this neck of the woods?'

Sophy looked into the lined face which seemed quite kindly under its coating of grime. 'I'm – I'm going to be an actress.'

'An actress, is it?' Dolly Heath surveyed the strikingly lovely young woman in front of her and shook her head slowly. 'I thought as much. Run away from home, have you? Don't bother to deny it, dearie, I've seen it all before. When a slip of a girl talks like you do and dresses nice, ten to one she's got a notion she wants to go on the stage. Did you leave under your own steam or did they throw you out?'

Sophy hesitated for a moment. 'There was a row and I left,' she said, which was true enough, just not the whole truth.

'And where's home?'

'In the north.'

'Well, this ain't the north, dearie, and I hate to say it but they'll eat you alive, given half a chance. I think you and me better have a little chat once you've moved in or it'll be a lamb to the slaughter.'

Sophy didn't know what to say. After a moment she fumbled in her bag and gave the landlady her first week's rent. 'Could I call back in a little while and' – she wondered how to put it – 'sort things out a bit?' She needed to scrub the room from top to bottom with a great deal of carbolic soap for a start, and then tackle the fireplace and clean the window. And she would whitewash the walls. If she bought some coal and lit a fire once she'd blackleaded the fireplace, everything would dry quicker. But getting rid of the smell was the first priority.

'You do what you want. Here' – the landlady gave her the key to the door – 'it's your place now, as long as you pay the rent on time. I don't put up with no shirkers. An' the front door's always unlocked, all right?'

'Thank you.' Sophy looked about her again, hiding her dismay at her new home. And then she metaphorically rolled up her sleeves. The sooner she went out and bought the cleaning materials, the sooner she could make a difference.

By the time she left the building later that night to get back to the guesthouse in time for her evening meal, the room was smelling sweeter and was cleaner than it had been in years. Everything had taken far longer than she had hoped and she hadn't had time to whitewash the walls, but she could do that tomorrow once she was in residence. She had decided she couldn't afford another night at the guesthouse; the cost of her train ticket and the subsequent three shillings a night had depleted her money enough as it was. She needed to conserve every penny she could.

★　　★　　★

When she let herself into her new abode the next day and dumped her valise and bag on the floor, she was pleased to find that the only odour was one of carbolic soap, and the view from the tiny window over a sea of rooftops was as clear as day, thanks to the elbow grease she'd applied to the glass. She stood for a moment looking around her. Mrs Heath's husband had come and disposed of the disgusting mattress the day before and she had washed the bedstead, so now she needed to buy a new mattress. She had no idea of the cost or where to go. After locking the door again, she went downstairs and knocked on the door at the back of the house where Mrs Heath lived.

'Oh hello, dearie.' Mrs Heath was dressed in a shapeless dressing gown, her hair in a net and her feet encased in what looked like men's slippers. 'What can I do for you?'

'I wondered if you could help me? Could you suggest a good place for bedding and a mattress, and I need to get a couple of other things while I'm about it.' Sophy tried not to wrinkle her nose. A waft of air full of the smell of cabbage, pipe-smoke and something similar to what had been upstairs surrounded the land-lady as she stood in the doorway.

'You want to see our Arnold – that's our eldest. He's done right nicely for himself, has Arnold. Owns Heath's Emporium, down near the market, and does a roaring trade in second-hand stuff and not rubbish either.'

Sophy didn't want the landlady to think she was going to be one of the shirkers she'd spoken about yesterday, but felt she ought to make her position clear. 'I can't afford much,' she said quietly. 'Not till – till I get employment.'

Dolly nodded. She had warmed to this young girl with the beautiful face and hauntingly sad eyes. She dare bet there was a story to this one. 'Tell you what, lovey. Give me ten minutes an' I'll come along with you to our Arnold's and we'll see what he's got. All right?'

It was bitterly cold and there was the smell of snow in the air as they walked along Endell Street and then Betterton Street, crossing Drury Lane. Heath's Emporium didn't look half as grand as its name when Dolly stopped outside a ramshackle shop at the end of Macklin Street. They had passed numerous snotty-nosed, barefoot children on the way, children with eyes too big for their faces and dressed in an assortment of rags from head to foot. Somehow, on the train coming south, Sophy had imagined London would be full of smartly dressed, well-to-do, fashionable folk, but even as she had stepped off the train in King's Cross she'd realised her naivety from the number of urchins begging for a penny from passengers or trying to sell them matches. And her three or four days of exploring parts of the city since had shown her depths of squalor to equal anything in the worst parts of Sunderland.

Arnold turned out to be a female version of his mother, and his wife a small, dumpy woman with a couple of little tots hanging on to her skirts, who immediately clamoured to get to Dolly. When Dolly explained the reason for their visit, emphasising that Sophy didn't have a farthing to throw around and that she'd prom-ised Sophy her lad would see her all right, Arnold smiled at his mother, revealing a mouth full of blackened teeth. 'Never have any profits if it was left to you, would I,' he said affectionately, before turning to Sophy. 'What is it you're after, love?'

The emporium turned out to be an Aladdin's Cave, albeit a dusty, higgledy-piggledy one, selling a wide variety of goods. Amazingly, in all the chaos, Arnold seemed to know exactly where he could put his finger on any one item. With no trouble at all he produced a new-looking, stain-free flock mattress from amongst a pile of items at the very rear of the shop, along with a selection of sheets and blankets and a very nice plump eiderdown. 'All came from a house clearance the other week,' he told them. 'Spinster lady, very clean and tidy. Want to see any more of her stuff?'

By the time Sophy left the shop she had bought the mattress and bedding, a thick hearthrug which would cover a good part of her little room, two flock cushions for the hardbacked chairs and a pair of bright yellow curtains for the window. Arnold had thrown in an old coal-scuttle, a knife, fork and spoon, a dinner plate and a mug. Sophy had been drawn to a small pink armchair in faded velvet but not only could she not afford it, it would barely have fitted into her small attic room. Arnold had only charged her six shillings for the lot, which even Sophy knew was a bargain, but he'd assured her he would make up his money with some of the other goods from the spinster's house which were all in excellent condition. He was going to deliver all the items after close of work, which for him meant ten or eleven o'clock, but Sophy was pleased about that as it meant she should have time to whitewash the walls and perhaps even get them dry if she lit a fire as soon as she got home.

Home. She savoured the word as she and Dolly walked back towards Endell Street. And ridiculously, the little room felt like home already, probably due to Dolly's kindness. She had seen several landladies over the last days and one or two had actually frightened her, and all the rooms had been too expensive anyway. She had already discovered that everything was more costly here than up north. Lamp oil was double the price at sixpence a quart, and candles a third more at sevenpence a pound. Even the piece of soap the shopkeeper had cut for her from a big bar had cost a penny; she could have had two pieces for that in Southwick. Half her money had gone already. She would have to concentrate on finding work now she had found somewhere to stay.

She had read the papers in the lounge of the hotel and made a list of all the theatres, deciding she would write to the managers asking for an interview over the next week or so. One thing she was absolutely decided on was that she didn't intend to work the halls. She wanted to be an actress, a serious actress.

It was only last year that Henry Irving, the actor-manager of the Lyceum, had been knighted, and she remembered reading an article at that time in one of the newspapers Jessica had smuggled into the dormitory. The reporter had stated that in one fell swoop the theatre had risen above the music halls and had become respectable, and middle-class children who had been taken to the matinées at the Prince of Wales and had performed in endless drawing-room amateur dramatics, would now contemplate acting as a career. This would be particularly true of girls, the reporter had gone on with a touch of disapproval. Young ladies had always been taught that women should be humble and obedient, and that ambition and independence were unfeminine attributes, but on the stage they could see women expressing passion and achieving fame. This was a double-edged sword, and might encourage women's suffrage – a dangerous notion, he had finished darkly.

'Here we are, dear.' Dolly interrupted her thoughts, and Sophy realised they were home. 'Would you like a nice cup of tea before you go upstairs? If I know my Jim, there'll be a pot on the go. Loves his cuppa, he does.'

When Sophy entered the quarters of the landlady she found Jim with his feet up in front of the range and a big fat cat purring on his lap. The kitchen-cum-living area was large, much bigger than Sophy had expected, and a portion of the room had been divided into what was obviously the Heaths' bedroom, with a big brass bed and wardrobe against the far wall. A curtain had been strung up to separate the bedroom area from the living area but this was only partially closed, and Sophy could see another two cats lying on top of the quilted eiderdown that covered the bed. The room was terribly overcrowded and more than a little smelly, but Jim beamed a welcome at them and Dolly pushed her down in the other armchair in front of the range, and Sophy felt herself relax. They were nice, this couple. She had been lucky to end up here. And then, for some strange reason, she had a great desire to cry.

She didn't, of course. She accepted her cup of tea and a piece of fruit cake thankfully – she hadn't eaten since the previous evening – and listened while Dolly told her about her twelve children and eighteen grandchildren and all their doings. After another cup of tea and an even larger chunk of cake – Dolly had noticed how quickly the first piece had gone – Sophy made her goodbyes and went upstairs to begin work.

The first thing she did was to light the fire. The little room was as cold as ice and it had begun to snow outside, big feathery flakes that swirled and danced outside the window. She had only purchased one small sack of coal and a bag of wood bits the day before, and she had barely been able to lug that up the three flights of stairs. In one way she thought it was lovely that she was tucked away all by herself at the top of the house, but the day-to-day practicalities of living in the attic room would be daunting for anyone less fit than herself. How old Mr Ferry had managed, she didn't know.

It took her the rest of the day to painstakingly whitewash the walls and ceiling, and by the time she had finished her arm was aching fit to drop off. But the effect was dramatic. Suddenly her tiny home was brighter, and when she lit the oil lamp as it got dark, the white walls reflected the light. By standing on the little table and stretching to her full extent she had managed to reach the top of the walls and then the ceiling, but as she put the last stroke to the ceiling – she had painted the walls first as she wanted them to dry before bedtime – the crick in her neck told her she couldn't have gone on a minute longer.

Climbing down, she put the table back in its place with the oil lamp in the middle of it and surveyed her work. She was tired and hungry and thirsty, she had nothing to eat or drink and she was covered in splashes of whitewash and had no water in which to wash, but she was satisfied. Yes, she was satisfied. Tomorrow she would buy a bucket so she could carry water from the yard up here for drinking, cooking and washing herself, but tonight she was too exhausted to do more than sit on the floorboards in front of the fire and wait for Arnold to deliver her things.

The rest of the house seemed to be asleep when Arnold came, although Sophy suspected they couldn't have remained so with the noise Dolly's son made on his three journeys up and down the stairs, cheerfully cursing and swearing about her rooftop abode. But he was kind, staying to put up the curtains on the piece of wire he had thoughtfully decided to bring, along with nails and a hammer, before clattering down the stairs for the last time, whistling tunelessly as he went.

Once he had gone, Sophy set about making her bed by the flickering light of the oil lamp, and when she had finished she stood admiring the first place she had ever really called home. The battered old brass coal-scuttle was reflecting the glow from the fire, the patterned hearthrug and curtains provided bright splashes of colour, along with the red flocked cushions on the hardbacked chairs, and her bed, topped by its faded pink eiderdown, looked warm and cosy. She gave a quiet, heartfelt prayer of thanks for Patience's quick thinking. But for her cousin she would have left Sunderland without a penny in her pocket, and even if she had sold her clothes and Miss Bainbridge's ballerina brooch, they wouldn't have provided sufficient funds for her train ticket to London, let alone anything else.

She would write to Patience one day. Not yet, perhaps not for a long time, but one day . . .

She sank down on her bed, staring at her whitewash-covered hands as a flood of mixed emotions stormed her breast. And then, for the first time since her aunt had screamed the truth about her beginnings at her, she let the tears come.

Chapter 10

It was Sophy's fifth week in London. She had written to umpteen theatrical managers asking for an interview, waited outside stage doors and in draughty vestibules hoping to catch someone who could help her, and spent a portion of her precious money having the cheapest cards possible printed with her details which she left at the theatres. She had quickly learned that the only way into the theatre was by the personal introduction and patronage of one of the actor-managers, and this often came by way of the acting classes some of the would-be actresses took. There was no drama training as such, these lessons came from working actresses and actors in their living rooms which doubled as the auditorium and stage for the purposes of the lesson, but the lessons cost money. Money she didn't have. Likewise, she had heard about an acting academy, the first in the country, which guaranteed successful students their first job in one of the touring companies owned by the founder, but it could have been on the moon for all the chance she had of finding the fees.

It had been during her second week, whilst waiting in one of the foyers of a theatre hoping to catch the manager when he left, that his assistant had indicated he might be able to help her. He had taken her into a side room, and when she had found out the price of this 'help' she had slapped his face and walked out, crying all the way home. It was then that Dolly had given her a little talk on what she called 'the birds and the bees', finishing with the warning that actresses – even young novices such as herself – were considered sexually sophisticated in the eyes of most men and therefore fair game.

Sophy had been embarrassed and horrified – as much from Dolly's candid account of what went on between a man and a woman as the assistant's designs on her, which apparently was only to be expected if she followed her chosen career – but the little talk stood her in good stead for the next time a man tried his luck, which was only a day or two later, as it happened.

None of this discouraged her, however. What did alarm her was the dwindling of her remaining money. Due to the years spent in Kitty's kitchen, she knew how to cook a sustaining broth with scrag ends and vegetables, and other such inexpensive meals, but having no oven she had to buy shop-baked bread at tuppence a pound loaf, and even dripping – butter or magarine was quite out of the question – was thruppence a half-pound. Then there was coal and candles – she had decided lamp oil was too expensive – and of course, Dolly's two-shillings-a-week rent.

She sat on her bed one morning, a snow flurry outside the window emphasising the unwelcome fact that the bad weather was far from over and spring was still a couple of months away, and contemplated the holes in the soles of her boots. She couldn't afford to get them mended. She had four shillings left and the rent was due. The last of the coal was burning on the fire and it was essential she got a another sack today, for not only did the fire provide warmth but it was her only source of cooking and making a hot drink. Since the four ounces of tea had run out which she had bought the first morning after moving in, foregoing the luxury of milk and sugar, she had been making do with half a teaspoonful of raw oatmeal in a mug of hot water to thaw her out when she had come in frozen from tramping from one theatre to another all day.

She shouldn't have bought the hearthrug and curtains and

cushions, she could have managed without them. She bit on her lower lip, anxiety flooding her. But one thing was clear. She had to put the ambition of becoming an actress to one side for the time being and find work of some kind. But what could she do? She wasn't trained for anything.

And then she remembered the notice in the window of a little restaurant she'd passed the day before, advertising the position of waitress. The restaurant was in one of the streets west of the Gaiety Theatre; she hoped she could find it again. She tended to get her bearings more by the theatres than the myriad of street names, which were confusing.

Having decided to try, she lost no time in getting ready. The only food she had was the stale end of a loaf, but undeterred she toasted it in front of the glowing fire and spread the last of the dripping on it. She was even out of the oatmeal, so a mug of hot water had to suffice, but she felt better for having something inside her as she set out twenty minutes later, her feet soaked through within seconds.

She found the restaurant without any trouble. It was sandwiched between a Roman Catholic church and a small row of houses at the back of the Vaudeville and Adelphi theatres. She made a mental note of the street name. Maiden Lane. Perhaps that was a good omen? The next few minutes would tell.

She'd taken special care with her hair, drawing it neatly into a shining chignon, and her coat – bought especially to the require-ments Miss Bainbridge laid down for her students – was of good quality. Fortunately no one could guess about the holes in her boots, she thought wryly, as she squelched into the restaurant which was quite full, considering it was only eight o'clock. There were no women among the customers, since respectable ladies dined in their own homes unless escorted by a gentleman, and most of these customers were clearly having breakfast before they went to work.

She stood just inside the door, uncertain of how to proceed and embarrassingly aware of the covert – and not so covert – glances of several of the men.

A small fat man with an harassed expression appeared from a

door at the back of the restaurant and on seeing her paused for a moment. Then he came towards her, a pair of shrewd black eyes surveying her from head to foot. Even before he spoke, Sophy felt herself bristling. There was something in his face . . .

'Don't tell me. You've come about the job as waitress.'

She stared at him, wondering what she had done to arouse such hostility. 'Yes. Yes I have.'

He put down the coffeepot he was holding, nodding slowly as he crossed his arms over his fat stomach. 'And why is that?'

'I beg your pardon?'

'Why do you want to come here and work as a waitress?'

Sophy knew she had gone as red as a beetroot; she could feel her ears burning. 'Are you the proprietor?'

That seemed to amuse him for some reason. He nodded. 'Yep, I'm the proprietor, my dear.' He emphasised the word *proprietor*. 'And I repeat, why do you want to come and work for me? No, don't tell me.'

She hadn't been about to.

'You want to go on the stage, and Mater and Pater have thrown you out in horror. Am I right? So you've decided to play at something else for a while.'

The strange feeling of aloneness which had been with Sophy all her life, even when she was in the midst of company, rose up at his aggressiveness, threatening to choke her. She wanted nothing more than to turn tail and leave, but she was blowed if she was going to give this nasty individual the satisfaction. Aware that everyone was listening, she glared at him, but her voice was crisp and without heat when she said, very clearly, 'I am not surprised you are looking for a waitress. I can't imagine anyone would suffer you for more than a day or two.'

'Is that so?'

At least he had stopped smirking, Sophy thought, but it was a pity about the job.

'Well, let me tell you I've seen plenty of your type, my girl. Born with a silver spoon in your mouth and—'

'That's enough, Horace.' One of the customers who had been

sitting at a table by the window spoke, his voice deep and low as he stood up. 'I fear you got what you asked for, old chap, and it's really not the way to speak to a lady, is it? Let me explain, my dear,' he added, looking straight at Sophy now. 'Our friend here has been caught twice in the last six months by young ladies who take the wonderful job as a waitress in this prestigious establishment, only to leave without notice when they get the offer of work in the theatre. Can you imagine that? Leaving this oasis of delight and the engaging company of Horace? It's hard to believe, I know.'

The other occupants of the restaurant were laughing openly now, and a man sitting a couple of tables away, called out, 'You always were a miserable blighter, Horace. If it wasn't for your wife's superb cooking you'd close this place within the month just by the look on your face.'

Sophy was surprised to see that Horace himself was smiling, albeit sheepishly when she glanced at him, but then her attention was brought back to her rescuer, when he said quietly, 'Please let me buy you a cup of coffee, my dear. It's cold outside.'

The smell of the coffee was intoxicating but Sophy took a step backwards away from him, a thread of alarm in her voice when she said, exactly as Miss Bainbridge had taught her girls when it was necessary to refuse an invitation but without giving offence, 'That's most kind of you, but I have a prior engagement.'

Kane Gregory knew exactly what was going through this lovely – and plainly terrified – young woman's mind, his voice quieter still when he said, 'An engagement that won't let you sit down for a few moments and warm yourself? You are quite safe, Miss . . .'

'Hutton. Sophy Hutton.'

'How do you do? My name is Kane Gregory.'

He was very smartly dressed, Sophy thought, hesitating. Obviously a gentleman. His frockcoat was of the best quality, and a gold watch gleamed on his waistcoat. And he had smiling eyes. They were smiling at her now as he murmured, 'I hate to eat breakfast alone, Miss Hutton. You would be doing me a great favour if you joined me.' He could see she was still on the verge of flying out of the door, and throwing caution to the wind he took her arm, leading her over to the small table by the window. There was a slight resistance at first but then she allowed him to pull out a chair for her, but she still sat perched on the edge of it as though poised for flight.

'I am about to indulge in one of Horace's wife's superb breakfasts. May I order two?'

The colour which had begun to subside flooded Sophy's face again. This was the sort of thing Dolly had warned her about; only bad girls allowed themselves to be picked up by strange gentlemen who always expected payment for anything they gave.

'Miss Hutton?' He had leaned forward, his voice so low no one else could hear. 'Please don't be frightened of me. I am sure you have encountered gentlemen who tried to take advantage of you, but I can promise you I am not one of them. I would simply like to share a meal with you, that is all.'

That wasn't quite true, Kane Gregory acknowledged to himself as he watched the slender shoulders relax slightly. He wanted to know how this enchanting girl came to be in Horace's restaurant looking for work. She spoke well, she held herself well and her clothes, although quite severely plain, were not inexpensive. He agreed with Horace, she clearly was the product of a middle-class upbringing.

'Th-thank you.' She had to swallow before she could speak, the smell of food was making her mouth water. Terrified at the way her money had drained away and desperate to keep a little by so she knew she could pay the rent, she had only eaten bread and dripping for the last week, and not much of that, filling up on hot water when the gnawing hunger pains became too uncomfortable. 'You are very kind.'

When Horace appeared at their table in the next moment, Sophy didn't dare to raise her eyes, sure she would read condemnation in the proprietor's face. She could imagine what the other customers were thinking too. And then the spirit which had carried her out of her aunt's house rose up. It didn't matter what they thought. *She* knew she wasn't bad. She listened to Mr Gregory ordering the food and when he said, 'I trust that is to your liking?' before Horace moved away, she looked at him and said politely. 'It sounds lovely, thank you.'

Horace had poured them two coffees, and when they were alone again, Kane gestured at the milk and sugar. 'I take mine black, but please help yourself.'

Again Sophy murmured, 'Thank you.'

'So . . .' Kane settled back in his chair. 'May I ask why you want to work as a waitress, Miss Hutton?'

For a moment she wondered if he was laughing at her, but the somewhat rugged male face gave no sign of it. He had the sort of face which made it impossible to determine how old he was, but she thought around the middle thirties. He was tall and well-built, and his hair was thick and dark, almost black, but his eyes were a bright blue. His complexion was severely pock-marked, but for that, he might have been considered good-looking. Aware that she was staring, she said quickly and with transparent honesty, 'I don't *want* to work as a waitress, I need to.'

'Ah.'

She poured milk into her coffee, adding two teaspoonfuls of sugar – a luxury – before she added, 'The proprietor was partly right, as it happens.'

'Call him Horace. Everyone does.'

'I – I do want to be an actress but I don't have wealthy parents as he suggested.'

'No?'

Her tongue was running away with her. It was the warmth and smell of food and not least the easy way Mr Gregory had with him. But he was a man, a stranger, and she shouldn't be talking so freely. She bowed her head, sipping at her coffee which tasted wonderful, and feeling uneasy again.

It was a moment or two before Kane went on, 'What have you done about furthering your desire to work in the theatre, Miss Hutton?'

Feeling this was safer ground, she told him of her efforts over the last weeks without mentioning when she had arrived in London or anything more about her personal circumstances. Their meal came, two large plates of ham, devilled kidneys, steak and eggs with a side plate of warm rolls and small slabs of butter. Sophy had to restrain herself from falling on the food, but somehow she managed to pick up her knife and fork and eat in a manner Miss Bainbridge would have approved of.

Nevertheless, as Kane watched her while appearing to concentrate only on his own breakfast, he thought, She's hungry. Damn it all, the girl was ravenous. What the dickens was going on?

It was towards the end of the meal, when Sophy had all but cleared her plate, that he spoke again. 'I hope you don't think I'm being impertinent, Miss Hutton, but you mentioned that your parents are not wealthy. Do they know you are here today?'

The question took her by surprise. Now her stomach was full for the first time in weeks, she was wondering how on earth she could have been so foolish as to put herself in this position. She should have walked straight out of the restaurant after the altercation with Horace, but it was too late now. Panic made her throat dry, and she took a sip of coffee. 'My parents died not long after I was born,' she said carefully. It was the story she had decided to tell if anyone asked. 'My aunt and uncle – my mother's brother – brought me up. They weren't in favour of my becoming an actress so I am at present in lodgings.'

'I see.' Not as much as he wanted to, but it was a start. He would guess she was roughly seventeen or eighteen, maybe a trifle younger, but the mantle of innocence that sat on her made him wonder how she had survived thus far. He could think of a handful of men on the fringe of the entertainment business who would snap her up if they got the chance, and for purposes other than putting her on the stage. She was tailor-made for one of the high-class brothels. Such men were like leeches, hanging round the theatres hoping to snare ingénues like this one, their naivety and freshness their downfall. And this girl was extraordinarily lovely.

His mind made up, he said, 'Forgive me for saying this, Miss Hutton, but I am assuming you are now outside the protection of your family and therefore in something of a delicate position.' As

Sophy went to speak, he held up his hand. 'I'm sure you are quite capable of looking after yourself in the normal way of things, but if – as I surmise – you are all alone in a strange city with limited funds, I think we could both agree that is not ideal.'

Her cheeks fiery, Sophy said stiffly, 'I have no intention of allowing myself to be' – she had been about to say 'used' but substituted it for the words he had spoken earlier – 'taken advantage of by men, I do assure you.'

Whether that was a warning to him or a statement of fact Kane didn't know, but his face expressionless, he went on, 'Unfortunately, there are occasionally circumstances when a young lady has little choice in the matter. But regarding your wish to become an actress, may I ask where your ambition lies? Do you intend to play fashionable dramas, ones where women who look like you do enjoy a heyday of popular success by exhibiting themselves in pretty frocks and playing gentle, virtuous wives and mothers? Or does your taste lie more in "new drama"? Plays like *Candida* or *The Master Builder*, for instance?'

Sophy stared at him. She had no idea what he was talking about, never having heard of these plays or the term 'new drama'. For a moment she thought about prevaricating. But only a moment. 'I'm sorry, Mr Gregory. I don't know what you mean.'

Inwardly Kane smiled. He'd thought as much. An innocent in every term of the word, and yet . . . There was something about this young woman that was different to the dozens of fashionable middle- and upper-class would-be actresses he'd seen over the last decade. Her face was undeniably beautiful but there was a depth in her eyes that spoke of . . . What *did* it speak of? he asked himself. Tragedy? Heartache? Desperation? If she could project that when on the stage, she'd bring the house down.

Putting his thoughts aside, he cleared his throat. 'My line of work is in the theatre, Miss Hutton.' He didn't go on to say he had a financial interest in several theatres and music halls and a touring company. 'One theatre is putting on a new play next week and the actor-manager is a personal friend of mine. I can arrange an introduction but the rest will be up to you.'

Again he stopped her with a raised hand as she went to speak. 'A word of caution. The theatre is a world within the world, and far from a glamorous world at that. For every Marie Tempest and Eva Moore, there are a hundred other girls who never make it beyond the chorus and struggle to support themselves all their working lives, often leaving the boards when they are too discouraged to continue, only to find that real life has passed them by. You will work hard and be paid little, and the touring side is harsh, but necessary if you want to learn your craft. Provincial theatres are ill-equipped and draughty, you will have to adapt fast to a nomadic existence in lodgings not fit for a dog, and the stage-door gallants will assume that because you are an actress you are fair game. I'm sorry to be so blunt, but that is how it is.'

Sophy's eyes were shining, she had barely heard anything beyond the magic words 'I can arrange an introduction'. 'I want to be an actress, Mr Gregory. It's the only thing I want.'

He smiled. 'That's what they all say, but time will tell.' He brought out his pocket-watch and glanced at it before standing up and throwing some money on the table, calling across to Horace, 'Tell Vicky that was even better than usual this morning,' and then adding in an aside to Sophy who had also risen, 'unless it's the company.'

Sophy was conscious of two things as she left the restaurant; one, Mr Gregory was even taller than she had realised, and two, her feet had only just got warm and now they were going to freeze again. Once in the street, Mr Gregory took her elbow, saying, 'Be careful, the pavements are icy under this latest snow and it would be a shame to break your ankle now, don't you think? The theatre is only a short distance away on the other side of the Strand, it's not worth taking a cab.'

'We're going there *now*?'

He looked down at her quizzically. 'Is that a problem?'

'No, no.' It was a massive problem. Huge. A sick agitation about the unknown was filling her as they walked on, and this wasn't helped when she saw that the theatre was none other than the Lincoln. It wasn't the largest theatre in the area – few could hope to compete with the Theatre Royal or the West End theatres surrounded by a host of supper clubs which stayed open until after midnight – but since being in London she had learned that the Lincoln was a cut above the other smaller theatres it competed with.

They didn't enter by the main doors but by a side entrance, which Mr Gregory unlocked with a key. Sophy found herself in a long narrow corridor with various doors leading off, but Mr Gregory led her right to the end and then down a few steps to another door which he opened without knocking. A middle-aged, very good-looking and rather distinguished gentleman was sitting at a large desk. He looked up as the door opened and then his face split into a grin. 'Kane. What are you doing here? I thought you had to be at the Empire first thing?'

'I'm on my way.' Kane drew Sophy in front of him. 'I'd like you to meet Miss Sophy Hutton. Miss Hutton, meet Augustus Jefferson, a fine actor and the manager of this establishment.'

Sophy was so covered in confusion she almost curtsied, just managing to restrain herself in time and say weakly, 'How do you do, Mr Jefferson.'

He didn't answer, looking straight at Kane with raised eyebrows.

In answer to the unvoiced question, Kane said, 'You still have one or two sylphs to find? Then perhaps Miss Hutton might do. I'll leave her with you.' And to Sophy's alarm, Mr Gregory smiled, nodded, and said, 'Goodbye, Miss Hutton,' turning and closing the door behind him.

Her eyes had followed him but when Mr Jefferson said, 'Miss Hutton?' she snapped them back to the man behind the desk. 'Mr Gregory has told you we open next week?'

She managed a nod.

'Rehearsals start at three this afternoon. Please be punctual.'

She stared at him, her mouth slightly agape. 'I— What— I mean, what am I—'

He cut her stammering short. 'What are you? A sylph, of course. Just follow the other girls and do what they do, it's not complicated. The dress rehearsal is today so you'll get some clothes from Wardrobe. All right?'

He looked down at the papers on his desk again, and when after a moment she was still standing there, raised his eyes to say, 'Three o'clock, Miss Hutton. All right?'

'Th-thank you.' Somehow she found herself in the corridor, although her head was spinning and she was in a daze. Then she nearly jumped out of her skin when a voice at her elbow said, 'Hello there, and what are you doing outside Jefferson's office at this time of the morning? Didn't I see you come in earlier with Gregory?'

Sophy swung round to see a young slim man with one of the most beautiful faces she had seen in her life smiling at her. She would never have thought of calling a man beautiful before, but his features, along with his mop of fair hair and bluey-grey eyes made him so. It added to the unreality of the morning.

'Well?' His smile widened, showing a set of perfect white teeth. 'You *can* talk, can't you?'

She tried to gather her wits. 'Of course.'

'Glad to hear it. It would be such a waste if a delicious creature like you were dumb. So, are you joining us? Is that it? I'm Toby Shawe, by the way.' He held out his hand.

Aware that he had said his name as though she should know of him, Sophy placed her fingers in his. 'How do you do,' she said weakly, her embarrassment increasing when he held on to her hand.

'And you are?'

'Oh, Sophy Hutton.' Somehow she managed to extricate her fingers and took a step backwards.

'Hello, Sophy Hutton,' he said softly. 'And am I right? Are you joining our merry little band?'

She nodded. His good looks combined with a slightly mocking air which, although not unkind, was making her shyer, rendered her mute.

'I thought as much when I saw you with Gregory. Taken you under his wing, has he, our noble benefactor?'

She didn't like the tone of the last words and her voice was stiff when she said, 'Mr Gregory was kind enough to introduce me to Mr Jefferson this morning because he thought there was a part in the play I might be suitable for. That's all.'

'Believe me, sweet lady, if Gregory brought you here himself, there *would* be a part for you. Our illustrious manager knows on which side his bread is buttered.'

Sophy found that in spite of his overwhelming attractiveness, she wasn't sure if she liked Toby Shawe or not. But then the next moment his whole persona changed as he took her arm in a friendly fashion, saying, 'Come on, I'll take you on a tour of everything while there's not too many people about. That way, you won't feel so strange when you come back later. What's old Jefferson given you – one of the sylphs? That'll be like eating cake so don't worry. What other things have you done?'

They were walking back along the corridor but when Sophy said, 'Nothing, I haven't done anything else. This – this is my first job,' Toby stopped, turning her to face him.

'Is that so?' he said softly. 'Then welcome into the big bad world of the theatre, little fledgling.'

He wasn't laughing now, and as Sophy stared into the angelic face it came to her who he reminded her of. Miss Bainbridge had been insistent her girls had an appreciation of art and culture, and to that end had introduced them to the works of many fine sculptors, painters, architects and poets. Sophy had been particularly taken with the creative genius of the Italian Buonarroti Michelangelo, and had pored for hours over the pictures of the Sistine Chapel and the Medici funeral chapel, but it had been his sculpture of David which had gripped her with its beauty and grace. And the same aesthetic purity of features was mirrored in this man's face.

And then he smiled again, breaking the spell, pulling her along with him as he said, 'They're painting one of the backgrounds in the theatre, come and see – and they've got some hot coffee on the go. We'll have a cup and then I'll take you on the grand tour. One thing's for sure, little fledgling. Your life will never be the same again after today.'

PART FOUR

Liberation and Subjugation

1897

Chapter 11

'Oh my goodness, can you *believe* this bedding? It's positively *dripping*. I shall have to go and have a word with the landlady, it's too much.' Christabel Ardington-Tatler – Cat to her friends of which Sophy was one – struck a dramatic pose in the middle of the grim little room on the second floor of the theatrical lodging-house in Shepton Mallet. 'We'll die of pneumonia before we even get on the stage of that wretched theatre at this rate.'

Sophy dumped her valise on one of the two single beds the room held and gazed about her. The room was no worse and no better than all the others they had stayed in during the tour, but Cat always had to have her little protest at the beginning of each new lodging-house. That was just Cat. She was vocal and militant and funny and fiercely independent, but her bold, self-sufficient exterior covered a heart of gold and Sophy was very fond of her.

'It's no good saying anything, Cat,' Sophy told her. 'It won't make any difference. You'll just annoy her.'

'Annoy her?' Cat plumped down on her own bed and then let out a little shriek. 'Look at my eiderdown, it's all holes. The mice have been having a feast. No, I'm sorry, this time I *am* complaining. I'll be back in a minute.'

After Cat had swept out of the room, Sophy opened the battered single wardrobe the room contained, wincing at the stale smell that assaulted her nose. She was definitely not hanging anything in there, it would reek for days. A slight movement in the corner of the room near the rotten skirting-board caught her attention, and a pair of bright round eyes stared at her for a second before the mouse shot back in its hole.

Mice again. Marvellous. That was another reason for not unpacking her valise. At their last stop she and Cat had found mice swinging from their clothes one morning when they had opened the wardrobe, and at another the walls had become alive with bugs at night.

She walked to the window which overlooked the street below and tried to open it, but it was stuck fast – the faded curtains hanging limply either side of the crumbling wooden frame. Lifting her eyes, she stared above the rooftops to where a bird was soaring high in the thermals, and smiled to herself. The company was playing three or four dramas a week, touring through many of the little towns of the south of England, but in spite of rehearsing all day, acting in the evening and arriving back at her lodgings in the early hours where she was lucky if she snatched five or six hours' sleep, she was happy.

Her salary at the Lincoln had amounted to fifteen shillings a week, rising to a pound when she had gained a little experience by having a 'walking-on' part after six months, but when Mr Gregory had offered her the chance of joining his touring company where she might be able to tackle larger parts, she had jumped at the opportunity, even though she was financially worse off. She still earned a pound, but now, as well as having to pay for her costumes and digs, she also had to pay Dolly's two shillings rent if she wanted to retain the tiny room which had become home.

Whilst at the Lincoln, she had managed to afford acting classes in the mornings, given by one of the working actresses from the West End. Sophy and several other girls had assembled in the actress's sitting room, learning the techniques of a good entrance and exit, and how to throw their voices without shouting. This had been wonderful experience, not least because the theatre was a hierarchical institution, and new recruits had virtually no contact with the established stars of the stage, and no idea how to negotiate even a minimum wage or what constituted a good or bad contract. By talking to the actress in question Sophy had discovered that the Lincoln was well regarded for paying a reasonable salary, unlike some other theatres.

As the door opened she was brought out of her thoughts by an indignant Cat. 'That ghastly woman!' Cat flounced over to her bed, her blue eyes flashing. 'Do you know what she said to me when I complained about the damp sheets and the holes in the eiderdown? She said she had a hole in her' – Cat stuck out her bottom and tapped her buttock – 'and it had never done *her* any harm.'

The two girls stared at each other, Cat outraged and red-faced and Sophy brimming up with the laughter that burst forth in the next instant. Within moments the two girls were howling with mirth and by the time they regained control their faces were wet.

They were still giggling on and off when they made their way to the theatre later that day. It was a very old-fashioned building but that wasn't unusual in the provinces. Only the number one tours played the major cities in the country; the number two and number three tours had to content themselves with visiting the smaller towns, some of which were merely large villages. Many of the provincial theatres were extremely ill-equipped, and the scenery, which the company always took with them on tour, often only just fitted on to the small stages.

Fortunately this tour was being conducted at the end of April – a perfect time, according to the old hands. Winter in the provinces was horrendous, with freezing cold theatres with inadequate heating and draughts of a magnitude second to none. Summer could be just as bad when the heat became unbearable and the clothes stuck to your back, and autumn could be a time of endless rain and mud. Spring was the best bet, they declared. Although you never could tell.

They were almost at the theatre when Cat said, casually as though it was of no importance, 'Heard from Toby lately?'

Sophy took a moment to reply. The subject was still a painful one. For the first little while at the Lincoln, Toby had made no secret of his interest in her and she had been both flattered and humbled that such a man, an accomplished actor who was greatly in demand, had even noticed her. He had taken her out to supper after the shows and been very attentive, even though those attentions had been a little too intimate on occasion, causing her to gently reproach him more than once. But it had been a magical interlude at the beginning of her career. And then had come the time when Toby had been offered the male lead in a new play on in the West End just after she had begun her first walking-on role at the Lincoln. He had told her he had secured a part for her too, a minor role admittedly, but still it *was* the West End. He had waited for her to throw her arms round him.

The play had been a conventional one, unlike the new drama the Lincoln favoured, such as Oscar Wilde's *A Woman of No Importance* where the poorly used mother of an illegitimate son is the heroine. When the son is offered a government post by his unknown father, the heroine reveals the son to the father and the father to the son. At the end of the play the son renounces the hypocritical society that makes an outcast of his beloved mother while condoning the actions of his father. This criticism of morality caused a storm of protest, and more than one personage left the theatre shocked to the core. But Sophy liked the Ibsen and Shaw heroines who were Joan of Arcs rather than pretty dolls. She had told Toby this before but he clearly hadn't been listening, or if he had, hadn't taken her seriously.

So she had told him again, that day, more forcefully. At first he had treated her with the indulgent, faintly mocking air he favoured. 'Sweetheart, you don't know what you're saying, believe me. This is a wonderful opportunity.'

'For you or for me?'

'Well, of course for me, that goes without saying, but for you too. You want to get on, don't you? You don't want to spend the rest of your career working for Jefferson and Gregory in their little tinpot theatre.'

That had hit her on the raw. 'The Lincoln isn't a tinpot theatre, you know it isn't, and Mr Gregory has been very kind to me. I don't know why you don't like him.'

That wasn't quite true. On the occasions when Mr Gregory came backstage at the Lincoln, he had made it clear that in his opinion, Toby still had plenty to learn about his craft. Toby had been angling for the male lead for a long time, thinking he could do better than Augustus Jefferson, and just before he was offered the part in the West End, he and Mr Gregory had had a heated exchange which had left Toby smarting and furious. Although Sophy adored Toby, she secretly thought Mr Gregory had a point. Toby *did* rely on his outstanding good looks when his acting ability wasn't up to scratch; he did forget his lines and expect the other actors to put up with it, and he did miss rehearsals when he felt like it. The charm and charisma which Toby used to good effect with everyone else just didn't seem to work with Mr Gregory, and the two tolerated each other at best and ignored each other when possible.

The upshot of their conversation that day was Toby leaving to work in the West End, and her remaining at the Lincoln. It meant they saw each other a lot less, and in the last two or three months Toby's name had been linked to that of his leading lady, an accomplished actress who, as Cat put it, had the morals of an alley cat in spite of being a married woman. He had denied anything other than a working relationship, of course, but all in all Sophy had been pleased when the opportunity to tour had arisen and she could leave London for some months. She hoped the time apart would convince Toby he couldn't do without her. If not . . . Well, she would deal with that when she had to.

Now she answered Cat with a forced smile. 'He's terribly busy and we agreed it's hopeless to try to write with me being on tour. But he's fine, I think.'

Cat made no reply to this. She thought Toby Shawe was an arrogant womaniser, but Sophy loved him and so she bit her tongue when they talked about him. It amazed her that Sophy seemed oblivious to the effect she had on men; she could have anyone she wanted with very little effort, but she seemed stuck on Toby. Even

Mr Gregory was smitten, she could tell – although he was always very correct and proper with everyone. But there was a look on his face sometimes when he thought no one was observing him . . . Still, it was none of her business. She was Sophy's friend and she'd back her to the hilt, but she wouldn't presume to tell her what to do.

When the two girls entered the back door of the theatre everyone was helping to put the scenery in place. It was like that on tour. Although they had a stagehand, there was too much for Bart to handle by himself so everyone mucked in. They were running late and there was no time for a rehearsal once everything was crammed on to the tiny stage, but they had been acting the play for weeks so it wasn't really necessary. Or then again, perhaps it was – in view of what happened when the play began.

The play was a work by Ibsen – 'glorious actable stuff', as Cat put it – with enough drama to satisfy the most fervent actors, but Sophy was on stage when all the set doors jammed, owing to the constricted space. She waited for Cat – the actress who was supposed to open the door and join her on stage – in vain, but she could hear the huffing and puffing as Bart and some others tried to force the door. In the middle of the stage there was a wardrobe. It was a bedroom scene and the wardrobe was never opened so it had no back to it; it went straight on to the rear of the stage. After a few minutes of ad libbing Sophy was just thinking they would have to bring the curtain down, when the wardrobe opened and Cat sailed out for her part. Throughout the whole of the rest of the play, Sophy and the other actors went on and off through the wardrobe, barely able to control their laughter on stage and giving free vent to it off stage.

It wasn't until the final curtain had come down that she realised Mr Gregory had been in the theatre when he joined them back-stage. He did this occasionally and always without notice. 'To keep us on our toes,' Cat said, and she was probably right.

He walked over to where she and Cat were watching Bart and a couple of the actors attacking the offending door with brute force. 'You handled that', he nodded towards the door, which suddenly gave way with a tremendous and ominous cracking sound, 'like true professionals, if I may say so. Well done, ladies.'

He smiled at them, and not for the first time Sophy thought what a difference it made to the craggy, somewhat stern face. She dimpled at him. 'I remember you did say to me that touring provides opportunities to learn the craft of acting like nothing else.'

'Did I?' His smile widened, his eyes lingering on the lovely face in front of him. 'That was uncommonly wise of me.'

'I don't think Henrik Ibsen would have appreciated the laughter from the audience tonight though, do you? He might have preferred us to bring down the curtain rather than use the wardrobe.'

'No doubt, but then he wouldn't be the one who would have to refund the ticket money.' Kane dragged his eyes away from the woman who haunted his dreams and tormented his days, saying to the cast in general, 'Anyone fancy supper on me? I think you all need a glass of something and a good meal after this evening.'

He didn't look directly at Sophy again, but he was vitally conscious of her as she bustled off with the rest of the group to change out of her costume. She had no idea in that beautiful head of hers how he felt about her. Which was good, in view of her attachment to Toby Shawe which had effectively tied his hands about presenting himself as a suitor.

That she was grateful to him was abundantly clear, and she didn't seem to dislike him. On the contrary, he imagined she saw him as something between a kindly uncle and an exacting benefactor, and being double her age he could understand that. But he didn't have to like it. And Shawe of all people. The man wasn't worthy of her. He was a philanderer and shallow into the bargain, she was throwing herself away—

He caught the thoughts, mentally shaking his head. Enough. With or without Shawe, she wouldn't have looked twice at him. If ever there was a case of Beauty and the Beast . . . He unconsciously raised his hand to the savagely pock-marked skin of his lower face where the smallpox which had nearly killed him as a twelve-year-old child had left its brand.

Kane Gregory was something of an enigma to his friends and

family – 'a lone wolf', as Augustus Jefferson, who knew him better than most, was apt to say. Born of well-to-do parents he'd had a privileged and happy childhood until the smallpox which disfigured his face killed his older and younger brothers, and his mother. The three boys had been inseparable, there being only a year between each of them, and Kane had been grief-stricken; however, his father had been inconsolable at the loss of his wife and two of his sons. After six years of heavy drinking, he had fallen off his hunter one day whilst drunk and had broken his neck, and Kane had inherited what was left of the family estate after his father's downward spiral into gambling and liquor.

Kane had gone into his twenties a troubled young man, devoid of a foundation in his life and given to wine, women and song. This state of affairs had lasted for three years. Then something had happened, something he never spoke about, and he had disappeared from all his old haunts for two years, only to return to London at the age of twenty-five with enough money to invest in two theatres. He'd proved himself to be a shrewd businessman, building on his success until now, at the age of thirty-four, he was very comfortably well off. He was also taciturn and cynical, and did not suffer fools gladly, with a well-earned reputation for having a tongue like a whip when he was displeased with something or someone.

'This is *so* good of you, Mr Gregory.' Sybil Brannon, another young actress in the company with fluffy blond hair and doe eyes, had positioned herself in front of him, and Kane sighed inwardly. The girl was a competent enough actress but he rather suspected she thought she might take a short-cut to playing the lead female role by sharing his bed.

'Not at all.' Kane took a step to the side but not towards Sybil, calling over to one of the actors who had already changed and returned promptly at the prospect of a slap-up supper, 'Mark, a word, please. I think your entrance in the second act needs to come sooner. Perhaps we can bring it forward a minute or two? When Christabel and Sophy have finished their dialogue about the sick child would be about right, I think. I'll have a word with

Leopold about it over dinner.' Leopold was the actor-manager of the touring company.

It was a merry little party who ate and drank in the private dining room at the inn Kane was staying at, but Sophy couldn't enter into the general jocularity as she might have done before Cat had brought up Toby's name. She didn't understand why he hadn't written to her. It had been a lie that they'd agreed not to correspond whilst she was on tour. She had written to him every day to begin with, but when after the first month she had only had one letter waiting for her, care of the theatre they were playing at on the itinerary of their bookings she had written out for him before she'd left, she had curbed her pen and tried to put a brake on her feelings. But it was hard. The more so because she couldn't share her despair with anyone.

She knew Cat didn't like Toby. Her friend had never said, but she knew. But Cat had never seen the side to him she had seen, the vulnerable, soft, sweet side. Perhaps she should have thrown all her principles and morals aside and followed him to the West End and ultimately into his bed? He had said more than once that if she truly loved him she would want to belong to him, body and soul. And she did. Except . . . Sophy's breath escaped her in a deep sigh. Her mother had followed that route and where had it got her?

She believed utterly in women having the vote, along with equal pay, equal job opportunities and equality before the law to free them from the domestic tyranny of men. She and Cat had talked often about such matters, and their seeing eye-to-eye on these issues had been one of the things which had cemented their friendship in the early days. But Sophy couldn't hold with the view of some suffragettes that women should be free to take as many lovers as men and act accordingly. She didn't personally believe it was right for men to use women for pleasure and then cast them aside when the attraction had worn off, so why would she condone women doing the same? Cat had agreed with her, and sensibly warned her not to let the view of a very small minority among the movement cloud what she felt about the real issues.

Look at Vesta Tilley and Bessie Bonehill and the other women in the music halls who impersonated men as male comedians, Cat had pointed out. They satirised men and a cavalier attitude to women through song and were applauded for it, but none of them were loose women in their personal lives. Rather, they pointed out how unfair society was, a society which labelled men as young bloods sowing their wild oats, and the girls they sowed them with as sluts and whores.

'My brother got one of our maids pregnant when I was still at home,' Cat had told Sophy quietly one day. 'The poor girl was shipped off to the workhouse, while my parents sent Alexander off abroad. There he was, enjoying himself with his cronies in Italy and France, while his child was being born in squalor and misery. It was the thing which finally made me leave home. That poor child will never amount to anything now – society will make sure of that, especially if it's a girl. Illegitimacy is the ultimate sin for the child and the mother, but the man, he walks away with his reputation intact. It's so wrong, so *unfair*.'

Cat knew nothing about her beginnings, no one in London did, but her friend's words, although spoken in innocence, were a sword through Sophy's bruised heart. Even Cat, if she knew about her mother, would look at her differently.

Sophy glanced around the table. Everyone was laughing at something which had been said, their faces happy and carefree. She mentally shook herself. What was she doing, brooding like this tonight? Dredging up the past did no good, she knew that, which was why she had determined to put it behind her and concentrate on the future. But some days this was harder than others.

Kane sat at the head of the table, joining in the conversation and paying everyone a little attention so no artistic feathers got ruffled. But little Sophy said or did escaped him.

Did she know that the new arrangement whereby Bart guarded the stage door and sent any stage-door johnnies packing was because of her? He had been meaning for some little while to do something about the impossible position his young actresses often found themselves in when touring but Sophy joining the company had prompted his hand. The number one tours playing the big cities with famous actresses provided chaperones as a matter of course – elderly ladies who dragooned the young women most effectively – but smaller companies couldn't afford such measures. Mind, in Sophy's case he didn't think it would be long before she was in such a position; her star was rapidly rising.

'What do you think, Mr Gregory?' He came out of his thoughts to find Sybil had brought everyone's attention to him. He'd been vaguely aware of Christabel – he considered the soubriquet of 'Cat' entirely inappropriate for a woman and always gave the girl the dignity of her legitimate name – engaged in a heated discussion with Larry, another of the actors, about the success of female stereotypes in the big West End theatres. However, his mind had wandered. He seemed to recall words along the line of '. . . horrible artificiality of the empty-headed doll wife and mother' from Christabel, and it had been clear that Larry was delighting in provoking the girl by making more and more outrageous statements about a woman knowing her place and so on. But he didn't intend to get into a discussion on the merits of parts for women in the independent theatre versus those traditional parts on the commercial stage. Not tonight.

He let his eyes pass over the assembled throng. He was weary and out of sorts. He was always out of sorts when in the company of Sophy. Why he kept torturing himself by seeking out the very thing that was the cause of his distress he didn't know. He hadn't been aware of masochistic tendencies before he'd met her, he thought wryly.

Forcing a smile, he said firmly, 'What I think, young ladies and gentlemen, is that it's time for you all to get some beauty sleep so you can be up bright and early in the morning to organise that scenery before the matinée.' He glanced at Leopold who immediately took his cue and stood to his feet.

Everyone thanked him again for the meal as they left, Christabel and Sophy bringing up the rear. He kept the smile on his face as he said goodbye, but looking at the two young women standing side by side, it only reinforced his earlier thoughts. Both girls were beautiful, both talented actresses as well as being clear-headed and intelligent, but Sophy had an extra quality which was indefinable. There was a depth to the amber eyes, an emotion that reached out and gripped the onlooker and held them transfixed. He had seen it on the faces of the audience tonight when they had looked at her, and on other occasions too. She had held them in the palm of her hand. She and Toby would make a stunning couple, he could see them being the toast of theatreland. How could he imagine, for one moment, that she would ever look at him in *that* way.

Chapter 12

Patience sat on the edge of her bed, the letter dangling in her fingers and tears in her eyes. Sophy was alive and safe. It had been over eighteen months since that snowy morning when her cousin had left, and many times since she had feared the worst, especially as month after month had gone by without a word. But she was safe and happy, although beyond that Sophy had said very little and there was no address on the letter. She read it through again, slowly this time:

Dear Patience,

First I must apologise for not having written before. I could say I have been too busy, but although that is partly true, it is not the whole truth. I think I needed time to come to terms with what I found out that day before I left Southwick. Your help the morning I departed was crucial and I want you to know that.

Looking back, I don't know how I imagined I would manage without a penny to my name, but I wasn't thinking clearly, of course. I am very happy in my new life but I will write more of that next time. For now, I wanted to thank you and to say that when I think of you, it is with fondness. Give the boys my best wishes and I hope you are all well.

Your cousin,
Sophy

Patience carefully folded the single sheet of paper back into the envelope before slipping it in her handbag, and then walked across to the window where she gazed out over the garden and drive. It was a sunny morning and the sunlight glancing over the grounds gave a tranquillity and beauty to the day. She drank it in, drawing strength from the birdsong and blue sky. And she would need strength in the coming hour, she thought grimly, when she faced her mother.

Her mother . . . Patience's thin mouth tightened into a line. How had her father put up with her all these years? Oh, she knew he wasn't perfect, far from it, but compared to her mother . . . In the space of the last eighteen months her mother had caused Sophy to run away to goodness knows where, and made life so impossible for John and Matthew when they wouldn't give up their girls that they now resided together in a small flat over a butcher's shop in Bishopwearmouth – the rent of which they could ill-afford as both were saving to get married. Even David saw to it that he was invited to his pals' homes over the hols whenever he could so he was rarely at the vicarage. And she had been left living at home, if you could call the four walls within which a silent war was played out day after day, 'home'. But no more.

Patience dried her face with her handkerchief and straightened her narrow shoulders. Today she was going to do something that would almost certainly result in the doors of the vicarage being closed to her for ever, and she couldn't wait. She had the rest of her life in front of her and she didn't intend to waste it. The seed of rebellion against her lot which had been planted the day Sophy had left, had come to flower. It was strange that she had received Sophy's letter this morning of all mornings, in view of what she intended to do – but she would take it as a positive sign. She was glad the letter had come by first post, which meant that Molly had brought it to her with an early morning cup of tea. It meant her mother knew nothing about it.

She glanced at her trunk packed full with all of the clothes and belongings she wanted to take with her, and her stomach fluttered, whether out of excitement or the thought of the ordeal ahead, she didn't know. She had arranged for the cab to call at nine-thirty after breakfast and it was now ten past eight. Morning prayers would begin in the drawing room at eight-fifteen and last for exactly fifteen minutes. As a child she hadn't minded the daily prayers; in fact, she had found them comforting. It seemed right to start the day by asking God to oversee it. But now this ritual grated on her as the height of hypocrisy. Her parents couldn't stand the sight of each other and yet they sat there in front of the servants every morning as pious and righteous as they came. However, from today she wouldn't have to endure that any more, along with many other things which regularly got under her skin.

Patience checked that everything was in order before leaving the room. She intended to break her news during breakfast, and if her mother reacted as she expected, she would have no time to do more than collect her trunk and handbag and leave.

When she entered the drawing room, Mrs Hogarth and Molly were already standing with their heads bowed, her mother was regally seated on one of the sofas with her eyes closed, and her father was droning on as usual. She was two minutes late. Heresy, as the swift piercing glance her mother gave her confirmed. Patience sat down but she didn't shut her eyes. Instead she glanced round the room she knew she was seeing for the last time, looking at the old familiar surroundings with a total lack of sentiment.

She had been happy in this house until the day her mother had whipped Sophy to within an inch of her life, but everything had changed from that point. It wouldn't be too extreme to say her eyes had been opened and she hadn't liked what she had seen, nor the person she herself had been then. And going away to school had driven home the fact that she was in grave danger of becoming her mother's daughter in every sense of the word. She knew she could be bossy and overbearing, 'a little prig', one of the girls in her dormitory had called her, but it was the narrowness of her vision which had alarmed her more than anything else. She had been so entrenched in her mother's way of thinking and doing things that she hadn't considered it could be wrong.

It had been a painful awakening. She nodded inwardly to the thought. But necessary. And now she thanked God for it, oh, she did.

She glanced at her father and not for the first time felt amazement that he could have come from the same parents as Sophy's mother. She wondered who Sophy's mother had taken after. The great-grandparents perhaps? Or maybe a free spirit reared its head in every family now and again? One thing was for sure, black sheep were never discussed or acknowledged, and all trace of them was effectively covered over.

When the prayers finished, Patience realised she hadn't heard a word of them. Mrs Hogarth and Molly trooped out, and she and her mother and father made their way to the dining room.

She found it enormously difficult to eat anything but forced down a few mouthfuls of porridge before buttering one of the soft rolls Mrs Hogarth made fresh every morning. Mrs Hogarth's cooking wasn't a patch on the meals Kitty had produced, but at least her bread was nice, Patience thought.

Her parents had started on their eggs and ham when Patience spoke. The meal had been conducted in total silence before then. 'I have some news.'

Her father raised his head but her mother continued eating.

Patience took a deep breath. 'I have been accepted as a nurse at the Sunderland Infirmary and I begin my training tomorrow. Probationer Nurses are provided with board and lodging and most of their uniform as part of their remuneration so I will be living at the hospital for the next three years until I obtain my nursing certificate. Of course, I can visit you on my half-day off once a week if you wish me to.'

If she had taken all her clothes off and danced stark-naked on the table she couldn't have shocked them more. Her father stared at her, his mouth slightly agape as he visibly tried to take in what she had announced, but it was Mary who sprang up, her chair falling backwards, as she cried, 'Never! I forbid it, do you hear me? Isn't it enough that your elder brothers have disgraced us without you attempting to do the same?'

Patience sat very still. 'John and Matthew are working hard and doing well at their respective jobs,' she said quietly, 'and their young ladies are pleasant, respectable girls. I see no reason for disgrace in any of that. As for me, my mind is made up. It has been for some time.'

'This is what comes from allowing her to demean herself working voluntarily at that dreadful Eye Infirmary in Stockton Road.' Mary had swung round to face her husband, her thin face flushed with temper. 'I told you no good would come of it, but you wouldn't have it. You could have been involved in all kinds of good works without coming into contact with sick people,' she bit out to Patience. 'It's not right for a young unmarried girl to see such things. But to get paid for it, to *work*. I shall never be able to hold up my head again. I won't have it, Patience. I mean it.'

'And *I* mean it, Mother. And you're quite right, the valuable experience I've gained at the Eye Infirmary has made up my mind where I see my future. I'm not squeamish and medicine fascinates me, moreover I've a natural affinity with the patients – everyone says so.'

'At the infirmary? But of course they would, girl. Cheap labour, they'll butter you up all they can.'

Patience stood up, white-faced. 'It was the head doctor who said it and he is not in the habit of "buttering up" anyone, believe me.'

'Is your mind made up?' Jeremiah entered the exchange. 'Are you absolutely sure it's what you want to do, Patience, because it will mean hard, relentless work, day in and day out. There's nothing romantic about nursing. You will be cleaning bedpans and giving bed-baths and seeing sights that will turn your stomach, and all for a pittance, remember that. It will be nothing like the voluntary work you've been doing. Are you prepared for that?'

'Of course she isn't, the stupid girl.' Mary was beside herself. 'Tell her! Tell her it's ridiculous.'

'Patience?' Jeremiah spoke over his wife.

'I know what I'm doing, Father. They were very explicit about all that at the interview. A full day's duty is ten and a half hours, more on occasion when emergencies dictate. On top of that we have to fit study in, and be prepared to work night duty one week in three. The wages are small, I agree, but to some extent I'm not doing it for the money although of course I need to earn enough to live.'

There was a snort from Mary which Patience, like her father, ignored.

'It was explained that a number of girls leave in the first twelve months, and of those who make it through to the close of the period of training, they must receive the approbation of the Matron as to their general conduct and efficiency. The Matron reports this to the physicians and surgeons, and the certificate is graded accordingly. From what has been explained to us, I understand this can be "fairly satisfactory" or "satisfactory" or "highly satisfactory", which can make a difference to one's future prospects. But I won't leave in the first little while and neither will I be fairly satisfactory or satisfactory. I promise you that.'

Jeremiah surveyed the daughter he had never particularly liked or understood until the last twelve months when she had amazed him by sticking resolutely to the voluntary work she had undertaken. He knew the Chief Physician at the Eye Infirmary – they were both members of the Gentlemen's Club – and the man had taken the trouble to seek him out on more than one occasion with glowing reports about Patience. He had once thought Patience to be the image of her mother in character as well as appearance. He had been wrong. At the bottom of him he didn't like the thought of a daughter of his joining what he considered to be a lowly profession more suited to the working class, but he sensed that if he said that now, he would lose her for good.

He smiled at her. 'I look forward to seeing the "highly satisfactory" in three years' time, my dear.'

He saw her blink and knew he had surprised her, but then Mary let fly with a tirade worthy of a fishwife, and as Patience slipped out of the room he took the full force of his wife's fury. Not for the first time – and he doubted it would be the last.

It was twenty minutes later when Patience left the house, her mother's last words, 'From this moment in time I have no daughter,' ringing in her ears. But it was her father who carried her trunk to the cab waiting on the drive – the horse munching on a carrot the driver had given it – who softened the leave-taking.

'I would like to say your mother will come round in time, but we both know that's not true.' Jeremiah helped Patience up into the carriage and when she was seated, pressed some pound notes into her hand. As she made to protest, he closed her fingers over the money. 'Please, it will smooth the way,' he said softly, much as she had said to Sophy eighteen months before. 'And I would like to see you sometimes on your half-day, if you agree? We could perhaps take tea together or a stroll in the park if the weather's clement.'

'I would like that, Father.' Patience hadn't expected to feel anything but relief as the driver clicked to the horse and they began to move down the drive, but as she leaned out of the window to wave to her father, she felt a moment's sharp pain in her heart at the sight of him standing alone outside the vicarage. He looked small and lost and suddenly older, much older than his years. And then the horse turned into the lane and the high hedge hid her father and the house from sight, and she settled back in her seat, excitement filling her once more.

She had done it, she had escaped the soul-destroying boredom which would have been her lot if she had stayed, and she didn't mind how hard she worked or what she did from now on, but one day she was going to be a fully qualified nurse. All things were possible, if you only believed.

The next few days were bewildering, frightening, demoralising and exhausting. Patience discovered her father had been right when he had intimated that a Probationary Nurse at the Sunderland Infirmary was treated quite differently to a volunteer at the Eye Infirmary. But every time she wondered if she had bitten off more than she could chew, she reread Sophy's letter, telling herself it had been no coincidence that it had arrived on the very day she had left the vicarage for good. Sophy had taken the bull by the horns and made a new life for herself, and she could do it too. And however difficult it was, Patience knew this was the right path.

The Probationer Nurses had been given a list of the lectures they had to attend in the next three months, a list of their day and night duties, a list of the papers they had to submit at the end of each three-month period, a list detailing all the wards and rooms at the hospital along with a plan of the building, and a list spelling out the timetable they were required to follow, set out as follows:

Rise	*Prompt at 6 a.m. No second call will be given.*
Breakfast	*6.30 a.m. in the Nurses' Dining Room.*
Wards	*7.00 a.m.*
Lunch	*10.00 a.m. Half-an-hour allowed from wards.*
Dinner	*2.00 p.m. ,, ,, ,,*
Tea	*4.30 p.m. Off duty until 6.30 p.m. Study time.*
Wards	*6.30 p.m.*
Supper	*8.30 p.m.*
Prayers	*9.30 p.m.*
Bedrooms	*10.00 p.m.*
Lights out	*10.30 p.m.*

There was yet another list for night duty, where it was noticed by several of the girls that they missed a meal:

Rise	*8.00 p.m.*
Breakfast	*8.30 p.m.*
Wards	*8.55 p.m.*
Off-duty	*8.15 a.m.*
Dinner	*9.00 a.m. followed by two hours study.*
Lunch	*11.30 a.m.*
Bedrooms	*12.30 p.m.*

'So we're expected to work longer and eat less on night duty?' Olive Tollett, Patience's room-mate, a big Wearside lass with arms as beefy as any docker, stared at Patience in horror. They were sitting on the narrow iron beds the small room held at the beginning of their second week at the Infirmary, having just got ready for bed. 'Why didn't I notice that before?'

Patience smiled. She had been a little unsure if she and Olive would get on when she'd first known she was sharing with the down-to-earth steelworker's daughter, but she needn't have worried. Whether it was a case of opposites attract, she didn't know, but the two of them had hit it off from the word go. 'Probably because you haven't had time to work it out?'

'Ee, you're right there, lass. Me feet haven't known what me head's doing and me backside has barely touched solid matter for more than ten minutes. They say they give us half-an-hour or so for meals, but by the time you've got to the dining room and sat down, ten minutes have gone, and then you've got to get back to the ward again most times. Still, the grub's not bad, is it, and they're not chary with the portions.'

Patience thought the food was verging on horrible but didn't say so. She was realising more and more just how privileged her life to date had been. Olive came from a family of fifteen children, five of whom hadn't survived past their first year. Their home was in the decaying slums of the East End in the heart of the community in Long Bank. Olive had invited her to go home with her on their first half-day off, and it had been a baptism of what true squalor entailed. Not that Olive's parents' two-up, two-down terrace had been dirty or smelly like some of the houses she had passed, their front doors open in view of the hot weather and the stink enough to knock you backwards. On the contrary, Olive's home had been as clean and tidy as plenty of carbolic soap and elbow grease could make it, but the filth and excrement in the streets outside in which barefoot children, their backsides hanging out of their ragged clothes and their faces covered in running sores, were playing, had filled her with pity mixed with revulsion. They had passed countless gin shops and bars on the way to Long Bank, and

Patience had to admit she was glad of Olive's stoic bulk at the side of her as thin, rat-faced individuals observed the two girls with dead eyes.

Nevertheless, it was an introduction into the fact that poverty is not necessarily synonymous with squalor. Olive's three younger sisters were dressed in white starched aprons and their hair was lice-free, and her brothers were polite and cheery. Olive's mother had presented them with a cup of tea and a shive of fruit loaf, and had been genuinely pleased to see her daughter, and Patience had left the crowded little house feeling envious of her new friend.

'Do you reckon we'll be able to stick it, lass?' Olive surveyed her with mild brown eyes. 'Me da was all for me starting at the kipper curing-house just down from us. It was better money, and heaven knows they need every penny at home.' Olive was the eldest child and although two of her brothers were now working alongside of their father at the steelworks, money was still tight. 'But me mam pushed for me to try for this when I got the heave-ho from Newtons.' For years Olive had been employed by one of the fishmongers in the East End, beginning when she was just a child of eight or nine after school and then continuing full-time once she had finished her limited education. According to Olive, Mr Newton and his wife had been kind to her, but when he had reached seventy he had sold up and the new fishmonger had two strapping daughters to help him in the shop so Olive's services were no longer required. 'Me mam says anyone can work with the kippers but I've got a bit more about me.' This was said with doubt. Olive, in spite of her bulk and cheery manner, wasn't the most confident of people.

'I agree with your mother.' Patience was speaking the truth. She'd observed her friend dealing with the patients a couple of times over the last days, and the big northern lass had a way with her that calmed the most agitated soul. 'You'll do just fine – I won't let you fail, I promise. We'll help each other through, all right? Bargain?' She held out her hand.

'I think you've got the worst of this bargain, lass, but aye, all right.' Olive shook her hand and they grinned at each other.

The bell sounded for lights out within moments and once the girls had settled down, Patience, in spite of being exhausted, lay staring into the blackness as Olive began to snore in her bed across the room. The nurses' rooms were small but clean, each holding two beds, one wardrobe and two tiny tables which served as desks with a hardbacked chair tucked under each. A series of shelves had been fixed to one wall on which books and papers and personal items could be stored, but the bare floorboards, walls painted a dingy green and paper blind at the window made the accommodation utilitarian at best. At least to Patience. For Olive, used to sharing a bed with her sisters, with a curtain separating their space from the boys' bed, it was the height of luxury. Likewise the Infirmary's flock mattress was as comfortable as the softest feather bed to Olive, who had been used to a sparse straw mattress all her life, but for Patience it felt as lumpy as lying on pebbles.

Patience tried to relax and let sleep take over her mind and body, but her thoughts went back over the day and especially to one of the patients on her ward. Gideon was a young man about Matthew's age, married with two small children, and after his leg had become tuberculous as the result of an accident four years previously and had to be removed, his wife had gone to pieces. She had sat with the woman for some time that afternoon, trying to instil into her that this wasn't the end of the world and the important thing was that Gideon's life had been saved, but the young wife had expressed revulsion at the thought of even seeing her husband, and had told Patience she intended to take the children and go back to her mother's house. She'd had a hard job not to shake the silly woman and had ended up being quite sharp with her, which unfortunately Sister had overheard, resulting in a lecture on the standards of propriety when dealing with patients' family.

She'd only been at the hospital a matter of days and had a black mark against her. Patience wrinkled her nose. And she suspected she'd already found what was going to be her Achilles heel to getting on in her career, because she couldn't in all honesty say she would do any differently if the same circumstances presented themselves. Well, apart from making sure Sister wasn't in earshot.

She smiled wryly to herself. She had all the time in the world for those family members who were bereft or anxious about their loved ones, but that silly, selfish woman needed a good slap.

Sister had tried to excuse Gideon's wife by saying the woman had been gently brought up, being a landowner's daughter with a privileged background, but that didn't cut the mustard with her either, Patience told herself. Florence Nightingale had been a gentlewoman of the upper classes – and look what she had accomplished, working in the worst of conditions in military hospitals in the Crimean War and transforming the most appalling state of affairs. Women weren't the empty-headed, weak creatures society – or perhaps she should say men – made them out to be, with lesser intelligence and fortitude than the male sex.

Patience nodded in the darkness, the thoughts she had been having more and more over the last months gathering steam. And marriage wasn't the be-all and end-all for a woman either. When she thought back now to how she had behaved with Mr Travis, who was her superior neither in intellect nor breeding, it made her hot with fury that she could have been so stupid.

She would never marry. Tiredness was overcoming her at last. Looking like she did, who would fall in love with her? And only love would do. And so nursing would be her husband, and the patients the children she'd never have. And she would be content with that. Given time.

Chapter 13

It was the beginning of a brand new year, and if nothing else, Rosalind and Christopher Robins knew how to throw a good party, Sophy thought, watching as everyone kissed and hugged and wished each other a Happy New Year. Rosalind had a reputation as a good actress, but when Kane had mentioned her once he'd been of the opinion that her looks, rather than her acting skill, had got her the leading roles for which she was known. Certainly she was beautiful, her golden-brown hair and eyes so blue they were almost violet setting her apart from many of her peers, and perfect for the traditonal, 'pretty' roles she favoured. Her husband, on the other hand, was a somewhat dour individual, but then if half the rumours about his wife were true, he had a lot to put up with. Of course he wasn't an actor so that didn't help, although there was no doubt his wealth hadn't done any harm in furthering his wife's career. Actresses with successful marriages tended to be married to fellow actors who did not expect them to conform to the conventional role of wife and mother, although in the Robins' case it was more Rosalind's cuckolding of her husband that was the problem.

Had Toby had an affair with Rosalind? Was he *still* having an affair with her? He said not, but then he would, wouldn't he. And then the next moment she found herself whisked round and into his arms as he said, 'I've been looking for you – where did you get to? Happy New Year, my darling,' and he kissed her hard. For an instant she returned the pressure of the kiss – it was always the same when he touched her, she melted – but then she pulled away. She tried to tell herself Toby was in love with *her* when thoughts of him and Rosalind came to torment her, that he wouldn't betray her, and when she was with him she believed it. There were always rumours about someone or other flying around in the theatre world, half of which weren't true. It was just how it was. But with Rosalind near, she felt . . . odd.

Quietly, she said, 'I didn't go anywhere. I thought you were getting us another drink?'

'I got sidetracked, you know how it is. People who wouldn't have bothered to speak a year ago now act as though I'm their best friend.'

This was said with a certain amount of satisfaction. Toby was enjoying his triumph in the West End and still couldn't understand the reluctance she'd expressed in following him there a year ago when she'd had the opportunity. He had told her more than once that the seat prices in his theatre ranged from one shilling in the pit to half a guinea in the stalls, and the theatre was full every night, with box-office takings of three thousand pounds a week. The play was an extravagant musical comedy with wonderful dancers and, of course, the famous Rosalind, but to hear Toby talk you would have thought the show's success was down to him alone. But she was being unkind, she told herself.

'Come on.' He took her hand, pulling her out of the magnificent drawing room and through the hall into another smaller room which appeared to be a morning room, whereupon he shut the door. She expected him to take her in his arms again, so when he dropped to one knee, taking her hand and looking up at her with the blue-grey eyes that had the power to make her weak at the knees, she was taken aback. She looked down on their joined hands. His was soft and finely boned for a man, the fingers long and thin. Quite different to Kane's hands, which were sturdy-looking, the backs covered in fine black hair. She didn't know why thoughts of Kane had intruded at such a moment, especially as she was now aware of what Toby was about to say.

'Will you marry me, Sophy? Will you make me the happiest man on earth and agree to be my wife?'

She had been longing for this moment, praying for it for months whilst doubting it would ever happen, but now it was here she felt strangely detached as though they were acting in a play. Perhaps it was because Toby's demeanour had the air of the theatrical about it, or maybe it was just that she had never been proposed to before and had imagined the moment so often it could never have lived up to expectation. Whatever, it tied her tongue and she gazed down at him, her eyes wide.

'Well, sweetheart, what is my answer?' His voice was laughing, playful; aware that he had surprised her, he probably thought she was overcome. But it wasn't that. Not exactly. She didn't know what it was.

His beautiful face swam before her eyes and somehow she managed to whisper, 'Yes, yes, I'll marry you,' through the numbness.

He stood up, drawing her to him and kissing her again before putting his hand in the pocket of his evening suit and drawing out a small box. Opening it, he presented it to her with a flourish, and again she felt they were acting a part. She looked down at the glittering gold band with a half hoop of two rubies and a diamond in the centre. Taking the ring from its velvet case, he slipped it on to the third finger of her left hand. 'A perfect fit.' He smiled at her, the smile that had the ability to make her forget everything. 'A good omen, don't you think?'

She nodded, smiling back through the frisson of disquiet that shivered down her spine. She had just realised what was missing from the moment she'd dreamed about for so long. Toby hadn't said he loved her.

The wedding took place in what would have been considered indecent haste to anyone outside the acting community. However, marriage was seen as both protection and respectability for young actresses, especially those like Sophy whose star was on the rise and who attracted a plethora of admirers with each passing week. Just three months to the day Toby had proposed, on a bitterly cold morning at the end of March, Sophy and Toby became man and wife. The service was held at a small parish church in Holborn, and afterwards the wedding breakfast for a small group of friends was a merry affair. Toby's parents had died years before and he had lost touch with his only sibling, a sister, so no family was present, although Sophy insisted that Dolly and Jim were invited. Otherwise the guests were all members of the theatre fraternity.

Sophy wore a long cream dress with tiny seed pearls sewn on the bodice and a large picture hat, and carried a small posy of cream and pink rosebuds, and as Dolly beheld her at the Savoy Hotel where the breakfast was being held, she said what everyone was thinking: 'You're the most beautiful bride I've seen in many a long day, lovey. And this place! I've passed it many times, of course, but never thought I'd set foot in it.'

Sophy smiled. 'We wouldn't be here but for Mr Gregory. He's given us the wedding breakfast as his present.'

'Which one's he?' Dolly glanced round the assembled company who were enjoying cocktails before they sat down to eat.

'He's not here.' A shadow passed over Sophy's face for a moment. 'He's away on business.' It had greatly disappointed her when Mr Gregory had said he couldn't come, and she had been upset he hadn't manoeuvred whatever business it was so he could join them. But it had been kind to give them such a generous wedding present, especially as she had just accepted a wonderful role in one of the West End theatres and would be leaving the Lincoln shortly. Instead of one of the sentimental dramas or the type of musical comedy Toby was playing in, the play – The Choice – was the story of a young upper-class woman's refusal to marry the man her parents had selected and her fight to make her own way in the world when she starts a drapery business with an inheritance her grand-mother left her. She falls in love with a working-class man, and he with her, but on learning of her beginnings he rejects her, only to return to her at the end of the play when he has made his fortune, stating that now they can begin their life together as equals.

The play was going to be controversial, challenging not only the class issue but that of women in business, and not least the idea of equality of the sexes which brought in a hint of Women's Suffrage with some of the lines Sophy got to say. She was excited but nervous. Toby had warned her not to do it, saying it was doomed to failure and she would be branded as an actress of the 'new drama' which would ruin her career. It was the first time one of the big commercial theatres had taken on such a contentious play; normally they were left to the independents like the Lincoln, but she had liked the role of Alice and felt she could do it justice. Surprisingly, in view of the fact it was taking her away from the Lincoln, Mr Gregory had agreed with her.

'The part is tailor-made for you and you'll be superb.' He'd smiled at her, his cornflower-blue eyes crinkling. 'And you can't always play it safe. It might fail, the press might be up in arms, especially as the Vote for Women is becoming more of a hot potato, but if you pull it off the world will be your oyster.'

She had smiled back at him, while thinking she didn't know if she wanted the world as her oyster. In fact, she didn't know *what* she wanted these days. Life had suddenly become very complicated and she wasn't sure why.

'Where's my wife?' Toby was calling from the head of the table where the guests were gradually being seated, and as she made her way over to him she thought he had never looked more handsome. He smiled at her as she joined him, his eyes soft and warm, and suddenly she felt better. Everyone was on edge before they got married; it was only natural – it was a huge step to take. But this was Toby, her Toby, and she loved him.

'We make a stunning pair, have you considered that, Mrs Shawe?' he whispered in her ear as she sat down beside him. 'The Golden Couple, that's what a couple of our friends have said – and who am I to disagree with them?'

He had already had two or three glasses of the champagne cocktails Kane had provided and his speech was slightly slurred. Sophy forced a smile and then, as Toby's best man – a fellow actor playing at the same theatre — stood up to make a toast, she took a deep breath. *Relax, relax,* she told herself. This was her wedding day and she was sitting in the most beautiful surroundings with the man she loved. She had been so incredibly fortunate since arriving in London, and she would always be grateful to Mr Gregory for giving her her chance. She wished he was here today so she could tell him so.

The meal was superb. Six courses, beginning with soup and finishing with a choice of desserts, half of which Sophy had never heard of before. She laughed and chattered, and, having had two further glasses of champagne after the champagne cocktail before the dinner, felt light-headed and giggly, but in a nice way. And then, as coffee and liqueurs were served and the party began to circulate once more, she saw Rosalind glide to Toby's side and take his arm in a proprietorial gesture that caused Sophy to become instantly sober. She watched as his face came down to that of Rosalind's, and after the woman whispered something in his ear, he threw back his head and laughed before saying something to her that caused Rosalind to smile in reply.

There was nothing to the exchange in one respect; in another it spoke of intimacy and the fact that the couple were extremely comfortable with each other. She found her eyes were riveted on them. It was Cat, appearing at her side and standing directly in front of her, blocking her vision, who caused Sophy to blink when she said, 'Don't look like that. It's nothing. She's nothing. He's married you, hasn't he?'

Sophy didn't try to pretend. 'You don't think they . . .'

'No, I don't,' Cat lied stoutly. 'Rosalind Robins is getting on, Sophy. She must be all of thirty-five. She knows the parts are going to start drying up soon and she likes to think every young man of her acquaintance is dancing to her tune. And Toby's not daft. He humours her. That's all.'

Sophy felt a sickness in the pit of her stomach. She hadn't been happy about inviting Rosalind and her husband to the wedding but had felt unable to say so. But she didn't like her. And in spite of the actress's gushing comments about her appearance today, she felt Rosalind didn't like her either. Was it because Toby wouldn't become the latest conquest in what was undeniably a long line, or – she swallowed deeply – because he had? But no, she wouldn't think that. And if she told Cat what she was thinking, her friend would say that Rosalind didn't like any woman unless they were in their dotage. That she was that kind of woman. Which was true enough.

Giving herself a mental shake, she hugged her friend, forcing lightness into her tone when she said, 'You're right as always, wise woman, but one thing's for sure. Whenever I thought about my wedding night as a young girl, I didn't imagine I'd spend it on stage.' Owing to their contracts, neither she nor Toby could take time off for something as unimportant as getting married, but they had promised themselves a proper honeymoon some time in the future.

Cat grinned. 'Only part of it, surely, darling, unless you're thinking of shocking the audience out of their tiny minds.'

Sophy laughed as she was meant to, but in truth she was more than a little nervous about the night ahead. Thanks to Dolly, she had a pretty good idea of the rudiments of what went on, and she wanted to belong to Toby, more than anything, but still . . .

They had rented a smart little flat in a house in Margaret Street close to Oxford Circus where the flower-sellers sold their blooms beneath their red umbrellas. Toby had wanted them to live in the West End and although Sophy had felt a huge wrench at leaving her little attic room up among the rooftops she'd known the two of them couldn't live there. And the West End *was* a fascinating place, from the massive shops in Oxford Street, such as Marshall & Snelgrove and Swears & Wells, to the colourful and slightly disreputable area of Soho, which drew artisans and artistes of all kinds, unlike the seedy Seven Dials rookery across the Charing Cross Road.

It was the area around Leicester Square which most bustled with life, however, especially since the building of Shaftesbury Avenue in the 1880s had removed some of the more dire slums. New theatres were being erected, small five- or six-hundred seaters which were already gaining a reputation as places where 'the play was the thing', rather than the conceit of being seen in one of the more splendid venues. Not that the new theatres could match ones like the Alhambra and Empire in most people's eyes – two great variety theatres which were essentially male resorts. Here young bloods descended in droves from the universities, Boat Race nights being legendary, and many was the ruse employed to regain admittance after being expelled for being too rowdy or offensive. As many of the young men were more than a little intoxicated, they weren't aware of the top-hatted bouncers who politely but firmly escorted them from the premises, patting them in a fatherly manner on the back, leaving a white chalk-mark as a signal that they weren't to be readmitted that evening.

But it was after the shows that the West End really came into its own. The supper clubs stayed open until well past midnight, but it was the less sophisticated cock-and-hen clubs such as the Red Beer Club, whose weekly dances frequently ended in high jinks in Soho Square as dawn broke, which catered for the university crowd. Some of these Hooray Henrys, used to a bevy of servants from babyhood and with more money than sense, could be dangerous to a young girl on her own, especially when showing off to their peers. Toby had already warned Sophy never to venture out alone but she wouldn't have done so anyway. She knew full well by this time that, due to the career she had chosen, many of these young men considered all actresses unconventional at best, and little more than high-class whores at worst. Cat had already been the victim of a series of obscene postcards from an 'admirer', and an actress they knew had been accosted by a man who had followed her home from the theatre. When she had refused to kiss him, he had accused her of being 'a female cad' who needed to be taught a lesson. It was only the girl's landlady, on hearing her screams, who had prevented the man from forcing himself upon her. And Sophy knew from Augustus, who still inspected any letters care of the theatre which the actresses received, that some of her mail was too 'passionate' to be considered suitable for her to read.

She did find this alarming when she thought about it, but had always felt safe both at the Lincoln and when on tour with Mr Gregory's touring company, due to the safeguards he had put in place for his female employees. But now she would have Toby to protect her. She was a respectable married woman.

He had left Rosalind and was making his way towards her, smiling the smile that turned the blue-grey eyes liquid. 'Happy?' he murmured.

She nodded. In this moment, when he looked at her like that, she was the happiest woman alive, she told herself, sending up a swift prayer of thankfulness for all that was hers. 'Are you?'

'Of course.' He gathered her into his arms, careless of onlookers, whispering in her ear, 'And I'll be happier still when it's just the two of us tonight.'

She blushed, and he laughed, hugging her again. 'My beautiful, innocent, radiant wife. I adore you, do you know that? From the top of your head to the soles of your dainty feet, I adore you. We're going to take the theatre world by storm, you and I. Mr Toby Shawe and the beautiful Mrs Shawe. We can't fail.' Glancing at his watch, he added, 'But for now it's work for both of us, my sweet. I'll come and pick you up from the Lincoln tonight, so wait for me. It's a pity you're not closer to home but it won't be long.'

Home. Sophy smiled although as yet she couldn't quite think of their modern little flat as home. It was very nice, possessing a small kitchen, a large sitting room and a lovely light bedroom amply big enough for a double bed, wardrobe and chest of drawers, and it also boasted that most newfangled of features, a bathroom complete with its own water closet. Each of the three flats in the terraced house had one, which was why the rent was so expensive, Sophy supposed. At seven shillings a week she could have rented a positive mansion up north, but when she had said this to Toby he had told her she couldn't compare the two. This was London, he'd declared, not some provincial little backwater, and if he had his way they would soon be moving to something much grander than Margaret Street. And the flats were smart and newly renovated; he didn't intend to start their married life in a couple of shabby rooms somewhere.

She hadn't argued, although she still felt slightly overwhelmed at the amount they would be paying out each month. But they could afford it, as Toby said. He was earning five guineas a week and she would be bringing home three guineas when she began her new part, although if the play failed that might be short-lived. Toby's play was due to end in the next little while but he was quite confident he would be offered something else before that happened.

Once outside the hotel, they went their separate ways. The Lincoln was only a stone's throw away so Sophy and Cat and a small group of other actors, including Augustus, went in one direction on foot, and Toby and his crowd hailed a couple of cabs. Dolly and Jim had already left a little earlier.

Cat slipped her arm through Sophy's as they walked, the two of them a little tiddly after the champagne. 'I shall miss you when you go, and I won't even have our evenings in Dolly's kitchen any more,' Cat said with a little sniff. 'Dolly will be sad too, you know that, don't you?'

Sophy nodded. It had been their habit, two or three times a week when she wasn't seeing Toby, for the two girls to take a box of chocolates or a cake and spend an hour or two with Dolly and Jim. The old couple were hilarious, especially Dolly, and had kept the girls entertained with stories from the past and present about their family and some of their odd doings. One of their sons was an undertaker and the tales connected with him verged on the macabre, and another two were 'into this and that' according to Dolly, although the girls suspected most of their dealings were rooted in the London underworld. They had drunk copious pots of tea and laughed a lot and Cat, whose upper-class parents had had very little to do with their children, had revelled in the family atmosphere.

'We'll still pop round and see Dolly and Jim,' Sophy said now. 'We're not going to lose touch, Cat. I've only got married, not disappeared to the other side of the world.'

Cat nodded and squeezed Sophy's arm but said nothing. She hoped she was wrong but she would be surprised if Sophy's friends saw much of her from this point on. Toby was determined to rise and he aimed to cultivate people who could make that happen, like Rosalind Robins. The woman was a major leading lady with many connections, and Toby knew as well as anyone else in the field that actors were paid according to their popularity, and that to get the right part was essential. Often the main criterion by which a play was chosen for production was the size and dramatic or comedic possibilities of the central male character, closely followed by the lead female role. Sophy was destined to be a star, Cat thought, but Toby? He was handsome enough and he could be charm itself when he chose, but there was a weakness to the man. He was flawed. She wished Sophy hadn't married him. More than that, she wished she had said so before the event, even if it might have resulted in Sophy drawing away from her. She wouldn't be feeling so wretchedly guilty now if she had.

'Cheer up.' Sophy unwittingly heaped coals of fire on Cat's head as she gave her a hug. 'We're friends for life, through thick and thin. I promise. What were those lines in the first play we did together at the Lincoln? Oh yes. "Nothing can separate us, dear friend. Neither the trials of life nor the blessings. Not husband or lover or foe, not surfeit or famine. Friendship is the golden cord of life."'

'"Oh sweet Patricia, that you would always cleave to such noble thoughts."' Cat struck a dramatic pose. '"And I pray that golden cord will bind us more surely in the years to come."'

They both laughed, walking on, but Cat wished more than ever she had spoken before it was too late.

Chapter 14

Sophy's first night of marriage was a mixture of pain and pleasure, but overall a feeling of surprise that men regarded this thing so highly. She knew Toby had sown his wild oats in the past, but she hadn't questioned him about it because she didn't want to know. It was enough that he had wanted to marry *her*, that she was the one he had asked to be his wife.

He had been gentle with her and understanding of her initial embarrassment, and she had been grateful for his consideration. It had engendered in her a deeper love for him, as had the act itself.

The next morning she had thought of her mother for the first time in a little while, wondering how Esther could have given herself away so cheaply. She couldn't imagine being so intimate with anyone but Toby, and surely love would have to be the main ingredient for a woman to allow a man to possess her? But then women were bought by men for money on the streets and in brothels, it was a fact of life. She had known about it, of course, but until now hadn't realised the significance of what was entailed.

She had told Toby only the bare facts about her past life, that her parents had died when she was a baby and her aunt and uncle had brought her up, and that she had run away from what was a claustrophobic and unpleasant existence and come to London. He had been satisfied with that and hadn't pressed for more. But now, as they sat together at their little dining-table in the sitting room enjoying their first breakfast as man and wife, she felt she needed to tell him the full story. Something had changed with the act of making love. She couldn't explain it but she didn't want any secrets between them.

'Toby, dear, I want to tell you something.' He was sitting behind his newspaper like an old married man, and as she placed a plate of sausages, ham and egg in front of him, he lowered the paper and smiled at her.

'Don't tell me.' He inspected his plate. 'You've burned the sausages? Or is the yolk of the egg hard? No, I know. You've forgotten my breakfast roll.'

She had, as it happened. After another trip to the kitchen she surveyed the food on the cheerful little gingham tablecloth she'd bought especially for their breakfasts. Everything was in order. She sat down, poured them both a cup of tea, and said again, 'Toby? I need to talk to you.'

Toby stifled an impatient sigh and lowered his newspaper again. He didn't like conversation first thing in the morning. He'd always been that way. Once he'd eaten and read the paper and had a shave and a wash, he was a different man. But Sophy would learn that in time. And this *was* their first morning together in the flat. For a moment recollections of the mornings he'd woken up in Rosalind's bed when her husband was away on business flashed through his head. Her maid had rarely opened the curtains before eleven o'clock, used to her mistress's habits when the master was away, and then had followed a decadent breakfast of champagne and caviar on tiny slices of toast most days. He had never heard of caviar before the first morning he'd stayed with Rosalind, but that was her all over.

He smiled at Sophy. 'What is it?'

'I want to tell you about my parents. Well, my mother, I suppose.'

'She died when you were a baby. Right?'

'Yes, but— but there's more. She . . .' Sophy took a deep breath, 'was a music-hall actress. She left her home like me and came to London when she was a young girl.'

169

Toby sat up straighter. This wasn't what he'd expected. He stared into the beautiful amber eyes watching him so intently, his eyes moving to the cloud of shining, silky hair she'd tied back with a blue ribbon for breakfast. 'Did she look like you?'

'A bit, I think.'

'Then she must have been a very successful music-hall actress.'

Sophy forced a smile. 'She wasn't married to my father, Toby. That's what I wanted you to know.'

He took a moment to digest this. He was shocked, she could tell, and suddenly she decided she wouldn't tell him the rest, that her mother hadn't been able to name her father because she hadn't known which of her lovers had impregnated her.

Toby stared at her. 'But you said your uncle was a minister.'

'He was. He is.'

'And your mother was his sister?'

She nodded.

He shook his head. 'I can understand why they were over-protective of you.'

'They weren't over-protective,' she said sharply, hurt tearing through her at the implied criticism. 'They were cruel. There's a difference.'

'Yes, of course.' He read what was in her face and stood up, coming to her chair and drawing her up and into his arms. 'I didn't mean anything, sweetheart. I know you were unhappy at home, that's all, and I was just trying to say they probably over-compensated for your mother's mistake.'

A mistake. Was that how he viewed her now? But no, she was being unreasonable. Reading too much into his words. And he had every right to be shocked, of course he did. She relaxed in his embrace, her arms going round his waist. Nevertheless, she wished she hadn't told him.

The next few months were not easy ones. *The Choice* was a critical and financial success, receiving favourable notices from the press and audiences alike. There was much praise and acclaim for everyone concerned, but it was generally acknowledged that Sophy was the new prodigy to conquer the West End. Words such as 'nonpareil' and 'sensation' were bandied about, which would have been wonderful except for the fact that Toby's play was finishing and he'd be out of work soon. He'd auditioned for the subsequent production, fully expecting it to be a mere formality, but another up-and-coming actor had been given both the part and – if rumours were to be believed – the delights of Rosalind's benefaction.

He had gone to see Rosalind the morning after he'd discovered he didn't have a part in the new production. They had arranged to meet at an apartment one of her friends owned. Of late Christopher Robins had taken to returning home unexpectedly, and Rosalind suspected he knew of their affair. Whether this was the last straw in a succession which had broken this particular camel's back, Toby wasn't sure, but certainly he felt his failure to gain the prize male part was due to the fact that Christopher Robins was a generous financial asset to the theatre concerned.

Rosalind had been waiting for him when he had knocked at the door of the sumptuous flat off Grosvenor Square. She had soothed him about the job, telling him that he was a fine actor and that he would pick up a leading male role with no trouble whatsoever, once the other prime theatres knew he was available. 'Darling, you're superb, everyone says so.' She was getting ready for a romp in bed, discarding her clothes with the complete lack of inhibition which always served to make him hungry for her. But not today.

He stared at her, feeling gauche and ridiculous but unable to stop himself saying, 'Bruce Thorpe, why did he get the part, Rosalind? Did you have anything to do with it?'

'How can you say that?' She sounded hurt but then she was an actress. 'You know I adore you, darling.'

'And Bruce? Do you adore him too?'

She was standing in front of him stark naked now and for a moment her eyes widened, then she turned and walked over to the bed the room held. It was a big bed with, of all things, black satin sheets. She slid under the top one, stretching like a cat before she murmured, 'No strings attached, remember, sweetie? That's what we promised each other at the start of our fun. I have enough problems in that direction with Christopher as you well know, and it's *so* unattractive in a man.'

'You didn't answer my question.'

The half-smile left her lips and her eyes hardened. 'I don't have to, but since we've had some good times together, I will be honest with you. Bruce got the part because he's a damn good actor for one thing. How much Christopher had to do with it I don't know. All right? But if I had insisted you were given the part it would have confirmed any suspicions Christopher has, and believe me, Toby, he makes a bad enemy. I've done you a service in keeping quiet although you may not see it that way right now.'

'You're right. I don't.'

'Oh for goodness sake, don't be petulant.' She sat up, pulling the sheet round her breasts and flicking back her hair. 'These things happen. You'll get another part soon enough.'

There was a sickness churning his stomach and causing his insides to shake. He had thought this woman loved him, he'd imagined he held her in the palm of his hand and she would do anything for him, but he'd misjudged the balance of their relationship. She held the upper hand. She had always held it. She had used him for her pleasure and now he was expendable. That was the truth of it. If she hadn't bedded Bruce already, it was only a matter of time.

'Look, come to bed, sweetie.' She held out her hand. 'I don't want to argue and spoil things. And this might be the last time we can see each other for a while. The play finishes this week and rehearsals begin straight away. We've been warned they'll be pretty gruelling short-term, as Christopher and the other backers want the show to start as soon as possible. You know how it is.'

He knew how it was all right.

His face must have spoken for him because now Rosalind swung her long shapely legs out of bed. 'Oh hell, you're going to be difficult, aren't you?' she said in the tone of voice one would use to a tiresome child. 'And I really don't see why. You surely knew we weren't going to last for ever, dear boy?'

She retrieved her clothes and dressed swiftly, and it was only when she was fully attired that she looked at him again. 'Can't we still be friends?' she said softly.

'What do *you* think?' It was churlish but he couldn't help himself.

She stared at him a moment more and then shrugged. Turning, she adjusted her hat in the bedroom mirror with deliberate slowness before leaving the apartment without another word. Toby walked over to the window and stared down into the street below, watching her walk away until she was lost from sight.

So that was that. All her promises of what she could do for him, the people she could introduce him to and the opportunities she could make happen had boiled down to this. He had even married Sophy because of her. Rosalind had suggested it would effectively allay any suspicions her husband might be harbouring if he was to take a wife.

He banged his fist against the wall next to the window, making the glass rattle. But he'd get another part soon enough, he told himself, nursing his bruised knuckles. And he'd been sick of currying favour with Christopher Robins and watching his ps and qs, as well as pandering to Rosalind's whims and fancies, in the bedroom as well as out of it. He had thought he knew it all sexually and that he had an open mind, but Rosalind had introduced him to things that had made him feel a novice in that department. But it was over. And now he had to tell Sophy he wasn't in the new play. He hadn't mentioned it last night, not wanting to say anything until he had seen Rosalind this morning. He supposed he had been hoping she would tell him it was all a mistake and that she had fixed things for him. Fool that he was.

He walked out of the bedroom and into the sitting room of the apartment, picking up his jacket which he has discarded on entering. He stood in the middle of the expensively furnished room, his mind assessing the quality of the furnishings and fittings. Rosalind knew some wealthy and influential people all right. He had thought he was going to have a meteoric rise to fame and fortune as her lover. She hadn't been able to keep her hands off him when they had first got together. But he'd succeed without her. She was just a woman, after all, like any other, and all cats were grey in the dark.

'Oh, Toby darling, I'm so sorry. Whatever are they thinking of? But it's like Cat always says, half the time in our profession it's not how good you are but whether the owners or the actor-managers have their own agenda and their favourites. I've heard of this Bruce Thorpe, I'm sure he's a relation of Christopher Robins. A distant cousin's child or something. But they'll live to regret it. He won't be a patch on you.'

Toby and Sophy were sitting eating breakfast the next morning, the windows wide open to catch any breeze the muggy August morning might afford them. He hadn't got in until the early hours, having gone for a drink with some fellow actors after his performance at the theatre. They had ended up in one of the more disreputable establishments in Soho much the worse for wear, and he had no recollection of how he'd got home. He did remember following one of the actors to the back of the club where they'd gained admittance into a room guarded by a pair of big burly ne'er-do-wells, however. He had never tried an opium pipe before and it had knocked him for six.

He smiled blearily at Sophy. She had been distinctly frosty this morning until he'd told her about losing the part in the next play, whereupon she'd leaped to his defence.

'I must admit I was a little put out at first,' he said, 'but there's other parts in other theatres.'

'Of course there are.' She reached across and took one of his hands between her own. 'And you'll be snapped up. You're such a wonderful actor.'

Toby looked down at his plate and tried not to shudder. He had forced down a breakfast roll and a cup of coffee, but he had a stinking headache and felt as sick as a dog. Putting his hand to his head, he muttered, 'I think I'll go and lie down for a while. I might have overdone things a bit last night.'

'Do that.' Sophy was all concern. 'I'll wake you in plenty of time to get ready for the theatre. When — when do you finish?'

'End of the week.' He stood up, touching her shining hair which she always wore flowing and loosely tied with a ribbon for breakfast. 'Thanks for being understanding.'

Once she was alone, Sophy let herself slump in her chair. *Thanks for being understanding.* She hadn't felt very understanding last night when the hours had ticked by. She must have fallen asleep after three o'clock and he hadn't been home then. She knew he liked to let his hair down after a show and relax with his pals, but he was usually home by midnight, one o'clock at the latest. She had been furious last night and her rage had brought to the surface all the doubts and fears she had about their marriage, and about Toby. She'd thought he might be with Rosalind, she had imagined them together and told herself she didn't believe there was nothing but friendship between them. And then this morning . . . She buried her face in her hands for a moment. Oh, she felt awful. Thank goodness he didn't know what she had been thinking. Poor Toby. He must be feeling wretched.

She sat quietly drinking a cup of coffee, letting the fresh air touch her face as she gazed out of the window and up at the patch of blue sky to be seen above the building opposite. It hadn't been the moment to tell him her news: last night, they had been informed that the play was doing so well they were going to run for another six months at least, and she had taken the opportunity to see the manager and negotiate a rise in salary. From next week she would be earning double her present rate. Six guineas a week. She hadn't quite been able to believe it when she had left the office, but of course she hadn't let the manager see that. But she had followed the advice Mr Gregory had given her when she had said goodbye to him on leaving the Lincoln.

'Value yourself, Sophy.' He had smiled at her and not for the first time she'd realised he was really a very attractive man and that his disfigurement added to his brooding appeal, rather than otherwise. 'If you don't, no one else will. Be courageous, especially when asking for financial satisfaction. Put a top price on your acting ability in any part you're asked to play, you can always agree to drop a little if necessary but it will be too late to negotiate up if you agree to a lower salary. All managers, mine included, will try to do their best for the owners rather than the actors. Remember that.'

She had remembered it last night, and instead of asking for five guineas – and she had thought that was on the top side – she had asked for six, never dreaming it would be agreed. But eventually it had. And they were going to need it now, with Toby out of work.

Not that it would be for long, she amended hastily, as though the thought had been a criticism. And they would manage quite well. Here a little frown came between her eyes. It had been a worry over the last months since they had become man and wife how Toby's salary seemed to drain away each week. They had agreed Toby would pay the rent, and that she would provide for their food and any household expenses out of her wage. Of course on top of this they both had to find travelling expenses, along with clothes and shoes and other living costs, but even so, it was rare that Toby had any money in his pocket at the end of each week. She knew he spent a considerable amount on drink with his friends when they frequented the gambling clubs now and again, and sometimes dined there, but when she had spoken to him about it, it had caused such ill-feeling between them she hadn't mentioned it again, not wishing to appear the nagging wife. But depending on how things panned out over the next weeks, she might have to raise the subject again.

Marriage wasn't what she had expected it to be.

The thought came before she could dismiss it and she realised it had been hovering at the back of her mind for some time. She had assumed they would do things together, spend most of their free time in each other's company, but it hadn't worked out that way. Half the time she didn't know where Toby was or what he was doing when he left the flat, and if she questioned him he always made her feel at fault. He was always telling her not to be so 'provincial' as though it was the greatest crime, and only last week, when she had asked him to accompany her to Cat's birthday party and he'd said he had a prior engagement and she'd got upset, he'd accused her of being a burden. She had been both upset and angry, and the anger had enabled her to go unescorted with her head held high and pretend to enjoy herself, ignoring the curious glances of those present who clearly wondered where Toby was.

Sophy bit her lip, telling herself post-mortems never did any good. They had got over that episode and it did no good to drag it up now. Dolly said men took a while to settle into marriage and she was probably right.

She finished her breakfast, forcing herself to eat and drink and then cleared the table. When she came to the muslin cloth which she always removed after breakfast, putting a vase of flowers in the middle of the table, she paused, staring at it for a long time. And then she folded it carefully as she did every day and put it away, setting the vase in place, which she could hardly see for the tears streaming down her face.

PART FIVE

The End of One Beginning
1908

Chapter 15

When does the end of a marriage begin? Is it when one half of what should be a whole witnesses their spouse rising to heights of renown they can only dream about? Or perhaps it's more insidious, a slow and largely inconspicuous drift into the fantasy world opium and its sister substances induce? Or yet again, it could be the disintegration of the part of man that makes him higher than the beasts when the darker side of the personality is given free rein, and a mind – naturally selfish and weak in Toby's case – cannot accept what it perceives as failure. But the rot in Sophy's marriage had set in even before the walk down the aisle. How can anything lasting be built on shifting sand?

The last ten years had been ones of enormous highs and lows for Sophy. By the time the new century had been ushered in on a wave of euphoria, extolling Britain's imperial powers and sovereignty, she had been acknowledged as one of the new glittering stars of the West End, the darling of the public and press alike. Queen Victoria's death a year later had seen King Edward VII take the throne and a more relaxed monarch in Buckingham Palace. When Sarah Bernhardt returned in triumph to London in the summer of 1902 in her best-known role as Marguerite Gautier, the consumptive courtesan, in *The Lady of the Camellias*, the critics raved over her performance and it added to the growing respectability of the theatre which the King regularly visited and enjoyed. But Sarah Bernhardt was also an advocate of the Vote for Women and was not afraid to say so. Sophy had attended a lunch given in the great actress's honour, and after Sarah had thanked everyone for attending and prettily entertained them with an amusing after-lunch talk, she had gone in for the kill.

Much of what the actress had said that day had resonated with Sophy. It *was* true that women possessing the vote was the merest kind of basic justice, and that all the weighty political philosophies which men had invented had no sensible argument against a woman's right to make her opinion and convictions known. The fashionable belief prevalent among the opponents of Women's Suffrage, that all intelligence in women was but a reflection of male intellect, that a woman had neither the discernment nor brain power to think for herself, *was* wrong, along with the tyranny of the law which favoured men in every regard. How could it be considered right in any humane society that a husband could divorce his wife for adultery as easy as blinking, whereas a wife had to prove adultery as well as cruelty or desertion of two years? A woman knew she would lose her home, her reputation and inevitably her children if she went to the divorce courts, and in consequence there were those who endured a living hell at home.

In truth, Sarah's words had been but a reflection of what Cat had been saying for years, Sophy thought to herself one fine day in the middle of March. The morning was bright and fresh, there was a nip in the air and the smell of spring was around the corner. It was the kind of day that made one feel good to be alive.

Dear Cat. Sophy smiled to herself as she thought of her friend. What would she have done without Cat's unswerving support through the last few years, as well as Dolly and Jim's, of course. Although their advice couldn't be more different. Cat's counsel was undeviating: 'Divorce the wretch.' If her friend had said it once, she had said it a hundred times. 'He's no good, Sophy. He never has been. He hasn't had a job in years and he never will again, not after the spectacle he made of himself rolling about the stage dead drunk when Mr Gregory gave him that last chance. Toby knew no one else would touch him and yet he couldn't stay sober each night until the performance was over.'

Sophy often thought that if Cat knew the half of it she would come to the flat and physically throw Toby out herself. If it had only been the drunkenness she had to contend with, it wouldn't be so bad. But she knew it was the opium which had really changed the man she had married. He was a different person. No, that wasn't quite right. It wasn't that he was a different person, more that the drug had destroyed his mind and intellect to the point that he was hardly there any more. He had gone through bouts of being violent in the past, but the one time he had hit her she had flown back at him with the first thing that came to hand – a small bronze statuette she had won for a performance – and belaboured him so wildly he had never touched her in anger again. Not that he touched her at all, these days. The effects of the alcohol and drugs had rendered him impotent years ago.

Dolly and Jim were of the old school in their advice. Once you'd made your bed you had to lie on it and divorce was wrong, full stop. However, Dolly had been quick to point out, that didn't mean you had to put up with any kind of nonsense. In their community, a father or brother wasn't above going round to sort out an errant husband for the wife, and if Sophy was willing, their Arnold and one of the other sons could do the job. They wouldn't hurt him, not the first time anyway, just frighten the living daylights out of him and wait to see if that worked.

Sophy had thanked Dolly but declined the offer. No one knew about the opium habit, and it would take more than Arnold and one of his brothers to stop Toby returning to the illegal dens like a dog to its vomit.

Sophy paused, lifting her face to the gentle rays of a spring sun. She was on her way to hear Emmeline Pankhurst's account of her recent imprisonment in Holloway Jail after she was convicted for obstructing the police within the Strangers' Lobby in Parliament. She had never attended a meeting of the Women's Social and Political Union before, although Cat had joined the new militant movement shortly after it had been formed five years ago. Their motto, 'Deeds not Words', had appealed to the recklessness in Cat, along with Mrs Pankhurst's determination for a radical change in future tactics. Previous Suffragists had met regularly with sympathetic Members of Parliament to plead their cause, but the frustration caused by Parliament's refusal to debate the subject or even consider the idea of female emancipation had led to the birth of the new society. Christabel Pankhurst, Emmeline's daughter, had been one of the first suffragettes to go to prison three years ago, and since meeting her, Cat had been even more fired up, spending most of her free time working for the Society. She even took minor roles in the theatre in order to devote more time to the cause. But, as she had said on more than one occasion to Sophy, 'I was never going to make it big like you, darling. I was never going to be a star.'

Sophy didn't know about that. What she did know was that her work demanded much of her time and what remained was devoted to holding what was left of Toby together. She was often exhausted, constantly worried and mostly heartsore. When he was in the real world Toby was either bitter and spiteful, or pathetically needy of her. Not as a wife, that had finished years ago, but as a nurse, a mother, someone he could cling to when the night terrors caused by the poison in his system turned him into a gibbering idiot, terrified of things only he could see.

He had killed all love within her, for nothing could survive the things he'd said and done, still said and did, but each time she told herself she couldn't go on, there would be another agonising night where he became a petrified child. And it was the child she couldn't abandon, not the man.

She began walking again, clearing her mind of her own problems and letting the first mild weather of the year caress her skin. She could have taken a cab to the meeting but she had wanted to walk in the sunshine along the streets, a chance to feel like any other woman, someone with a normal existence and a happy home life.

She didn't glance at the couple making their way down the steps of a small hotel to her right; the lovely weather had brought the world and his wife out and the pavements were bustling with Londoners. Since she had become a success, Sophy had found that fame could be a two-edged sword on occasion, so if she ever took a walk alone – which was rare – she tended to keep her head down and walk swiftly, thereby remaining largely unnoticed by her fans. So when her arm was grabbed, and a voice in her ear said, 'Sophy? It *is* you, isn't it?' she was taken aback, the more so when she saw who had accosted her.

'Patience?' She stared at the woman who was Patience and yet not Patience.

'Yes, it's me.' Patience was holding on to her as though she was afraid Sophy would disappear if she let go of her arm. 'Oh, Sophy, I can't believe it's you! I've longed to see you again. Thank you for your letters. Father passes them on to me and it's been good to know you are all right.'

Sophy didn't know what to say. For one thing this Patience, with her bright face and sparkling eyes, was as different to the girl she'd known as chalk to cheese. For another, she had always felt a little guilty about the letters – not only their infrequency, since she had only written five or six in the years since she had left the north-east, but also the fact that she had never given a return address. Her mind caught at Patience's last words. 'You're not living at the vicarage then?'

'No, no. I left there about eighteen months after you had gone, to train as a nurse.' Patience now blushed, turning to the tall, rather distinguished-looking gentleman at her side. 'This is my husband, Dr Aldridge. William, this is my dear cousin, Sophy Shawe. You did say your husband's name is Shawe when you wrote to say you had got married?'

Sophy nodded, smiling as she took the doctor's outstretched hand. 'It's nice to meet you, Dr Aldridge.'

'William, please.'

Sophy liked Patience's husband immediately. His handshake was firm, his brown eyes were warm with a twinkle in their depths and his smile was open and friendly.

Still reeling mentally from the shock of discovering that Patience was not only married but had left the vicarage years ago to enter the nursing profession, Sophy stared at her cousin. She could see where the transformation had occurred now. For the first time in her life Patience looked happy. 'Do you live in London now, or are you visiting?'

'Oh, only visiting. It's our wedding anniversary. We've been married two years this week, and as Florence Nightingale is having the Freedom of the City conferred on her on Monday, we thought we'd spend a few days here and try to catch a glimpse of her. She's such a wonderful woman and absolutely amazing for eighty-seven years old.'

Sophy nodded. 'Are you still working as a nurse?'

'Of course.' Patience glanced up at her husband with adoring eyes. 'William has no problem with me continuing with my career even though it does sometimes mean we're ships that pass in the night. William's a paediatrician at the same hospital and with night duty and such . . .' She shrugged. 'But we get by, don't we, William?'

'Splendidly, most of the time.' William smiled, and there was no doubt he doted on his wife.

'I don't suppose . . .' Patience hesitated. 'You wouldn't like to have dinner with us one night? You and your husband? We leave London on Tuesday morning and it would be so nice to catch up a little. John and Matthew are both married now, you know, and John is the father of one-year-old twin boys.'

Sophy didn't know how to reply. Part of her was glad to see Patience, and the other part of her wanted to take to her heels and run. With an effort she pulled herself together and injected warmth into her voice when she said, 'I'm sorry, Patience, but dinner's not possible as I'm on stage each evening, and furthermore, Toby is . . . is unwell.' Seeing the disappointment in her cousin's face, she added quickly, 'But we could meet for lunch if you like, the three of us?'

Patience's face lit up. 'Really? That would be lovely. Come and join us at the hotel then. Shall we say tomorrow at twelve o'clock? Does that suit?'

Sophy nodded. 'Tomorrow it is.' She turned to Patience's husband again and extended her hand, saying, 'It's been lovely to meet you, William,' but before she could make her goodbyes to Patience, her cousin was hugging her tight, murmuring, 'You won't change your mind, will you? You will come?'

'Of course I'll come.' Even as she said it she was reflecting that Patience knew her better than she knew herself.

The suffragette meeting was more harrowing than Sophy expected, revealing, as it did, an inside view of the horrors of prison life. Emmeline Pankhurst's vivid account of the drudgery and misery of her imprisonment was harrowing. The meagre rations, the coarse, scratchy clothing with its convict's arrows, the dismal surroundings and the desperate unhappiness of her fellow inmates was compelling hearing, and it was hard to acquaint such dreadful happenings with the beautifully dressed and aristocratic-looking woman talking to the large crowd that had come to see her.

'All the hours seem very long in that place,' Mrs Pankhurst said calmly, her perfectly pitched voice carrying to the back of the hall where the meeting was being held. 'The sun can never get in, and every day is changeless and uninteresting. Within a very short time one grows too tired to go through to the exercise yard and take the air, even though the yearning for the smell and feel of the outside world is paramount.'

'And what was her heinous crime?' Cat whispered at the side of Sophy. 'Conducting a peaceful march through the streets of London, that's all. Like she said in court, the disturbance that developed was the fault of the authorities who'd instructed the police to use strong measures. Mounted police riding into the march to break it up, I ask you! Women were knocked down and bruised and their clothes torn, and that lasted for five hours. There's Finland giving women seats in the Finnish Parliament this year, and here we have the Prime Minister saying we have to be patient and wait rather than act in a pugnacious spirit! Women have been waiting for decades and where's it got us? Nowhere, that's where.'

'You don't actually have to convince me,' Sophy whispered back. 'I'm a woman, I'm on your side, remember?'

Cat giggled. 'Just checking.'

They left the hall to find the weather had changed dramatically during the two hours the meeting had been in progress. The sky was overcast and grey, and a cold drizzle was misting the streets. There had been the usual number of hecklers and ne'er-do-wells inside the hall – men who favoured the MP who had openly declared two or three years ago that 'men and women differed in mental equipment, with women having little sense of proportion, and giving women the vote would not be safe'. One or two of the more unpleasant types a meeting such as the one today always seemed to attract eyed Sophy and Cat as the two women hugged on the steps of the building.

'Let me give you a lift back to your lodgings,' Sophy urged Cat, having decided to take a cab home in view of the weather. 'It's beginning to rain quite hard now.'

'No need. I'm going straight to the theatre – it's only a street or two away, so it makes sense. I'll buy something to eat before I go in, as I've got a matinée and I'll be cutting it fine if I go home first.' Cat smiled at her, pulling her felt hat further over her head and opening her umbrella. 'What did you think of Mrs Pankhurst?'

'She's an amazing woman.'

'I know. Promise me that somehow you'll come and see the play I'm doing at the moment. It's Elizabeth Robins' second work and it's sheer propaganda for the Cause, which is wonderful. It finishes with a suffragette rally in Trafalgar Square, and the political speeches are tremendous. We regularly have one or two men escorted from the premises in the evening when they've had a few drinks, and there's a number who are barred from the theatre now because of their obnoxious behaviour. They only come to disrupt the performance but it doesn't work. Everyone's all the more determined to see it through and make the point.'

Cat was bright-eyed and bushy-tailed and clearly pleased with herself, but Sophy felt a stab of unease. 'Have you ever been threat-ened personally?'

'We all have,' Cat said airily, giving Sophy another hug before turning and saying over her shoulder, 'I'll see you at Dolly's on Saturday morning. You haven't forgotten it's her birthday?'

'Cat, please let me give you a lift to the theatre,' Sophy called after her friend as she began to walk away.

'No need,' Cat said again, raising her hand without turning round. 'See you at the weekend.'

Sophy stood hesitating for a moment or two before hailing a cab. The meeting had been held in a hall off Ludgate Hill near St Paul's Cathedral, and she knew Cat's theatre, a tiny one in comparison to the West End giants, was only a short distance away by foot. Nevertheless, as she sat back in the cab and settled her damp skirt about her legs, she wished Cat had agreed to ride with her.

Quite when Cat became aware of the footsteps behind her she wasn't sure. There were a few people about although the rain had driven some folk indoors and it wasn't as busy as when she'd walked to the hall from her lodgings earlier. She had kept glancing over her shoulder then, feeling she was being followed, but the amount of people on the pavements had made it impossible to be sure. She had told herself that the vile letters she had received from someone who called himself 'A devotee of your art' had made her uneasy and that she was imagining things, but now the feeling was stronger than ever and the hairs on the back of her neck were prickling.

She had turned off Ludgate Hill into one of the side roads leading down to Queen Victoria Street, and had just reached the back of a printing works which was probably midway between the two main streets, when she was grabbed from behind by one of the two rough-looking men she thought she'd glimpsed at the hall that morning. Lifted right off her feet and with a large hard hand across her mouth, she was held against the man's front as he carried her into the narrow alleyway at the side of the building which appeared to have a dead end, his companion following him. She kicked and struggled but it had no impact on the burly body.

'Calm down, calm down.' The man holding her spoke above her

head. 'There's someone who wants to meet you, that's all. Seems you didn't reply to his letters, even though he asked you to reply in the Agony Column of *The Times*. Not polite, that. Ignoring him. Upset him, it has. Especially with how you flaunt yourself on stage, saying women should be able to choose where they give their favours and that you're as good as men. Little tease, aren't you, an' you've excited him, see?'

Fear was making Cat light-headed. Her feet still weren't touching the ground, and he was holding her as casually as though she weighed nothing at all, the other man not looking at them but peering towards where they'd entered the alley.

The man holding her now said, 'You told him where we'd be? That we'd have her?'

The second man grunted a reply, and then, as the clip-clop of horses' hooves came to them, Cat gathered all her strength and kicked out viciously with her boots at the same time as twisting her body.

She almost got free and she knew she'd hurt her captor from the groan he made, but as she opened her mouth to scream, the hand clamped even more firmly across her mouth. He was muttering foul curses as he carried her to the end of the alley and thrust her into the open door of the carriage that was waiting. She sprawled on the floor, but as she tried to scramble towards the opposite door, the man climbed in beside her and hoisted her up none too gently.

'Gently, Charley, gently. Is that any way to treat a lady?'

The man sitting in the seat facing her was clothed all in black; black frockcoat, black trousers and a black top hat. Cat was now frozen with terror, and although her mouth was free she couldn't cry out or move. Not that she would have got very far with the two men who had accosted her now sitting either side of her.

'But we haven't been formally introduced, my dear.' The man leaned forward and Cat instinctively shrank from what she saw in his face. 'My name is Henry, and yours is Christabel. Such a very beautiful name.'

The carriage was moving but the curtains at the windows made it impossible to see out. That alone increased Cat's dread. It was inconceivable that she was being abducted in the middle of a normal working day, but it was happening, and no one would know.

Somehow she found her voice. 'Stop this carriage this instant.'

'Why should I do that?' The man leaned back again, the slender walking stick with a silver top he was holding resting between his knees. 'I've been waiting for this opportunity to talk to you for some time. It's unfortunate it had to be this way but you've only brought it on yourself, my dear, ignoring my letters and requests that we meet.'

She knew but she still had to ask. 'Letters?'

'"A devotee of your art"?'

Oh God help me, help me, help me. Those disgusting letters detailing what he wanted to do to her, the 'fun' they could have. 'They were not the sort of letters a gentleman sends to a lady,' she said, aiming to keep the trembling in her body out of her voice.

'On the contrary, a lady of your profession must receive such accolades all the time, surely?'

'They weren't in the nature of an accolade, they were offensive and detestable.'

'They were a compliment, my dear. To your beauty and the free spirit you talk about on stage. You are magnificent in your unrestraint, your shamelessness.'

She stared at him. If he had come to see her as he proclaimed, then how could he possibly have twisted the fight for liberty and the vote and the other issues in the play like this? Swallowing hard, she tried to inject cool politeness into her voice. 'It is a play and I am an actress, that is all.'

'Such modesty.'

'I have to be at the theatre shortly so will you kindly stop this carriage,' she said again, warning herself not to lose control. With this man's henchmen sitting either side of her she had no chance of escape, so she had to talk her way out of this, but it was hard when she wanted to shout and scream. Whoever he was, he had money, that much was evident, but for all his fine clothes and this carriage, which she had to admit was beautiful, he was no gentleman to behave this way.

'All in good time.' He smiled the smile that wasn't a smile. 'All in good time, m'dear.'

She would escape. He would have to stop the carriage at some time, and no matter where she was she would scream and make a run for it. Her mind made up, Cat tried to get her bearings. The carriage had been pointing in the opposite direction from the Cathedral, towards the Strand, but already she had been conscious that they had twisted and turned a couple of times so they could be going back whence she'd come for all she knew.

Was his name really Henry? She moistened her lips which were dry with fright. He was a big man and heavy with it, and she would put his age at about fifty or so, although it was difficult to tell with the full beard he wore in the style of the King. He wasn't ugly, but there was something distinctly repellent about him, something that made her flesh creep. Whether it was the redness of the thick, full lips beneath the moustache or the look in his eyes when he stared at her, she didn't know, but whatever it was, everything in her recoiled from any contact with him.

The two men either side of her were apparently relaxed, but she sensed the slightest move from her and they would pounce. Quietly, she said, 'Where are you taking me?'

'You'll see shortly.'

'Why are you doing this?' She hated the pleading note in her voice. 'If you admire me as you say you do, why are you treating me this way?'

'This way? What way is that?'

'Kidnapping me.'

He laughed, a dry sound. 'Christabel, Christabel, such accusations. I am merely ensuring I enjoy the pleasure of your company as you seemed determined to thwart me. And really, you intrigue me more than a little. All this passion and openness on stage and yet you shrink from my letters? Why is that? I wondered. In all my observations over the last months I see no constant male beau, and so, I began to wonder, does your fancy lie in a different direction? Or perhaps you simply enjoy pleasure from wherever it comes? Certainly I, myself, consider nothing unnatural. You could say I am the most liberal of men in that regard.'

She stared at him, only half-understanding what he was implying. 'You've been watching me? Outside the theatre, I mean?' The creeping feeling he induced spread over her scalp as if the hairs on her head were rising.

He sat, half-smiling, watching her.

The rest of the journey was conducted in silence and lasted no more than ten minutes or so. When the horses' trot slowed down and then stopped, Cat prepared herself for flight, but no one in the carriage moved. And then the wheels were rolling again but only for a moment or two before the carriage turned at an angle and then stopped once more, but this time for good.

The man who called himself Henry got out, and she heard him say to someone, 'Lock those gates,' before adding, directly to her, 'May I help you, my dear?' as he held out his hand.

Ignoring him, Cat climbed out of the carriage to find she was in the walled yard of what looked to be a fairly substantial house, and another man was busy locking two huge wooden gates set in the eight-foot-high wall. She opened her mouth, but the scream never had voice because the man who had grabbed her had followed her from the carriage and now lifted her as before, his hand over her mouth as he carried her straight through an open doorway into the house. She kicked and struggled for a moment before becoming still, realising the futility of wasting her strength.

Cat saw she was in a large kitchen but she was carried through this into a passage. Halfway along the passage the man called Henry had unlocked another door, and as her captor took her down the steep stone steps she realised they were descending into the cellar. She fought again, nearly sending them both headlong, and as the man holding her uttered a string of oaths, Henry, now at the bottom of the stairs, laughed. 'I think we'll have to give her something. See to it, would you?'

'I know what *I'd* like to give her.'

'All good things come to those that wait, Seamus.'

Henry stood aside at the bottom of the steps. An enclosed room had been constructed, the door of which was open, and now Cat was pushed into it with enough force to send her to her knees. She crawled forwards and then scrambled to her feet, turning to see Henry watching her from the doorway. 'Scream all you like,' he said mildly. 'This room was made to certain requirements.' And then he shut the door and she heard the bolts slid into place.

The gas-lights burning in several holders mounted on brackets on the walls of the room told Cat she had been expected. It was the colour that hit her senses first. A deep scarlet red; walls, carpet – covering all of the floor; even the ceiling was painted in the same brazen shade. There were no windows, no natural light, but as Cat stared about her, her face white and terrified, the implements the room contained froze her blood. Whips, handcuffs and other items were hanging on the wall close to the huge bed, and it was then she began to whimper like a child.

When the man Seamus returned he had his companion with him who was holding a cup. Cat had heard the bolts being slid, and had braced herself to fly at whoever entered the room, but Seamus had clearly anticipated such a reaction. He subdued her with little effort, and the other man held her nose, brought her head back at a painful angle and forced her to swallow the contents of the cup. It tasted bitter, and when she had ingested it all Seamus hauled her to the bed and flung her on it. 'I'll wager you won't forget this day in a hurry,' he said thickly, surveying her sprawled limbs hungrily. 'The things he does . . .' He grinned. 'Still, you'll find out soon enough.'

When they left the room, locking the door once more, Cat had a feeling come over her she'd never experienced before. Her limbs were heavy and her mind wasn't her own, but the panic and agitation had subsided somewhat and she wanted nothing more than to sleep. Knowing she couldn't give in to the deadening potion, she tried to fight it, but it was worse with each minute that ticked by, and by the time the door opened again she was barely able to stand.

Henry Chide-Mulhearne, a member of the aristocracy and a follower of Donatien Alphonse Francois de Sade, had been anticipating this moment for a while. He had come across one of the Marquis de Sade's novels, *Les 120 Journées de Sodome* in his youth, and the works of sexual fantasy and perversion had gripped him like nothing else in his pampered and profligate life. Wealth and power he took as his right, and the privileges they accorded him a divine prerogative. He considered himself above the law and the narrow views of men, and although he usually took his women from the brothels where they would not be missed should his 'games' go too far, occasionally, as in the case of Cat, a woman who was not a prostitute caught his eye.

His servants, such as Seamus, he chose very carefully and paid extremely well. He had a country estate, this large townhouse, a grand chalet in France and a villa in the Italian Alps, and divided his time between them, never staying too long in one place. Each of his homes had what he called his 'special' room, like the one Cat was in now. Actresses interested him, they always had. In an age where the paragon of womanhood was the humble, obedient wife, mother or sister of some man, a woman who flagrantly displayed herself on the stage of the theatre was anathema and therefore exciting to his jaded palate – whatever the puritan morality of the play. And lately, the 'new drama' where conventional attitudes were challenged excited him still more.

He saw that the drug Seamus had given her had done its work. Even as she backed away from him, she stumbled and almost fell. He was wearing nothing beneath the long velvet dressing gown he had on, and as he reached her, he said softly, 'Will you take off your clothes, my dear, or shall I?'

Chapter 16

The lunch with Patience and William went well, but Sophy was glad when it was over. Patience did most of the talking. By the time they parted, Sophy was well-acquainted with most aspects of her cousins' lives. She knew John and Matthew had houses in the same street in Bishopwearmouth and were blissfully happy with their respective wives, and that John's boys were darlings but a handful. David had done splendidly at university and was now an archaeologist working somewhere in Egypt. Patience and her husband lived close to the children's hospital on the southern outskirts of Bishopwearmouth where William had recently taken up the post of Head Consultant, after eighteen years at the Sunderland Infirmary. Patience had told Sophy that she and her brothers saw their father on a regular basis, but their mother rarely.

Sophy gave Patience her address before they said goodbye. It would have been churlish not to. But seeing her cousin had brought up the wounds of the past, especially the feeling of loss she'd felt when Bridget, Kitty and Patrick had been dismissed. Consequently she left the hotel sad and disturbed.

Two days later, however, when she waited in vain for Cat at Dolly's, and then went to the theatre where Cat was appearing

only to find her friend hadn't shown for the last few performances, she felt more than disturbed. It was the same story at Cat's
lodgings. No one had seen her since the morning Cat had
attended the suffrage meeting.

Sophy left Cat's lodgings and went straight to the local police
station. From there she tried several hospitals. Everyone she spoke
to tried to be helpful but Cat had apparently disappeared into
thin air. During her performance that night, all Sophy could
think about was her friend. She sensed that something was terribly
wrong. Single actresses were vulnerable. Everyone knew that,
which was why many married for protection as much as for
respectability. True, the theatre was more reputable than the music
halls, and the social status regarding male actors had changed for
the better in the last decade or two, but a segment of society
persisted in viewing actresses as scarlet women. Henry Irving,
the actor-manager of the Lyceum, had done much for male
actors when he was knighted thirteen years before, but actresses
were still suspect. Ambition and independence were unfeminine
attributes, male logic argued, and when women expressed passion
and a lack of restraint on stage, it stood to reason they were
females of a certain sort.

Sophy had heard these views in various forms over the years.
Most of the time actresses could laugh at the bigotry they
represented, but occasionally, like now, they were more worrying.

Toby didn't come home that night. This was not an uncommon
occurrence. Sophy had long since insisted on separate bedrooms
so he did not wake her in the early hours. But it wasn't her
husband's absence which had her pacing the floor. She felt sick
about Cat. At one point she sat on her bed holding Maisie, who
normally reposed on her dressing-table, staring at the doll Bridget
had given her so long ago and praying that another dear friend
hadn't been taken from her. And as Bridget had been more
mother than friend, so was Cat more the sister she had never
had. She loved her dearly. How dearly, she hadn't realised till
now.

As soon as it was light Sophy bathed and dressed, refusing the breakfast Sadie – her maid-cum-cook – tried to press upon her before she left the house. With Sophy's success had come a move to a large terraced establishment overlooking Berkeley Square, and when she'd come across Sadie, an ageing ex-actress who'd spent the last decade living in abject poverty, it had seemed right to offer her the job even though some of the other applicants had been more suitable. It had proved a happy arrangement. Sadie was endlessly grateful for her changed circumstances, and Sophy was glad of the other woman's company, especially with Toby being the way he was. It was good to have another woman living in the house.

Sadie now fussed over her as she hailed Sophy a cab. 'You ought to eat something, ma'am,' she scolded gently. 'Even if it's just a slice of toast.'

'I'll have something later, when I've spoken to Kane.' 'Mr Gregory' had become 'Kane' some years ago. The entertainment world was a small one, and after meeting several times at various functions on a social level, he had requested she address him less formally.

'We're friends, aren't we?' he'd asked one day at a dinner for a respected actor who was retiring from the profession and going abroad to end his days in the sun. 'And I always think of you as Sophy. It's silly to stand on ceremony.'

Toby hadn't liked it, of course, but by then Sophy had ceased to worry about annoying her husband. If Toby had had his way, she would have had no friends of her own and would have sat at home twiddling her thumbs when she wasn't at the theatre. She had become used to attending the numerous receptions and social occasions alone, when Toby was either off goodness knows where or in a state of drugged senselessness, and it was nice when Kane invited her to be his partner for some event or other. He was always very proper, and most meticulous about her reputation, making sure that no one misconstrued their friend-ship for anything else. And he'd proved himself to be a good and faithful friend over the years, although Sophy sometimes felt she knew as little about him now as when she'd first met him.

She never spoke about Toby and Kane never asked, although she suspected the state of their marriage was common knowledge in the incestuous theatre world.

She had never visited Kane's home before, although she knew where he lived, and during the cab ride to Russell Square at the back of the British Museum she found she was a little nervous, although she was sure he wouldn't mind her calling unannounced in the circumstances. When the cab deposited her outside a large, three-storeyed terrace with black painted iron railings separating the snowy-white front steps from the pavement, she stood for a moment, composing herself before she mounted the steps and used the shiny brass knocker on the front door.

The door was opened almost immediately by an individual who gave Sophy something of a shock. The man was big; in fact, to use northern terminology he was 'built like a brick outhouse' with a squashed, well-lived-in face to match. Taken aback, Sophy hesitated for a moment before she said, 'I – I've come to see Mr Gregory. Is he at home?'

The man's eyes narrowed but otherwise his face was impassive when he said, 'An' what's your name, miss?'

Sophy blinked. 'Sophy Shawe.' And then in case he got the wrong idea: '*Mrs* Sophy Shawe.'

It was clear he recognised the name, if not her. His manner undergoing a change, he smiled, standing aside as he said, 'Come in, Mrs Shawe, and I'll tell Mr Gregory you're here.'

He showed her into a beautifully decorated and furnished drawing room which was quite devoid of the dark colours and heavy curtains and aspidistras favoured in the previous few decades. Instead the space was light and unburdened and free from clutter, the furniture of a pale wood and the curtains and cushions on the sofas and chairs the room contained pastel shades of green and blue and lemon. Japanese vases and oriental-looking ornaments were dotted here and there, and the light, dove-grey walls held several fine paintings, but again these were different from the normal landscapes or stiffly posed portraits. One picture showed a young woman with coffee-coloured skin washing her long black hair under a waterfall; another, a solitary fishing boat in a sea turned brilliant scarlet from the setting sun, and yet another, a group of raggedly clothed black children playing on the edge of a cotton-field where their mothers were working under a burning sun.

As Sophy gazed about her, her mouth slightly agape, Kane's manservant – if that's what he was – waved her towards a sofa set at an angle to the fire burning in the enormous marble fireplace. 'Take a seat, miss – Mrs Shawe,' he corrected himself, 'and I'll let Mr Gregory know you're here.'

As he left, pulling the door closed behind him, it swung open again and stood ajar a few inches. Sophy heard him walk upstairs and knock on a door, presumably Kane's bedroom. Then she heard nothing else for a few moments, but just before the sound of a door shutting again she thought she heard a woman's voice and then Kane's deep, unmistakable smoky tones.

The sound brought her sitting bolt upright. *Kane had a woman in his bed.* She felt a heat in her body that rose up to stain her neck and cheeks bright red. Oh my goodness, and she had arrived like this. She looked about her frantically as though she wanted to hide. Which she did.

First this strange and beautiful room which showed him in a totally different light, and now this. It was too much. She couldn't face him, she really couldn't. For a moment the fear and anxiety about Cat was forgotten. Kane and a woman . . .

By why not? Her hands gripped tightly together, she tried to bring reason to bear. He was a man, wasn't he? And men had needs, desires. She stood up and walked over to the wide windows; the heat from the fire was strong and wasn't helping her colour. Pressing her hands to her cheeks she willed them to cool down. She knew women threw themselves at Kane on occasion, she had seen it, but because he had never mentioned anyone in *that* way she had thought . . . What? That he was celibate? No, not exactly. She supposed she hadn't thought of him in that way at all, that was the truth of the matter. He had always been Mr

Gregory to begin with – if not a father figure, then definitely a kind of benign benefactor. And then he'd become a friend. A valued and precious friend. How precious she hadn't realised until this moment when she'd recognised she didn't know him as well as she'd imagined. *She had to pull herself together.* She drew in several deep breaths, staring out over the tree-lined square beyond the windows. It wasn't for her to judge if Kane entertained women. He was a single man, he could do what he liked. It was ridiculous to feel let down like this.

It was another few minutes before Kane walked into the room, and by then Sophy's acting ability had come to her rescue. She was able to greet him quietly and calmly, even if this new Kane – who clearly hadn't yet shaved and whose black stubble accentuated the unfamiliar and disturbing side of him tenfold – was slightly unnerving. 'Sophy?' He had a worried frown on his face. 'What's wrong? What's happened?'

'Hello, Kane.' When he took her hands in his she forced herself not to react. 'I'm sorry to arrive uninvited like this, but it's Cat.'

'Cat?'

'She's missing. That is, she hasn't been to her lodgings or the theatre she's appearing at for days. It's not like her. Cat wouldn't leave without letting me know where she was, and she certainly wouldn't miss a performance, let alone several.'

'Slow down, slow down.' He stopped her voice which had risen with every word by drawing her over to the sofa she'd vacated earlier. He pressed her down on it before sitting beside her, but without touching her now. 'Start at the beginning,' he said. 'When was she last seen, for a start?'

'I think I must have been the last person to see her. We went to a meeting together . . .' She told him it all, finishing with her visits to the police station and the hospital. Taking a deep breath, she added, 'And she said she'd been threatened.'

'What?' Kane sat up straighter. 'By whom and when?'

'She didn't say.' Sophy was bitterly regretting not making Cat ride in the cab with her. 'In fact, she made light of it. She said all the actresses were subject to the same thing.'

Kane nodded slowly. Cat was right. It was this very thing that gave him nightmares regarding Sophy and caused him to provide protection for the actresses in his theatres. But Cat hadn't been working for him, and he knew that the manager of the establishment where Cat had been playing couldn't give a damn. Behind his calm facade, his mind was racing. One part of his brain was dealing with Sophy's presence in his house – something he had fantasised about for years; the other was reflecting that it was Murphy's Law it had to be on a morning he'd brought a woman home the night before. Eliza was a young, busty wench happily devoid of inhibitions, and they'd enjoyed a pleasant if energetic night together, both of them aware it meant nothing beyond a gratification of bodily need. He was no saint, he admitted it, but this morning he wished he was when he looked into Sophy's amber eyes.

'You think some harm's come to her?' he said slowly.

Sophy nodded, eternally grateful he hadn't dismissed her fears or played down the possibility that Cat was in trouble. 'The police were all ears until I said she was an actress, and then I could tell they thought she'd gone off for some frivolous purpose somewhere, but Cat isn't like that. They said they'd investigate, but . . .' She shrugged. 'Something's terribly wrong. I know it.'

Kane thought she could be right.

'I'm sorry to burden you with this,' Sophy went on, 'but I didn't know who else to come to. I – I should have called at a more reasonable time.'

So she knew. Kane's jaw clenched but beyond that he made no outward sign, his voice calm and cool when he said, 'You are welcome here any time, you know that. I'll make a few enquiries of my own, all right? Ralph, the man you met at the door, is an old hand at such things and not easily intimidated, which is why he makes such an excellent manservant for someone like me. His background is . . . unorthodox, but he gets to hear of any rumblings of trouble, and sometimes that can be the success or failure of a production. You'd be surprised how many plays are sabotaged by anxious rivals.'

Nothing would surprise her after this morning. 'But – but this isn't a play.'

'He has contacts, Sophy.'

He didn't add, 'in the criminal fraternity', but Sophy knew what he meant.

'And he can move easily in places where you or I would stick out like a sore thumb.'

Sophy didn't ask what sort of places; she didn't want to know. 'So you don't think I'm being silly?'

He smiled, his cornflower-blue eyes crinkling, and suddenly it was the old Kane, the tried and trusted friend. 'No, I don't think you're being silly, but try not to worry. There might be a simple explanation for her absence.'

She couldn't think of one and she didn't think Kane could either. The sick churning was back but stronger now he had taken her seriously. She realised part of her had been hoping he would pooh-pooh the likelihood of Cat being in trouble. But Kane was a realist. She thought back to the safeguards which had been in place when she'd worked for him, and suddenly wished herself back a decade. She would make different decisions and not be swept off her feet by stunning good looks like a giddy schoolgirl. Alarmed at the way her thoughts had gone, she stood up. 'I must go.'

He didn't invite her to stay, which wasn't surprising in the circumstances. Instead he said, 'Ralph is a surprisingly good cook. You must come to dinner sometime. You and Toby, of course.'

And to this Sophy coolly replied, 'Thank you.'

'Ralph will stop a cab for you.'

'There's no need, I can catch one on the corner and—'

'Ralph will stop a cab for you,' he repeated quietly, and his voice was grim when he added, 'Take every care over the next little while, Sophy. Be alert and on your guard. This sort of thing doesn't happen very often, but it does happen.'

Again, she didn't ask him to explain himself because she couldn't bear to think of what it might mean for Cat.

★   ★   ★

Toby had recently arrived home when the cab dropped her outside the house. Sadie opened the door to her, whispering, 'He's a bit the worse for wear, ma'am, but I can't get him to go upstairs yet. He wanted to know where you were and I said you couldn't sleep and had gone for an early morning walk.'

Sophy nodded. Toby had become increasingly paranoid about other men over the last years since the opium had affected his physical capability in the bedroom. He had accused her of having affairs with each of her leading men over this time, along with any other male she came into contact with. Preparing herself for yet another inquisition, Sophy opened the door to the drawing room. It was about half the size of Kane's splendid drawing room and although she had always been pleased with the furnishings she had chosen, the room seemed cluttered this morning.

Toby was slouched on a sofa on the far side of the room, a cup of coffee at his elbow. He scowled at her and she could see he had trouble focusing. 'Where've you been?' he muttered as she stood looking at him.

Sophy found she was angry. He stayed out all night whenever he felt like it, was forever critical of her and everything she did, spent money like water and would never admit where he'd been and what he did, and now he had the nerve to question her in this manner? Stiffly, she said, 'I've been to see Kane.'

It clearly wasn't what he'd expected. He shook his head like a boxer after a heavy blow, running his hand through his mop of fair hair as he sat up straighter. 'You what?'

'I've been to see Kane Gregory. Cat's missing. She hasn't been seen for days and I'm worried about her.'

'So you went to see *him*?' It was aggressive.

'Yes, I did, as you weren't around to talk to. As usual.'

Toby stood up, stumbling slightly as he walked across to her. As he drew near, Sophy became aware of the smell of him: a sweet, musty, faintly obnoxious smell that was on his breath and clothes. It told her exactly how he had spent the night. Not that she needed proof. He was still clearly under the influence of the drugs he'd imbibed. 'Don't you talk to me like that. I'm your husband,' he said thickly.

There were many replies she could have made to that. Biting her tongue, she said again, 'Cat's missing. Do you understand?'

'Her? Huh. She's likely with someone who's caught her fancy. And I mean a woman, incidentally. Your great friend is nothing more than a—'

'Stop it!' Her voice was almost a scream. 'Don't you dare talk about Cat in that way.'

'I'll say what I like in my own house,' he shouted back. 'And you, you're no better. Daughter of a whore and with the same inclinations—'

Nothing could have stopped her hand shooting out and making contact with the side of his face in a ringing slap. And there was no doubt he would have hit her, his doubled fist coming up to strike even as Sadie virtually burst into the room, causing his hand to hover in the air for a second. Sadie reached Sophy in a moment, standing slightly in front of her as she glared at Toby.

He surveyed the two women; Sophy as white as a sheet and Sadie red with anger, and then, his words coming as though sieved through his teeth, he hissed, 'To hell with you. To hell with you both.' Swearing foully, he staggered from the room, banging the door violently behind him.

Sophy sank down on a chair, her knees all but giving way. She wanted to cry but she wouldn't let herself. That Toby had thrown the secret she'd confided about her mother into her face so cruelly had cut her to the quick, and she knew it was the final blow to their marriage. Where her love for him had been was a great void; she didn't even feel bitter or resentful or angry any more. For the first time she had to acknowledge that Cat was right. She must leave him and start divorce proceedings. It was now a matter of self-preservation.

The thought of Cat brought her mind back to the immediate worry. She turned to Sadie who was patting her shoulder.

'Could I have something to eat, Sadie? Something light. And a hot drink. Tea, not coffee.'

Obviously glad of something to do, Sadie bustled off, muttering something under her breath about feckless husbands and what she'd like to do with them.

Sophy lay back against the chair. She was tired in mind and body. So much had happened in the last few days. Patience, Cat, and now this with Toby. She didn't let herself think of Kane Gregory, that was a road too complex and disturbing to go down.

She shut her eyes, her head aching through lack of sleep. *Please, God, please let Cat be found alive and well. Let there be some kind of simple explanation for her going away, like Kane suggested.* But Kane hadn't believed it, she knew he hadn't. And neither did she.

Chapter 17

Once Kane had sent Eliza home in a cab, he called Ralph into his study and explained the circumstances which had driven Sophy to call on him.

The big man's face was sombre when Kane finished speaking. 'Don't like the sound of it, boss,' he said gruffly. Kane was normally 'boss' when they were alone, other times he was 'sir' or 'Mr Gregory', but always he had Ralph's absolute loyalty. 'Usually means only one thing when a young woman disappears.'

The two men stared at each other, each knowing what the other was thinking. They had met through a similar situation twenty-two years before, when Kane had been a young man of twenty-three, still grieving from the loss of his brothers and mother, and bitter by what he'd seen as rejection by his father. He had been wild in those days and dissolute, spending his inheritance on wine, women and song. Ralph's sister had been a music-hall actress and Kane had taken up with her. Lily had come to live with him at the rooms he rented, and when one day a few weeks later her brother had turned up on the doorstep demanding to know his intentions, he'd laughed in Ralph's face. The subsequent fight had put him in hospital for forty-eight hours, and when he had returned to the rooms it had been to a scene of unspeakable horror. Lily had been brutally murdered, and the police — who were still hunting for Ralph with regard to the attack on Kane — had decided Ralph was guilty when they'd cornered him a little while later.

Kane had gone to visit Ralph in prison to tell Lily's brother he would personally see to it that he hanged for the crime. Instead he'd left convinced of the man's innocence. Lily had been raped before being bludgeoned to death, and whatever else Ralph was, he wasn't a pervert. Moreover, as Kane had talked with him, he'd understood that Ralph's attack on himself had been the desire of a brother to rescue a beloved sister from what he saw as an immoral life which would lead to ruin.

He had contacted various acquaintances of Ralph — most of whom lived outside the confines of the law — and paid them hand-somely to prove Lily's brother innocent and bring the real perpe-trator to justice. He had also hired top lawyers to fight Ralph's case, and all against the background of the police being convinced they had got their man. Kane had got to know Ralph well over the subsequent weeks, and the two men had become friends, something which had surprised both of them. Kane learned that Ralph had virtually brought Lily up when their parents had died of the fever when Lily was ten years old, and although Ralph didn't deny being a member of the criminal fraternity, he'd sacrificed much to enable his sister to become a respectable woman, only to have Lily herself rebel against his constrictions when she was old enough to leave home.

The horror of what he'd witnessed in the rooms when he'd returned from the infirmary, the vision of which would be with him to his dying day and which haunted his dreams, and not least his part in encouraging Lily to defy her brother, was a turning-point in Kane's life. He fought hard for Ralph — the first time he had fought for anything — with a tenaciousness of which he wouldn't have thought himself capable. He was still fighting when the case came to court and, in spite of the lawyers, Ralph was found guilty and sentenced to be hanged. It was at the ninety-ninth hour before the execution that the hundreds of pounds he'd spent buying information brought results. Lily's real murderer — an 'admirer' of

hers from the music halls – was arrested after Kane provided sufficient proof to have the man questioned. He had confessed soon
afterwards as though pleased to relieve himself of the secret he'd
been hiding. He had apparently followed Lily home from the music
hall and when she'd fought him he'd raped and killed her.

Kane's inheritance was severely depleted by the time Ralph was
released, and when he announced his intention to try his luck
abroad – having bought a piece of land in the west of America,
which was gold country, with the last of his wealth – Ralph pleaded
to accompany him. Two hard years followed, years in which Kane
often thought he'd die destitute in the dust of foreign soil, but
then they hit the seam which lifted him out of the dirt and on to
a ship bound for England as a relatively wealthy man once more.
And this time he *was* a man, not a spoiled youth in search of
aimless pleasure.

Looking at Ralph now, Kane said quietly, 'Make enquiries, but
discreetly. Any leads, no matter how small, follow. Money's not a
consideration. She might have gone away for a few days with one
of the Hooray-Henrys who've got more money than sense, but I
doubt it. Cat's not that sort of woman. I don't like this, Ralph. I
don't like it at all. She left Sophy saying she was going straight to
the theatre and then she vanished. Check all the hospitals and the
morgues, every one. No stone unturned, all right?'

Ralph nodded. He was fully aware that it wasn't just demons
from the past prompting Kane's fear. He had been in the company
of this man for more than two decades and he had never seen a
woman affect him like Sophy Shawe had. On the day of her
marriage to that wastrel Toby Shawe, Kane had got blind drunk
and remained so for twenty-four hours. He'd never spoken about
how he felt about her, but Ralph knew. And what might have
happened to this friend of Sophy's could so easily happen to any
of the actresses.

Ralph's grisly tour of London's hospitals and morgues over the
next forty-eight hours brought the result Kane had been dreading.
A woman's body had been discovered dumped in a filthy alley
deep in the heart of the East End's dockland. It was an area rife

with brothels and slum tenements, where disease and death haunted young and old alike, and it wasn't uncommon for bodies to be pulled from the water or found in the gutters and back alleys. This one was slightly unusual in that it was naked and devoid of any means of identification.

When Ralph informed him about his find, Kane went straight along to the police morgue, hoping against hope it wasn't Cat. The identification didn't take long. It was early evening when he entered the building, and when he left he welcomed the bite of the cold March air on his face. He'd heard it said that death smoothed out the evidence of pain and suffering. It hadn't with Lily, neither had it with Cat.

Ralph had accompanied him to the morgue and to the public house where Kane had two stiff whiskies. Then Kane sent Ralph home. He had to see Sophy alone, and now the identification had been made he didn't want her hearing about Cat from the police. He knew she would be at the theatre preparing for the evening performance but it couldn't be helped. Her understudy would have to take over.

When he reached the theatre he found the manager and explained he was the bearer of bad news and that Sophy would be unable to go on stage that night. Then he found her dressing room and paused outside. How was he going to tell her? He raked his hand through his hair. How the hell was he going to say it?

In the event, he didn't have to. Sophy was sitting at her dressing-table putting the finishing touches to her stage make-up when he entered the room, and as she looked at him in the mirror she froze.

'Sophy—'

'No.' Childishly, she put her hands over her ears as she shook her head. 'No.'

'Sophy, I'm sorry.'

She swung to face him then, her eyes filled with tears. She still shook her head as she whispered, 'Are you sure?'

He nodded. 'There – there's no doubt.'

'Oh, Cat, Cat.'

It was a moan and nothing could have prevented him from

crossing the space between them and taking her into his arms. She fell against him, her head bowed and resting on his chest and it was all he could do not to crush her to him. He could never have imagined or wished for these circumstances, but, terrible as they were, they were the means by which he was holding his beloved in his arms for the one and only time.

The funeral was well attended. Sophy held the reception at her home, and on top of the tensions of the day and the harrowing facts she had learned about the manner of Cat's last hours, which were at the forefront of her mind day and night, she was on tenterhooks lest Toby would do or say something to smear Cat's name and dishonour her friend. By the time friends and acquaintances had left she felt like a limp rag, but although Toby had been surly, he'd behaved himself.

Arranging Cat's funeral and dealing with the hundred and one matters appertaining to her friend's death, along with her performances at the theatre, had meant that Sophy was flying from pillar to post every day, but even so she hadn't been able to sleep much at night. She didn't think she would until the person who had done those wicked things to Cat was caught and brought to justice. Kane had been so against her seeing Cat before the funeral that she hadn't persisted in her wish to visit the undertakers once the police had released Cat's body, but now, with the funeral over, she regretted this. She didn't feel as though she had said goodbye. She felt she'd let Cat down.

Cat's family had had no such qualms about not paying their respects, however. Sophy's soft full mouth pulled tight. She had written to the Ardington-Tatlers after the family had made it clear to the police that they did not wish Cat's body to be returned home and did not intend to give her a decent burial. A short terse letter from Cat's father had arrived by return, stating that as far as the family was concerned, Christabel had been dead to them from the minute she had left to take up a degrading life on the stage, and they would thank Mrs Shawe not to communicate with them again in any form.

She glanced at Toby who was sitting in a chair by the fire, a glass of brandy at his side. He had been drinking steadily all day, and as soon as the last mourner had gone, had collapsed in the chair and promptly fallen asleep. Not for the first time she reflected how the life he had led for the last decade had changed the handsome man she'd married. His face was puffy, his skin blotched and the once athletic body unnaturally thin, but then he rarely ate properly. The opium he craved deadened his appetite and if, like today, he was forced to go without it for a time he drank excessively instead.

She had done nothing about the decision she had made regarding her marriage, telling herself she would think about that once the funeral was over. Due to the circumstances of Cat's death and the police investigation, the necessary paperwork had been slow in coming. It was now the second week of April, and the police were no further forward in their inquiries than on the day when Cat's body had been discovered. Inspector Bell, the nice middle-aged policeman who was leading the murder case and who had attended the funeral that afternoon, had told her it might be a lengthy process, so she couldn't use that as an excuse to delay. She had to take the bull by the horns.

Sophy's stomach turned over. In order to disentangle herself from this marriage she would have to go through the courts and she knew it would be a tortuous process. She had no doubt that Toby had committed adultery; she'd had her suspicions about Rosalind Robins but she had been sure about another actress he had worked with briefly after Rosalind, when this woman's husband had warned Toby off. Proving this might be difficult, along with the charge of gross cruelty the law insisted on, but she had to try. If nothing else, she could live separately from him once proceedings were under way, even if it might be years before she was legally free.

A gust of rain splattered against the window and a few drops found their way down the chimney, causing the fire in the grate to hiss and spit. The weather had become wintry again in the last forty-eight hours after a prolonged mild spell, but Sophy had welcomed the icy wind and rain. She didn't think she would have been able to stand it if Cat had been buried on a sunny day with the birds singing.

Becoming aware she was wringing her hands together, she stood up and walked over to the window, staring blindly ahead. How could Cat and she have imagined it would end like this? Cat having fallen into the hands of some madman, and she with her marriage in tatters? She had married fully expecting to fulfil her role as a mother. Traditionally in the theatre an actress was not expected to give up her career when she had a child. She had thought she and Toby would do what other couples did and bring their babies with them to work. Even when an actress was touring, every theatre had the equivalent of a nursery in what was called the green room, where children could sleep or play during rehearsals and performances. Some actresses employed nannies and sent their offspring to boarding schools as soon as they were old enough, but she had always imagined she would keep her children with her and employ governesses and tutors when the time came to further their education.

She had wanted Toby's babies once. Been entranced by the idea. Now it disgusted her. How could she have been so wrong?

Turning from the window, she was startled to find Toby's slatey-blue eyes fixed on her. He sat up in the chair, his voice flat when he said, 'Are you satisfied with how you played your part today, my talented little wife?' before he drained the last of his brandy, smacking his lips as he finished.

She genuinely didn't understand. 'I'm sorry?'

'Lady Bountiful. Virtuous, grieving friend. Sweet, gentle, docile wife. Take your pick. You incorporated them all into the performance at various times, and I have to take off my hat to you. You're a damn good actress.'

She had seen him like this many times when he was under the influence of drink or drugs, but tonight there was a viciousness in his face that frightened her. He was mad. He had to be. She said nothing, remaining perfectly still as she held his gaze.

'But of course you're used to playing to a packed house, albeit a smaller than normal one in this case.' He threw his arms in an expansive gesture, encompassing the room. 'The great Sophy Shawe, the darling of the West End. Isn't that right, my sweet?'

'You're drunk.'

It was not so much her words, more the look on her face which acted on him like an injection. He leaped up from the chair, his face infused with angry colour and all pretence of composure melting from him as he yelled, 'Drunk, you say? And who wouldn't have to be drunk to put up with what I do? Parading your conquests in front of my face and all the time looking down your saintly nose at me. But I know what you are, under the skin, don't I? Oh yes. I know, I know. I've got more talent in one little finger than you've got in the whole of your body, but you're clever with that body, aren't you, sweetheart? You know how to use it to get what you want, same as your whore mother.'

She had always known that the only way she could tell him would be when he was at his worst, like now, even if on those occasions he was also at his most dangerous.

'I am going to see a solicitor tomorrow,' she heard herself saying. 'I am going to divorce you.'

He stared at her for a moment, amazement etched on his mottled face. 'Don't be ridiculous.'

'Ridiculous or not, that is what I'm going to do.'

'Over my dead body.' His spring towards her took her by surprise, as did the punch between her eyes which knocked her clean off her feet and caused her to fall backwards on to an ebonised wood cabinet containing a collection of small figurines.

She couldn't have said if she screamed or not; afterwards it was a blur, but something brought Sadie running into the room. Before Sophy lost consciousness, she heard him say, 'You won't make a fool of me like that, do you hear me? I won't be made a laughing-stock, I'd kill you first.'

And then there was nothing but a consuming darkness.

When Sophy became dimly aware of sound and feeling again, she felt herself being rocked, in the same manner one would use with a child. Fighting the nausea which had accompanied the consciousness, she struggled to open her eyes through the blinding pain in her head.

'Oh, ma'am, ma'am.' She was in Sadie's arms on the floor and tears were running down the woman's face. 'I thought he'd done for you.'

Sophy tried to sit up but as the room swam and she felt herself slipping away again, she lay back. She felt ill, so terribly ill. What had happened? And then she remembered. Feebly, she murmured, 'Toby?'

'He's gone, ma'am. Oh, ma'am, your poor face.'

'Help me sit up, Sadie.'

It took several attempts, because each time she raised her head the blackness took over, but somehow, with Sadie taking her weight, Sophy managed to reach a chaise longue. She knew she was going to be sick and Sadie just had time to grab an ornate bowl holding pot-pourri, emptying the mixture of dried petals and spices unceremoniously over the floor, before Sophy gave in to the nausea. She was aware of Sadie wiping her mouth afterwards and of her saying, 'Lie back, ma'am, that's right, and shut your eyes. You'll be all right in a minute,' and then she must have lost consciousness once more.

When she next became aware of anything, she could hear a voice saying, 'I'll have him hung, drawn and quartered for this, the swine. You did absolutely right to send for me, Sadie, and Ralph'll be here soon with the doctor.' She sensed Kane was kneeling at her side and his hand felt cool on her hot forehead, but she couldn't find it within herself to move or talk. She knew she was drifting back into that deep sleep again and she welcomed it.

On the perimeter of that other world she heard Sadie say, 'I know Mrs Shawe needs a doctor, sir, but she wouldn't want you to send for the Constable like you said. She's a very private person, sir.'

'Private or not, this needs to be documented.'

She had never heard that note in Kane's voice before. He must be very angry.

'There is no way Mr Shawe is coming back into this house, you understand that, Sadie?' the same grim voice continued.

'But the police won't be able to stop him, sir, and—'

'The police will have nothing to do with it.'

Kane couldn't do that, he mustn't do it. Toby was capable of anything when he was thwarted. Now she tried to surface from the fog but it made the blinding pain that was threatening to break her head apart worse, and this time when she went under she knew nothing for a long, long time.

Chapter 18

The concussion Sophy had sustained was serious. It was a full two weeks before the doctor would allow visitors, and a further week after that before she was able to leave her bedroom and venture downstairs. She hadn't argued with the doctor's orders, mainly because she felt too exhausted and ill to object, but also because she didn't want to see anyone until the bruising to her face had gone down. Kane had been the only exception to the doctor's rule simply because he would not have it otherwise. He had visited each day for a short period, treating her with the same friendliness he'd always shown and often just sitting by the side of her bed while she slept. This embarrassed her once she thought about it when she was getting better, but at the time it had seemed perfectly natural for him to be there when she awoke.

Sadie had told her that Toby had returned home the morning after the attack. Kane and Ralph had been waiting for him. They had taken him into the drawing room and closed the door in Sadie's face. Sadie didn't know what had been said but when the three men had emerged, Toby was clearly shaken. He'd quickly packed a case and left the house, and that afternoon Kane had told Sadie he wouldn't be back in the forseeable future. They'd since been informed he was staying at his club, but nothing more.

The subject of her husband was not mentioned between Sophy and Kane until the first afternoon she came downstairs. She was still feeling shaky and some vestige of the severe bruising to her face had yet to fade completely, but now the terrible headaches and nausea had all but gone she felt much more like herself. Sophy was lying on a chaise longue close to the window where she could see a little of the comings and goings in the square when Sadie showed Kane into the drawing room. It was a beautiful day and the May blossom was drifting in the air like summer snow, but the bright sunshine and blue sky merely emphasised the darkness in her life, and once Kane was seated and Sadie bustled away to prepare a tea tray, she said, 'I need to know exactly what you said to Toby, Kane, but first, is there any news about Cat's murderer?'

The vivid blue eyes narrowed for a moment. 'We can discuss all this when you're feeling better.'

'I am feeling better.'

This was said impatiently and the tone convinced Kane more than a thousand words that he couldn't prevaricate. He looked at Sophy. He had been dreading this moment. 'Ralph's enquiries have borne fruit,' he admitted softly.

'Ralph's? Not the police's?'

'Ralph can go places and ask questions the police can't,' Kane said shortly. And money was a great persuader. He'd spent a small fortune buying information, and Ralph had put himself in peril and to what end? He'd given the police enough reason to apprehend the man in question and the same day he'd skedaddled abroad. It stank of friends in high places. The aristocracy looked after its own, there was no doubt about that, and closed ranks when scandal threatened.

Aware Sophy was waiting, he cleared his throat. 'I think the man who hurt Cat knew we were on to him and has gone abroad.'

Sophy stared at him. 'Are you sure? That he was the man, I mean? Who is he? What's his name? Did Cat know him?'

'Yes, I'm sure it's him. His name's Chide-Mulhearne. And no, I have no reason to think Cat was acquainted with him before she was taken captive, although he may have been the individual who wrote certain obscene letters to her in the weeks before her murder,' said Kane, answering her questions in order. 'He's rich enough to buy loyalty, but one of his servants made the mistake of talking a little too freely to a woman he later got with child and then abandoned. Her terror of the workhouse was greater than her fear of the man in question, and on being assured she'd be provided with enough money to make a new start far from London with her baby, she was very helpful. But Chide-Mulhearne was too clever, I'm afraid. He's left and no doubt covered his tracks in the process so nothing can be proved. I'm sorry, Sophy.'

'But that's so wrong, so unfair! Can't anything be done?'

Kane shook his head. 'The only satisfaction gained out of this is that he probably won't risk returning to England again if he's as wily as I think he is, but I admit that's not much comfort.'

Sophy shook her head in bewilderment. What sort of world was this? It seemed as though, if you were a man and you were rich enough, you could do anything you liked with impunity. Marriage, society, even the law was weighted on the side of men; she had never seen it so clearly before or resented it so bitterly.

'This is a horrible world,' she said slowly. 'Where is the protection for the innocent? I always thought the law was supposed to help in the fight against wrongdoing, but half the time it doesn't seem like that to me, not if the transgressor is rich or influential. Children can be imprisoned for stealing a loaf of bread to keep their family from starving, and someone like this man can do the things he did and get off scot-free.'

'Most of the time the law works.'

'No, it doesn't. It doesn't, Kane. Not for one half of society, the female part.' All the talking in the world wouldn't bring Cat back, but she couldn't bear to think this man was somewhere – eating, drinking, laughing, enjoying life – and her friend was dead.

She stared at Kane. 'So he's got away with it, this man? He could do unspeakable things to Cat and probably other women too, and then just leave the country?'

Kane's discomfort showed as he strained his neck upwards, adjusting the collar of his shirt. 'Like I said, he's clever. And very wealthy. When the police went to the address we'd been given, they found the cellar room the female informer had described, but it held nothing incriminating and had been newly whitewashed.'

Sophy drew in a sharp breath. 'A cellar room? Cat was held in a cellar? Was she killed there?'

'Possibly.'

Sophy repeated the word but only in her mind. She felt sick and furiously angry, and this showed in her voice when she said, 'I shall go and see the police myself and demand that more is done. I shall shout it from the rooftops if necessary.'

'It will do no good, Sophy. Believe me. Everything that could be done has been done. Cat is gone and nothing can bring her back, and if you continue to torture yourself like this, you'll only delay your recovery.'

She glared at him, incensed by the male logic, incensed by everything male, including Kane. For the moment he wasn't Kane, her friend, but a member of the sex responsible for the outrage on her dear friend.

Sadie knocked on the door and entered immediately with the tea tray. She fussed about, pouring the tea and plying Kane with cake before bustling off again, a little put out by the atmosphere she sensed.

As soon as they were alone again, Sophy said stiffly, 'And Toby? I understand you and Ralph spoke to him the morning he returned. Can I know what was said?'

'Of course.' Kane was well aware of how she was feeling and not altogether surprised by her reaction to the news about Chide-Mulhearne. He had said to Ralph it might well be a case of shoot the messenger when he broke it to her, but that couldn't be helped. He'd done his damnedest to see to it that the man was brought to justice, and he hoped Sophy would eventually come to see that. 'I told him what would happen to him if he laid a finger on you again and suggested he removed himself from this house until such time as you saw fit to invite him back.' He had also told Toby that certain acquaintances of Ralph would pay him a visit if he so much as came within a hundred yards of Sophy without her summoning him, but he had no intention of admitting this, or that one of these acquaintances had been to see Toby a few days later to remind him to behave himself.

Sophy nodded. 'Thank you,' she said tightly. She wanted to tell Kane that she had already made arrangements for her solicitor to call in a few days with a view to starting divorce proceedings, but somehow she couldn't voice it. She also knew she was being uncharacteristically antagonistic and unfair, and she didn't understand why, except that an echo of the woman's voice she'd heard that morning in Kane's house frequently came to mind when she was in his company. Kane wasn't who she'd thought he was. No man seemed to be. And she didn't know if she was on foot or horseback.

A week later, against the advice of her doctor, Sophy returned to work, much to the disappointment of her understudy. Her solicitor had personally gone to see Toby at his club but had reported back that Mr Shawe had been sullen and non-committal. Indeed, Mr Brownlow of Brownlow & Son had added, he was doubtful if the gentleman in question had understood what was happening, so withdrawn had he seemed, and when he had given him the necessary papers he had stared at them with the strangest expression on his face before tucking them into the inside pocket of his suit jacket.

Sophy had half-anticipated a visit from Toby, but one had not been forthcoming. Nevertheless, Sadie made sure the doors and windows to the house were always locked and bolted, and checked at least three times at night that everything was secure before going to bed.

Despite feeling so exhausted she could barely put one foot in front of the other at the end of each evening, Sophy was glad to be playing at the theatre again. When acting her part, for a brief time she was someone else, and the long speeches and complicated interaction with the male lead meant she had to put everything else out of her mind. She rose late every morning and after an early lunch of something light arrived at the theatre in good time for the afternoon performance, not leaving until the evening performance was over. This meant Kane's daily visits had come to an abrupt end, for which she was thankful. As she had got better she had found he unsettled and disturbed her in a way she couldn't describe, even to herself.

And so May gently led into June, with just one or two events registering from the world outside Sophy's tiring routine. She attended the meeting presided over by Lord Lytton calling for a UK national theatre to be built by 1916 so as to commemorate the three-hundredth anniversary of Shakespeare's death, rubbing shoulders with Bernard Shaw, H.G. Wells and other influential celebrities, some of whom were remarkably self-effacing and others less so. And when France introduced a new law whereby automatic divorce was granted after three years' legal separation, she took note, due to her own situation. On the whole, though, her life consisted of sleeping, eating and working at the theatre, an insular existence, and something she could never have imagined on the day she had got married. She had thought her life was set on a course of togetherness, encompassing children and family life, and now she found it had taken the opposite direction. But there was nothing she could do about it. It would be years before she was free of Toby. And the last decade had taken its toll. She had no wish to marry again, to come under the headship of a man, any man, after the misery she had suffered. It would be enough to be unrestricted by the bonds of matrimony, to be independent and footloose. With that she would be content.

Grieving for Cat was a daily process, that and coming to terms with the way her friend had died and that the man responsible had escaped justice. And so, when she heard about a Votes for Women rally being held in Hyde Park in the middle of June, she knew she had to go to represent Cat and her beliefs.

Sadie stared at her askance when she announced her intentions at the breakfast-table, the day of the rally. She had risen early and been downstairs at nine o'clock. Already the morning was hot, the sky blue and high. The perfect day for a rally, she told Sadie cheerfully.

When Sadie had realised she couldn't dissuade Sophy from attending, she declared she was accompanying her and nothing Sophy said could convince her otherwise. So it was, at just after ten o'clock, the two women set off.

Huge crowds were jamming Hyde Park when they got there. Bugles blew and banners waved, and although most of the crowd seemed sympathetic to the cause, there was a minority of individuals who had clearly come to heckle the speakers. The leading speakers were positioned round the park on twenty different platforms wearing sashes in the campaign colours of purple, green and white, and each platform had a policeman or two beside it. The morning was bitter-sweet for Sophy. She was roused by the inspiring speeches of Christable Pankhurst and Annie Kenney, and the fellow-feeling in the crowds which encompassed women from all walks of life and all classes was like nothing she had experienced before, but Cat should have been there beside her, her lovely face aglow with passion for the cause and her voice joining in the cheers for the speakers. The sea of pretty hats and summer dresses worn by the tens of thousands of women present, the bright sunshine and the almost carnival atmosphere, brought home her loss even more, and Sadie must have been feeling the same because she whispered in Sophy's ear, 'She's in a better place, ma'am, that's what you've got to keep remembering,' as she squeezed Sophy's arm.

The rally finished with a resolution calling on the government to bring in an official Women's Suffrage Bill without delay which was passed overwhelmingly, and although there were one or two ugly moments when trouble flared, the police came to the rescue immediately.

There were the usual groups of Hooray Henrys dotted about the fringe of the park as the rally broke up – rich, ineffectual young men who made a nuisance of themselves at such events because they had more money than sense, drank too much and had little respect for women outside their own class. Since Toby had become unemployable due to his drink and drug addiction, he had drifted into the company of such types now and again, but however freely he spent Sophy's money, he was still unable to keep up with the profligate lifestyle of most of them, who were recklessly extravagant and wild.

It was as Sophy and Sadie approached the line of horse-drawn cabs waiting for hire at the perimeter of the park that she heard her name bandied about by one such bunch of wastrels. 'Hey, chaps, isn't that Sophy Shawe the actress, good old Toby Shawe's wife? She's even more of a beauty close to, and willing to entertain, according to Toby.'

'Ignore them, ma'am,' Sadie murmured at her side.

Sophy nodded. The words had been spoken loudly, and clearly meant to reach her ears.

The next moment, the two women found themselves surrounded by a group of laughing young men who were eyeing Sophy in an insolent manner as they jostled each other. Aware that they only had a few yards before they reached the cabs, Sophy glanced at them coldly. 'Please let us pass.'

Disregarding this, the foppish young man who seemed to be the ringleader and who had spoken before, swept his hat off his head in an exaggerated bow. 'Let me introduce myself. Rupert Forester-Smythe at your service, Mrs Shawe.'

Sophy allowed no expression on her icy features. 'I said, please let us pass.'

'Hoity-toity.'

From the laughter which followed from his cohorts you'd have thought Forester-Smythe had said something extremely witty.

Sadie jabbed at the man nearest her with the end of her parasol, causing him to jump to one side. More laughter followed.

'We have a mutual acquaintance, Mrs Shawe.'

Sophy had no intention of holding a conversation with Rupert Forester-Smythe and stared at him without speaking.

'A certain Toby Shawe?' he carried on, undeterred. 'And he's been very . . . vocal about your – shall we say *willingness* – to show a fellow a good time.'

This was too much for Sadie. Using her parasol again she lunged at Forester-Smythe and prodded him in the stomach. 'Get away, you foul-mouthed creatures!' she hissed furiously, before using the light umbrella to clear a path to the first cab, the driver of which had jumped down from his seat behind the horse and was saying, 'Can I be of any assistance, ladies?'

The group of young men were now hooting with laughter and blowing kisses to the two women as the cab driver assisted them into the carriage, but as it drew away Sophy caught a fleeting glimpse of Forester-Smythe's face, and he wasn't smiling like the others.

'What are things coming to?' Sadie was highly indignant and bristling like a porcupine. 'I'd like to take their silver-topped canes and stick them where the sun don't shine; that'd take the smiles off their silly faces and make their eyes pop, sure enough.'

Sophy had to smile. But the incident had shaken her. The more so now she had time to think about what the man had said. That Toby had been saying such things about her, hurt her to the quick – but perhaps she should have expected it.

She instructed the cab driver to take her straight to the theatre before he drove Sadie home, and as she was a little late she didn't have time to dwell on the episode before the afternoon perform-ance. In the interval before the evening show, several members of the cast, including Sophy, had a light meal brought in from a nearby restaurant, and the usual jocularity and clowning around from one or two of the younger members of the cast banished the last of her distress. If nothing else the incident had shown her she was right to distance herself from Toby, she told herself when she was back in her dressing room getting ready for the next performance. Not that she had doubted it. Yet, she asked herself, how could she have been so mistaken about the man with whom she had thought she would share the rest of her life? When she looked back over those first two or three years of their marriage, she could see a hundred different times when she should have realised what he was really like, but loving him as she had, she'd made countless excuses for him. Perhaps she herself had contributed to his decline into the habit which had mastered him body and soul? If she had challenged him earlier, forced him to get help, maybe he could have risen above his addiction? She had tried, heaven knows she had, but perhaps not hard enough . . .

The five-minute curtain call came and she mentally shook herself. Toby had made his decisions and nothing she had done or said could have persuaded him otherwise. She had loved him, she had genuinely adored him, but love hadn't been enough.

No more heart-searching. She had to look forward now. But even as she thought it, she dreaded the fight which would undoubtedly ensue in the next months and years before she could gain her freedom.

Chapter 19

The day had started dismally for Toby, like the ones before it since he had left the comfort of the house overlooking Berkeley Square. He didn't remember coming back to his room at the club but when he awoke, fully clothed and lying on top of the covers, he could smell the vomit splattered on the floor at the side of the bed.

Dragging himself into a sitting position with his back resting against the iron bedhead, he lit his first cigarette of the day and drew the smoke deep into his lungs. Then he reached for the whisky bottle and glass on the bedside cabinet. He poured himself a good measure and drank it straight down, and after a minute or two his hands stopped shaking. Shutting his eyes, he finished the cigarette and lit another with the stub, and had another glass of whisky but he sipped this one, making it last. The bottle was almost empty.

The angle of the shafts of sunlight slanting in through the high window told him it must be late morning, and when he glanced at his watch he saw it was, in fact, two in the afternoon. He finished the last of the whisky in the bottle and sat for some time thinking of nothing in particular, his mind in the empty vacuum it retreated into these days.

After a while he stirred himself. There was a small washstand holding a bowl and a jug of cold water in the room, but the bathroom was at the end of the corridor and shared by anyone staying at the club. There were ten guest rooms in all, but only half of these were normally occupied at any one time.

He swung his legs out of bed on the side opposite to the mess. He'd have to clear it up before he went out. A housemaid came in every day to clean and straighten the rooms, but he had been warned by the manager of the establishment that if she reported finding puddles of vomit one more time he would be asked to leave the premises. Silly little scut. He straightened his aching back and glared around the room. It was her job to clean up after paying guests like himself, wasn't it? To hell with her. To hell with all women.

He left the club at four o'clock and made straight for the barbers where he had a shave and a spruce-up. From there he made his way to a fashionable little café favoured by the young blades and those such as he, a place where gossip and character assassination was the order of the day. Ordering his first bottle of wine, he sat and drank it at one of the tables outside, half-asleep in the sunshine. He was about to call for a second bottle when he was clapped on the back by one of a group of young men who joined him, pulling up chairs and sitting down as they shouted to the proprietor to bring more bottles and glasses.

'Toby, old fellow. We thought we might find you here.' Rupert Forester-Smythe was all smiles, and as the owner of the café bustled out he took an opened bottle of wine from him and filled Toby's glass to the brim.

The talk was inconsequential at first; it was only when Rupert refilled Toby's glass that he said, 'Saw your wife today, by the way. Did you know she was at the rally in Hyde Park? I'd have thought you'd have kept a tighter rein on her, old fellow. Doesn't do to let their heads be filled with all this nonsense about women's rights and the rest of it.'

Toby peered at Forester-Smythe. He had never liked the man, mainly because he felt that as far as Forester-Smythe was concerned, he was an object of ridicule. The man had a way of making fun of folk and sometimes his derision was downright nasty. Did he know Sophy had thrown him out? Word was getting about. It would be just like him to rub a man's nose in it. He drank half of his glass of wine before he said, 'Nothing to do with me. I've had enough of her whoring. Washed my hands of her.'

'Is that so?' Rupert topped up Toby's glass. 'Now that's a shame as I had a little proposition to put to you regarding the fair lady.'

'Proposition?'

'I thought you might persuade her to come to one of the supper clubs after the show tonight, one with a private room for a little . . . entertainment? She seems a spirited young baggage and I'm sure she could accommodate us all in turn without too much trouble.'

Toby stared at him. He knew what went on in some of these private rooms, he'd even been to one or two such escapades in his time. 'She wouldn't listen to me. We're— I'm staying at my club.'

'I see. Now that's disappointing, very disappointing. I, we' – his nod took in the group of smiling men – 'would be prepared to pay handsomely for such pleasure as I'm sure she can give, but if you don't think you can oblige us . . .'

Toby's lower jaw moved from one side to the other as he thought rapidly. She'd thrown him out, humiliated him, ruined his life. He had been doing all right until he'd married her, and then it had been like she'd put a curse on him. She'd stood by when the theatres had refused to give him parts tailormade for him and hadn't lifted a finger, and why? Because she was too busy having her fun with every Tom, Dick or Harry. He knew. He wasn't as stupid as she thought he was. As for Gregory, she'd been his mistress for years, he could see it all now. She'd kept the man sweet and feathered her own nest along the way, and what did he – her lawful husband – have? A stinking room in his club and a notice of her intention to divorce him.

He glanced at Rupert. 'How much is handsomely?'

Rupert smiled. He knew when he'd nailed his man. 'Name your price, old fellow.'

Toby nodded. 'All right, but like I said, she wouldn't listen to me, supper club or no supper club. I've another suggestion, however.'

'Oh yes? I'm all ears.'

Toby reached into his pocket and held aloft a key. 'This opens my front door. You could be waiting for her when she gets back from the theatre and who's to say she didn't invite you home with her?'

Rupert liked it. If the baggage complained, it would be his word against hers that she hadn't been game for a bit of hanky-panky, and who would take the side of an actress? They were teasers, all of them, and this one in particular. He was itching to bring her down a peg or two. She wouldn't be so haughty when they'd finished with her.

'She has a maid–cum–housekeeper living in – you'd have to deal with her.'

One of the other men guffawed. 'An ageing crone? We met her this morning, didn't we, Rupert,' he added slyly.

Rupert scowled. His stomach was still tender from the steel tip of Sadie's parasol. 'We'll deal with her, all right – we might even allow her to watch the fun. So' – his hand reached for the key but Toby held it just out of reach – 'what's your price?'

An hour later the deal was done and Toby had his blood money. Rupert and his cronies had sauntered off, glancing back at him once and then sniggering as one of them murmured something. Toby watched them go as he finished the last of the wine they had left. Let them look down their aristocratic noses at him, he thought morosely. He didn't care. If any of them traced their family tree back far enough they'd find they came from murderers and rapists and scoundrels; the aristocracy was littered with dubious ancestors.

His fingers caressed the wad of notes in his pocket contentedly. Tonight, he could go and see Chan. Chan's place was a cut above some of the other opium dens and he provided a degree of privacy if you could pay for it. And he could. But first he needed a drink, a proper drink. Whisky. Or brandy perhaps. He could afford a good malt.

He stood to his feet, holding on to the back of his chair to steady himself once he was upright and then tottered off in the direction of a public house he frequented, swaying slightly as he walked.

The proprietor of the café watched him go, shaking his head slightly. How could someone who was married to one of the most successful and beautiful actresses in the theatre end up like that? But that was the demon drink for you. So thinking, he gathered up the plethora of empty wine bottles and glasses and, humming a merry tune to himself, walked back into the cafe.

Sophy left the theatre immediately after the last curtain call without bothering to change or remove her stage make-up. She wanted to get home and lie in the hot bath Sadie always had waiting for her when she walked in. It was times like tonight when she realised she still wasn't completely well, even though all visible signs of the attack which had left her dangerously ill for some time were gone. But it wasn't just that, or even the tiring day and the confrontation with those awful men when they were leaving the park earlier that had her feeling tired and depressed. She had had a letter from Patience yesterday in which her cousin informed her she was expecting a baby. And she was glad for Patience, genuinely glad – but it had brought home that such an avenue was now closed to her.

She had read the letter twice and then put it away and refused to think about it, but tonight every word Patience had written was printed on her mind.

We're thrilled, of course, and William has already gone out and bought the most splendid perambulator, even though the baby isn't due until October. In truth I am so surprised I can scarcely take it in. I suppose I had never thought I would be a mother, Sophy. It is something so wonderful, so womanly, and I have never felt worthy for such a role. But William thinks I will be an excellent mother, and as he is always right about everything . . .

In spite of how she was feeling, a small smile touched Sophy's lips. Dear Patience. No one could doubt that her cousin's marriage was a love-match. Lucky baby, to be born into such a happy home.

She had been so lost in her thoughts she hadn't realised they'd reached the house until the driver of the cab jumped down from behind the horse and opened the carriage door.

'Here we are then, Mrs Shawe,' he said cheerfully, helping her down onto the cobbled pavement. Sophy was one of his regulars and he liked her, not least because she always tipped well. 'Another minute or two and you'll be able to put your feet up.'

'Thank you, George.' Over the months and years he'd been collecting her from the evening performances at whichever theatre she was playing at, she'd found out he had ten children, thirty-nine grandchildren and two great-grandchildren, and knew most of the goings-on in their lives. She always sent George and his long-suffering wife a large hamper at Christmas, knowing most of their brood descended on them Christmas Day and that money was tight.

After paying him, she said goodnight and let herself into the house, wondering why the hall was in darkness. Calling Sadie's name, she opened the door of the drawing room and stepped into the room. Several things happened in quick succession. As she took in Sadie sitting between two young men, one of whom had his hand across her mouth, someone grabbed her from behind. She uttered a piercing scream which brought another man out of the shadows on the far side of the room, saying, 'Shut her up, for crying out loud.'

As the two men who had been waiting behind the door tried to hold on to her, she screamed again, twisting and turning in their hands and kicking out with all her strength. She managed one more scream before the hand came across her mouth and nose in an iron grip, a voice in her ear saying laughingly, 'She's a real little wild cat, this one. She'll take some taming.'

She recognised Rupert Forester-Smythe as he came towards her and her terror increased. She knew why these men were here and what they were about to do. Her frantic eyes met Sadie's for a moment. This couldn't be happening. Not here, in her own home.

When the front door burst open and George charged into the room wielding the heavy wooden cudgel he kept tucked behind his seat, Sophy was on the verge of fainting. The hand across her face was cutting off her air supply.

George didn't wait to ask any questions. He brought the lethal-looking weapon straight down on the head of one of the men holding Sophy and he went down like a stone, and as Sophy jerked herself free of the second man George struck him too, causing him to stagger backwards with blood pouring from his smashed nose and teeth. George wasn't a small man and he was built like a wrestler and as tough as old boots, neither did he hold to fighting within the constriction of the Queensberry Rules.

The two men who had been holding Sadie had jumped to their feet but seemed uncertain as to what to do, and as Rupert shouted, 'Get him! Get him!' they still hesitated, clearly intimidated by the fury and prowess of the man in front of them. Rupert had grabbed his walking-stick, which he brought with a thwack round the side of George's shoulders, and as the other two men made to join him, one was hit from behind with a heavy vase which Sadie had picked up and used with unerring accuracy.

George was bellowing like an enraged bull and as he swiped wildly with the thick club and caught Rupert on the arm, the crack of bone and Rupert's shriek of pain added to the mayhem.

Leaving their two cronies who were out cold on the floor, Rupert and the other two who could still walk fled the scene, with George following them and still aiming blows halfway up the street, before he turned and ran back to the house. By now the neighbours either side of the house had been alerted and were on the doorstep, and lights had gone on in several other residences.

It was ten minutes before someone returned with two burly constables. By then, Sophy and Sadie were sitting swathed in blankets on one of the sofas drinking a cup of tea that Mrs Webb, from next door, had made. George was standing guard over the two unconscious men who were still stretched out on the carpet amidst blood and splintered pieces of fine Meissen porcelain, a couple of the neighbours at his elbow.

The two constables surveyed the scene in front of them as Sophy explained what had happened, and then looked at George who was still holding the cudgel in case one of his victims came to and attempted to make a run for it. 'We could do with you on the force, mate,' one said dryly.

George didn't smile. 'Thank God I was checking one of Maggie's hooves and hadn't driven straight off, else I might not have known anything was amiss.'

Sophy echoed the sentiment. But for George this night might have ended very differently. Now the danger was over, she found she couldn't stop shaking.

Over the next hour or two the assailants were taken away in the police wagon to hospital, statements were taken and descriptions given of the three men who had escaped. The fact that Sophy knew the name of one of them caused the constables to smile in satisfaction. They were solid, working-class men and had little time for the idle Hooray Henrys of the world, especially those who abused their position and wealth.

It was four o'clock in the morning before everyone left, and Sophy and Sadie sat looking at each other in the kitchen where Sadie had made the umpteenth pot of tea of the night. 'And you say they came in using a key?' Sophy asked for the third time in as many minutes. 'But how? Where would they have got it and how did they know it was the key to this house?'

Sadie bit her lip. Sophy wasn't a stupid woman, far from it, and it had been clear the way the constables' minds had been working when she'd told them about the key and they had asked all those questions about Mr Shawe, but Sophy was shutting her eyes to it. Deciding plain speaking was in order, she said gently, 'As far as I know there's only you, me and Mr Shawe who's got a key to the house, ma'am. I've got mine and you've got yours, so . . .'

'No.'

'I think it's a possibility we have to consider.'

'No.' Sophy was working the fingers of her left hand into the skin of her throat, and becoming aware of this, she made herself stop. Toby was weak and foolish and had become increasingly unpredictable and violent over the latter days of their marriage, but he would never do anything like this to her. He wouldn't. It was unthinkable. There was a different explanation, there had to be.

'No,' she said for the third time. 'I know him, Sadie, and all his faults, but this? He wouldn't.'

Sadie made no reply. She felt in her water that Mr Shawe was behind this and her water was never wrong. She was going to send for Mr Gregory in the morning and ask him to arrange for the front door to be mended and the locks changed, and see what he said. Herself, she wouldn't put anything past Toby Shawe. If ever a man was going to hell riding on a handcart, it was him. But Sophy wouldn't see it, she'd never see it.

Toby was woken by something furry running over his face. He opened his eyes and stared into the inquisitive ones of the rat for a moment before it scampered off. And then the pain hit. In every part of his body. Whimpering in his throat and in agony he tried to move but it was beyond him. And then he remembered. The men he'd been chatting with in the Horseman's Hounds, they'd followed him when he'd left to go to Chan's. They had knocked him to the ground and gone through his pockets, and when he'd tried to get up they'd used their feet on him, kicking and stamping and jumping. The pain brought a red mist in front of his eyes as he tried to take a breath and the metallic smell of blood was in his nostrils.

He must have lost consciousness again because when he next became aware of anything beyond the excruciating pain, it was the rat just inches from his face. His eyes, which seemed to be the only thing he could move without passing out, took in several more browny-grey shapes behind the leader.

The shout he tried to muster was merely a soft gurgle in his tortured throat, and when the big male, bolder than the rest, took a tentative bite from the piece of flesh nearest to it – Toby's bloody arm – he could see the yellow teeth as they fastened on his body.

Chapter 20

Kane stared at the policeman. 'You want *me* to tell her that? Why me? Can't you or one of the others do it?'

The Inspector shuffled his feet. 'We thought it might be kinder coming from you, sir. That's all.'

Kinder? Kane ran a hand through his hair. How did you break the news to a wife – and Sophy was still Toby's wife, or his widow, to be exact – that her husband had been found beaten to death in a squalid, filthy alley and half-eaten by rats? Moreover, this was the same husband who had virtually sold her to be raped and goodness knows what just days ago. *He* had been barely able to believe the statements made by the two men George had apprehended; how it had affected Sophy he didn't dare to imagine. And now all five men involved were in custody.

Kane looked into the Inspector's eyes. They were world-weary but kind. 'I suppose you see this sort of thing every day of the week?'

'Not quite like this, no, sir.' The Inspector didn't go on to say that this case had shocked even the most seasoned policeman among them. 'If you would prefer me to speak to Mrs Shawe . . .'

'No, I'll tell her. Does Sadie, the housekeeper, know?'

'Not yet, sir.'

'Then I'll see her first and have her with me when I speak to Mrs Shawe.'

'As you think best, sir.'

Think best? How could there be any best in this hornet's nest? It seemed he was forever destined to bring the woman he loved the worst kind of news. When Sadie had sent the note explaining that Sophy had been attacked in her own home four days ago, he had been on the doorstep within the hour. He had still been there when the Inspector and a police constable had arrived bearing the news that the men in custody had confessed to the crime and implicated Toby in the matter of the key. Sophy had listened to what they had to say without uttering a word, and had spoken only in monosyllables after they had left. And that had set the pattern thereafter. As far as Sadie was aware, Sophy hadn't wept or broken down since the incident, nor mentioned Toby's name. In fact, she'd barely spoken at all and would see no one besides himself, and George, when the latter had called to see how she was, the day after the attack. It was worrying. In truth, he was worried to death and didn't know what to do about it, nor how to reach her.

The Inspector cleared his throat and Kane came out of his thoughts, saying quickly, 'I'll go and see Sadie now before Mrs Shawe comes down. Thank you, Inspector. Are you going to stay around for a while?'

'I don't think so, sir. There's nothing more we can do at the moment.'

Kane nodded, and once he had shown the policeman out he walked through to the kitchen where Sadie was preparing a break-fast-cum-lunch for Sophy. It was eleven o'clock in the morning. Sadie had confided in him the day before that Sophy stayed up until three or four in the morning since the attack, only going to bed when she was so exhausted she couldn't keep her eyes open. 'It's awful, Mr Gregory,' Sadie had whispered. 'She paces.'

'She does what?' he'd asked.

'Paces. You know – walks backwards and forwards, but not just once or twice. It goes on for hours. She sends me to bed, but how can I sleep when I know the state she's in? I sit on the stairs until

I see the drawing-room light go off and then I nip to my room. This can't go on. Not without her losing her mind. You have to do something.'

He had stared at Sadie, utterly at a loss. He was still at a loss.

Sadie had stopped what she was doing as he walked into the kitchen and was now looking at him with fearful eyes. 'What did the Inspector say?'

'They've found Mr Shawe's body.'

'He's dead?' Hearing the relief in her own voice, Sadie quickly added, 'How? When?'

'It appears he was flashing a wad of notes around in a public house the night Forester-Smythe and his motley crew came here. That's what the landlord of the public house told the police anyway. I would imagine a person or persons unknown took note and followed him when he left the Horseman's Hounds.' Kane shrugged. 'What happened then is fairly clear. No money was found on the body so it's a straightforward case of robbery.'

'Where – where was he?'

'In an alley.' A muscle clenched in Kane's jaw. 'He had been beaten ferociously. They can't say if he was still alive when the rats found him.'

Sadie stared at him in horror. 'Rats? Oh my, oh my.' She had a terror of any kind of rodent. 'That's terrible, just terrible. I mean, I know he was a wicked so-and-so, Mr Gregory, but to go like that . . . Well, it don't bear thinking about.'

Kane stilled his tongue. He had had murder in his heart for the last four days, but someone had saved him the job.

After a moment, Sadie raised her eyes. 'That's what the Inspector has come to tell her?'

Kane nodded. 'But he's asked me to do the job and I want you present, Sadie. To tell you the truth, I have no idea how this latest news is going to affect her, but – but I'm worried.'

'She's not herself, that's for sure,' Sadie agreed, 'but is it any wonder?' They stared at each other helplessly for a moment. 'The poor lamb, and her that wouldn't hurt a fly. This has never been a happy house, Mr Gregory, but I don't need to tell you that.

You've got eyes in your head. But this, this is something beyond . . .'

When words failed her, Kane finished, 'Beyond belief, Sadie. Most definitely beyond belief.'

'I'll be with you, sir, and you know I'll look after her all right. She'll get through this. She's stronger than she looks – she's had to be.' Sadie was remembering the words Toby had shouted at Sophy the day he had punched her in the face – wicked words about Sophy's mother. They might or might not be true, and she would never dream of mentioning it to the woman who had lifted her out of a life of drudgery and despair and brought her into an existence that was comfort itself; she didn't even know if Sophy realised she had heard what Toby Shawe had said, but if it was true, it would explain a lot. Sophy never talked about her life before she came to London, never mentioned family or friends from that time. Yes, it would explain a lot.

Thinking that Sadie's words related to the life Toby had led Sophy, Kane nodded again. 'Yes, she's strong, but this on top of Cat . . . well, it would be enough to turn the strongest person's reason.'

'She has her work, sir.'

Kane closed his mouth against the words in his mind. Her work. Always her work. Damn her work. He wanted her to lean on *him*, to look to *him* for comfort and sustenance, but of course it was not the time to say it. He drew in a deep breath which caused his waistcoat to expand then slowly sink back into place as he said quietly, 'Quite so, and I know I can trust you to take care of her.'

Their eyes met for a moment in total understanding.

'That you can, Mr Gregory. And all things pass. That's what my old mother used to say and she was right. All things pass. There'll come a day when all this will be behind her.'

He wanted, he *needed* to believe that. A grain of hope was better than no hope at all.

Sophy watched the Police Inspector leave the house from her vantage point at the bedroom window, one part of her mind noting how the sunshine lit up the bald spot on top of his head. He was a nice man, the Inspector. Stolid, fatherly.

Her gaze moved to the trees in the square opposite, their green leaves fluttering in the light breeze. All the May blossom had fallen now, the last of it blown away by the strong winds which had seen the month out. Today, though, the wind was simply a gentle caress as befitted a summer's day in June. Her eyes followed a young nursemaid in her black and white uniform entering the square holding two small children by their hands. The little girls looked to be twins and were dressed in flouncy white dresses, straw bonnets sitting on their heads below which fair ringlets bounced as they walked.

She must write to Patience and congratulate her; she should have done it by return. Patience would expect that. And she should send her something for the baby; a bassinet perhaps? And some flowers for Patience.

She glanced at the tiny gold watch pinned to the front of her bodice and told herself she should go downstairs. Kane had arrived some time ago, a good half-hour before the Inspector. It was rude not to make the effort to see him. But still she continued to sit by the window as her tired mind took refuge in inconsequentials.

When Sadie knocked on the bedroom door and then popped her head round it, saying, 'Mr Gregory's here, ma'am, and I've done a light lunch for the pair of you,' Sophy stood up resignedly. She didn't allow herself to wonder why the Inspector had called, because to do so would pierce the protective bubble.

'Thank you, Sadie. Would you tell him I'll be down directly, please?' she said, before smoothing her hair in the mirror.

Kane stood up as she entered the drawing room, coming across to take her hands as he said quietly, 'How are you this morning?'

'I am well.'

She didn't look well. Her amber eyes had lost their light and the pale creamy skin of her face seemed as if it had been drawn tight over the bones beneath it.

His voice even softer, Kane said, 'Sit down a moment before we go through to the dining room. I want to talk to you.'

When Sadie didn't leave the room but moved close to the sofa where Kane had drawn her, Sophy stiffened. She wanted to say, 'Whatever you're about to tell me, I don't want to hear it,' but instead she sat down and didn't remove her cold hands from Kane's warm ones when he seated himself beside her.

'The Inspector called a short while ago.' Kane waited for a response and when none was forthcoming, added, 'He had some news about Toby.' He felt her fingers jerk slightly as he said the name. Otherwise she could have been cast in stone.

'I'm sorry, Sophy,' he said gently. 'They've found his body. It seems he must have been set upon the same night as the incident here.' And then, in case she didn't understand in her present state, he added, 'He's dead.'

Sophy's gaze moved from his face to Sadie's and then back again. She knew they were waiting for a reaction. Tears, perhaps – he had been her husband, after all. Or maybe anger. Through the numbness which blanketed her mind, she said, 'I see. Where was he found?'

'In an alley. The police are sure he's been there all this time while they've been looking for him.' He didn't add that the Inspector had remarked that the body would be there still, but for the smell which had become overpowering.

Sophy tried to think what she should ask. 'Do they know who was responsible?'

Kane shook his head. 'The Inspector said they'll do everything they can, but reading between the lines I don't think he is particularly hopeful of tracing the perpetrators.'

Again she said, 'I see.'

'I'm meeting the Inspector later.' The body had to be formally identified but the Inspector had told him it was a grisly sight for even the strongest stomach, and they had agreed Sophy shouldn't be put through such an ordeal. The police had found an outstanding account from Toby's club in one of the jacket pockets, along with a couple of other papers that confirmed who the victim was. There was also an initialled signet ring. 'At the police morgue,' he added when Sophy's brows wrinkled.

241

'Oh, yes, of course. But shouldn't it be me?'

'That's not necessary. It's merely a formality.'

For the first time there was a touch of animation in her voice when she said, 'I can't put upon you like that, it's not fair.' First Cat and now Toby; he shouldn't have to do both identifications.

'Nonsense, what are friends for?' And when she opened her mouth to object again, he said, 'It's all arranged and you'll have enough to do over the next little while.'

He meant the funeral. Another funeral, another coffin being lowered into the ground. And people would expect her to play the heartbroken widow. 'I hate him, Kane.' She hadn't meant to say it, it had just popped out. But now she repeated it. 'I hate him.'

'Oh, ma'am, you don't really—'

Kane cut off Sadie's voice. 'That is understandable and perfectly natural in the circumstances,' he said quietly.

'Perhaps, but it's not right, is it?' Sophy stood up, walking over to the window and standing looking out with her back to the room. 'It frightens me how much I hate him, if I let myself think about it. I've wished him dead the last few days, not once but many times.'

'Again, no one would blame you for that.'

She turned to look at him then. 'Oh, but they would. When someone dies they acquire sainthood. Isn't that how it works? But he was a weak, vicious and cruel man and I don't intend to pretend a grief I don't feel. It will offend people.'

'Not me.'

A glimmer of a smile touched her pale lips. 'No, not you.'

Sadie was finding this conversation difficult to deal with. Toby Shawe had been a devil, that much was for sure, and this last act of his in sending those men to the house had been wickedness itself, but to speak ill of the dead in this way was asking for trouble. She cleared her throat. 'I'll go and bring the things to the dining room, it's all ready.'

'Thank you, Sadie.' Once Sadie had left the room, Sophy looked at Kane. 'That's the first person I've offended.'

'Don't worry about it.'

Worry about it? She didn't think she would ever worry about anything again if this numbness held. Even the hate for Toby had become a thing of the intellect rather than the heart. She wanted to sleep, to lay her head on the pillow and never wake up, never have to deal with this evil, horrible world where good people like Cat could meet such a terrible end and someone whom you had loved and trusted with all your heart could betray you so completely. She would never put her faith in a man again.

Looking at her, Kane was pretty sure he knew what she was thinking. Walking across to the window, he stood in front of her but without touching her or taking her hands. 'It's a cliché, I know, and I hate clichés, but time really is a great healer, my dear. I've proved it in my own life. You're tired and spent now, and no wonder, but you will recover from this and be the stronger for it.'

The words of understanding were almost too much. They were weakening and she couldn't afford to be weak. There was a second's pause before Sophy stepped away from him, and her voice was cool when she said, 'Lunch is ready. And I shall return to the theatre today, Kane. I've been away long enough.'

'No one will expect that, not in the circumstances.'

She turned with her hand on the door knob. 'I know it isn't seemly, Kane. Certainly not before the funeral. But from this moment on, I'm going to do what *I* see fit. My friends won't understand, but those who are really my friends will take me as I am. The others . . .' She shrugged her slim shoulders.

It was rare Kane didn't know what to say but this was one of those times. He wanted to gather her up in his arms, to tell her all men weren't the same and he would give his life for her without a moment's hesitation, that he wanted to protect and cherish and love her.

Instead he nodded, and as she led the way to the dining room, he felt a weight descend on his heart. It was only now he admitted to himself that when the Inspector had told him of Toby's death he had felt a surge of elation that she was free and the way was now open to him. In reality, asking her to look on him as anything more than a friend was now further away than ever.

Chapter 21

Patience sat at the breakfast-table in a state of shock, staring at the letter she had just opened and read. When William said, 'What is it, my love? Are you unwell?' she simply thrust Sophy's letter into his hand.

She watched his eyes scan the words written on the single piece of paper before she said, 'I have to go to her, William. Now, today.'

William looked at her in alarm. Although they were both thrilled about the baby, the pregnancy had been a far from easy one. The chronic sickness in the first four months had been so debilitating it had frightened him, even though Patience had remained cheerful throughout. That had eased in latter weeks and she was now able to eat normally again, but she was nothing but skin and bone, apart from the gently rounded swell of her belly. 'I don't think that's wise. She's said here the funeral is over and done with, so I really don't see why you need to make such a journey in your condition. You can write, send flowers. She'll understand.'

Patience smiled. He was a dear and she loved him with all her heart, but for a medical man he wasn't handling the problems of her condition very well. Perhaps it was because he *was* a doctor and knew what could go wrong? But she felt well now, better than she had in a long time actually. 'I must go,' she said again. 'It's not just that Sophy has lost her husband but the circumstances – well, it's horrific, William. What must she be feeling? And it was only a little while ago she wrote about the murder of her friend.'

'Darling, you need to build your strength up and do nothing more strenuous than sit in the garden each day at this time. Think of the baby.'

'I think of the baby *all* the time.' She took his hand across the table. 'And I'm not ill, William. Just expecting a child. I understand your concern and I promise I'll be sensible, but I have to go to her and perhaps stay for a while until she's a little better.'

'You don't know she isn't all right.'

'Oh yes, I do. The way she's written, it's – well, it's not Sophy. And people need family at such desperate times.'

'But you hadn't seen each other for years until we met by accident.'

Patience lowered her gaze to their joined hands. 'I know,' she said softly. 'And I was deeply unhappy about that. I – I've always felt so guilty about how I behaved towards her until we went to school. I was hateful, William. A little beast. And perhaps if I'd been different, Mother wouldn't have thought she could get away with so much.'

'Now don't get upset. And I have to say hand on heart that nothing you could have done or said would have influenced your mother's actions.' In truth, he thought his mother-in-law unbalanced and was thankful they had little to do with her.

'Perhaps.'

William looked into her eyes and sighed. 'Come on, no tears. Dry your eyes. If you are going to go I will come with you and fetch you when you want to come home, all right? And you must take Tilly with you.' Tilly was their housekeeper, a widow who had never had children of her own, which was a pity because she was a warm, motherly soul.

'But Sophy might not have room—'

'If Tilly doesn't go, you don't go.'

Patience tried one last time. 'But how will you manage?'

'Perfectly well. I shall eat at my club and Maud will see to the house.' Maud was Tilly's sister who lived close by and came each day for a few hours to do the washing and ironing and any other jobs Tilly designated. Maud's husband, a miner, had been severely injured in a fall at the pit some years ago, and the generous wage William paid her had made all the difference to their standard of living. 'But don't stay away too long.'

Patience stood up, walking round to her husband's chair and putting her arms round him as she rested her chin on the top of his head. 'Thank you,' she said tenderly. 'You're a wonderful man.'

'And flattery will get you no more concessions.'

When Sadie answered the knock at the door in the late afternoon, she stared in surprise at the well-dressed couple standing on the doorstep, another woman peering out of the horse-drawn cab standing at the kerb. 'Can I help you?'

'I've come to see my cousin, Mrs Shawe. My name is Patience Aldridge and this is my husband, Dr Aldridge. She wrote to me about – about what's happened.'

'I'm afraid Mrs Shawe's at the theatre but if you would like to come in?' Sadie stood aside as the couple entered the house, and when she glanced at them and then back at the woman in the cab, it was William who said, 'My wife was wondering if Mrs Shawe would like her to stay for a few days. Family, you know? And due to my wife's condition, I was insistent our housekeeper accompanied her. I have to get home immediately, I'm afraid.'

Sadie thought quickly. She remembered Sophy saying something about a cousin who was expecting a baby about the time all the trouble occurred, but other than that she had no idea who this person was. Sophy never discussed her past. But she couldn't very well say that.

'How is she?' Patience had taken a step forward. 'Really, I mean?'

Making a swift decision, Sadie said, 'Mrs Shawe would tell you she is all right, ma'am, but to my mind she's far from well. I think you staying for a bit would be just the ticket, if you don't mind me saying so.'

Patience's thin shoulders relaxed. 'Then that's what I'll do. And there's room for Tilly?'

'Of course, ma'am.'

The next few minutes were all bustle. The cab driver helped William bring Patience's and Tilly's bags into the house, and then Patience and William said a fond farewell and he set off back to the train station in the same cab. Blessing the fact that on Sophy's instructions, Toby's bedroom had been emptied of all his possessions, and new curtains and bedlinen bought in a pale lemon shade as befitted a guest room, Sadie placed Patience's bags in it. Tilly was to have the other, smaller room, similar to hers, at the back of the house.

A few minutes later when she brought a tea tray into the drawing room Tilly jumped up, saying, 'Let me help you with that, lass. And I'll be obliged if you allow me to help you with the load, us turning up like this. I can't abide sittin' twiddlin' my thumbs.'

The two women smiled at each other, each liking what the other saw, and Patience relaxed a little more. She didn't want to tread on anyone's toes, least of all Sophy's servant's.

By the time Sophy returned home from the theatre after her evening performance, Patience had been acquainted with the full facts concerning the happenings of three weeks ago, along with the life Toby had led his wife before the fateful night. She had listened open-mouthed, hardly able to believe what she was hearing, and then cried a little. But when Sophy walked in the door, Patience was calm and composed.

'Patience?' Sophy stared at her cousin in amazement as Patience rose from her comfy chair where she had been reading and came across to hug her. 'What are you doing here?'

The two embraced, Patience holding Sophy tight for a long moment before she murmured, 'I had to come as soon as I heard. I'm so deeply sorry, Sophy. William, too. He sends his fondest love and said if there's anything he can do . . .'

'Where is he?' Sophy glanced about her as though she expected William to leap out from behind the furniture.

'He brought me here but he had to go straight home, due to

work commitments. I thought I would stay on for a few days, if that is convenient?'

Sophy was stunned. The last person in the world she'd expected to see sitting in her drawing room was Patience, and to be truthful she didn't know how she felt about having her here. She spoke to few people these days, and then only when it was absolutely necessary. She rose even later in the mornings than she'd been accustomed to, went to the theatre and said her lines and returned home straight after the performance. In the interval between the matinée and evening show, she kept her dressing-room door closed and discouraged visitors. She knew she had retreated into herself and that Kane and Sadie, probably others too, were worried about her, but it was the only way she could cope. She didn't want to see anyone and she didn't need anyone. She wouldn't let herself *ever* need anyone again.

Politely, she said, 'Of course you must stay,' but with no enthusiasm in her voice.

Ignoring the tone, Patience said, 'Thank you.'

Sadie knocked on the door and then came in with the usual tray of sandwiches and coffee which Sophy ate on returning from the theatre, Tilly following behind with a similar one for Patience. Patience introduced Tilly, explaining it had been William who insisted the housekeeper accompany her, and after the two servants had left the room, Sophy looked more intently at her cousin. 'You've lost weight.'

'I couldn't keep anything down for what seemed a lifetime.' Patience smiled, her hand unconsciously going to her swollen abdomen, and as Sophy's gaze followed the action she became aware for the first time of the mound beneath Patience's loose-fitting dress.

Fascinated, she found she couldn't tear her eyes away. 'How many more weeks are there to go?'

'Eleven or so, but the way it kicks and moves about I wouldn't be surprised if it comes early. It seems impatient to see the world. It's kicking now. Do you want to feel?'

Without waiting for a reply, Patience took Sophy's hand and

placed it over the baby, who obligingly kicked for all it was worth. Sophy froze, but inside her something was happening to the lead weight plugging her emotions as though the core of it was melting. 'Don't be in a hurry to be born into this world, little baby,' she whispered, so softly Patience could barely make out the words. 'Stay where you're safe and warm and protected.'

The baby kicked again and now Sophy removed her hand to cover her eyes with both hands. She felt as though she was drowning in pain made up of a sadness and despair that came from the depth of her. It was cracking her ribs, a flood of molten misery that had its origins before Toby's betrayal, before Cat's death, even before finding out the truth of her parentage. It was the hurt and helplessness of a small child knowing itself to be unloved, of knowing it didn't belong to anyone, that it was scorned and held as undesirable, but without knowing why.

When the release came it was on a wailing cry which brought Sadie and Tilly running from the kitchen. Sophy was aware of Patience's arms about her, of Sadie's voice saying, 'She hasn't cried, that's the thing. It's not good if you don't cry, is it? This'll do her good in the long run, you mark my words,' but she was beyond responding.

After some minutes, the nurse in Patience took control. Still cradling Sophy in her arms, she looked up at Sadie. 'Has she been prescribed anything to help her sleep?'

'The doctor gave her some pills but she won't take them.'

'She'll take them tonight,' said Patience grimly. 'Go and fetch them, please, with a glass of warm milk, and once they begin to take effect we'll get her upstairs. I'll stay with her tonight – she mustn't be left.'

It was another few minutes before Sadie and Tilly half-carried Sophy to her bedroom where they undressed her like a child and got her into bed, a stone hot-water bottle at her feet. Patience came into the room a minute or two later in her nightdress, by which time Sophy's crying had diminished to the odd hiccuping sob.

'She'll be all right, ma'am, won't she?' said Sadie, tears in her voice after Patience had thanked the two women for their help and told them she would take over now.

'Of course she will. Didn't you say yourself this will do her good?' said Patience briskly, although she wasn't feeling as confident as she sounded. This breakdown, if that's what it was and she rather thought so, wasn't just a result of the last few months, although no doubt they'd brought it to a head. She had been horrified when Sadie had confided what Sophy's husband had put her through since their marriage, and of course Sadie wouldn't know all of it. And this last act of his, the utter callousness of selling his wife to be made sport of by a group of young men – well, how did a woman recover from something like that? But for the cab driver Sophy had befriended, the unthinkable would have happened.

Once Sadie and Tilly had left the room, Patience climbed into bed, saying softly, 'I'm here, Sophy. You're not alone. Try and sleep now, there's a dear,' as she extinguished the light.

She wasn't sure if Sophy was already asleep; she had given her an extra pill, knowing it was safe and would only send her cousin into a deeper sleep which was all to the good in the present circumstances.

But after a moment, a small voice came in the darkness. 'I can't go on, Patience. This is the end. I thought marrying Toby, him loving me, was a new beginning, but it was all a lie from the start.'

'Listen to me.' Patience propped herself up on one elbow as she faced the mound under the coverlet. 'This is only the end of one beginning, that's how you have to think of it. You've made a wonderful life for yourself as a successful actress, you have a lovely home and lots of friends who care about you, not to mention myself and William – and Sadie, of course. What Toby did was unforgivable, but he's paid for it. As William would say, if you live by the sword you are likely to die by it.'

There was another pause before Sophy mumbled tiredly, 'It's not just Toby.'

'I know, my dear. I know.'

'How can you know?' It was a whisper. 'You had a mother and father who loved you, brothers, a family. And then William came along too. I – I've never had anyone who really loves me for who I am.'

'I love you, Sophy. Not just as a cousin but as a sister, a dear sister. Please believe that. And you have so many friends—'

'I don't mean that sort of love.'

'Sophy, you're still young. You'll meet someone else.'

'That's just it. I don't want to.' Through the exhaustion, a fierceness emerged. 'I won't ever put myself in that position again, Patience. I mean it. If you knew what the last years have been like, you'd understand why.'

'But all men aren't like Toby.'

'And how do you know what a person is like until you are married? You can't know, not really. No one can know. There are things you have to take on trust and I can't do that again. I *won't* do it.'

'The way you are feeling now will pass, I promise you. I have nursed people who felt the same for various reasons, and as their bodies and minds healed, so did their emotions. You have been through a terrible ordeal, two terrible ordeals, and those against a background of years of unhappiness. At the moment your mind is saying it can't cope, and no wonder, but as you recover you'll feel differently, my dear.'

Sophy let Patience talk on. She knew Patience meant well, perhaps her cousin thought she was losing her mind – she'd thought the same thing herself – but deep in her heart of hearts she knew the desolation she was feeling would prevail until the day she died. That's why she had fought against feeling anything at all the last weeks. But unexpectedly, in a way she didn't understand, Patience's unborn child had opened Pandora's Box and there was no going back to the state of numbness she'd been existing in.

What she couldn't explain to Patience, to anyone, was the feeling that she should have prevented some of what had happened. She *should* have made Cat ride with her that day; *should* have made Toby seek help for his addictions. The pills were dulling her mind, shutting out Patience's soft voice and relaxing her limbs so that she felt she was sinking right through the bed.

But Toby had never loved her, that was the thing. He had told her that many times over the last few years. If he had loved her, perhaps he would have listened to her. Why hadn't he loved her? she asked herself muzzily. What was it about her that had made her unlovable to her husband, to her aunt and uncle? It had to be something in *her*, her fault . . .

Her last thought before sleep overtook her was the prayer she'd prayed every night since the evening she'd returned home and found Forester-Smythe and his cronies waiting for her: *don't let me wake up, God. Take me while I sleep.*

Patience stayed on in London for six weeks. When Sophy looked back over that time in years to come, she knew she could never repay her cousin for her kindness. It wasn't an exaggeration to say that Patience saved her reason. For the first week, Patience didn't leave her side for a moment, encouraging her to talk out all her hurt and despair, letting her cry when she wanted to, insisting she ate and drank all the tasty meals and soups Sadie and Tilly provided, and making her take the sleeping pills each night.

'You need to rest your mind, dear,' she said, when Sophy protested after the third night. Sadie had told Patience about the pacing. 'In a week or two you won't need them, but just at the moment you do – and you will take them.'

Sophy thought Patience must have been a formidable nurse.

The second week, Sophy was allowed out of bed in the afternoons and she was surprised how this tired her. It was then she began to realise how physically exhausted she had been, and that Patience had been right to dispatch Sadie to the theatre the morning after her collapse with a note informing the manager that Mrs Shawe wouldn't be well enough to return to work for at least a month, possibly two.

The third week, Kane was permitted to call, and a few days later, Dolly and Jim. It touched Sophy that Patience hovered like an anxious hen with one chick the whole time, and by the fifth week Sophy was feeling better than she had in a long, long time.

The day before William was due to take Patience and Tilly home, the four women spent a delightful afternoon shopping for the bassinet Sophy wanted to buy for the baby, along with so many other items, Patience was forced to protest. 'Please let me,' Sophy said quietly, when Patience demurred at the number of tiny outfits in Sophy's arms. 'I feel I am part of the family, doing this.' Patience said no more after that.

The day of departure was bitter-sweet for Sophy. She had known her cousin couldn't stay for ever, and with Patience's baby due in just over a month, it was high time her cousin returned home and prepared for the birth. Also, in the last few days, she had begun to look forward to returning to the theatre and letting life resume its normal pattern. It would signify the beginning of a new chapter in her life. Whereas, just weeks ago, this would have filled her with foreboding, now she found she could look to the future if not with optimism, at least with a clear idea of what she was going to do.

She and Patience had had many long talks over the time they were together. They had talked about Cat and the manner of her death, the danger young women in the theatres and music halls could find themselves in from unwanted admirers and men like Forester-Smythe, the inequality which existed in the world between the sexes and how the Vote for Women would be the first stage of addressing this to some extent. Sophy had told her cousin how Cat and other actresses, dissatisfied with a male-dominated theatre and the manipulation of women, had entered the fight for the vote, sometimes at the cost of their career. And as they had talked, and argued on occasion as Patience did not support the militant tone the Women's Suffrage movement had taken of late, Sophy found her own opinions and views solidifying. Because Cat had cared so passionately about the vote she had gone along with supporting it without really thinking deeply for herself. Her work, the struggle of trying to make her failing marriage succeed, had taken centre stage. But now she *was* thinking for herself and she was angry. And yes, when Patience had gently suggested it, Sophy had agreed she was embittered too. What was more, she didn't intend to apologise for it.

As she stood on the doorstep in the late-summer sunshine waving Patience off, Sophy squared her shoulders. Never again would she let any man reduce her to the state she had been in when Patience had arrived. But that time was gone now: she was better, she wanted to live again. Her life had to have some purpose to it other than entertaining people in the theatre; she not only owed that to herself, she owed it to Cat. She would make a difference. She wasn't quite sure how yet, but that would come.

She had made a great mistake when she had married Toby. She had let love make a fool of her, and in a way she had perpetuated that mistake by trying to be a trusting wife, by supporting him and standing by him when in truth she should have left him years ago. But it was no good looking back. She had learned by her mistake and she wouldn't make the same one twice. She was successful in her own right, she didn't need a man to support her and she certainly didn't need one in her home or in her bed.

The cab disappeared round a corner and Sadie, who was standing just behind her, said, 'Well, ma'am, it's just the two of us again.'

Thank God for Sadie. And that's what she had to do. Count her blessings and get on with life. Turning, she smiled. 'As you say, Sadie, it's just the two of us.'

PART SIX

A Woman of Substance

1909

Chapter 22

On the last day of September, Patience's baby arrived a few days early. The birth had been a difficult one and the labour exhausting, but as soon as Patience saw her son the previous thirty-six hours were swept away in the rush of love she felt for her tiny little boy. Although he was small at six pounds, the baby was perfect and had a fine pair of lungs on him, which he used whenever he wanted feeding or changing. As William remarked after a week, he'd had no idea one so tiny could so quickly have a whole house-hold dancing to his tune.

When Sophy heard the news she would have loved to have been able to make a trip to Sunderland then and there, but having only recently returned to the theatre she felt she couldn't justify such an indulgence. She had to content herself with sending Patience armfuls of flowers and a promise that she would try and travel up to see little Peter William in the New Year.

There had been one or two changes in Sophy's work-life, the main one being Kane taking on the role of her agent. He had recently sold his partnerships in several theatres, along with his travelling company, to take on the new venture as theatrical agent, and it was already proving hugely successful. He had many contacts within the entertainment industry and was extremely well thought of, and within three months his books were full. When asked what had prompted such a move, Kane was non-committal, airily passing off such enquiries by saying he'd felt the need for a change for some time and fresh stimulus. Not even to Ralph would he admit that the prime motive had been a wish to inveigle himself more firmly into Sophy's life.

Sophy had decided to go back to her roots in the theatre. As an established and firm favourite of the West End, she could command a role in any of the major theatres and they would have been delighted to have her, but she felt she wanted to return to the smaller companies which dealt with the taboo subjects such as divorce, sex, women's rights and prostitution, by little-known playwrights as well as established dramatists like Shaw, Ibsen and Barrie. Kane warned her it was something of a risk. Fans could be fickle and there was no guarantee they would follow her on the strength of her name, but she was determined that when her present contract finished at the end of the year, she would consider her next part very carefully and do something meaningful.

She had also taken up Cat's baton with regard to the Vote for Women cause, not just because of her friend or the events of the last months, but because the gross inequality women faced in all walks of life had begun to stir her fighting spirit more and more.

So it was, on a cold mid-December afternoon, she attended the first public meeting of the Actresses' Franchise League which was held at the Criterion Restaurant, a prestigious establishment in the heart of London. Stars of the West End stage arrived dressed to the nines and surrounded by hordes of fans, male and female. It was a truly glittering occasion, and inside the restaurant, four hundred actresses, actors and dramatists listened to numerous telegrams of support from influential men and women of the decade.

The two speakers were both women, but despite the exclusively female membership of the League, the chair was taken by the efficacious actor-manager, Johnston Forbes-Robertson, who was a firm supporter of women's rights. As would be expected at a meeting made up of a good number of men and women from the entertainment industry, including Shakespearean actresses like Ellen

Terry, the darling of the Lyceum Theatre, and comediennes of the calibre of Mrs Kendal, both in their sixties, the speeches were given with flair and a certain amount of facetiousness. However, no one present, including the cynical newspaper reporters, could doubt the genuine passion and determination of those involved.

Sophy had been asked to give a short word of support and she kept it light and amusing – but with a sting in the tail when she asked why the actress's life was a paradox: off stage she could marry and divorce, even take lovers if she was so inclined, but on stage she was expected to play a dutiful wife and daughter or a 'scarlet woman', conventional roles in a predictable mould.

She sat down to a standing ovation, and even Kane – who had escorted her to the event whilst expressing his doubts about Sophy getting too involved in the organisation – had stood to his feet. Sophy enjoyed every minute of the meeting and afterwards, when Kane took her out for a meal before her evening performance at the theatre, had waxed lyrical about her new crusade.

The next day the newspapers had been full with the names of the West End stars who had publicly demanded the vote, and when the manager of the theatre Sophy was presently working at tried to put pressure on her to withdraw from the League, she told him she was going to get more involved, if anything. She wasn't surprised when her contract wasn't renewed, neither was she concerned. Kane had negotiated an excellent part for her as the leading lady in one of the smaller but well-respected theatres, and the part – which kept clear of specific Suffrage party politics and concentrated on the generalised sexual inequalities of Edwardian society – was one she felt she could get her teeth into.

There was a two-week interval between finishing at the present theatre and taking up her part at the General, so on 2 January, the day after thousands of Britons over seventy years of age went to the Post Office to draw their first weekly pension of five shillings, Sophy set off for the north-east with Sadie at her side to keep her promise to Patience. She found she was immensely grateful for Sadie's company; she hadn't expected to feel so nervous about returning home. No, not home, she corrected herself for the umpteenth time as the train steamed its way through the bitterly cold countryside. London was her home now. Southwick was merely the place where she had been born and lived the first sixteen years of her life.

It got colder the further north they travelled, and it had just begun to snow and the darkening sky looked full of it as the train chuffed its way into Central Station. Sophy had been able to eat little on the journey, her stomach tied up in knots. She had left this town thirteen years ago, heartsore and determined never to return, and yet here she was.

She glanced at herself in the train window, her fingers nervously stroking the little silver ballerina brooch Miss Bainbridge had given her and which she wore always. Her grey suit was both expensive and tasteful, and with her fur coat, muff and hat, she looked every inch the wealthy gentlewoman, but that was just on the outside. Inside she felt like the bewildered, frightened young girl who had fled these shores. This, returning home – she didn't check the word this time – was harder than she had expected it to be. She wished now she had accepted Kane's suggestion that he accompany her. His solid support would have been a comfort.

She didn't ask herself why she had refused his offer, she knew that only too well. There could be a chance – remote, maybe, but still a possibility nonetheless – that he might find out about her mother, her beginnings. And she wouldn't be able to bear it if he looked at her differently. She now accepted that something had happened the morning she had gone unannounced to Kane's house. It was then that she had been forced to think of him as a man, rather than her friend and one-time benefactor. She had felt disturbed at the time but she'd pushed her feelings to the back of her mind, having more – as she had put it to herself – important things to think about.

She had never asked him about his private life and would rather die than do so, but at the oddest moments since that morning she found herself imagining him with a woman – any woman – and when she did so, her feelings were plunged into a turmoil of which she was ashamed. Kane had always been so good to her, fatherly even, and she was sure he thought of her as something between a daughter or a fond niece – and a friend, of course. And she was further mortified that this had become increasingly irritating to her. She didn't want any involvement with anyone on a romantic level, she was sure about that after the years of being trapped in a marriage that had been a mockery from the start, so why did it matter how Kane regarded her? It didn't. Of course it didn't. She was being ridiculous and perverse.

She'd imagined she would be able to see him in the way she once had when she'd agreed to his proposal that he become her agent. It would set their relationship on more of a business footing, she had argued to herself, and she had been thinking about employing an agent for some time. Some of the actresses she worked with had agents and some did not, but there was no doubt that a good agent was of considerable benefit to an actress's career. And so she had been all for his suggestion. But it hadn't helped. To be fair to Kane, he was still the kind, benevolent gentleman he'd always been, somewhat patriarchal and protective but he had been well brought up and was that way with all women. At times she sensed a reserve about him, but that had probably been there since she'd known him. Cat had called him enigmatic once, and she had been right. And yet when Patience had stayed with her and Kane had visited, he had seemed more relaxed with her cousin than he ever was with her. To her great chagrin, she had found she was jealous, jealous of dear Patience, and it was then she had told herself enough was enough.

'There's Dr Aldridge, ma'am.' Sadie was peering out of the train window. 'And he's buttonholed one of the porters.'

The next few minutes were hectic but eventually the luggage was loaded on top of the cab William had waiting and the horse was clip-clopping its way through the now fast-falling snow. Sophy looked out at familiar landmarks. She had gone to see Dolly and Jim at Christmas, her arms full of presents, and had confided in the motherly Dolly her apprehension about the visit back to her roots. Dolly's advice had been the usual mixture of homespun commonsense and optimism. 'Blood's thicker than water, lovey, and to my mind it's a blessing you came across your cousin that day. I don't know what you were running away from when you left the north and I don't need to know, but you're your own woman now. It won't do no harm to lay a few ghosts in the long run, even if you're a bit jittery. You go and have a nice time and see that little one. That'll cheer you up.'

Dear Dolly. Sophy smiled to herself. There were some things that never changed, and Dolly was one of them. Every time she walked into that kitchen it was like stepping back thirteen years ago, and she would never forget the old couple's kindness to a petrified young girl who hadn't had a friend in the world.

Patience must have been waiting at the window because as soon as the cab drew up outside the imposing semi-detached house in Barnes View, she was on the doorstep, her face alight. It was a lovely welcome. The six-bedroomed house was also lovely. The garden – what Sophy could see of it under its mantle of white – was lovely, too. But baby Peter, he was exquisite. He had been asleep when she arrived, but as they were finishing the tour of the house he began to stir and Patience took her into the beautifully decorated nursery. With little ado, she whisked the baby out of his bassinet and plonked him straight into Sophy's arms, taking her by surprise. She stared down into the tiny face looking up at her, wonder filling her heart as she saw the minute eyelashes, the little snub nose and blue-grey eyes. A small hand, complete with the tiniest fingernails imaginable plucked at the air for a moment, and then, like a ray of sunshine which brightened the whole room, the baby gave her a big toothless smile.

'There,' said Patience, pretending not to notice the tears in Sophy's eyes, 'he knows his Aunty Sophy already. He doesn't smile for everyone, believe me.'

'He's utterly adorable, Patience, and so beautiful,' said Sophy, her voice husky.

'I know.' Patience smiled happily. 'I still don't know how we managed to have such a pretty baby. If we are fortunate enough to have more, I hope they are as bonny, especially if we have a girl. I always thought it was so unfair I had three good-looking brothers, looking like I do.' And then, as Sophy made to protest, Patience added, 'It's all right, Sophy. I don't mind that I'm plain now, truly, because I know William doesn't see me like that. You know, when I was a young girl and I realised for the first time what sort of a trick nature had played on me, I used to pray that my guardian angel – Father had always taught us that we each had a guardian angel who looked over us – would work a miracle and change me into a beauty while I slept. And each morning I woke up with my heart fluttering and looked in the mirror. I was so jealous of you, not just because you are so beautiful but because I knew everyone – everyone except Mother and Father, of course – preferred you to me. The boys never made a secret of it, and I knew Bridget and Kitty and our governess didn't even like me. Looking back, I can see it wasn't my appearance that was the problem.' She grimaced. 'I was a horrible little beast. And then came the day when Mother beat you half to death and I saw something of myself in her.'

'Oh, Patience.' Sophy didn't know what to say.

'It frightened me. Terrified me. And although I wouldn't have wanted my moment of truth to come at the cost of you nearly dying, it was the lesson I needed. And then we went away to school and I discovered I liked you, but – but I didn't know how to say it, I suppose. When you left after that last row with Mother I missed you terribly, and it was then I realised you'd become the sister I'd always wanted, but it was too late to tell you. And I didn't think you'd have believed me anyway.'

Sophy smiled through her tears. 'I believe you now.'

'We were going to ask you together but I know William won't mind; we want you to be Peter's godmother. Will you, Sophy?'

'Me?' Sophy was astounded.

'Will you? William's best friend is going to be his godfather.'

'But your parents? Your mother won't stand for it.'

A hard look came over Patience's face. 'My mother will have no say one way or the other, but I doubt she will attend. She has already taken offence because we are not holding the christening at Father's church, but William wanted it at the one we go to.'

Sophy's gaze returned to the baby in her arms as Peter gave a little gurgle. He'd won her heart for ever with that first gummy smile. 'I'd love to be his godmother.'

'Good. That's settled. Now bring him downstairs, as I think Tilly's prepared tea and cakes in the drawing room. We can catch up on all the news. Oh, Sophy' – Patience beamed at her – 'we're going to have such a lovely time.'

Sophy did have a lovely time. For the first few days she enjoyed herself helping Patience with the baby, bathing him and putting him to bed. At the weekend, John and Matthew and their wives came to dinner, and both of them invited her back to their respective homes the following week. On the last day before she was due to return to London – a Sunday – Peter's christening was held at the parish church in Bishopwearmouth which Patience and William attended. A family get-together took place afterwards; this included Jeremiah, who had missed the christening, having his own church service to see to.

Sophy was shocked at how old and frail her uncle looked when she saw him. He was approaching seventy, but could easily have been mistaken for a man of eighty years or more. She had been secretly dreading meeting him again, but he simply kissed her cheek and politely asked after her health before retreating to a comfy chair in one of the alcoves bordering the large drawing-room windows. There he sat, surveying the assembled company through the steel pince-nez perched on the end of his nose and saying little to anyone.

It was later in the day after the buffet tea Tilly and Sadie had prepared that Jeremiah approached Sophy. John's twin boys were asleep on her lap, and sitting down beside her on the sofa he said, 'You've a way with children. Those two are little imps usually.'

Sophy's heart was thudding and her mouth dry, but her voice was remarkably steady when she said, 'They're high-spirited, that's all, and very bright, but then their father and uncles are above average intelligence so I suppose it's to be expected.'

'Yes, I suppose it is.' He didn't look at her as he said, 'You have no children, I understand? I'm sorry about that. They would have been a comfort to you after the death of your husband.'

Sophy had agreed with Patience and William at the time of Toby's death that they would merely tell the family her husband had met with an unfortunate accident and leave it at that. Now her voice didn't falter: 'I would have liked children, of course, but my husband's death was not the blow it would have been if we had been happily married. We were separated at the time of his accident.'

She had evidently surprised him as his quick glance at her showed. 'Again, I'm sorry.'

Sophy shrugged. 'In hindsight I made bad choices. The evidence of what he was really like was always there but I ignored it to my cost.'

'Ah, hindsight. I know all about hindsight.' He sighed deeply. 'And bad choices. My life is littered with them. I thought I knew it all when I was a young man, what I wanted to achieve in my life and how to achieve it. Looking back, it was all dross of course – worldly acclaim and so on. This' – he waved his hand at his children and grandchildren – 'is what is important, and it is only by the grace of God I can have a measure of it now. The mysteries of human nature are manifold, and considering our Creator knows exactly what we are like, I find it more amazing as I get closer to meeting Him that He bothers with us at all.'

Now it was Sophy's turn to be surprised. Her uncle had changed and she hadn't expected that.

'I am glad I have seen you again before He calls me home.' For the first time that evening Jeremiah looked her full in the face. 'I want you to know that your mother – my sister – *wasn't* a bad woman at heart. I thought so once, but as I have reflected on it, I realise our parents unwittingly instigated much of her rebellion. I was an easy child to handle – put up the line of least resistance, you know? But Esther was spirited from a baby. My parents were frightened by this, they didn't understand her and so, thinking they were doing the best for their daughter, they imposed so many restrictions that I believe she felt like a caged animal. When she escaped the cage . . .' He sighed again. 'She was a beautiful young girl but innocent when she left the vicarage, ill-prepared for the outside world.'

It was the first time she had been able to talk about her mother. Painfully, she swallowed. 'She . . . she had lovers.'

'Yes, my dear, she did. And I cannot condone that. But let us face facts here. There are women, supposedly happily married, respectable women with a place in society who make a habit of illict relationships. I'm sure you know of one or two. I certainly do. Perhaps your mother was more honest than such as they and this was her downfall.'

'I think you are being kind.'

'If that were so, it's not before time, is it?' His eyes, deep in his sockets, held hers.

She had to ask. 'Did she want me? Was – was she looking forward to having a baby in spite of the circumstances, or – or was she looking at it as a burden?'

Hoping his God would make allowances, Jeremiah put one parchment-dry hand over that of his niece's for a brief moment. 'She wanted you so much she had returned home to make a different life for herself and her child,' he lied softly. 'It wasn't to be, of course, but thankfully Esther didn't know this.'

Sophy had shut her eyes but as a tear seeped from under her closed lids, she whispered, 'Thank you.'

If he had been a stronger man, a better man, Jeremiah would have asked for her forgiveness at this point, but as he himself had said, it was his nature to take the line of least resistance, and in case she should refuse, he didn't obey the prompting of his heart. Instead he described Esther as a little girl and the escapades she had got up to, painting a picture of her until the time she had run away. Sophy drank it in, asking questions about her mother she had never thought she would be able to ask.

At the end of the evening Sophy found she was able to kiss her uncle goodnight with genuine warmth as she again whispered, 'Thank you.'

'Oh, my dear.' Jeremiah shook his head. 'Too little, too late.' He had half-turned away but then swung back on the icy doorstep. 'She would have been proud of you, your mother. Very proud of the fine young woman you have become.'

She watched him as he tramped through the snow to where his horse and trap were waiting under the lean-to at the side of the building. The impression she'd had earlier, of a man far older than his years, intensified as he climbed stiffly into the seat and sat hunched over the reins, his black hat and coat making him appear like an ancient crow as the trap disappeared into the night.

Jeremiah wasn't surprised to find the vicarage in almost complete darkness when he drove the horse and trap through the open gates and on to the drive. It was another of the subtle ways in which Mary delighted in showing her contempt for him – instructing Mrs Hogarth and Molly not to wait up for him. He had often thought their housekeeper was so like his wife they could have been sisters, both being without any natural human warmth or womanly softness.

After settling the horse in his stable, Jeremiah had to walk round to the front of the house again rather than entering by the immediate route, the kitchen door. He knew this would be locked and bolted. He didn't doubt Mary would have relished bolting the front door against him too, if she had dared, but to date she had not gone this far on any of the evenings he visited their children's homes. As he did each time he accepted an invitation from one of them, he had asked his wife if she wished to accompany him today. He told himself this was in an effort to bring about some sort of a reconciliation between Mary and her daughter and sons; not even to himself did he admit that he enjoyed letting her know where he was going, knowing it incensed her more than anything else could do. He had left the house shortly after lunch and it was now ten o'clock, and he was quite aware that Mary would have been seething all that time.

The familiar smell of beeswax and lavender oil greeted him as he stepped into the hall after scraping his boots against the thick cork mat at the entrance. At one time, so many years ago now it was difficult to remember, he had enjoyed coming home after leaving the vicarage even for an hour or two. He had been the master of an orderly and well-run ship then. The house was still orderly and well-run, he supposed, but he knew, and so did the servants, that he was no longer the master of it. Mary had emasculated him more effectively than any bullock.

Why had he put up with her behaviour? He knew men who had half-killed their wives for far less than Mary subjected him to, every day of his life. He had been made to feel a usurper in his own home, degraded, humiliated. Her every action, every look held him up as weak and spineless, and that's what he was. He had always been afraid of her, he knew that. And although his children might have some affection for him, they did not respect him. Why would they? Yes, indeed, why would they?

Climbing the first flight of stairs, he did not continue to the second which led to the bedrooms. Instead, he entered his study and poured himself a glass of whisky from the decanter he kept on his desk. There was no fire burning in the grate despite the bitterly cold night, although he didn't doubt that in Mary's private sitting room – which had been the children's schoolroom at one time – the fire would be banked up high for the night and the room as warm as toast. Mary had decided some years before that the household budget couldn't run to a fire in his study any more, along with his bedroom, of course.

He threw back his head and downed the whisky in one swallow before pouring another. He was cold, inside and out, and weary, but overall bitterly ashamed. Seeing Sophy again had brought the past to life, stirring the canker of guilt and remorse that had grown in his latter years. She was his sister's child, his own flesh and blood, and yet he had stood by from when she was a baby and seen her ill-treated and abused without lifting a finger. His knuckles white as he gripped the heavy crystal glass, he stared at his hand before suddenly throwing the glass at the empty fireplace where it shattered into a hundred pieces.

Shivering – the room was like an ice-box – he stood up. At least in bed he could get warm eventually. He mounted the narrower,

268

steeper stairs which led to the bedrooms with his head down, and so it was he didn't see Mary standing on the landing until he reached the top step, whereupon he started and nearly fell backwards. Her bedroom door was open and a shaft of light was coming from it.

Assuming the sound of the breaking glass had awoken her, he said tersely, 'I broke a glass. Get back to bed.'

'I wasn't in bed. I have been waiting for you.' She had moved forward as he made to pass her, causing him to step down one step and crane his head as he looked up at her. 'I think you have something to tell me, don't you?'

He peered at her, his eyes narrowing. She was angry, furiously angry, he knew the signs. If he wasn't mistaken, she'd found out Sophy was back and staying with Patience.

When he didn't reply, she said in the same clipped tone which vibrated with fury, 'I had visitors while you were out. Mrs Fletcher and her daughter.'

He knew Rachel Fletcher and he couldn't abide the woman, nor her spinster daughter who was as plain as a pikestaff and had a coquettish manner all at odds with her appearance. The two were avid gossips and great friends of Mary. He didn't doubt the three of them spent many happy hours in malicious vocal muck-spreading, all done under the guise of being concerned for their fellow man, of course. Quietly, he said, 'There is nothing unusual in that.'

'True.' Her thin face with its sharp nose was mottled in the dim light coming from the landing window. 'But what they had to tell me was unusual, or perhaps the fact that I was not aware of it. Oh yes, Rachel took great delight in that. How long was it going to be before you did me the courtesy of informing me that the girl was back?'

All this time and she still couldn't bring herself to say Sophy's name. It was unbelievable, the hate that drove her. He knew she hated him and there were times when he thought she hated Patience and the boys too. She was riddled with it. How else could you explain her refusal to have anything to do with John's boys, her own grandchildren? And she had never mentioned Peter once since the day he had told her that Patience had given birth to their third grandson.

Keeping his voice flat, Jeremiah said, 'I didn't tell you because many years ago, you forbade the mention of her name in this house, remember? Besides which, she is not back in the way you imagine, for good. She is visiting Patience for a short while before returning home.'

'You're telling me Patience has had contact with her? For how long?'

'I don't know. Ask Patience yourself. Now if you'll excuse me, I'm going to bed.'

Mary didn't move. 'You've been there today, condoning Patience's treachery, haven't you, you weak-kneed excuse for a man. That girl ruined our lives and turned my own children against me, but all that doesn't matter, does it? *Does it?*'

'Keep your voice down, you'll wake the servants. And what are you complaining about anyway? You could have come with me today. You could have come with me in the past.'

'You knew I wouldn't.'

'Then that is your choice, isn't it, Mary? And no one turned your children against you, you did that all by yourself. You have three beautiful grandsons you've never seen. Doesn't that concern you?'

'Listen to yourself.' Her voice was a hiss now, filled with loathing. 'You're spineless. You stood by and saw your sons marry beneath themselves and make us a laughing-stock among our friends, and your daughter debase herself by working as a skivvy and said not a word.'

'A skivvy? What are you talking about? Patience was a nurse, as you know full well.'

'And what are they if not skivvies, doing the most menial tasks whilst exposed to sights no well-brought-up young lady should experience. It's a disgrace. *She's* a disgrace. I can't hold my head up any longer in polite society and you talk about grandsons? I *have* no grandsons! Our two eldest sons are as dead to me and Patience too, and if you had any self-respect, you would feel the same. But no. Not only do you persist in ingratiating yourself with them, but you humiliate me by acknowledging that girl after the misery she has caused.'

'There is no reasoning with you,' Jeremiah said wearily. He was tired. He was always tired these days, and at this moment he wanted nothing so much as his bed. He made to step up on to the landing again but still Mary held her ground, and short of manhandling her out of the way there was nothing he could do.

'She has beguiled you, hasn't she? Like she beguiled our boys and turned them against me. That sort of woman is born knowing how to make men dance to her tune, and I have no doubt how she has been keeping herself since leaving this house.'

Jeremiah's eyes had adjusted to the darkness, and the light coming in the window from the white shining world outside the house enabled him to see his wife's face with some clarity. He took in the twitching lips, the globule of spittle in one corner of her mouth and thought, *She's deranged, she's become unhinged.* And it was in response to this thought that his voice took on something of a placatory note when he said, 'Of course she hasn't beguiled me, Mary. She's a pleasant young woman, that's all − and one who's recently suffered the loss of her husband, I might add.'

He would have gone on but for his wife's 'Huh!' of a laugh. 'And you believed that? You think she was married? And the others, I suppose they fell for that too?' She bent forward slightly, her eyes gimlet-hard. 'If ever there was a case of history repeating itself, this is it. A husband! Don't you see? She's obviously in trouble and has come creeping back with her tail between her legs and her stomach full.'

It was rare Mary spoke so explicitly; bodily matters were never mentioned. Knowing he should leave it − turn away and return to his study or bodily move her out of the way, Jeremiah did neither of those things. Sophy's face as they had talked about Esther was still fresh in his mind, the softness in her eyes as she had kissed him goodnight and the note in her voice when she had whispered, 'Thank you.'

He straightened, easing his neck in its stiff clerical collar. 'I'm sorry to disappoint you but she was most certainly married. Furthermore, she has made a very successful life for herself in London and has a beautiful home, according to Patience who has visited. Sophy is a respectable woman, Mary, and—'

'You.' His mention of the despised name was the last straw. Mary wasn't a big woman but the suddenness of her attack as she thrust out her hands and caught Jeremiah on his shoulders took him by surprise. It was purely a reflex action that caused him to grab at his wife as he lost his balance. The stairs were narrow and steep, and the stair-runner in the centre of each step did nothing to cushion the impact as the two bodies bounced and rolled, plummeting to the landing below. Mary was dead before she reached the polished floorboards, her neck broken. Jeremiah survived the fall but not the massive heart-attack which followed within moments. By the time Mrs Hogarth and Molly reached the scene there was nothing they could do. Jeremiah and his wife lay in a tangle of limbs, closer in death than they had ever been in life.

'Sophy mustn't know.'

'What?' John stared at his sister, taken aback. He had been informed of his parents' demise by a solemn-faced constable who had knocked on the door as the family were rising. After sending the policeman on to Matthew's house a few doors away, he had made the journey to Barnes View on the other side of town himself.

'She's leaving this morning and I don't want her to know. For it to happen while she's here – oh, I don't know. I feel she might think it's somehow something to do with her, and she's had enough to deal with over the last months.'

John looked at William. They were sitting in William's study and Sophy was in the nursery, making the most of her last hour with Peter. William nodded. 'I agree with Patience.' He didn't voice what he was thinking out of respect for John and Patience – Mary had been their mother, after all – but as far-fetched as it seemed, he felt as though his mother-in-law was continuing her vendetta against Sophy beyond the grave. And regardless of what the police constable had said, he didn't think this tragedy was a straightforward accident either. He didn't know what had gone on at the vicarage last night, they'd never know, and maybe that was something to thank God for, but Mary Hutton had been capable of anything.

John was staring at them in bewilderment. 'She'll have to know sometime.'

'Of course she will.' Patience wiped her eyes. She was shocked and upset, but through the turmoil she knew this was the right thing to do. 'I'll write and tell her in a few weeks and let her assume it happened then. I'll say that due to special circumstances – I haven't thought about that yet, but I'll come up with something – the funeral had to be quick. Sophy may not have wanted to attend anyway, but just in case . . .'

John stood up, and as Patience and William rose he hugged his sister. 'As you see fit. I made my goodbyes to Sophy yesterday, so would you prefer me to slip away so she doesn't know I've called this morning? Yes, I think that's best. I can come back this evening with Matthew; there'll be things to discuss.'

For the next hour Patience was on tenterhooks, but then the cab arrived and all was bustle and activity. She accompanied Sophy and Sadie to the station with William, and once they had settled the two women into a carriage, she hugged her cousin tightly. 'I'm so glad you came.'

'So am I.' As the guard blew his whistle and William stepped down on to the platform, holding out his hand for Patience to descend, Sophy hugged her again. 'Thank you for everything,' she whispered. 'It was good to talk to your father last night. I – I liked him.'

Her throat full, Patience couldn't reply. Knowing Sophy would put her distress down to their parting, she joined William and he shut the carriage door, putting his arm round her. They stood waving until the train had steamed out of sight, and then as William drew her against his chest, Patience gave free rein to the sobs shaking her body.

Chapter 23

Over the next weeks Sophy felt as though the visit to Sunderland had set a seal on the next phase of her life. Seeing her uncle again, talking about her mother and the life she had led as a little girl in Southwick and why Esther had done the things she had, had settled something inside her. The shame and bitterness which had accompanied thoughts of her mother for so long was gone, and the relief was overwhelming. Even when news came of the accident, her main feeling was one of thankfulness that she had spoken to her uncle before it was too late, although she grieved for Patience and her other cousins that they had lost both parents in one fell swoop, even if they had been estranged from their mother. She didn't know how she felt about Mary. She would have liked to think that she had forgiven her aunt for the things Mary had done and said, but when she looked into her heart she knew that wasn't so. And so she pushed it to the back of her mind and refused to think about it.

The company were playing to full houses at the General Theatre and the initial eight-week run had been extended to twenty. Her work, along with her enthusiasm to support the Actresses' Franchise League and other suffrage societies kept her fully occupied, with little time to think about her feelings for Kane. In the spring of

1909, when a member of the Women's Freedom League sailed over the House of Commons in a balloon painted with the slogan *Votes for Women*, Sophy was at the forefront of the crowd cheering her on from the ground. She was one of many actresses selling the suffrage newspaper *Votes for Women* on a regular basis, and on a rainy day in the middle of April she and several other suffragettes drove round the London streets in a prison van marked EP, in support of Emmeline Pankhurst, before dispatching themselves as human letters to 10 Downing Street. She knew Kane disapproved of such escapades, more by what he didn't say than what he did, but such is the perversity of the human spirit that this made her more determined, if anything.

When the play at the General was extended again, it was officially pronounced a resounding success, much to everyone's delight. Sophy was pleased, although she was aware that the newspapers were far more interested in the antics of the more militant suffragettes than in the performance of a play which pointed out the hardships and injustices women suffered under the present laws of the land. Inevitable clashes with the police were beginning to become widespread, and although this worried her and other members of the Actresses' Franchise League, it was not enough to stop her joining in the marches.

At the end of July, the Women's Social and Political Union held their own Women's Parliament at Caxton Hall, which concluded with a deputation to the House of Commons led by Mrs Pankhurst. The day was bright and sunny, and Sophy enjoyed the walk through the dusty London streets in spite of some of the more objectionable hecklers who always surfaced on such occasions.

The meeting had been rousing and Mrs Pankhurst inspiring, but when the women arrived at Parliament Square and Asquith, who had taken over from Campbell Bannerman as Prime Minister the year before, refused to receive them, the mood changed.

If she had stopped to consider, Sophy had to admit afterwards she probably would have thought twice about getting involved in what followed, when quite a few windows in government

275

buildings were deliberately smashed and scuffles with police ensued. A number of actresses in the League had recently resigned due to this kind of thing happening, but although Sophy sympathised with their decision, she had to agree with Mrs Pankhurst that decades of the softly-softly approach with regard to women's liberation had got the cause precisely nowhere.

When several suffragettes were arrested, to the indignation of marchers and the crowd who had gathered, the situation turned ugly. The mounted police arrived to help their comrades, and as Sophy was jostled so she lost her bonnet and almost fell under the hooves of one of the horses, a hand jerked her out of the way of the big beast.

'What the hell do you think you're doing?' Kane glared at her, hauling her unceremoniously into a doorway. 'I know you don't care about your safety, but spare a thought for your friends. This is madness, woman. To attack government property won't win the vote.'

Sophy stared at him, her cheeks flushed and her hair tousled. 'What are you doing here?'

'Looking for you.' His glare intensified. 'I knew if there was trouble you'd be in the thick of it.'

He made her sound like a common delinquent. Stiffly, she said, 'There were precautions taken to avoid any injury to the people inside the buildings. We wrapped the stones in paper and tied them with string, and we tapped them against the glass and then dropped them through the holes. We didn't throw them as such.'

If he hadn't been so furious Kane could have smiled, but the sight of Sophy teetering on the edge of falling under the stamping hooves had taken any amusement out of the situation. 'How lady-like,' he said with scathing sarcasm. 'And do you think it will be reported like that in the papers tomorrow?'

Sophy matched him glare for glare. 'How do I know? They print what they want to print. You know that as well as I.'

'And how would it have helped further the cause of women's liberation if you had got yourself trampled to death by a horse?'

'Oh, for goodness sake!' He had no right to speak to her like this. He was as bad as the magistrates who refused to treat suffragettes as political prisoners when they were arrested, and instead labelled them common criminals. There was talk of hunger strikes in protest from those currently in detention. 'I'm standing up for what I believe in, that's all. If I was a man, you'd think that was perfectly all right.'

'I hate to point out the obvious, Sophy, but you *aren't* a man.' He'd deftly steered her into a side road as they had been speaking. 'And while you may not think so, I agree absolutely with women having the same rights and privileges as men regarding the political system, but breaking windows and acting like children is not the way to get sympathy for the cause. You've been a part of taking the establishment theatre by storm with some of the taboo subjects you've tackled, and I admire you for that. But this, this is foolishness.'

Sophy drew herself up, visibly bristling. 'I don't have to listen to this.'

'Oh yes, you do. I'm speaking as your agent rather than your friend. You're a working woman, not a high society debutante. If you get arrested, even if it's just one night in a cell, it will be sufficient to damage your chances of future employment once the reason for the missed performance is known. By all means support the cause, but not by being directly involved in the sort of foolhardiness that happened today. Most of the militants are able to do what they do because they have a husband or a father who supports them. You do not.'

Kane watched her considering his words. He wondered what she would say if he told her he didn't give a damn about her damaging her career compared to her safety. There were going to be casualties soon, everyone was saying so. He hadn't known a moment's peace since she had thrown herself into this suffragette business. Her golden-red hair was hanging in tendrils around her face, and the scene she'd been involved in as he'd arrived had put rosy colour in her cheeks. She looked as though she'd been thoroughly kissed rather than breaking windows, and his body was as hard as a rock in response to the thought.

Determined not to give Kane the satisfaction of acknowledging he had a point, Sophy tossed her head. 'I shall do what I think best,' she declared icily.

'Which means?'

'Exactly what I said.'

And with that he had to be content.

It was only the following week that the incident occurred which was to influence the direction of the rest of Sophy's life, although she didn't know it at the time. She had been to a late-night party thrown by one of the actors who was celebrating his thirtieth birthday, held at a supper club close to the theatre. It was two in the morning and she was getting into a cab with another member of the cast, when a woman appeared out of the shadows of a nearby shop doorway, saying, 'Spare a penny or two?' before stopping abruptly. With a shock, Sophy realised she knew the heavily pregnant, poorly-clad creature. Harriet Crawford had been one of the actresses working at the Lincoln when she had first started in the business, and more than once they had shared tea and toast at each other's lodgings before a show.

As Harriet made to turn swiftly away, Sophy sprang after her. 'Wait. Harriet, wait!' She caught the other woman's arm, and it was then she realised that in spite of Harriet's distended stomach, the rest of her was as thin as a rake. 'What are you doing here like this?'

Harriet kept her head averted as she muttered, 'Isn't it obvious?'

'You – you're sleeping rough?' Sophy knew it went on, of course. Londoners were becoming increasingly aware of the problem of the homeless and unemployed. Many of them congregated on the Embankment at night, making it an unpleasant place. The men and women who crowded the area were attracted there because they knew it offered a chance of food and shelter. The Salvation Army was reported as feeding as many as seven hundred vagrants every night and providing some shelter during the early hours of the morning. There had been talk that the police at Scotland Yard, which was only a few yards away from the squalor, should disband the queues, but this only drove the men and women further afield into shop doorways and dark alleys.

Harriet shook her arm free. 'I'd better go.'

'No, wait.' She couldn't let Harriet go like this. Throwing caution to the wind, Sophy said, 'Come home with me for a meal. You could do with something to eat, couldn't you? And a bed for the night? It's all right, there's only me and my housekeeper and she's a dear soul.' She kept talking as Harriet collected a pitifully small bundle from the shadows before walking with her to the cab, feeling that if she stopped, the other woman would take flight. Once in the cab, Harriet said not a word. It wasn't until they had dropped the other actress off at her lodgings that Harriet said, 'I heard about Toby. I'm sorry.'

'Thank you.'

They continued in silence, Harriet shrunk in a corner of the seat, her thin cotton dress and stained jacket doing nothing to hide the mound of her stomach.

Sadie had gone to bed, but came downstairs when she heard them in the kitchen. She bustled about, setting a crusty loaf and a pat of butter on the table before frying some eggs, sausages and bacon, and making a pot of tea. Harriet ate as though she was starving, which she probably was. There followed a story which was only too common, a litany involving casting couches, broken promises, licentious actor-managers and finally being thrown out of her lodgings when she became pregnant, lost her job and couldn't pay her rent. The father of her baby was a married man who wanted nothing to do with her; in fact, he had threatened violence if she approached him again. The baby was due in a few weeks and it was clear that rather than go in the workhouse, Harriet would do something desperate.

Sophy and Sadie talked far into the night once Harriet had had a bath and washed her hair and was tucked up in bed fast asleep in one of Sadie's voluminous flannelette nightdresses. The next morning, Sophy told her that she was welcome to stay until after the baby was born and she could find a job of some kind to support herself and the child once she was fit again. She could help Sadie in the meantime, Sophy said gently when Harriet burst into tears of gratitude, and she would be company for the older woman. She was away at work for so much of the time and Sadie got lonely.

Sophy had a luncheon appointment with Kane that day. A new restaurant had opened recently on the Strand and the food was reported to be wonderful. He hid his surprise at finding a heavily pregnant Harriet in residence when he called to pick Sophy up, and was charmingly polite and gentle to the embarrassed woman, making conversation as though he had only seen her the other day rather than some thirteen years ago.

Once in the cab, Sophy told him Harriet's story and how she had come across her the night before. 'And so I couldn't just let her leave today,' she finished. 'She really wants to keep the baby and she's done with the theatre. If she and Sadie get on, the answer might be for her to stay on with us. Sadie is getting older, and although she won't admit it, she feels her age. We'll just see how things pan out over the next little while.'

Kane stared at her. 'You're a remarkable woman.'

Something in his eyes made her blush. To hide her discomfiture, she looked out of the window as she said, 'Not really. I'm just very aware that, but for the grace of God, and — and you too, that could be me. When I came to London I was very naive, I had no idea it was such a predatory place. I suppose all big cities are the same, but the entertainment business seems especially so — for women, that is.'

Telling himself not to make too much of her acknowledgement of the part he'd played, Kane said, 'You would never have found yourself in Harriet's position. You are too strong, too principled.'

'My mother did.' She hadn't meant to say it and yet she had been wanting to since she had returned from Sunderland. She felt differently about her mother now; she felt she understood Esther better after the talk with her uncle. She still couldn't completely dispel the feeling of embarrassment, but now she knew her mother had wanted her, that she'd been prepared to give up her life on the stage for her, the hurt had gone.

Her eyes returned to Kane. Not for the world would she have admitted to herself that this was some kind of test, but she found she was holding her breath as she searched his craggy features. The cornflower-blue eyes held their normal warmth and no vestige of shock showed on his face. Quietly, he said, 'Do you want to talk about it?'

Strangely, she didn't. He had passed the first hurdle with flying colours, she didn't want to say anything which might change that. Nevertheless, she nodded. 'My grandfather was a vicar and my mother was brought up very strictly. She rebelled and ran away to come to London when she was fifteen years old. She wanted to go on the stage . . .'

She kept nothing back. She related the misery of her childhood, the time her aunt had beaten her half to death, which had been the catalyst for the change in her relationship with Patience and their going away to school, the revelation which had brought her following in her mother's footsteps to the capital, even the last conversation she'd had with her uncle in the New Year.

She finished as they arrived at the restaurant. Kane had taken her hand part-way through the story but had listened without saying a word. Now he said, very softly, 'I am glad your aunt and uncle are dead because I would have wanted to kill them with my bare hands for what they did to a sensitive little child. And when I called you remarkable just now, I didn't know *how* remarkable.'

Sophy gulped in her throat, telling herself she couldn't cry, not here, not now. His reaction was all she had wanted Toby's to be. The doorman standing outside the restaurant saved her by walking to the kerb and opening the cab door.

The restaurant's interior was the very latest thing and had already had personages such as Winston Churchill as its clientele, but Sophy was oblivious to her surroundings as she followed the waiter who led them to their table for two. She was drawing on all of her acting ability to maintain a pose of calm composure.

Kane ordered her favourite cocktail which she sipped as she studied the menu, and gradually her thudding heart returned to its normal beat. They ordered the food and a bottle of wine, and then Kane leaned forward. 'I am honoured you have confided in me,' he said gently, 'and I will support you in all you want to do for Harriet. I know how easy it is for girls such as her to lose their way. May I tell you something now? Something I have not talked about with anyone else. It does not reflect well on me, I warn you.'

Sophy stared at him in surprise. She knew a little of his background, how he had lost his brothers and mother to the smallpox, and then his father's death a few years later which had provided him with the wealth to forge the life he had built for himself. 'I am sure nothing you could say could make me think any the less of you.'

'Do not be too hasty.' He smiled, but it didn't crease the lines at the corners of his eyes and Sophy realised he was nervous.

As he began to talk, she became aware that she was hearing some of his own bitter truths – the pain of losing his brothers and mother in one fell swoop – his anger and feelings of rejection as his father took to the bottle – his dissolute youth and then the meeting with Ralph's sister and its terrible outcome . . .

'America was my salvation,' Kane said soberly, 'although I cursed it many times in those two years grubbing in the dirt under a blazing sun. But I got to know myself, the good and the bad. Maybe that's what every man needs.'

'And then you came back to England and invested your money in the theatres and travelling company.' Sophy had been silent throughout, fascinated by this insight into a man who had the reputation of being a mystery.

'Just so.' This time Kane's smile was real. She hadn't been disgusted or repulsed by what he'd revealed, but then he should have known she wouldn't be. Sophy understood the variables of human nature; he felt as though she had been born older than her years in that sense.

They had eaten their first course while he had been speaking, now their waiter arrived with the galantine and side dishes they had ordered.

The conversation was light and inconsequential for the rest of the meal. In truth, they both felt somewhat overwhelmed at the direction the day had taken, but when Kane dropped her off at the theatre later that afternoon they both knew their relationship had undergone a subtle change. Kane drove away in the cab elated, feeling he was a step nearer to achieving his goal of persuading Sophy to see him in a different light, that of suitor rather than friend. Sophy was disturbed and confused. Kane's revelations had highlighted the conundrum at the heart of her association with him, the impossible task of reconciling her heart and her head.

Chapter 24

Harriet's baby was born at the end of the second week of a blazing hot September when the newspapers were buzzing with the fact that Lord Northcliffe, the owner of *The Times*, had claimed that Germany was rapidly preparing for war with Britain. The furore caused by Kaiser Wilhelm's II interview with the *Daily Telegraph* the previous year, in which he expressed more than usually indiscreet opinions on foreign affairs, mentioning the secret talks which had apparently taken place between Russia, France and Germany on finding a way to end the Boer War and to 'humiliate England to the dust', had just calmed down. King Edward VII, in full German military uniform and accompanied by Queen Alexandra, had enjoyed an official visit to Berlin at the beginning of the year, during which he and the Kaiser had reaffirmed their friendship and pledged to work for lasting good relations between their countries. Great Britain didn't want to hear anything to the contrary. The Kaiser was the King's nephew, after all, and everyone knew blood was thicker than water.

The occupants of the house overlooking Berkeley Square were not concerned with the political situation between England and Germany on the morning of 11 September. Harriet had gone into labour just after midnight, and when Sophy had sent Sadie for the midwife at three in the morning, the birth had been imminent. So imminent, in fact, that Sophy had delivered the baby herself. Not that little Josephine Sophy was any the worse for the experience. Weighing in at a chunky nine pounds, she was the epitome of a bouncing baby girl with a shock of black hair and bright black eyes. Sophy had been terrified when she'd realised the baby was coming, but there'd been no complications, and as she gazed at Josephine, still covered in blood and mucus but bellowing for her mother, she acknowledged that nothing in life thus far had been so rewarding. Harriet was radiant, and as she cuddled the baby to her breast she instinctively began to suck. Harriet and Sophy were still dewy-eyed when Sadie and the midwife arrived ten minutes later.

Josephine was a contented baby and Harriet an excellent mother, and by the time Sophy undertook her next part as her current play finished, a happy routine had been established at home. And having a baby in the house had made it so much *more* of a home.

The new play, a spectacular event, involved many stars of the West End stage, and all the national newspapers had reviewed the production. It was entitled *A Pageant of Great Women* by Cicely Hamilton, and Sophy had known she had to be involved in it as soon as a part was offered to her. It was first performed in the Scala Theatre on 10 November, two months after Gladstone had instructed the prison doctors to forcibly feed suffragette hunger strikers. The main character in the *Pageant* was Woman, who demands freedom from Justice, while Prejudice – a man – argues against her. Prejudice's objection to Woman's case is that her innate stupidity makes her incapable of mature thought.

Written and directed by two women, the *Pageant* paraded an array of women warriors, artists, scholars, monarchs and saints who show the physical, intellectual, creative and ethical strength of womankind. It was powerful stuff, giving fifty-two actresses the opportunity to stand up for what they believed in.

The play proved so popular that suffrage societies all over the country clamoured to perform it, and the League involved themselves in these local productions, providing the costumes and leading performers where they could. Sophy offered herself as one of the actresses who could direct such undertakings, having no children of her own or family commitments as some actresses did.

Although her prime motive was wanting to encourage women to express themselves through theatre and to stand up for what they believed, there was another reason for her decision to take to the road again and leave the comforts of home and the delights of little Josephine, who was the sweetest baby imaginable. She needed to put some distance between herself and Kane. She knew she had been avoiding him since their shared confidences, making excuses when he invited her to lunch or dinner and refusing any invitations to social occasions he might also attend, but she couldn't help it. She was in turmoil, the more so since she had become unsure of exactly how he viewed her. She hadn't liked it when she'd thought his feelings were fatherly; now she suspected they might be of a different nature, it had thrown her into a state of panic. All the misery she had endured with Toby had come to the fore again, haunting her dreams and colouring her days.

She was a mess, she acknowledged ruefully, which was why, for the first six months of 1910, she travelled the country, encouraging local suffrage societies to go beyond performing the *Pageant* and put on their own plays. The tradition of drawing-room amateur theatre dating from the Victorian era made it comparatively easy to break down the delineation between amateur and professional theatre, and with the policy of the League to provide scripts and expert assistance in the form of experienced actresses and directors, Sophy felt she was really making a difference, albeit a small one, in the fight to open up men's – and women's – minds to the wind of change sweeping the country.

In the middle of June she returned home to join a demonstration in support of the latest Women's Suffrage Bill. The King's unexpected death from pneumonia in the first week of May had plunged the country into mourning, thus delaying the first reading of the important Bill, but after a month's delay it was introduced to the House of Commons on 14 June.

Sophy arrived home three days later, the night before the huge march which had drawn together all the suffrage societies. She had been away since before Christmas. On entering the house, she felt a strange little pang at how life had gone happily on without her. Sadie and Harriet were a team now. Harriet had taken over the more demanding physical jobs which Sadie, who was getting on for seventy-two, had begun to find difficult. Sadie had settled comfortably into the role of cook and supervisor to Harriet, who saw to the cleaning, washing, lighting the fires and other household chores. Little Josephine had flourished in the convivial atmosphere, and Sophy fell in love all over again with the dimpled tot who gurgled and held out her fat little hands to her as though she knew Sophy had helped deliver her into the world.

When Harriet had gone to bed, Sophy sat with Sadie before the fire in the kitchen as she had often used to do, and the two talked – of the things Sophy had been doing – at how well Harriet had been absorbed in the household – of little Josephine, who was, according to Sadie, the most remarkable baby who had ever drawn breath. The one thing they didn't mention was Kane. Not, that is, until Sophy rose to go to bed herself. It was then Sadie, with the privilege of an old friend, said quietly, 'He's called by every week without fail since you've been gone, ma'am.'

Sophy could feel herself flushing. 'You mean Kane?'

Sadie nodded, her eyes tight on Sophy's face. She had known for a long time how Mr Gregory felt about Sophy – you only had to catch him unawares when he was looking at her – but until recently she hadn't been sure if Sophy returned his affection or not. Of course, while she had been married it wouldn't have been right to mention such a thing, and afterwards, with the nature of Toby's passing and the ramifications which had gone on and on, well, the last thing Sophy had been thinking of was another husband. But all that was two years ago. And heaven knew, the poor man had been patient.

'He got the man in when the drains got blocked and the smell was enough to knock you backwards, and when Josephine fell out of her pram and bruised her head, he sent for his own doctor and wouldn't let us settle the bill,' she told Sophy. 'He's ever so good with her – Josephine, I mean. It's a crying shame he hasn't got children of his own, don't you think, ma'am?'

If there had been any doubt in Sadie's mind as to whether she was on the right track, it was dispelled when Sophy didn't answer but, walking to the door, said coldly, in a tone she had never used before, 'I shall need an early breakfast in the morning. A cab is calling at nine o'clock,' and left the kitchen without another word.

Well, well, well. Sadie smiled to herself but then almost in the same breath, her face straightened. What was to be done? She knew Sophy, and for all her good traits she could be stubbornness itself. She sighed, lifting herself out of her comfy chair by the range. Her dear old father used to say that even the most stubborn donkey could be moved by a red-hot poker up its backside, but what was the particular poker that would move Sophy? She'd have to put her thinking cap on. And in the meantime, when the opportunity arose, she'd give Mr Gregory the nod, but discreetly like, that she was on his side.

Ten thousand women, dressed in white, had gathered at the Embankment to walk in a two-mile-long procession to the Albert Hall when Sophy joined them the next morning. The sky was cloudless and the sun already beating down; it was going to be a baking hot day.

The AFL were playing a prominent part in the demonstration in support of the Bill. Sophy took her place with the other actresses, all dressed in fashionable white gowns and elegant, wide-brimmed white hats, behind the huge banner embroidered with the linked comedy and tragedy masks. Although everyone was in mourning for the King, for this event white dresses and hats had been called for, and as they walked in the dust and heat of the roadway, Sophy had to admit it was a stroke of genuis. Most onlookers were dressed in black or the darkest clothes they possessed, and the contrast was striking.

Like an orderly and well-drilled army and carrying banners and flags of the different societies represented, the women walked to the Albert Hall.

'Look at them two.' Gertie Price, an actress Sophy had worked with on a number of occasions, nudged her as they passed a group of well-dressed men standing outside a gentleman's club. Two of the men, ridicule in their eyes and smiles of superiority on their sneering lips, had got hold of a parasol from somewhere and were imitiating the women's walk in an exaggerated manner, calling forth guffaws from the crowd. Gertie, a rough and ready Manchester lass, left the procession and spoke briefly to the two men, and when she joined Sophy again the men were no longer laughing.

'What did you say to them?' Sophy asked curiously.

Gertie grinned. 'I told them they looked a mite too natural with that walk, and if they weren't careful they might get offers from the Oscar Wilde set to shove that parasol where the sun don't shine.'

'Gertie, you didn't!' Sophy had to laugh, although she didn't doubt Emmeline Pankhurst would have been horrified at such behaviour.

Sophy was feeling exhausted by the time the procession began to disperse later in the day. The last six months had been gruelling, the journey home the day before tiring, and she hadn't slept well. Kane had written to her several times while she had been away, as had Patience. She had replied to Patience's letters by return. Kane's she had left for some days and then written brief business-like notes as befitted a client to her agent. His letters had remained warm and friendly, and at least twice he had said he missed her.

She sat down on a bench in the sunshine a short distance from the Albert Hall, watching women walk past her in their twos and threes and small groups, mostly talking about the success of the procession. She knew she had reached a crossroads in her life which would determine her future, and now she was home again she couldn't put it off much longer. She was fond of Kane. She bit her lip, refusing to acknowledge more than fondness. And if his feelings for her were more than that of a friend — and she didn't know that for sure, nothing had been said — then sooner or later he would ask her to make a decision. That was only fair.

Could she join her life to that of a man's again? Make that huge step of trust, of faith? Did she want to? However well she thought she knew him, it was a step into the unknown. If he loved her – she closed her eyes for a second as her heart thudded at the thought – it might be all right, but how did she know what he was really like? People only showed you what they wanted you to see, and she was as guilty of that as the next person.

No, she couldn't do it. She sat quietly, letting the decision settle on her. One part of her wanted to get married and have children of her own, but the other part – the stronger part – felt sick at being caught in a trap. And that was what marriage was, if it went wrong. For a moment she wished she was like several of her actress friends who defied convention and took lovers when they felt like it, but she knew she wasn't like that either. In that respect she was not her mother's daughter.

So . . . She lifted her eyes to the sun which was more gentle now it was late afternoon. She would follow that other path which seemed to have become clearer over the last months. In the course of her recent travels she had met one or two women who were managing their own companies and making a success of it. Although it had been exhausting, she had enjoyed helping to produce and direct plays since Christmas, and she knew she was good at it too. She had even helped write some material a few times. Women were beginning to make their mark in the theatre and she wanted to be part of that. She was successful and wealthy. Her chin lifted. If she was going to buy and run her own theatre somewhere, now was the time to do it. And women like Harriet weren't isolated cases. Actresses had been suffering from great wrongs and would continue to do so until the balance of power become more equal. And how would that happen if women like her, who had the fame and fortune, didn't stand up and make it possible for their less fortunate sisters?

That night two years ago, she could have been used and cast aside as though a night of rape and violence didn't matter because she was a woman, and an actress at that. And Cat, dear Cat. It was all so unfair, so wrong.

She had learned a great deal by producing and directing and

performing to suffrage audiences in the last six months, but off stage the theatres were controlled almost exclusively by men. She stood up, deciding to walk a while rather than take a cab. She wanted to think.

Why not a theatre where the business management and overall control would be in the hands of herself and other women? Women who could and would enjoy stepping up to the roles of stage-managers, producers and production assistants, directors, scenic artists and the rest of the jobs that had to be done, and done well, for a theatre to be a financial success. Actors and authors could be drawn from both sexes, of course, but in the main it would be women who were the driving force.

Could she do it? Did she have the experience needed to under-take such a venture, or would she find herself overwhelmed by the business side? She shrugged the doubt off. She knew Kane had employed accountants and so on when he had owned his theatres; it wasn't necessary to do everything yourself. And of course she could do it! If she set her mind to it, she could run a theatre and more. She had to believe in herself. That had been one of the things Patience had said to her over and over again when she was recovering from her collapse after Toby had died.

'Believe in yourself, Sophy. You must believe in yourself. None of this, Toby and what's happened, was your fault. It was his. You don't know your own worth, you never have. You're an amazing woman.'

She didn't feel like an amazing woman. Someone like Emmeline Pankhurst or Florence Nightingale was an amazing woman. They had no doubts, no uncertainty about what they were doing, whereas she was racked with them. They had probably never woken in the middle of the night feeling they weren't worth loving.

The sound of her name being called lifted her out of the mael-strom of her thoughts. There, on the other side of the road, waving with all his might, was Kane. It had been over six months since she had seen him and she didn't think beyond that in the surprise of the moment. Her lips forming his name, she stepped out towards him, oblivious of the carriage and pair bearing down on her. She saw him shout, turned to see the horses almost upon her, and then she was flying backwards out of the path of the hooves to land at the side of the kerb. The lunge Kane had made to push her out of harm's way was not enough to carry him clear. As she raised her head she saw him bowled underneath the horses and then the carriage went over him, to the accompaniment of screams and shrieks from onlookers. As the carriage came to a halt a little way down the road, Sophy struggled on to her hands and knees. She was looking straight at the crumpled body lying ominously still, a rivulet of red running into the dust of the road.

It had all happened in a moment of time.

Chapter 25

'I blame myself.' Sadie repeated the words she had said umpteen times. 'I should never have told him where to find you. He could have sat and waited for you to come back and this would never have happened.'

Sophy shut her eyes for an infinitesimal moment. The small hospital waiting room was painted a sickly green and smelled strongly of antiseptic, its immaculate walls and floor as clinically clean as only plenty of disinfectant and elbow grease – and a healthy fear of Matron – could achieve. She wanted to scream at Sadie that if she said the same thing one more time, she would go mad. Yet when she looked at Sadie's quivering lips her innate kindness overcame her own guilt and fear, and, putting out her hand, she patted Sadie's. 'It's not your fault. I was the one who stepped out into the road without thinking.'

They had been sitting huddled together for what seemed like an eternity but in reality was only a matter of hours. A young nurse had brought them cups of tea at regular intervals, which they had drunk without tasting, and twice a middle-aged Sister had put her head round the door and tried to persuade them to go home and rest. Kane had not regained consciousness before they had taken him down to theatre to attempt to save his crushed legs, and there was talk of other serious injuries too. The surgeon had held out little hope when he had spoken to them earlier.

Sophy was always to look back on those hours and the ones that followed as the worst of her life. They eclipsed anything that had happened in her childhood, the revelations about her mother which had driven her from the north-east, the misery she'd endured in her marriage with its terrible conclusion when Toby had sold her to be violated, even the horror of Cat's death at the hands of a madman. Those things she had been unable to prevent, they had been out of her control. But Kane . . .

When she had crawled over to him in the road and seen what the carriage had done to him she had begun to whimper his name over and over but he hadn't heard her. He'd lain deathly still, bloodied and broken in the dirt. One of the women who had been on the march had come running over and, after explaining that she was a nurse, had torn pieces of cloth from her dress and applied tourniquets on Kane's legs where the blood was pumping freely. The doctor had told her Kane wouldn't have reached the hospital alive but for this lady's action, but the woman had disappeared when the ambulance had arrived and Sophy had never thanked her.

Dazed, and her white dress stained red with Kane's blood, she had travelled with him to the hospital, willing him to open his eyes so she could tell him she loved him. Why hadn't she realised it before? she'd asked herself, only to have the answer in all its starkness: she had realised it, deep down in the depths of her. For months now she had known she loved him in a way she had never loved Toby, and because of that, Kane could hurt her more. If she had admitted to herself that she loved him, it would have given him a power over her that she found terrifying, and so she had substituted affection and fondness in all her deliberations, weak versions of the real thing.

Ralph had joined them at one point for an hour or so and, in an effort to comfort her, had added to her silent screams of protest and self-denigration when he'd told her he knew Kane had loved her for years. 'He's never said, mind,' Ralph elaborated quickly as though his knowing might cause offence, 'but it tore him in two the day you got wed. He went out and got blind drunk – paralytic, he was, and that's not like him. He's a man of few words, is Mr Gregory, but he feels things more deeply than most and that's a fact. He's a fine gentleman—' Ralph, great hulking Ralph, had broken down at this point and it had been she who had comforted him, all the time wishing she could cry too. But the agony inside was too acute for the relief of tears.

Giving Sadie's hand a last pat, Sophy straightened in the uncomfortable hardbacked chair. 'I think you should go home and get some sleep for a few hours,' she said quietly. She had sent a messenger boy to the house to inform Sadie and Harriet what had happened, saying she didn't know when she would be home; she hadn't expected Sadie to drop everything and rush to her side, but maybe she should have.

'No, I'm staying with you.'

'What good is it going to do if you make yourself ill? I don't want to have to worry about you as well as Kane. Please, Sadie, go home.'

It took a little more persuasion but eventually she saw Sadie off in a cab and returned to the waiting room. She saw several people looking at her askance and realised her bloodstained dress must appear disconcerting, but she wasn't about to go home and change. However long it took, she had to stay until she knew he was going to be all right. He had to be all right. But his legs, if they amputated his legs, how would that affect him? But she wouldn't think like that. *Please, God, please save his legs, but if he has to lose them to live, then please grant him life. I can't bear it if he dies, God. I'll do anything, anything, but don't let him die.*

She sat on, praying and beseeching and, when the desperate pain within got too much, pacing the waiting room for an hour or more, only sitting down when she felt too weak and faint to continue. She was frightened, so very frightened.

At midnight, the surgeon came. Sophy had been surprised when she had seen him before Kane had been taken to the theatre earlier in the day. He looked to be about thirty-five, maybe forty years of age, which she thought young for such an important post. She wasn't to know that any of the other surgeons whom Kane might have had wouldn't have hesitated before amputating both legs, so severe were his injuries. But Edgar Grant was not only a brilliant young surgeon, he had the advantage of a formidably intelligent and empirical mind and was bang up to date with the most advanced thoughts and techniques. Kane's injuries had presented him with the perfect opportunity to try out some experimental surgical procedures at which a lesser man would have baulked. Added to this, Grant was an avid disciple of Joseph Lister, a British surgeon who'd pioneered antiseptic techniques in surgery to prevent the infection of wounds following an operation, and who'd introduced carbolic acid to dress wounds and clean equipment. Through observing various patients, Grant insisted his serious cases be isolated in side rooms within a ward, and that any nurse or doctor attending to the wounds of such patients must wash their hands in a solution of diluted carbolic acid before touching their charge. Grant was not a popular man among his peers and subordinates, having a cold, analytical mind which suffered fools badly, but he was a respected one.

Sophy rose to her feet as the door opened. The surgeon looked tired and he wasn't smiling. Again, she wasn't to know that Edgar Grant almost never smiled. Her heart filled with dread, as she stared at him.

'Please sit down, Mrs Shawe.' Grant waved at the seat she'd just vacated and Sophy automatically sat. He pulled up a chair and sat down himself, stretching his neck out of the collar of his shirt as he did so. Sophy found she still couldn't speak.

'Mr Gregory is a fighter,' he said quietly. 'He has just survived a very long operation which in itself would have finished most men, but he is a very sick man.'

'His – his legs?'

'I have done the best I can but, should he survive this trauma which I have to tell you is by no means certain, whether he'll walk again, I don't know. Apart from the damage to his legs, he also has several broken ribs which I think are due to the horses' hooves rather than the carriage. He also has some concussion which is not unusual in the circumstances.'

'Can I see him?'

Grant shook his head. 'Maybe tomorrow if he' — he had been about to say 'lasts the night' but something in the extraordinary amber eyes holding his made him change it to — 'is well enough. He's asleep now and I don't expect the effects of the anaesthetic to wear off for at least twenty-four hours.'

The relief which had flooded her at the surgeon's first words had quickly abated as he'd gone on. He didn't expect Kane to live. She could tell.

Grant stared at the lovely young woman in front of him. He knew who she was. One of the doctors who had been to see her in a play had said she was a fine actress, but he had no interest in anything besides his work. She was certainly beautiful, but she had the saddest eyes of anyone he had ever seen. He briefly wondered what had happened in her life to put such a depth of grief in such a relatively young woman. It had to be more than her concern for this fellow Gregory.

His thoughts caused him to say, in a voice that would have amazed the junior doctors on his team who were terrified of him to a man, 'The will to live is a powerful force, Mrs Shawe, and one that we doctors cannot always understand. I have seen men and women who should have died make a good recovery, and others who should have lived simply fade away. Mr Gregory is fighting back. It's a good sign.'

'Thank you.'

His reward for the uncharacteristic thoughtfulness was her smile. As he found himself smiling back, he thought to himself that in Gregory's position he would do battle to come back to the land of the living too.

After a few hours' sleep and a wash and change of clothes, Sophy was back at the hospital at ten o'clock in the morning. She was allowed into Kane's room with a nurse at her side at twelve o'clock for five minutes, after being warned that he was still unconscious.

His face was deathly white on the pillow and the huge contraption to keep the covers from his damaged legs was alarming. She sat down, taking his limp hand which was resting on the counterpane and told him, over and over again, how much she loved him, even though she knew he couldn't hear her. She still hadn't cried.

Taking her seat in the waiting room again, once the nurse had gently told her she had to leave Kane, she sat on. She knew Edgar Grant had relaxed the strict visiting hours in her case and she was grateful, but she didn't want to leave the hospital again until she had to. He might wake up, and if he did, she wanted to be near.

She was allowed in Kane's room for another five minutes before she went home that evening, and the same pattern was repeated the next day. Kane remained absolutely still, so still she had to lean forwards to check if he was still breathing.

It was a full forty-eight hours before Edgar Grant was sure Kane was winning the fight he'd talked about. Until then his patient had remained in that other world but his temperature had gone up and down with alarming suddenness and his blood pressure had been all over the place. A man who prided himself on remaining detached from his patients, Grant found himself taking a particular interest in this case. Not only because of the difficult and gruelling hours he'd spent putting Kane's legs together again, but because of his patient's heroic battle to live against all the odds, and the beautiful woman waiting for him.

Sophy was in her usual place in the waiting room when Grant walked in just before midday on the third day after Kane had been admitted to the hospital. She was alone, although over the last two days Sadie had joined her on occasion, along with Ralph who had proved a tower of strength. Ralph was so sure Kane would pull through it was difficult to think otherwise when he was present. It was when she was by herself that the demons came. If she had faced it once, she had faced a hundred times the thought of a life without Kane in it, and she knew if he died it would be the end of her. Oh, she might continue to exist, to function on a day-to-day basis and go through the motions of life, but she knew the core of her, the place from whence came all joy and happiness, would shrivel away.

Now everything had become so crystal clear, she wondered how she could have got it so wrong before. Kane had showed her in a million different ways over the years the sort of man he was. Who he was had been there, in front of her eyes, the whole time. And his last act, and she prayed with all her heart it wouldn't be that in reality, of saving her at the cost of himself, wouldn't even have entered Toby's mind.

She was sitting in a shaft of sunlight from the small window in the waiting room when the surgeon walked in. She had been half-dozing, so tired her limbs felt like lead and her mind fuzzy, but even so she had kept up the steady begging and pleading and wild promises to God she'd engaged in since the accident. She had got to know the routine of the hospital a little during the last days, and she knew that this consultant – this *god* as the medical staff seemed to regard him – did the rounds of his patients every morning between eleven and twelve o'clock. She jumped up, with an alert-ness she would have thought herself incapable of a second before.

When he motioned for her to sit down again she did so, but on the very edge of the chair. She could read nothing from his face. He was the most reserved individual she had ever come across. And then he contradicted this thought when his face split into a smile, the second since she'd known him. 'Mr Gregory is back with us, Mrs Shawe, and waiting to see you. Only a few minutes though, I'm afraid. We mustn't tire him. There's still a long way to go.'

She was glad now she was sitting down. And she must have looked as she felt because Mr Grant said, with some concern, 'Are you all right, Mrs Shawe? Can I get you a glass of water?'

'No, no.' The faintness was receding. 'Oh thank you, thank you so much. I don't know what to say.'

His smile was back. '"Thank you" is more than adequate. Now as I say, ten minutes at the most.'

She sat for a moment more when he had gone, endeavouring to overcome the choking sensation that was filling her breast as she told herself she couldn't cry. This wasn't the time to cry. He was going to be all right. He was conscious and in his right mind, and he was going to get better. Ralph had been right.

No nurse accompanied her into the little room off the main surgical ward this time, although as she walked across the highly polished floor towards Kane's door, the Sister called, 'Ten minutes, Mrs Shawe. No more. Doctor's orders.'

She hesitated for one moment as she reached the room, her heart thudding so hard she couldn't breathe. When she pushed open the door and stepped inside, his gaze was waiting for her. He had been propped up slightly by a wad of pillows under his back and his face was as white as the pillowslips, but his eyes were brilliantly blue as he looked at her. She thought he breathed her name as she covered the distance between them in one second, bending, and with no sense of decorum, pressing her lips against his.

Kane remained absolutely still for one moment and then his arms came out to pull her close, only for him to wince with pain as his broken ribs made themselves felt. 'Damn it.' It was a whisper. 'I've waited to do this for years and now look at me.'

'Oh, Kane, Kane.' She was half-laughing, half-crying. And all the laws of propriety went out of the window as she murmured, 'I love you, I love you so much and I've been so frightened I wouldn't get the chance to tell you. And it's my fault you nearly got killed, trying to save me. If I hadn't gone on the tour, if I'd stayed here and faced what my heart was telling me . . . Oh, Kane . . .'

She was sobbing in earnest now, the pent-up anguish of days pouring out as she half-bent, half-lay on the side of the bed, wanting to hold him but terrified she'd inadvertently hurt him.

'Ssh, ssh.' Oblivious of the pain in his chest he folded her against him, his mouth seeking hers so the first real kisses they exchanged were salty from her tears. His lips covered her face in small burning kisses a few moments later as he murmured passionate words of endearment between each one, words which Sophy repeated as her hands came up to cradle the rough, pock-marked skin of his cheeks.

It was minutes before, still within the circle of his arms, Sophy whispered, 'Do you forgive me?'

'Forgive you?'

'For nearly getting you killed, for avoiding you and running away, for – for being such a coward.'

'That you have never been.' As she sat up, rubbing at her wet face with the back of her hand, he smiled at her. 'And although I didn't like it, the fact of you running away, as you put it, gave me hope that you might be beginning to see me as a man at long last, rather than some old gentleman on the perimeter of your life.'

'You're not old.'

'I'm forty-seven, Sophy.' His face was straight. 'Seventeen years older than you.'

'What does age matter?'

'A great deal when you are still an active and beautiful woman pushing an old man in his bath-chair.'

'Kane, I wouldn't care if you were twenty-seven, thirty-seven years older than me.' Her voice was soft, as were her eyes. 'I love you.' She could see he was exhausted and knew it was painful even to breathe. 'Go to sleep now and I'll be back later.'

'Sophy?' He held out his hand and she put her fingers into it. 'When I can walk out of here, and I will walk again, whatever the doctors say, believe me, I will ask you a question. But I won't ask lying on my back. Can you wait for me?'

'Forever and a day.' Her smile was luminous. 'And when you ask your question, my answer will be yes.'

Sophy didn't have to wait forever and a day – just four months, in fact. On a mild but windy day towards the end of October, Kane left the hospital on his own two feet, flatly refusing a wheelchair or crutches although he did compromise by having a walking stick. Edgar Grant had predicted Kane might be walking again in nine months initially when Sophy had asked him, then Ralph had suggested that knowing 'the boss' as he called Kane, it would be more like six – and Kane did it in four. He was still in considerable pain most of the time, although Edgar Grant had assured him that would diminish over the next six months as muscles and sinews strengthened, but the bones in his legs had knit together extremely well. He would always walk with a stick, the surgeon had told Kane, but he would walk. They both agreed it was an excellent outcome.

Sophy and Kane had talked frankly during the time he had been incarcerated. She had told him about her dreams of opening a theatre run mainly by women, and as they'd discussed the possibilities, the idea of returning to the north-east had evolved. Sophy's cousins and their families were there, and Kane had no family ties of his own; furthermore, Sunderland was a fast-growing town which had absorbed many of the small villages on its outskirts into the fold. The town centre, with its fine buildings, busy shops and urban streets, along with the beaches, piers and promenades and bustling docks, meant the music halls and theatres would find plenty of customers. And, although neither of them voiced it, London held too many painful memories for Sophy.

But all these plans and discussions had been somewhat abstract. The all-important question still had to be asked. So it was, on the morning he left the hospital, standing on the Infirmary's steps with his head lifted to the windy sky and racing clouds, Kane told Sophy he was taking her out that evening, refusing to listen to her protests that he should rest on his first day at home.

The Hippodrome was no longer a variety theatre after its reconstruction the year before, and he told her he had tickets for the Russian Ballet performing there, after which they were having dinner at a secluded little restaurant in Leicester Square. Ralph had arranged it. It was done and dusted. No argument.

Sophy spent some time with Kane at his home, helping Ralph to settle him in and making sure he ate the tasty lunch Ralph had prepared. Then, Kane having reluctantly agreed to an afternoon nap, she flew home to tell Sadie and Harriet she was going out that evening.

'I knew it.' Sadie looked in triumph at Harriet. 'I told you he wouldn't waste any time, didn't I? And he's doing it proper, I like that. You'll come back with a ring on your finger, ma'am, and no mistake.'

'He might not ask me to marry him, Sadie.'

Sadie snorted. She had a repertoire of such sounds which were far more effective than words. 'And pigs might fly, ma'am, but it's not likely, is it? No, he'll ask you, and a better man than Mr Gregory doesn't draw breath, bless him.'

'What are you going to wear, Sophy?' Harriet had been busy ironing when Sophy had burst into the kitchen, Josephine fast asleep in her pram outside the back door so she got her quota of fresh air.

Sophy looked at her two friends. 'I don't know. Nothing too fancy, although, if we're going to the Hippodrome . . . But I don't want him to think I expect him to ask tonight, do I? It wouldn't be seemly.'

Sadie, forever the one to speak her mind, said, 'I think you're past that stage with Mr Gregory, ma'am. Telling him you loved him and whatnot saw to that.'

Sophy giggled. Dear Sadie. Dear Harriet. Dear everybody. This was a wonderful, wonderful day.

For the next hour the three women had a lovely time as Sophy paraded in one outfit after another. Eventually they decided on a pale green evening gown in crushed silk which had a matching coat trimmed with ermine. The shade brought out the burned honey of Sophy's eyes and her magnificent golden-red hair.

When Josephine woke up, Sophy spent some time playing with the baby who was now crawling and into everything. A happy little girl with a mass of dark brown curls and big brown eyes, Sophy adored her as much as Josephine adored her Aunty Sophy. She hadn't seen Peter since her visit to Sunderland over eighteen months ago, and although Patience wrote regularly to keep her up to date with all the doings of her godson, it wasn't the same as being involved in the child's life on a day-to-day basis. Josephine satisfied a need in her, and she was grateful to Harriet in a way she couldn't express. Harriet, in her turn, with the memory of the terrifying time she'd spent trying to survive on the streets before Sophy had rescued her burned into her mind, couldn't do enough for Sophy. In fact, Sophy and Sadie were continually having to persuade her to do less; she would have worked every moment she was awake if they had let her.

At six o'clock Sophy had a long hot bath in soapy bubbles, and once Josephine was tucked up in her cot fast asleep in the room she shared with her mother, Harriet came to help Sophy fix her hair. Sophy normally wore her hair in a simple chignon at the nape of her neck, but tonight Sadie and Harriet had persuaded her to put it up in a mass of curls and waves secured with tiny jewelled pins which twinkled like diamonds when the light caught them. The result was better than they could have imagined.

When Sophy was ready, she stared in amazement at the woman staring back at her from the mirror.

'Oh, Sophy.' Harriet was openly emotional. 'He'll be bowled over when he sees you.'

'Not again, I hope,' said Sadie dryly, who had come up to see the end result.

'Sadie,' said Harriet reproachfully, but the black humour broke what had suddenly become a tense moment for Sophy. She wanted Kane to ask her to marry him, she was living for the moment but, at the same time, she was as jumpy as a cat on a hot tin roof now the possibility was about to become a reality.

The front doorbell rang, causing Sophy to swing round from the mirror. The look on her face brought Sadie stepping forward to take her hands as she said, 'It'll be fine, just fine. Harriet, go and let Mr Gregory in and tell him Mrs Shawe will be down directly.' However informal the three women were together, Sadie and Harriet made it a policy to give Sophy her full title when referring to her in front of visitors, even Kane. 'Now' – as Harriet hurried downstairs, Sadie chafed Sophy's cold hands – 'this is Mr Gregory, remember? And he worships the ground you walk on, anyone can see it. You're going to be very happy, ma'am. I feel it in me water.'

'Oh, Sadie.' Sadie and her water. The expression was used for everything, from her suspicions that the butcher wasn't above diddling his customers now and again, to predicting changes in the weather. Smiling, Sophy hugged the older woman, careless of her dress. 'What would I do without you?'

Sadie forgot the mistress/servant role she adopted most of the time and hugged Sophy back. 'I think the boot's on the other foot.'

Harriet wasn't the only one who was aware of how different her life would have been if Sophy hadn't come across her. Then, gently pushing Sophy away, she said, 'Go and have a wonderful evening. You deserve it and so does he.'

Kane was waiting in the hall as Sophy descended the stairs, her coat over her arm. The expression on his face made her suddenly shy, and to cover her confusion she said quickly, 'I'm sorry to keep you waiting, is the cab outside? I didn't mean to—'

'You look beautiful.' He cut through her babbling, his deep voice husky, and then turning to Harriet and Sadie who were watching them with beatific smiles, he said, 'I shall look after her, so don't worry.'

He could have been referring to their evening out but Sadie knew better, and as her smile widened, she said, 'I know that, Mr Gregory. She couldn't be in better hands.'

The Ballets Russes was breathtaking. The technical brilliance of the Russian dancers, led by Vaslav Nijinsky and Anna Pavlova, electrified the audience, and the choreography went far beyond the vocabulary of classical steps, stressing the male dancer's role. Nijinsky seemed to defy gravity in his airborne leaps, his muscular energy stunning, and the decor and costume designs were like nothing London had seen before with their boldness and brilliant, exotic colours. It was a new experience for all the spectators at the theatre and one that would have normally had Sophy spell-bound. As it was, in spite of the incredible performance on stage, her senses were almost completely tied up in the big dark man sitting quietly at her side.

Kane had always looked good in evening dress – his brooding air lent itself well to formal attire, but tonight there was something about him which caused her to tremble inside. He was altogether a very masculine man, as different in stature and build to Toby's slight, slim physique as chalk to cheese.

He had ordered refreshments to be brought to their box in the interval – ice-cold champagne and strawberries – partly, she supposed, because he would have found it difficult to mingle with the crowd, still being a little unsteady on his legs, but also so the poignant, almost tangible emotion between them would not be broken. They talked of inconsequentials while they sipped the champagne and ate the strawberries, their eyes holding for long moments.

Just before the second half began, Kane leaned across and took her hand, turning it over, palm uppermost, as he kissed the pulse beating in her wrist. 'I've dreamed of being with you like this every night in that damn hospital bed,' he murmured against the scented warmth of her skin. 'But the reality is so much better than the dream.'

The second half was even more spectacular than the first, and the curtain went up and down several times before the audience let the performers retire, the stage strewn with flowers the crowd had thrown. Sophy and Kane waited until most of the throng had dispersed before making their way out of the theatre. Once they were standing on the pavement, a cool night wind ruffling tendrils of hair across Sophy's flushed cheeks, Kane drew her hand through his arm. It was only a two-minute walk along Cranbourn Street to Leicester Square, and when they arrived at the restaurant, their table was waiting, tucked away in a quiet corner of the glittering room. Kane ordered more champagne, ignoring Sophy's protest that she would be tipsy, and after the waiter had left them to peruse the heavily embossed menus, he again took her hand. 'I was going to do this at the end of the meal,' he said softly, 'but I find I cannot wait. However, one thing I must make very clear before I continue. I'm aware I'm no catch for a young and beautiful woman, a woman of substance' – when she would have spoken, he raised his other hand, palm facing her – 'and there is the matter of age to consider. I will not hold you to anything you might have said when I was in hospital and you were feeling sorry for me, and nothing you say tonight will prevent us continuing as friends.'

She stared into his craggy face. Now the moment had come her mind was clear. Her only regret was for the wasted years when they might have been together, but she would make up for them, she told herself fiercely. She would love him as no man had been loved before.

'I love you, Sophy. I think I have loved you from the first moment you put Horace in his place, to the delight of everyone in the café. I knew then my life would never be the same because, until then, I had never fallen in love. I am a man, I have needs and they have been met on occasion, but love is a thing apart. I will devote the rest of my life to making you happy, I can promise you that, and I will never do anything to hurt you. Forgive me for not kneeling but I fear I may not be able to rise again,' he added with a fleeting smile as he brought a small box out of his jacket pocket. 'Sophy, will you do me the great honour of becoming my wife?'

'Yes, oh yes.' She didn't have to think about it, neither did she care that throwing her arms round his neck and pressing her lips against his wasn't the done thing in public. And apparently neither did he, for his arms came round her like a vice and he kissed her until the breath seemed to leave her body.

'Oh my love, my love.' The formality with which he had previously spoken had fallen away and he suddenly looked ten years younger as they eventually parted. 'Here.' He slipped the engagement ring on to the third finger of her left hand. She looked down at the sparkling stones. It was a gold band with five large diamonds set into it, and it felt heavy on her finger. She had stopped wearing her other rings the day after Kane's accident, handing them to Sadie and telling her to sell them and give the proceeds to the men and women who ran the soup kitchens down on the Embankment.

'It's beautiful, Kane.' She raised shining eyes to his.

'You're beautiful.' He touched her slightly parted lips with the tip of his finger and then straightened as the waiter appeared at their side.

Sophy never could remember what she ate that night but as Kane put it, they feasted on love. They sat close together in the cab which took them back to Berkeley Square where Sadie and Harriet were waiting. Without a word, Sophy held out her left hand, secretly hoping Sadie wouldn't say, 'I told you so.'

She didn't, of course. There were oohs and ahhs from both women, and then Sadie made a quaint little speech which she and Harriet had obviously rehearsed, wishing them both happiness and long life.

Kane had kept the cab waiting so he only stayed for a few minutes, but after Sadie and Harriet had discreetly disappeared into the kitchen his kiss goodbye was everything Sophy could have wished for. She stood on the doorstep and watched the cab until it disappeared, then glanced down at the ring on her finger. He had called her a woman of substance and she supposed she was, in a way. Certainly that would be how the rest of the world saw her, even Kane. But she didn't feel like that in her heart.

She closed the door slowly and then leaned against it. *Give me a child until it is seven and I have it for life.* That was what the Jesuits had said. And until she was seven, and beyond, she had lived knowing she was of no account and barely tolerated within her family home. Would she ever rid herself of the feeling, deep, deep inside, that she didn't know where she fitted in the world? She had thought her career, then her marriage, even her involvement in the League and women's rights would settle the issue, but somehow it hadn't.

But she was going to be Kane's wife. As the door at the end of the passageway opened and Sadie and Harriet appeared, beaming all over their faces, she straightened and went to meet them, smiling. This, on top of all her other blessings, was enough. She would make it enough.

They were married nine weeks later on the last day of the year. The wedding was a quiet affair, they'd both wanted it that way, but as Sophy glanced about her at the reception held in the same restaurant where Kane had proposed, she knew that everyone she cared about was there.

Patience, John and Matthew and their respective families – Matthew and his wife now had a baby daughter – had made the journey from Sunderland, along with Tilly, of course, whom Sophy wouldn't have seen forgotten. Sadie, Harriet and Ralph – who was Kane's best man – and Dolly and Jim, along with a few personal friends, made up the party, and it was a merry one. David, still in Egypt, had sent a telegram expressing his good wishes and congratulations, and there had been others from work colleagues too.

Sophy looked quietly radiant in a pale peach dress and jacket with matching hat, and Kane — as Sadie eloquently put it — was most definitely the cat that got the cream, unable to wipe the smile off his face the whole day.

They were honeymooning in Brighton for two weeks and when, mid-afternoon, everyone accompanied them to the station to wave them off, they left amid hugs and kisses and a shower of confetti. Sophy's last sight was of Ralph holding little Josephine high above his head as the child waved with all her might, although she probably wasn't sure what the day was all about. She settled back in her seat and snuggled close to Kane, who put his arm about her. She was Mrs Gregory. And what more could she wish for in this life?

Chapter 26

The honeymoon was a blissfully happy one. Kane proved to be a caring and tender husband, a generous and passionate lover and an amusing companion. The weather threw everything at them – rain, hail, sleet and snow – but it didn't matter. It was two weeks out of time, a magical interlude when they got to know each other as man and wife and cemented a union which had been thirteen years in the making.

The happy couple returned home knowing huge changes were in front of them. Ralph, Sadie and Harriet had all agreed to accompany them in a move up north, and in the weeks preceding the marriage, Kane had wound up his agency business. Both Kane and Sophy's houses were up for sale and offers had been made on each of them which were more than acceptable. For the time being, until the legal formalities were finalised and monies exchanged, it had been agreed that Ralph would continue living in Kane's house and deal with boxing up any items of personal value and furniture his employer wanted to keep. Kane would join Sophy in what would be their marital home until the move.

Patience and William, on hearing their plans, had volunteered to look for suitable accommodation in Sunderland for them.

Patience had undertaken this task with relish, thrilled that Sophy was returning to her roots.

A letter from Patience was waiting for Sophy and Kane when they sat by a roaring fire checking their post on the day they got home. She and William had found the perfect place, Patience had written excitedly. It had just dropped into their laps as though it was meant to be. A doctor friend of William's had converted a farmhouse some years before, about half a mile west of where they lived. He'd sold most of the land to a neighbouring farm, but the place had a wonderful garden and a couple of terraced cottages set in what had been the farmyard. These were in a state of some disrepair but it wouldn't take too much time or money to bring them up to scratch, and they would be snug little homes for Ralph, and Sadie and Harriet. The doctor, who had been offered a wonderful post in a large Edinburgh hospital, was anxious to sell immediately and would therefore take a reasonable offer. Could Sophy and Kane come up and see the house as soon as possible? Time was of the essence, Patience had urged.

The next letter they opened was one from an actor-manager Kane knew who now ran a touring theatre company based in the north. Kane had written to him asking him to spread the word within the industry that a buyer was looking to purchase a theatre Sunderland way. It appeared he'd heard of two possibles, one in Seaburn which was a very nicely presented music hall at present, and another in Bishopwearmouth itself which had recently suffered fire damage and was something of a wreck. He'd been assured, he added, that this would be reflected in the asking price of the building.

'Oh, Kane, we have to go and see them both, the house and the theatre in Bishopwearmouth. It's a sign, don't you see? Them both coming to our attention on the same day and both at a reasonable price.' Sophy, swept away on a flood of excitement, looked at her husband with shining eyes.

Kane, ever the pragmatist, was less enthusiastic. 'We don't know what "a reasonable price" is in either instance,' he pointed out. 'What the seller may consider reasonable is quite different to what the buyer thinks is a good price.'

Sophy wouldn't be dampened. 'You didn't think Ralph and Sadie and Harriet would want to up sticks and move away from London, did you? But they do, all three of them. That was the first sign this was meant to be. This is the second. We have to go without delay before the house or the theatre are snapped up by someone else.'

'What about the one in Seaburn?'

'No.' Her voice was adamant. 'It's the one in Bishopwearmouth we should have, I know it. We must go straight away, Kane.'

'We've just walked in the door, sweetheart. We'll need a day or two sorting out here. We'll go next week sometime, I promise.'

They left the next morning. Ralph arrived as Sophy was saying goodbye to Sadie and Harriet in the kitchen, and as Josephine – who had learned to walk the month before and was now running her mother ragged – saw him, she waddled towards him, face beaming and arms raised to be lifted. And Ralph whisked her into his arms as though it was an everyday occurrence, his tough face tender as he murmured, 'And how's my big girl then?'

Sophy glanced at Harriet who was watching the tableau with a fond expression, then at Sadie who nodded her head in the direction of the hall. When the kitchen door was shut, Sadie whispered, 'He's been round every day since you've been gone on some excuse or other. I've thought for some time he's had his eye on Harriet.'

'And what about Harriet?' Sophy asked, bemused.

'Oh, she's taken with him, that's for sure. And he's absolutely marvellous with Josephine.' Sadie smiled. 'I wouldn't be surprised if he says something soon, but he's a bit bashful, is Ralph. Bless him.'

Sophy stared at Sadie. She'd had no idea anything was going on, but it would be wonderful for little Josephine to have a father and for Harriet to have someone to love and protect her. Knowing how close Sadie and Harriet had become, she said hesitantly, 'You wouldn't mind? If they made a match of it?' It would inevitably mean Sadie would be alone in the evenings when the work was done, as Harriet and Ralph would want to live together in the other cottage – *if* they bought the farmhouse near Patience, that was. Or perhaps Sadie could live in the main house, but then she'd still be by herself once Harriet had gone home. It wasn't what Sophy wanted for Sadie, who was a garrulous soul who thrived on company and could talk the hind leg off a donkey.

'Mind? Of course not,' Sadie said stoutly. 'A pretty young thing like Harriet doesn't want to live the rest of her life with an old crone like me, and besides, the child needs a father. No, I don't mind.'

Oh dear. Sophy gave Sadie a hug. Kane was calling her: the cab had arrived to take them to the station so she said no more. When she broached the matter of Ralph and Harriet to Kane on the way to the station he was as surprised as she had been, but told her, in typical man fashion, that what would be, would be, and if it was to be, he thought it was an excellent state of affairs.

Sophy didn't mention her concern over Sadie. The latter would be the first to say she was an old woman who had lived her life, and Harriet must have her chance at happiness, Sophy knew that, and of course it wasn't as if there wouldn't be folk around Sadie most of the time. It was just . . . not what she'd imagined for her friend.

The house was perfect, right down to an indoor privy in the bathroom upstairs which the doctor had had converted from one of the five bedrooms, leaving four. But four was enough, Sophy assured Kane excitedly, and if they ever needed more in the future there was always the possibility of building a new wing on to the original building. Downstairs comprised of a typically large farmhouse kitchen, a separate dining room, a large sitting room with a huge walk-in fireplace, and a study. The doctor's wife showed them round the property and made them very welcome, and over a cup of tea in the sitting room told them she was sorry to leave because it was a quiet, peaceful house and they had been very happy there.

The theatre was a different kettle of fish. It turned out to be situated in Holmeside, not far from the Olympia Exhibition Hall which had closed the year before. Sophy remembered the Olympia from her childhood when, unbeknownst to her aunt and uncle,

Bridget had taken her there one day for a forbidden treat which would have cost her her job if the deception had been discovered. The giant Pleasuredrome had been a wonderful place to Sophy the child, the roundabouts and gondolas brightly painted, and the circus and skating rink it held providing endless hours of entertainment for Wearsiders. She had never forgotten the magic of that day and she felt sad the Olympia was no more. However, Holmeside was still a bustling, busy place with the museum, the newly-extended Victoria Hall and plenty of shops in the area, like Piper's the grocer's shop where Bridget had bought her an orange before they had gone home. She still remembered the smell of coffee beans, the barrels of butter and the little blue bags of sugar lined up on the counter, and the taste of the orange on her tongue as they had walked home. She felt that a theatre, advertised properly and run well, would thrive in the hurly-burly of life in Holmeside.

Nevertheless, Sophy had to admit her heart dropped a little when the estate agent the owner had hired opened the door of the building to reveal a blackened interior which smelled strongly of smoke, overlaid with a fusty odour from the water used to put out the fire. Kane said nothing as he walked round the premises, the estate agent quick to point out that the rear of the property – where the office and dressing rooms and so on were situated – was relatively unscathed, and Sophy's spirits fell further still, each time she glanced at his expressionless face. He hated it, she could tell. And it was awful, but she still felt deep in the heart of her that this was the right place.

Once outside again, the bitingly cold north-east wind cleared the smell of smoke from their nostrils in moments. Kane thanked the estate agent politely and said they would be in touch before sending the man on his way. Sophy looked at him miserably. 'What do you think?'

'It looks terrible which is in our favour, but the damage is mainly superficial. I like it.'

'You *do*?'

'Don't you?'

'Yes, yes, but I thought— You seemed so dour, uninterested.'

'Sophy, this is business. I have to negotiate the best price I can, so the last thing I want to do is enthuse, but I think this could work very well. It's your money as well as mine going into this though, and you do understand the cost of refurbishment? In blood, sweat and tears too, I might add. This kind of project always throws up hidden problems and gets worse before it gets better in my experience.'

Sophy nodded. 'Nevertheless, I think it's the one.'

'Then, my love, I think we've found your women's theatre.'

'Oh, Kane.' She looked at him with shining eyes. 'I love you.'

Sophy and Kane stayed with Patience and William a further ten days. By the time they returned to London, the purchase of both the farmhouse and the theatre was settled, and Kane had arranged for local builders to begin work on the cottages immediately with the permission of the doctor and his wife. Sophy wanted the two-up, two-down dwellings to be refurbished throughout, and the addition of an extension at the back of each providing another bedroom upstairs and a bathroom downstairs with an indoor privy. Sadie was getting older all the time, and already arthritis was taking its toll; if, in the future, she found the narrow steep stairs of the cottage too much, then a bed could be moved down to the sitting room and her old friend would still have relative independence in her own home.

They arrived back to the news that Ralph had proposed to Harriet and she had accepted. As Sophy had half-expected, the couple wanted to be married before they left London. And so it was, at the end of March — a month which had seen the first woman Member of Parliament in Norway take her seat in government amid great celebrations, and which gave hope to Sophy and other women in England that their government would have to listen to their voice before too long — the move to Sunderland took place, with Harriet and Ralph moving straight into their new home.

The first night in the farmhouse, when the others had retired to their cottages for the night and Sophy and Kane sat before the fire in the sitting room, Kane took his wife into his arms. They were surrounded by boxes and crates which still had to be unpacked, and everything was topsy-turvy – unlike the cottages which Patience had seen were furnished beautifully from top to bottom. However, this didn't matter.

Kane echoed what Sophy was thinking when he murmured, 'Our first home we've bought together and it's going to be a happy one, my love. I promise you that.'

Sophy snuggled into him. 'I know.'

Above her head he sighed before he said, 'I'll support you in everything you want to do with your theatre. I just wish I could be more involved physically.'

Sophy moved to look up at him. Kane had finally accepted that he would never be able to do what he did before the accident. Thanks to Edgar Grant he had the use of his legs, but he would always walk with a stick and his mobility was restricted. She knew he found this frustrating but he rarely complained, even on the bad days – which were becoming fewer – when his joints were so stiff every movement was painful. But he was getting better. Albeit slowly, but he *was* improving. She said this now, finishing by kissing him hard.

'You're right.' His brief moment of despondency was gone. 'I'm a fortunate man. Every morning when I wake up beside you I know that.' He kissed her back in the way which always made her wonder how she had survived for most of her life without him, and when they slid down on to the big thick rug in front of the fire and made love in the flickering glow of the flames, it seemed a fitting end to the first day of the rest of their life in their new home.

Sophy allowed herself a few days to get straight in the farmhouse before she and Kane visited the theatre in Holmeside again. Along with the house, they had bought the doctor's horse and carriage, knowing they were going to have a great deal of to-ing and fro-ing to do in the future. It was going to be one of Ralph's jobs to tend to the horse, which had a fine stable in part of the square cobbled yard at the back of the farmhouse where the cottages were situated. He would also be driving Sophy and Kane about. The upkeep of the gardens was his domain too, and he, Harriet and Sadie had already decided they wanted a greenhouse in one part of the grounds, with a mushroom house and a large vegetable garden alongside. Sadie was to continue as cook, and Harriet would see to everything else. Sophy was a little worried this might prove too much for Harriet, who had her own home to attend to as well as caring for Josephine, but Harriet wouldn't hear of anyone else being brought in to help her.

Kane had been instructing Sophy on the intricacies of the business side of running a theatre since she had first discussed the possibility of owning one with him. At first he had been frankly apprehensive about a venture where women, and solely women, ran the company – something, he admitted, that was to his shame. It wasn't that he didn't think women could accomplish such an undertaking, he'd stressed to Sophy in the early days. More that the male owners of the theatres and the actor-managers they employed wouldn't let them. To his credit, when Sophy had argued back that the status quo would forever remain as it was unless more and more women took the proverbial bull by the horns, he had agreed without further reservation. They were buying the theatre together, but Kane was fully prepared to be more of a sleeping partner who could be called upon in an advisory capacity if required. If Sophy hadn't loved him to distraction already, this would have tipped the balance.

From the inception of her idea to run her own theatre, Sophy had known it wouldn't be easy. Quite how hard the reality would be gradually dawned on her over the next weeks. In the main part of the theatre the stage was still intact but the wood had to be stripped back and varnished. The walls, the fancy plasterwork, the decorative woodwork, *everything* – needed to be cleaned and renewed, and the high ceiling and chandeliers proved a nightmare. Several rows of seats were completely destroyed, and the others had to be stripped of their upholstery, cleaned and restored. Curtains and carpeting the same. And although the back of the building where the dressing rooms were situated wasn't damaged, the smoke smell had permeated every nook and cranny, necessitating as vigorous cleaning as the auditorium itself.

Determined to start as she meant to carry on, Sophy had advertised for women workers. However, after a while she had to compromise on the carpentry work as she couldn't find a woman carpenter in the whole of the north-east. She was amazed at the initial response to the cards she paid to have in shop windows around the town. Most of the women who applied were curious and had no real idea of what was required, and a good number of them were drawn from the wretched filth and poverty of the East End. The old river-mouth settlement of Sunderland had once been a thriving and bustling area where much of the wealth of the town was generated, but when the rich merchant families moved away from their big townhouses in the commercial part of the area to live in the more fashionable and genteel Bishopwearmouth in the first half of the nineteenth century, the East End became a dire place of tenement slums. But for every drunkard and slattern of a mother and wife in the ghettos, there were ten women battling against the odds to bring their children up properly – often in only one or two rooms – and keep them from the worst of the vices rampant in the East End. These women worked their fingers to the bone from noon to night, some with husbands who worked in the docks when shifts were available, others with husbands who had never done an honest day's work in their lives. And there were others, as Harriet would have been, struggling to raise their children alone.

Sophy saw each woman who applied personally. Several took one look at what was required and walked out, one or two were shifty and, Sophy felt, couldn't be trusted, but over a period of a week or so she had brought together a little team who were prepared to work hard for the generous wages she was offering. Sophy had already decided that those who proved themselves, she would keep on once the inaugural work was done, in some capacity or other. She was going to need cleaners, stagehands, people to serve refreshments and so on, and it didn't take her long to realise that for some of these women, the money she was paying was a lifeline. Especially for one or two who had no husband at home.

She also provided a facility which, had she known it, won her employees' loyalty to a woman. She had set aside a small room at the back of the theatre and furnished it with a comfy sofa and a few toys, and here, if they so wished, any of her employees could bring their children while they worked. A rota system was set up so a different woman each day cared for the little ones, and any breast-feeding mothers could pop into the room when the babies were hungry.

During the next weeks Sophy learned a very important lesson which she never forgot. Win your employees' hearts and they will work for you in a way they never would for mere money. Kane was constantly amazed at the progress being made when he called in, but more so by the happy atmosphere. Some of the women, who had never had anything to be joyful about for years, sang as they worked, and the sense of a little community was strong.

As the women were working full days, Sophy had decided that during this initial phase, each lunchtime Ralph and Harriet would bring food to the theatre. She had noticed in the first day or two that some of the women had had nothing to eat all day and suspected – rightly – that any food available at home went to the man of the house and the children first. So Sadie prepared ham and egg pies, meat rolls and pickled eggs, along with loaves of bread and scones, rice or fruit cake and the odd batch of apple pies. The first morning Sophy was amply rewarded for her generosity by the looks on the women's faces as Ralph and Harriet laid out the lunch, but she found she had to go into one of the empty dressing rooms and shed a few tears at the sight of women who were clearly half-starved trying not to fall on the food but eat politely.

And so the work progressed, time ticked on and April turned into May and May into June. With the help of the Actresses' Franchise League Sophy had found her stage-manager, an able producer, a director, and a general assistant to all three. The business side of the theatre, she was taking on herself. The League also put her in touch with two stagehands and a scenic artist.

In the middle of June, just before the Coronation of George V which took place amid sumptuous church and state pageantry, another procession took place which Sophy would have loved to attend, had she had the time. Sixty thousand or so supporters of the enfranchisement of women marched through the streets of London in a five-mile-long line, many dressed as famous women such as Boadicea, Joan of Arc and Queen Victoria. One of the most impressive groups was the seven hundred suffragettes who had been imprisoned for the cause, each proudly displaying a silver arrow as a mark of their suffering and carrying a banner which read *From prison to citizenship*.

The marchers were drawn from all walks of life and all classes: factory girls and aristocrats, actresses and university graduates, but when Sophy – full of enthusiasm – read the account from the newspaper to her workers the following lunchtime, their reaction was mixed.

'All that vote stuff won't make no difference to the likes of us,' Flo, one of the strongest and best workers, muttered. 'My Harold will still knock the living daylights out of me if he feels like it.'

'An' I wouldn't know how to vote anyway,' Peggy, another woman, chimed up. 'It's all right for the likes of you, Mrs Gregory. You're educated and clever, you know about these things. But a vote'd be wasted on me.'

Before Sophy could say anything, Amy, a pretty woman who was married to a brute of a husband and who already had five children at the age of twenty-two, spoke up. Normally quiet and retiring, her voice trembled a little but gathered pace as she said, 'No, you're wrong, Peg, you mustn't say that. A vote wouldn't be wasted on you. We're as good as men any day, but until the law's changed we'll never have any say. It's not right how women are treated.'

'Aye, I know it's not right, lass, but I'm saying me havin' the vote'll make no difference one way or the other.'

'But it *will*, don't you see? And you don't have to be educated or clever to know the difference between right and wrong, and us not being allowed to vote like a man is wrong. And there's women like Mrs Gregory, clever women, who can speak proper and argue with them up in London. I'd vote for someone like her, wouldn't you?'

'Well aye, aye, but women'll never be in Parliament, lass.'

'I wouldn't be so sure about that, Peggy.' Sophy entered the discussion. 'A woman was elected to Parliament in Norway not so long ago. Did you know that?'

Peggy looked at her in amazement, but it was Flo who said, 'Aye, well that's Norway, Mrs Gregory. It's not like here, is it.'

'It's just like here, Flo. Women wanted fairness, that's all. Not to take over so men didn't have a say, but merely to be able to have *their* say. And so women, ordinary women like you and Peggy and me, because I'm no different to you except I've been lucky, that's all, they rose up and stood for what they believed in. Like the suffragettes here who are prepared to go to prison, to be force-fed even, for what they know is right.'

'My Harold says the lot of 'em are frustrated spinsters who need a good—' Flo stopped abruptly, remembering who she was speaking to.

Sophy had to smile. 'And you, Flo? What do *you* think?' she asked quietly. 'You have a mind of your own, you know. Your Harold can't stop you thinking. You work all day as well as running your home and bringing up your children, you make a penny stretch to two and keep the wolf from the door. To my mind that's heroic, let alone clever.'

Now it was Flo who stared at her in amazement until Peggy chipped in, 'That means brave, lass.'

'I know what it means!' Flo glared at her friend. 'I'm not daft, you know.'

'No, you're not, Flo.' Sophy's face was straight now. She glanced at the others as she added, 'None of you are. So think for yourselves, that's all I'm saying.'

She told Kane about the conversation when she got home that evening and he grinned at her, shaking his head. 'I don't think some of those husbands know what's going to hit them if their wives continue working for you,' he said dryly.

Sophy smiled back. 'Peggy has already told Flo to hit her husband over the head with the frying pan next time he comes home drunk and knocks her about. It worked for her, apparently. She only had to do it the once and he keeps his hands to himself now. Peggy says Flo's husband is a little rat of a man and she's twice his size, but she's always let him get away with murder. Funny that, isn't it?'

They stared at each other, the spectre of Toby suddenly in both their minds. 'Or perhaps not so funny,' Sophy murmured. No. Not funny at all. It was amazing what people put up with when it became commonplace in their lives.

Chapter 27

At the beginning of July the theatre was almost ready, the stage-manager and everyone had arrived, actors and actresses had been hired and rehearsals had begun. The first play they were putting on was one by Mr Arncliffe-Sennett, entitled *An Englishwoman's Home*. The central theme of the play was the artificial division between women's work and that of men, highlighting the fact that although inflation and unemployment had forced many women to take in work in their homes or take work outside where they could find it, there was resistance on the part of husbands and older sons to help with housework or childcare.

The play was a mixture of styles which was one of the reasons Sophy had chosen it for the all-important opening of the theatre. The opening scene carried a serious look at the effects of poverty on the relationship of the two main characters, a married couple, but this contrasted with the monologues in which each appeals to the audience for sympathy, and with the slapstick elements which came in with other characters demonstrating the inability of men to deal with 'women's work'. She wanted a play which would speak to the mainly working-class audience she was aiming for, and a couple of lines in particular – when the wife in a conversation with her husband says, 'You don't believe then, that what is sauce for the goose is sauce for the gander?' and his reply of, 'I don't know nothing about goose's sauce 'cos we never have none,' had made her little army of women workers howl with laughter, which she took as a good sign.

Their first night in the middle of July was to a full house and was enthusiastically received by audience and local press alike. Originally Sophy had thought she would like to take the lead female role when they had first begun work renovating the theatre, but over the last two or three months she'd felt increasingly that she wouldn't be able to do it justice. She had thrown herself into the cleaning and hard physical work as vigorously as anyone else, wanting the women to see her as part of the team and not as a remote figurehead they couldn't talk to. She was the first one to arrive in the morning and the last to leave at night, and once she got home she often had further work to see to – checking accounts, making lists of materials and items still to buy, settling bills, sorting out the women's weekly wages, answering letters, writing letters – the list was endless.

She had lost weight and she knew Kane was worried about her, as she was tired all the time and very emotional, but she kept reassuring him that things would settle down once the theatre was ready and the show under way. They had known the first few months would be sheer hard work, she told him. It would all be fine in the end. Nevertheless, she hired another actress for the lead female role and was glad she had done so on the opening night. Kane had insisted she sit with him in one of the boxes and watch the show from the auditorium rather than clucking like an anxious hen with one chick in the wings. She sat, in an exhausted stupor, unable to judge whether the show was a success or not, and when it ended and the audience rose to their feet cheering and clapping, she stood automatically, feeling very strange. And then she fainted clean away.

'Well, my dear.' The doctor friend of William's whom Kane had had brought to the house the next morning was very kind and thorough, and his voice was gentle as he looked at her after his examination which had seemed to go on for ever. 'Your husband tells me you've been working very hard over the last few months.'

Sophy gripped Kane's hand tighter and nodded. Now the show was up and running and she could begin to relax a little, she had admitted to herself what her body had been trying to tell her for weeks. She felt unwell. Unwell and so exhausted she hadn't argued with Kane when he had made her stay in bed. Terrified now that something was seriously wrong, she didn't dare ask what was the matter.

'Forgive the intrusion but I need to know,' the man went on. 'Your monthly cycle – has it been normal?'

Blushing furiously, she stammered, 'Not-not really, Doctor. But I've been so busy . . . I – I think it's been three months since – since I—'

'Yes, that would be about right. You are expecting a baby, Mrs Gregory. Have you noticed any changes in your abdomen?'

A baby. Now it was Kane's hand that squeezed hers until it hurt. 'Changes?' Sophy repeated vacantly, unable to take in the news. 'I suppose it's a little swollen but I put it down to not eating properly, flatulence . . .'

'Well, I think this little piece of flatulence will be born some time in December.'

'Are you sure?' Kane's voice was thick with emotion.

Dr Palmer smiled. He liked giving good news. 'Quite sure, Mr Gregory. I definitely felt a baby in there.'

'Oh, my love.' As Kane crushed her to him Sophy's eyes widened. A baby. A *baby*. A flood of protective joy caused her to put her hands to the swell of her stomach, but almost immediately, she said apprehensively, 'But I haven't felt sick, Doctor. Just tired and generally unwell. Are you sure?'

Not at all annoyed at being asked to repeat himself, Dr Palmer's smile spread. 'Quite sure. Now I'll make an appointment for you with a colleague of mine who is a specialist in this area.' He didn't add. 'There is something I would like him to check', because he didn't want to worry them.

Kane saw the doctor out and then dashed back to the bedroom

as fast as he could, his stick clattering on the stairs. Sophy was waiting for him with shining eyes. Taking her in his arms, he said huskily, 'To think of all you've been doing.'

'I know, I know. And I should have thought, when my monthlies stopped, but I put it down to all the hard work and tearing about. And I've lost weight, not gained it.'

'There were days when you didn't bother to eat, you were so busy, now weren't there? And other times when you were so tired you came home and just picked at your meal.' He shook his head. 'I blame myself. But now, young lady, you are going to do what *I* say, and behave. If you won't look after yourself, I will do the job.'

'Oh, Kane.' She looked radiant. 'A baby. Our baby.'

Everyone was thrilled at the news. Patience and William, who had been worried to death when Kane had gone to see them that morning asking William to recommend a good GP, arrived with chocolates and flowers. Sadie cried. Harriet and Ralph beamed, and the women at the theatre let out a cheer when they heard which could have been heard in Gateshead.

Sophy rested at home for a few days and slept a lot, but then she was itching to get back to the theatre. Because Kane had been so concerned about her, she agreed to wait until they had seen the specialist Dr Palmer had spoken of. This occurred one week after Dr Palmer had been to the house and this time they saw the consultant at the Sunderland Infirmary. They left somewhat stunned. In the consultant's opinion Sophy was between four and five months' pregnant but from his very thorough examination he was sure there was not one baby but two. And in the next few weeks, he warned, her stomach would begin to expand rapidly as they grew.

'That settles it.' As Ralph drove them home in the sweltering heat of a July heatwave, Kane was adamant. 'We're going to have to get extra help for you.'

'But I've told you, I'll manage. Harriet and Sadie will help and I can take the baby – babies – into work with me when necessary.'

'Sadie is the cook, not a nursemaid, and Harriet has enough to do, and whether you take the babies with you to the theatre or not, you will need another pair of hands. You know I felt this way when we thought there was only one baby, but now twins are confirmed there is no way you can manage. The theatre will still take a great deal of your time, Sophy. Be realistic. Without a sound, capable nursemaid to take some of the burden, you will make yourself ill, and how will that help you, me or the babies?'

Sophy stared at him miserably. She knew he was right but she didn't want a stranger coming into her home and living with them, and that was what it would mean. Furthermore, *she* wanted to look after her children, but at the same time she didn't want to let the theatre go, not now, not after the wonderful women she'd found who relied on her. Her hand rested on the mound of her stomach wherein her children lay. She nodded. 'All right, but I'll write the advertisement in my own way. Agreed?'

Kane eyed her suspiciously. 'What are you going to say?'

Sophy giggled at the look on his face. 'Nothing untoward, I promise. You can read it if you like. But I don't want one of those officious types of nannies for my babies, someone who thinks they know better than me.'

Kane smiled. 'I'm sure you'd put her right immediately, but do as you see fit.' He put out his hand and stroked the side of her face, his eyes soft. He just wanted the best for her. He hadn't thought he could love her any more than he did, but since he had known she was carrying his child – children, he corrected himself silently with a surge of inexpressible joy – he'd felt so protective, all he wanted to do was to wrap her up in cotton wool until the confinement. But Sophy was the last person to agree to that. Which was partly why he so adored her. He knew better than anyone how her beginnings had affected her, but she had fought back every inch of the way. She was a strong woman, but strangely, he knew, she didn't see herself in that way. He also knew that although she was enough for him in every way, there was still something in her, a sadness, an aloneness, something, which afflicted her at times and which his love had not been able to banish.

She said now, 'Two babies, Kane,' with a gurgle of laughter.

'Patience and David are twins, you know, so perhaps this has stemmed from my side.'

'Are you pleased?'

'That it's twins?' She smiled serenely. 'Double the blessing.'

'And double the crying, the feeding, the changing, the sleepless nights . . .'

She pushed into him with her shoulder. 'And of course you, as a man, have to worry about all that,' she said with gentle sarcasm.

Suddenly serious, he turned her face to his, his fingers holding her chin as he murmured, 'I don't want to be a distant father, Sophy. As youngsters we, my brothers and I, were left to the nanny and the nursemaids. We had an hour each evening before bedtime when we were brought to the drawing room to see our parents, but more often than not it was only our mother who was there. We were lucky if our father joined us for ten minutes. It was the way it was with many families such as mine, I suppose. And then there was prep school, followed by other boarding schools, and as often as not when we returned home for the holidays our parents were elsewhere – in Scotland for the shooting or taking the waters at Bath or holidaying on the continent.'

'We won't be like that.' She kissed him, cradling his face between her hands. It hadn't taken her long to realise, even before their marriage – while they'd still been engaged – that his reserved, enigmatic air was a front he'd erected to hide behind. The real Kane, the Kane she knew, was warm and spontaneous and endearingly vulnerable, with a heart as big as the ocean. 'And you'll be a wonderful father.'

By the end of September Sophy was feeling as big as a house. Her appetite had returned shortly after she had found out she was expecting twins, and with the theatre up and running and doing very nicely, the latter part of the summer had been enjoyable. At the beginning of October she placed an advertisement in the *Sunderland Echo* and the *Newcastle Journal*, as well as contacting three agencies in the north-east. Her advertisement did not follow the pattern of most such notices, but she was satisfied with it:

Wanted. A capable and friendly nursemaid to assist in the care of newborn twins. An affinity and liking for children as important as experience. Generous remuneration for the right applicant.

Her advertisement in the papers brought fifteen replies. From these she chose five, and on interviewing them deemed none of the women to be what she had in mind. The two Sunderland agencies she'd visited sent her seven interviewees between them but it was the same story. One stiff-faced matron told her straight out that she worked on the principle of 'spare the rod and spoil the child'; another was a fluffy-haired girl who giggled a lot and whom Sophy was sure wouldn't know one end of a baby from the other; yet another lady, well past middle-age, smelled strongly of stout at eleven o'clock in the morning, and so it continued.

By the end of the month, the evening before she was due to see the Newcastle agency's offerings, Kane asked her – kindly – if she was perhaps being a teensy-weensy bit too particular. Sophy, tired from an unproductive day and feeling huge and unattractive, promptly burst into tears. The babies had kept her awake most of the night for the last week with their gymnastics, but as it was the start of a new play at the theatre she had insisted on going in each day, which meant most evenings she had been dealing with office work at home.

The Newcastle agency were sending her four women they thought might be suitable and that was all she knew, she told Kane through her sobs, but if they were like the others she would not, *would not* be pressurised into taking someone about whom she wasn't a hundred per cent confident.

Kane drew her out of the study where she had been sitting going over the theatre accounts and into the drawing room, where he made her put her swollen feet up on the sofa as he chafed her cold hands.

'New rules,' he told her gently but firmly. 'From now on until the babies are born I take over the business side of the theatre. I know you want to do it yourself, but it's too much at the moment and after all, I have been doing this kind of work most of my adult life. Your baby will be in good hands, and these babies' – he touched her stomach tenderly – 'need a rested mother. All right? You can visit the theatre with me as often as you wish, but no more work. I mean it, Sophy. Dr Palmer was worried about the swelling in your legs and feet last week and it's got worse, not better.'

She lay back against the cushions of the sofa, too tired to argue with him.

'Regarding the nursemaid, I have no intention of forcing you to make a choice that doesn't suit. We will manage. Somehow. And now you are going up to bed and I will bring you a dinner tray later.'

'But it's only seven o'clock!'

'Bed, Sophy.'

He was worried, really worried, she could see it in his face, and it was this that made her nod and let him help her to her feet. They were crossing the hall, Kane holding her arm, when the doorbell rang. Harriet came hurrying out of the passageway which led to the kitchen, and on seeing her, Kane said, 'I'm taking Sophy up to bed, she's exhausted. Get rid of whoever it is and then warm some milk and bring it upstairs, would you.'

They were halfway up the stairs when Harriet opened the door. They heard her say, 'Can I help you?' and then a woman spoke in reply. They couldn't hear what she said but as Sophy stopped dead, Kane glanced at her in surprise. 'What's the matter?'

Harriet was saying, 'I'm sorry, but Mrs Gregory is indisposed. You'll have to come back another time,' as Sophy turned round and descended, Kane still holding her arm.

'Bridget?' Sophy's voice was a whisper, and then as she reached the hall, she said more strongly, 'Bridget? Is that you?'

Harriet stood to one side, clearly bemused, as the woman at the door pushed past her, saying, 'Sophy? Sophy, lass! Aw, Sophy.'

In spite of her bulk Sophy flew across the hall and into Bridget's arms. The women hung on to each other, both making unintelligible sounds which made their listeners wrinkle their faces against the mixed pain and joy they contained. It was a full minute before they drew back to look into each other's faces and both had tears streaming down their cheeks. 'Oh, me bairn, me bairn, look at you.' Bridget was smiling through her tears. 'I knew you'd be as bonny as a summer's day.'

Sophy couldn't talk. Here was her Bridget and hardly any different to what she remembered. The same bright brown eyes and curly light brown hair and not a trace of grey, although Bridget must be fifty-five, fifty-six now.

Such was the look on Sophy's face that Bridget said, 'Now come on, lass, don't take on so, not in your condition. Ee, I couldn't believe it when Miss Patience told me. Twins, she said. Look, come an' sit down.' Bridget glanced helplessly at Kane who now stepped forward, taking Sophy's arm once more as he escorted her into the drawing room with Bridget following and Harriet making up the rear.

When Sophy sat down she held out her hand to Bridget who came and sat beside her. Sophy hung on tight. She had the feeling that if she let go of Bridget's hand, it would all turn out to be a dream. Looking up at Kane, she whispered, 'This is Bridget, you remember I told you about her?'

'I do.' Kane smiled. 'And you're very welcome, Bridget. Harriet, I think we could all do with a cup of tea, don't you?'

'I never thought I'd see you again.' Sophy squeezed Bridget's hand and then, remembering her manners, she said, 'Oh take off your hat and coat. You can have dinner with us, can't you? Where are you staying? Are you living in Sunderland? Where's Kitty and Patrick?'

Bridget smiled. When Miss Patience had told her that Sophy was a famous actress married to a wealthy man and living in a great big house, she'd wondered if her lass might have changed – got a bit uppity – but she needn't have worried. 'I only heard you were living in these parts today, lass,' she said quietly. 'The last I heard, you'd gone off somewhere but no one knew where.'

'When was that?'

'Years back, just before I went across the water with my mam an' da.'

'You went back to Ireland?'

331

Kitty nodded. 'But I'd asked about you before then. I went knocking at the door of the vicarage one day about a year or so after your aunt had thrown us out, and she threatened to have the police on me. Vicious, she was.'

'She's dead now, my uncle too.'

'Aye, I know, lass. Miss Patience told me.'

'Bridget, why don't you start at the beginning and tell us the full story,' Kane suggested, as Harriet came in with the tea tray.

'Well, there's not a lot to tell, sir. When your aunt,' she turned to Sophy again, 'got rid of us, we hung about these parts for a bit. I didn't want to move too far afield because of you. But then we got the offer of work from a farmer at one of the hirings. The pay wasn't much but it was Silksworth way so still close. The cottage he let us have was no more than a pigsty of a place, holes in the roof, all sorts, but we stuck it for a while. Then on me half-day off one Sunday I went to the vicarage. I wanted to let you know I was thinking of you, lass. That I hadn't gone far. Your aunt was there. She said you'd been sent away and you weren't coming back, and if I came again she'd have me locked up for stealing. Well, I've never stolen anything in me life, as you well know.'

Sophy nodded. 'She was a hateful woman, Bridget.'

'Then me mam got poorly, the cottage was so damp and cold, terrible it was, and then as luck would have it, we got set on at a big house in Newcastle.'

'Newcastle? Oh, Bridget, I was at school in Newcastle! We might have met.'

'You were? Well, I never. Well, me mam never really got better, not like she'd once been anyway, and she'd always had a hankering to go back to Ireland to see her sisters an' that, and in the end she got right poorly and me and Da knew if we didn't go soon, that'd be that. But I came back to the vicarage before we went, just in case. This little maid answered the door and when I asked after you she said there'd been a big row and you'd gone and no one knew where, but you weren't coming back. I gave a letter to her to give to you on the off-chance.'

'I never got it.'

'No, well you wouldn't if your aunt had anything to do with it,' said Bridget darkly. 'Anyway, we went back to Ireland and me mam died within the year but Da wanted to stay on, and as I was all he'd got . . . He went a month ago, God rest his soul, so I thought I'd come back and see if I could find out if you were all right. I've thought about you all the time, lass, and that's God's honest truth. I went to the vicarage but there's new folk there and the lady – nice soul, she was – didn't know anything about you, but told me Miss Patience had married a Dr Alridge and they lived Barnes Park way. I booked into a bed and breakfast last night and then went knocking on doors asking, but when I found the right house Miss Patience was out for the afternoon. So I went back tonight.'

Bridget didn't add here how amazed she had been at the welcome she'd received. She remembered Miss Patience as a spiteful little madam with a tongue on her like her mother, but the warm, friendly woman who had invited her in and told her about Sophy's success and given her Sophy's address had been kindness itself.

'And here I am,' Bridget finished softly.

'Here you are.' Sophy hugged her again, she couldn't help it. 'Can you stay, Bridget? I don't mean just tonight, although we'll get your things picked up from the bed and breakfast in a little while, but for good? Can you?'

Bridget looked at Kane, clearly taken aback. He smiled broadly.

'We're looking for a nursemaid for when the twins are born and somehow I think we've found her,' he said. 'If you're free, of course?'

'Oh yes, sir.' Bridget looked at Sophy. 'Oh, lass, lass, I can't believe it. I've been a bit low since my da went, not having bairns of my own, but I've always thought of you as my bairn . . .' And then she stopped, again glancing at Kane as she said, 'Not wishing to take liberties, sir.'

'Take all the liberties you want, Bridget. You've done my wife the power of good. Now, give me the address of where your things are and Ralph will go and fetch them,' he said briskly, pretending not to notice the tears in Bridget's eyes. 'And then we'll see about settling you in. I'm sure my wife will want to show you the nursery later, but for now I'll leave you two to chat.' He put out his hand and touched Sophy's cheek before leaving the room.

'He seems a grand man, lass,' Bridget said softly.

'He is a grand man, Bridget.'

'And you're an actress, Miss Patience said? Fancy that.'

Sophy nodded. 'I went to London when I left the vicarage once my schooling had finished. The row, it was about my mother. My beginnings. Did – did you know that the story about her marrying a Frenchman wasn't true?'

Bridget bit her lip. 'Not till you've just said, lass, although I have to admit I always had my suspicions. Me mam an' da believed it, but they didn't have as much to do with your mother as I did when she came home.'

'She wasn't married to my father.'

'Well, all the same for that she was a real lady, lass, and nice with it, if you know what I mean. I liked her.'

Sophy put out her hand and clasped Bridget's once again. 'Thank you. Anyway, I went to London . . .' She told Bridget everything, about Cat, about Toby, Kane's accident, filling in the missing years as they sat by the fire drinking another cup of tea together. Then they went through to the kitchen and Sophy introduced Bridget to Sadie and Harriet, explaining their shared background. When Kane came out of the study where he had been finishing the accounts Sophy had been working on earlier, the four women were laughing at one of Sadie's witticisms, and he said again, but to himself, 'Yes, the power of good,' as he looked at his wife from the kitchen door. And, although not a churchgoing man, he sent up a swift prayer of thanks for the little Irishwoman who had come knocking at their door.

Chapter 28

The next few weeks passed without mishap and the house ran more smoothly than it ever had. Bridget fitted into the household as though she had always been there, and she and Sadie hit it off immediately, for which Sophy was thankful. Harriet had Ralph, and although Harriet was very fond of Sadie, she obviously preferred to sit by her own fireside with her husband once Josephine was tucked up in bed and her work in the house was finished for the day. Now, instead of Sadie retiring to her cottage at some point after she and Harriet had served dinner to Kane and Sophy and then made the kitchen spick and span, she and Bridget sat by the range drinking tea and putting the world to rights.

It had been agreed that, for the present and until the twins, once they arrived, were old enough to go through the night, Bridget would sleep in the room next to the nursery so she was always on hand to help with night-feeds and so on. But once the children were older, Bridget would join Sadie in her cottage and the two women would share the little home.

The only cause for concern as the last weeks of the pregnancy progressed was the swelling in Sophy's feet and legs. This persisted, to a greater or lesser degree, during the whole of the month of

November. A bitterly cold November, with thick frosts and ice and the odd snow flurry.

Dr Palmer had flatly forbidden his patient to leave the house, and in truth Sophy didn't think she could have done so even if she'd had his blessing. Looking at herself in the bedroom mirror, it was amazing to think she hadn't known she was pregnant at first. Once her stomach had started to expand it hadn't known how to stop, and even Harriet, the most tactful of creatures, had to admit Sophy looked as though she was going to burst. Sophy agreed with her – over the last weeks she felt as though she was going to burst too. She slept half-sitting up, propped against a pile of pillows because if she lay down flat she felt as though she couldn't breathe, and she waddled rather than walked. In the last weeks her appetite had all but vanished, because, as she said to Kane when he worried about her small portions at the dinner-table, there was no room for anything but babies in her abdomen.

But Sophy was happy and it showed.

On the afternoons when Kane was working in his study or out checking on how things were going at the theatre with Ralph, she would join the three other women in the kitchen and sit in Sadie's comfy armchair in front of the glowing range. The four of them would drink endless pots of tea, gossip about this and that, discuss names for the babies and generally enjoy themselves while the Arctic conditions outside made the kitchen all the more cosy. Sadie and Bridget's knitting needles kept up a steady click–clack while they talked, and the pile of baby clothes grew week by week. Josephine revelled in all the attention she got, playing on the big thick clippy mat at their feet with her toys or having stories read to her. It was a halcyon time and despite her enormous bulk, Sophy was utterly content.

She felt slightly guilty at times that she was detached from the outside world, the things that had mattered so much just weeks ago were fading into the background. It wasn't that she didn't care about the theatre, the women there, the bigger picture of the fight for the vote – just that it was difficult to concentrate her mind on anything but the forthcoming event. Her physical discomfort made sure of that. But the wonder of having Bridget back had given her a reassurance about the birth and caring for the babies afterwards, that nothing else could have done. Bridget had been with her from the beginning, she felt as though the little Irishwoman was part of her in a way that no one else was, and she loved her every bit as much as a mother.

It was on the first day of December, when the snow flurries of the previous month attacked the north-east in earnest, that Sophy woke up from an uneasy doze. It was just after midnight and she felt distinctly unwell. The griping backache which had been making itself felt for the last forty-eight hours had worsened and spread to her abdomen, on top of which she felt nauseous.

She lay in bed, trying to persuade herself that if she went back to sleep she'd feel better, but after half an hour or so the pains seemed to be strengthening. She was wondering whether she should wake Kane and ask him to get Ralph to fetch Dr Palmer when her whole stomach seemed to be gripped in a vice. She arched in the bed, gasping, and when Kane's voice murmured, 'Sophy? Is everything all right, sweetheart?' she couldn't speak for a few moments.

Kane shot up in bed. 'Is it the babies?'

'I think so.' Mercifully the pain was receding. She could now smile and say, 'I think very shortly you are going to be a father, my darling.'

Within a short while, controlled panic reigned.

Ralph was dispatched to fetch Dr Palmer in the midst of the first real snow blizzard of the year. Sadie was roused and told to boil lots of hot water, and Bridget joined Sophy and Kane in the master bedroom. Harriet was fully occupied for the present seeing to little Josephine who had been awoken by the hustle and bustle and had decided it was morning, protesting vigorously at being put back to bed and crying for her daddy. Ralph spoiled the little girl shamelessly and Josephine had soon learned that if she wanted something, Daddy was the person to ask. Probably the calmest person in the whole mêlée was Sophy.

The spasms of pain were excruciating at their peak, but in

between the contractions she tried to reassure Kane who was as white as a sheet and visibly shaking. She would never have dreamed in a million years that her calm, unflappable husband could fall to pieces, but his distress at her pain was obvious. He recovered his aplomb after a while but she loved him all the more for his brief lapse.

By the time Ralph returned with Dr Palmer, Sophy's pains were coming every four minutes. After ascertaining a few facts, Dr Palmer told them that he was sure Sophy had been in mild labour since she'd experienced the strong backache. There was nothing to worry about, he assured Kane. All was normal.

The contractions continued fairly regularly until five o'clock in the morning when the time between pains changed with some rapidity. Now it seemed to Sophy that one contraction hadn't ended before another began.

At this point, Dr Palmer tried to send Kane out of the room, telling him he would be better served waiting downstairs. Kane's reply to the good doctor was not repeatable, and as Sophy was gripping her husband's hand for dear life, the doctor didn't argue further. He muttered something about never having had a husband present at a birth in all his days as a physician, but no one was listening.

Bridget was holding Sophy's other hand and proved a tower of strength, as did Harriet who had also come to help, along with Sadie, once Ralph had returned.

The first baby was born at seven o'clock. It was a strong-limbed male child who yelled for all he was worth and caused his mother to smile when she heard him. A good weight for a twin at six and a half pounds, Bridget had just cleaned his face and wrapped him in a warm blanket and placed him in the crib waiting by the fire, when his brother made his appearance into the world. At just under six pounds his cry was no less lusty. Kane, the tears running down his face, showed him to Sophy before handing the baby to Harriet who began to do what Bridget had done.

'By, lass, they're bonny.' Bridget was bending over an exhausted Sophy, gently wiping her face with a warm flannel. 'You rest now, you deserve it. I'll bring them to you in a minute.'

'They're beautiful, my love.' Kane had come to the bedhead, and now he bent and kissed her. 'Our two sons, sweetheart – can you believe it?'

Sophy had been about to say yes, she could believe it after what she had just been through, when a familiar pain made her groan.

'What's wrong?' Kane looked to Dr Palmer. 'Is this normal?'

'After-pains, Mr Gregory.' And then the doctor's face changed as Sophy let out another long groan and pushed with all her might. 'Good grief, I do believe there's another one.'

There *was* another one – a little girl, smaller than her two brothers but still able to make her presence known as she cried loudly, her tiny wrinkled prune of a face screwed up in protest at being expelled from her nice warm place beside her siblings. Pandemonium reined for a few moments, but once the cord was cut, Bridget wrapped the baby in a blanket and placed her in her mother's outstretched arms. 'Is she all right?' Sophy whispered dazedly to the doctor.

'She's quite wonderful.' He was clearly as surprised as they were. 'She'll need to be kept very warm for a few weeks and fed more often than the boys, but she's breathing well and there's nothing to worry about, nothing at all. She must have been lying behind the other two. Triplets. Good grief. This is a first for me.'

'And me,' said Sophy with a weak giggle.

Bridget looked at her and then began to laugh, and Harriet and Sadie who had been too shocked to say a word, grinned at each other. Even Dr Palmer, in between saying several times, 'Triplets. Good grief. Triplets,' was chuckling. It was only Kane who was quiet, but the look on his face as he gazed down wonderingly at her and his baby daughter made Sophy reach out her hand to him.

'We'll need another crib,' she murmured, smiling.

'She can have anything she needs,' he said huskily. 'Anything at all. She's exquisite, like you.'

After a minute or two Dr Palmer checked Sophy and the babies over and then went downstairs with Sadie who had offered him bacon and eggs and a warm drink before he left. Harriet changed the bed while Bridget helped Sophy wash and put on a clean nightdress, and then they too left the room so Sophy and Kane could have some time together.

Kane opened the curtains as Sophy sat back against the pillows, her daughter cradled in her arms. It was eight o'clock on a cold winter's morning and dawn was breaking, the mother-of-pearl sky streaked with charcoal and rivulets of pink, and the fresh white world beneath quiet and still after the storm of the night before.

Kane brought his sons over to the bed, little cocoons in the crook of each arm, and the proud parents examined their children's minute faces. They were the most beautiful things Sophy had ever seen. The boys were identical and ridiculously like their father, her daughter tinier, more feminine.

This was what she had been waiting for all her life. She couldn't tear her eyes away from the little downy foreheads, the small snub noses, the tiny mouths and chins. They were hers, her family, hers and Kane's. She felt a truth being pressed upon her from somewhere outside herself, and as she did so the root of aloneness, the feeling of being on the outside looking in, of not belonging, melted away. She knew who she was, she recognised these little people, she had known them from the beginning of time and loved them for as long.

She glanced again at the window. Dawn had broken. It was a new day.

Bonds Hospital